The Man She Loved Was Back in Her Life . . . at Her Daughter's Side!

Bronwyn glanced to the sofa where Asher sat, his head back, his eyes closed.

Elizabeth followed Bronwyn's eyes, but she saw Asher as he had sat that first night when he had said: "I'd much rather make love to you."

She closed her eyes against the longing surging in her and took a long swallow of her drink.

Bronwyn watched her mother drain half the glass; she had never seen her drink neat like that. This is as good a time as any, she thought, and softly, Bronwyn said:

"Asher's not my friend, Mother. He's my husband. . . ."

Choices

Judith Keith

PUBLISHED BY POCKET BOOKS NEW YORK

Another *Original* publication of POCKET BOOKS

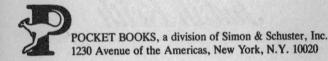

POCKET BOOKS, a division of Simon & Schuster, Inc.
1230 Avenue of the Americas, New York, N.Y. 10020

For
My Mother and My Daughter

Special thanks to:

Elisa Fitzgerald and Beverly Lewis for their astute editorial direction and encouragement.

And to: Dr. Robert L. Letcher, New York City; Dr. Allan Dunn, Miami, and the doctors and nurses of the spinal cord injury department of Jackson Memorial Hospital, Miami, for medical information beyond the author's ken; and to Michael Stinson, R.N., for sharing his medical texts.

And very special thanks to my agent and sister free spirit—Roslyn Targ.

Chapter One

ELIZABETH Banks had been celibate for five years. She had settled ever deeper into a cocoon of silken detachment, checking, confining her emotions, curling inwards as a caterpillar curls against danger. But she could not deny all instincts, especially her appreciation for beautiful men, and the tall stranger who edged his way towards her when she called "Single!", in search of someone to share the chairlift, brought a tentative smile to the fine, oval face framed in a red fox hat.

As he drew near her through the long line of skiers, she saw that the lean, chiseled face was grim. He acknowledged Elizabeth with a nod and said testily, "You'd think by now the line would have thinned."

"Twenty-five-dollar lift tickets make everyone ski to the bitter end," she replied, raising her collar against the wind which spun around the corner of the loading shed, lifting

1

snow from the roof and swirling it crazily onto the skiers inching forward, as cadenced as a corps of cadets.

He didn't reply. She lowered her goggles and peered towards the mountain. How quickly the sun had gone. Bloated clouds tumbled and collided, turning the once clear sky into thickened gruel.

She thought of the Englishman she had met at St. Anton years before. "My dear," he had said, "I ski only between twelve and two and when the sun is shining." She looked at the sky again and decided to quit after this run. Glancing at the man beside her, she noted his face held no joy, no enthusiasm for the excitement of a downhill run, and she wondered why he stood in line.

Sliding his skis impatiently, the man, too, wondered: *Why the hell don't I pack it in? Just step out of this goddamned line and head back to New York!* But it was too late—they were at the chairlift. Elizabeth moved quickly to the marker. The man stepped beside her, stomping the snow from the bottom of his skis, placing them smartly across the white loading line. The chair swung to them, and they slid back onto the slats and began the ascent. As they left the shelter of the loading shed a whirlpool of wind smacked them. The man reached up swiftly and lowered the safety bar. With each blast of wind, they huddled deeper into their parkas.

The chair creaked across a rock-strewn gully; far below, a few stunted trees clung precariously to the jagged ledges. A frenzied gust slammed the chair and it swayed alarmingly.

Elizabeth gasped as the force threw her against her partner; she clung to his arm and buried her face in his down jacket. He pulled her close and as the wind stung sharply, sank his face into her fur hat. The clouds could no longer hold their burden and they split, spewing heavy flakes. The wind caught the deluge, whipping the snow into slanting, stinging shards. The two people huddled close. Buffeted and blown about, the chair inched towards the summit.

As the chairlift approached the landing, the man raised the safety bar and they rose to ski off. A fierce funnel of

2

wind swiped the lift and the chair swerved, knocking them headlong.

"Damn!" he swore. They fell in a bizarre, slow-motion movement of flailing arms, legs, skis, and poles—grotesque ballet dancers gone amok.

"Oh no!" Elizabeth cried, imagining herself in a cast for Christmas. With relief she felt her bindings snap open. Landing hard, she lost her goggles and with them her fur hat, and with the hat, her wig, which rolled and rolled and rolled down the ramp—a curly mop of red hair with no face.

The lift operator stopped the line of chairs immediately. Attendants rushed to disentangle Elizabeth and her disgruntled companion, hustling them off the ramp, restarting the chairs which unloaded storm-tossed skiers. Off to the side, Elizabeth and her partner gathered their gear and stepped back into their bindings. Someone handed Elizabeth her hat and goggles. The wind blew her loosened hair across her face. A skier coming off the ramp speared her wig on the end of his pole and with a wide grin extended the snow-covered mass of hair to her. She burst out laughing, and the sound soared above the wind. Blithely she lifted the wig from the tip of the shaft, shook the snow from it, and tried to rearrange it atop her head, but the wind caught the tendrils, blowing them crazily.

Her laughter pealed as she struggled. Skiers paused as they tightened their buckles and adjusted their poles; they couldn't help laughing with her. She turned her back to the wind and caught the astonished look on the face of the handsome stranger. She shrugged helplessly. She looked like a rag doll come alive and at the sight of her, a smile broke through the irritation on his face.

"Come on," he exclaimed, jamming the wig and hat on her head. "Let's get a cup of coffee and warm up." Taking her firmly by the arm, he guided her towards the summit shelter.

The lodge was smoky and steamy from a blazing fire, thawing bodies, and drying parkas. As they entered, the tall man pulled off his hat and goggles and Elizabeth stared at the strong-planed face. She felt suddenly uncomfort-

3

able, knowing how unkempt, how windblown she must look.

As if he read her mind he said, "I'll get the coffee while you freshen up."

It was an order delivered by a man used to being in charge and momentarily she bristled, but his teasing glance at her hair mollified her.

"I'll give it a whirl." She smiled, feeling a quickening inside as she stared into dark, green eyes.

The ladies' room was crowded with skiers, many holding parkas, mittens, hats, and boots in front of the hot air dryers. Elizabeth found two inches before the mirror. She looked at herself in dismay. What a mess! Her auburn hair hung like overcooked spaghetti from under the wig. She pulled the tousled wig off and the girl next to her swiveled her head sharply, staring. Taking a small brush from the inside pocket of her parka, Elizabeth brushed her fine, shoulder-length hair back from her forehead; deftly she curled the strands into a French twist, securing it with pins. The classic, close-to-the-head style accented large hazel eyes framed by arching brows; her wide forehead was unlined and the slender oval face had such high color she seldom wore makeup. Shaking moisture from the short, tight curls, she brushed out the wig and put it on. Suddenly the sleek, sophisticated woman turned gamine. The girl watching exclaimed, "Wow, that's terrific!"

"Thank you," Elizabeth said, laughing as she headed for the door.

The stairway was filled with skiers clunking heavily up and down. Upstairs it was even more congested and noisier as skiers took shelter from the storm. Elizabeth tried to seek out her companion, but dozens of multicolored bulky bodies blocked her view. She felt a hand at her elbow.

"I've found us a corner," he said, leading her towards the fireplace. He had put his parka, hat, and goggles on the end of a long table to secure a space; now he took her outerclothes and put them atop his own. Taking two cups of steaming coffee off the mantel, he handed one to her.

4

She thanked him, looking at him over the rim, her eyes mirroring her appreciation for the taste of the hot brew.

She noted the set lines of his mouth, the edge of a frown between his eyes. His skin was drawn tightly over high cheekbones; he had a strong, straight nose and a square jaw. He looked like one of Remington's cowboy bronzes, she thought, liking the way he returned her gaze. His eyes did not travel the room; they concentrated on her with a contact that was steady and confident. The flames of the fire illuminated his face, softening the hard edges. But it was his eyes which fascinated her. They were green, like shoal water surrounding a reef, shadowed by black lashes. Why did men have the thickest lashes? And his hair! Thick, wavy, the grey running through the black like fine, multiveined silver in a hidden mine. His skin was ruddy from the biting wind—it was skin attractively etched with years and living. He was older than he had seemed on line, but age had enhanced his looks. Age was so kind to men—and so merciless to women. Even Mother Nature tilted the scales in favor of men, Elizabeth reflected.

The unconscious, rueful smile which crossed her face at the thought brought a half-smile to the man observing her just as closely.

"You have a terrific sense of humor," he said. "Most people would shrivel at losing their hair in public."

A hint of mischief stole into her eyes. "When a great-looking man shares your chairlift, then falls at your feet, you're bound to lose your head."

He felt the laugh begin inside him. He hadn't laughed freely in days and it felt good. His gaze went to her hair.

"Why do you wear a wig? Even with your own hair mussed by the wind, you're an attractive woman."

"Thank you," she said. "But I don't *feel* attractive with my hair messed up. A wig comes in handy, especially for skiing—it keeps me warm, and I like the look—it's so different from *me*. Sometimes we need a change from the person we are."

"It's so easy for women," he said quietly. "Men don't have that advantage."

Her eyes tried to see beyond the words, beyond the

5

scrim of green iris and black pupil, seeking to read what lay within.

She discerned only what he would allow.

In her eyes grew the mischief he had seen before. "If I looked like you," she said, smiling, "there'd be little I'd change."

Her eyes went to his hair. Reaching up, she lightly ran her fingers along its thickness. "What I wouldn't give for hair like that," she said, unabashed.

He was a man used to the response his looks evoked in women, and he knew she intended nothing more than a simple compliment, but to him, her touch was erotic, intimate. It stirred him, and his eyes held hers.

She flushed.

And then they both laughed.

She had such an open, unpretentious quality, he thought. And she was intriguingly chameleonlike. On the lift, startled by the wind, she had seemed fragile, in need of protection—but when they had fallen and she had lost her hair, she had braved the wind whipping her, like some fearless earth mother challenging the storm. Inside the lodge, with her hair straggling and her hat askew, she had been touchingly vulnerable—but now she faced him with an honesty that was exciting and the assurance of a vital, experienced woman. Perhaps this day, which had begun so badly, would end more pleasantly.

"Why do you look at me that way?" she asked.

He touched the curls of her wig.

"I like it. It's very Parisian—like ZiZi Jeanmaire. Do you remember her?"

"Of course!" She smiled. "I never missed a Roland Petit ballet."

Something shared. A remembrance—a place—a time. And two strangers no longer feel strange.

"There're two seats by the fire," he said, taking her arm, leading her to a bench near the large, rough-cut stone fireplace which rose two stories high through the sharply peaked roof. They sat down and removed their boots, stretching their toes to the warmth of the fire.

Her skin shone in the glow. The firelight caught in her eyes, lighting orange specks in the hazel depths.

"You've a happy face," he said, feeling himself relax, warmed not only by the fire but by a good feeling beginning to flicker in him.

She laughed. "You should have seen me this morning."

His own chuckle was knowing.

"You too?" she asked.

He nodded. "But tell me about you. Why is a woman like you skiing alone?"

She wondered why a man like *him* was skiing alone.

"That's a boring story," she said.

He smiled. "Go ahead—bore me. After today's interminable lift lines, I can take anything."

He drank the last of his coffee and flicked the foam cup into the fire. Elizabeth, too, drained her cup and tossed it beside his. She watched the cups flare brightly, hissing until they disintegrated into blackened ash. Then she said, "You're right about the lift lines—that's why I rarely ski on weekends. But I'm lucky—I can ski during the week. I wanted to sleep late today, have a lazy breakfast, and catch up on some reading, but frustration woke me very early and I couldn't get back to sleep. Bleary-eyed, I went to the kitchen to make orange juice. I threw the oranges in the trash, the spoon in the blender, and the egg in the sink."

He laughed out loud. "What the hell were you doing last night?"

Elizabeth was having a fine time. It was years since she had bantered and flirted with a man. She didn't even know his name and that made it more interesting. She rolled her eyes in mock dismay.

"I had a heated encounter with my typewriter. I've had a writing block for days and finally broke through—I stayed up late writing, and then in the midst of an intense climax, my typewriter went '*boing—boing—boing*' and died. It just petered out."

His eyes were devilish. "That happens to the best of us."

And again they laughed—in unison.

"I hope there's more," he said.

"There is—are you sure you want to hear it?"

"Please."

"I made more juice, took it to my desk, and began to

7

read what I'd written last night—before the typewriter died. The phone rang, and when I reached for it I spilled the juice all over the typed pages."

He chortled. "Forgive me—I don't mean to laugh—I hope the call was worth it."

"It was a wrong number."

He turned and impetuously hugged her, surprising them both.

"What a tonic you are," he said. "I can't remember when I've laughed like this. I thank you sincerely."

"I'm glad." She smiled, still feeling the hug, feeling the *rightness* of it, and feeling, also, a sense of familiarity. Did she know this man? The thought amused her. Certainly if they'd met, she could not have forgotten. He had an élan not often seen in the men who skied Cable Mountain; even in ski clothes, he wore an air of authority. And he had an edge, which, to her keenly observant eye, meant he was a man without a woman. But why? Why would so attractive a man be alone?

She would love to ask him why. Had he not asked *her?* A wry expression touched her lips. That was different. Men could ask personal questions and seem attractively interested, but if a woman did the same, she *pried*. How she resented the double standard!

The man sitting beside her, watching the firelight play on her face, saw her drollness and was about to speak when a demanding voice interrupted:

"LIZZIE! What the hell are you doing here on a Saturday?"

Elizabeth turned quickly and when she saw a tall, burly man barging through the crowd towards her, holding a draft of beer above his head, a warm, welcoming smile lit her face. She rose, as did her companion.

"Hello, Tom," she said. "This is a surprise."

"Welcome to the land of the masochists," he said, giving her a damp kiss on the cheek. "I never expected you to fight the weekend lift lines. I called you and when I got the message machine, I thought you'd taken off for Palm Beach to spend the holidays with Paul and Arnold."

"I'm not sure I'm going. It's kind of nice to be home."

8

"Good, we'll make some time to ski together," he said with a quick glance at the man standing close to Elizabeth.

In his wool plaids, Thomas Peter Calhoun looked more like a lumberjack than a skier. His red beard glistened with melted snow. He was a giant—in size, in ego, in talent. He was also a man of giant contradictions. He looked like a log-splitter, but he was a neurosurgeon. On occasion his voice could still an SST, but in the halls of the university hospital where he chaired the Department of Neurosurgery he spoke softly. On the ski slopes, aboard his Swan racing yacht or hiking backcountry, Tom Calhoun dressed carelessly, but in the city he wore impeccably tailored, stylish clothes. He adored women but had never married—his eclectic pursuits precluded close intimacy with any one person. He was arrogant and egotistical with those he disliked but almost self-effacing with those he admired. And he admired Elizabeth.

They'd first met when Calhoun was a resident and Elizabeth a young patient admitted for a back injury. She had asked questions, important questions most patients never asked, and her grit and intelligence impressed him. When she refused the surgery urged by her doctor, a man whose reputation earned him the scrub room name of "Dr. Quickcut," Calhoun's respect mounted, and when the doctor withdrew from the case, Elizabeth asked Calhoun's advice. He had suggested therapy and exercise, which she had pursued with such dedication she had remained fit all these years. Their friendship was a platonic, easygoing relationship that made no demands.

Curiosity lit Calhoun's dark brown eyes as he glanced from Elizabeth to the man beside her. He measured Elizabeth's companion, his eyes dissecting the tall man as though he were a glioma. Calhoun stuck out his hand, the fingers spatulalike—it was difficult to believe they performed delicate surgery.

"Calhoun," he said. "Tom Calhoun."

Responding, the man gripped his hand with equal vigor. "Asher Jacobs."

Elizabeth's eyes widened. Of course! That was why he seemed so familiar. She wondered that she had not

9

recognized him at once. But then, who would have expected Asher Jacobs to be skiing at Cable? Aspen and Gstaad were more his style. Wryness twisted her lips. Had she set such a scene in a novel, it could not have been more contrived. Asher Jacobs! She pulled the name and its history from the back of her mind as if the man standing before her were a card in her research file.

Jacobs, Asher: President, ICC (International Communications Corporation). Frequently called on by presidents. Born, Poland; raised in Switzerland and England. Married once (for twenty years) to Eleanore Cassidy, heiress to ICC empire, avid sportswoman; E. Cassidy killed hang-gliding accident. Jacobs takes leave of absence from ICC, accepts government assignment to Third World countries, abroad two years.

Interests: Music, art, ballet, theatre—skis with Redford, sails with Kennedys, treks with Hillary.

What was he doing here? Elizabeth wondered. The gossip columns had reported him in the Caribbean, sailing on a private yacht. A small, amused smile touched the corners of her mouth. Bumping into Asher Jacobs at Cable Mountain was like bumping into Jackie Onassis at Burger King.

Asher saw the recognition in Elizabeth's eyes and smiled derisively.

"Guess I've blown my cover. And you, my two-headed lovely lady, who are you?"

Elizabeth extended her hand. "Elizabeth Banks."

He lifted the fine-boned hand to his lips. Her fingers were slender and she wore no nail polish. The nails were cut short, softly rounded. He kissed the top of her hand lightly. For Asher Jacobs the gesture was unaffected, and Elizabeth, enjoying the European elegance of his manner, responded with a natural grace. He held her hand just for a moment before releasing it.

Calhoun noted the interplay between them. He sensed

10

the attraction. He was pleased. Elizabeth had been a recluse too long.

"Are you up for the weekend, Tom?" she asked.

He shook his head regretfully. "Wish I were, with all this new snow, but my lady friend doesn't ski, and I promised I'd be back in New York tonight. I'm stealing some time at New Year's and I'll give you a call. If you stow the typewriter for a day or two, I'll come up and we can wiggle and giggle."

Asher's eyes flickered.

Calhoun caught it and grinned. He downed the last of the beer in a long, appreciative swallow. Putting his arm around Elizabeth's shoulder, he hugged her warmly. "I'd better head back before this storm destroys my new romance." He turned to Asher. "Nice to meet you. Enjoy your run."

"Thank you," Asher said. "You too."

Calhoun shouldered his way towards the door, pulling his hood over his head. The snow outside swallowed him.

Asher turned to Elizabeth. "Wiggle and giggle? Does he mean in bed?"

Elizabeth laughed, a lilting laugh that crinkled her eyes. It was so infectious Asher laughed with her. How charming she was.

"No, that remark was perfectly innocent," she said. "Tom loves to dance and he loves square-dancing most of all. Can you imagine a Manhattan neurosurgeon and a Bronx-born cynic square-dancing?"

Asher's eyebrows rose at the news that Calhoun was a neurosurgeon.

"He's an unusual man."

"Without a doubt," Elizabeth acknowledged. "Unique, in fact."

"And you, Elizabeth, are unique as well. But you're too warm and funny to be as cynical as you claim."

"Thank you," she said, pleased at the compliment and pleased at how comfortable she felt in his company. Ordinarily she would find a man of Jacobs' reputation off-putting. She was uneasy with fame.

The room around them was emptying. They chatted amiably, unaware that workers were preparing to close the summit lodge. In the huge hearth, the fire which had blazed now simmered, the wood's once massive bulk disintegrating into powdery cinders.

Outside it had grown dark, and when the mercury lights came on, both Asher and Elizabeth looked up in surprise, and then they smiled. Each had lost track of time. Asher went to the window and peered into a night turned golden by the banks of lights.

"It's still blowing out there, but there's a lot to be said for the Banana Belt. I'm glad we're not up on the Valluga in a storm like this."

Elizabeth bent to put on her boots. She stamped her heels back into the high-topped Langes and looked up at him.

"I was caught up on the Valluga once at three-thirty with just one ski boot."

His eyes quickened with interest.

"Sounds fascinating. Why not tell me about it at dinner?"

She hesitated.

"Do you have other plans?"

A whimsical smile parted her lips. "Not really. I intended to work tonight, but if anyone learned I'd turned down an invitation to dinner with Asher Jacobs to sit at a burned-out typewriter, they'd put me away."

He chuckled and held her parka as she slipped into it.

"Let's get going then," he said.

They both adjusted their hats and goggles, and taking her arm, he led her out into the storm. They easily found their skis on the emptied rack, and when they had cleared them of snow, they stepped into the bindings, which clicked shut smartly, the ski brakes lying flat against their heels. Grasping their poles, they bent their heads into the wind and pushed off towards the slopes. Elizabeth headed for Corkscrew. If Asher skied the Valluga at St. Anton, Corkscrew was no problem for him.

The snow was deep but light, unusual for the East, where humidity weights the flakes. Elizabeth tested herself and the snow, bending her knees, her ankles, shifting her weight, making quick, short turns.

Asher, skiing behind, noted her swift, sure movements;

she was a fine skier. They came to the top of Corkscrew. He had skied it earlier in the day and enjoyed its challenge, but then it had been crowded and icy, its snow sheared by unskilled skiers. Now it lay pristine, a steeply winding, narrow trail edged with thick forest that broke the wind. He had been surprised to find such a demanding slope this close to New York, but all day it had been jammed with too many skiers, long on daring and short on skill. He had not been at all surprised by the ski patrol toboggans containing the injured, which snaked down Corkscrew at frequent intervals. But now, the trail looked like a skier's dream, and the thrill of a run surged in Asher.

Elizabeth swung over the crest and he followed her closely, skiing with a smooth, effortless rhythm. The mercury lights sliced the darkness, turning all into misted silver, and all around them the snow sparkled like powdered diamonds. Elizabeth slowed, opening her senses to the beauty around her, as if opening an unexpected gift. Taking long, deep breaths of the cold night air, she listened to the swish of her skis break track, saw the tips sink beneath the powder, felt the deep snow smooth the jagged trail. How lovely—how lovely! *It's almost like Alta,* she sang silently, *so dry—so light!*

Skiing to the side of the slope, she stopped. Below, the mountain fell steeply to the base lodge and the parking lots. Were it a clear night, she could have seen her house to the east, across the creek.

Asher slowed also and slid to her side, the edges of his skis arching into the snow, catapulting a crescent of powder high into the air. He was pleased she had stopped. He wanted to prolong this moment—it was what he had sought all day. A quietness, a peacefulness. His muscles lengthened and relaxed, his scalp loosened, the tension behind his eyes dissolved. Even the steel-like collar that had been tightening the back of his neck for months began to give way.

Elizabeth looked up at him. The light caught the serenity of her face, and he saw her eyes shining happily behind the goggles. The joy in them reached out to him. She stood downhill, coming barely to his shoulder. With a

13

quick slide he spun around so that he stood on the downhill side and their height was equal. The light now reflected on his face, turning his green eyes tigerlike behind the yellow lenses.

Eyes on eyes, they shared the silence, their minds embracing the solitude. Slowly, they smiled in understanding. The snow drifted about them, whitening their jackets, burying their skis. Asher put his hands on her shoulders; his ski poles dangled loosely from his wrists. He drew her to him. They came together gracefully despite their skis. His arms encircled her waist. He drew her closer and she felt his warmth.

Taking her head in his gloved hands, he turned her face to his and bent to kiss her. Their goggles crashed, sending a shock wave of sudden sound into the stillness. It startled them, and Elizabeth felt mirth well in her. She strove to suppress it. Again, Asher tried to reach her lips, but again, the goggles got in the way. Bending lower, he tried to avoid the goggles, and Elizabeth erupted into full-throated laughter that echoed beyond the trees.

Asher grinned at her.

"Just for that," he said, laughing, "the last one to the bar buys the drinks."

He turned his skis into the fall line and waved for her to follow him.

14

Chapter Two

THE base area seethed with people. Many headed towards the parking lots, skis on their shoulders; others made their way to the bars in the huge complex. Asher and Elizabeth skied up to the front of the main lodge and got out of their gear. Through the glass facade misted with the heat of many bodies, they saw a crowd clustered about the bar in the lounge. The blare of a rock band spilled from inside, drowning the beautiful silence they'd just left; their eyes met and they silently agreed—neither wanted to be part of the din.

"Do you know a quiet place?" he asked.

She nodded and lifted her skis onto her shoulder. "Follow me."

A man in front of her changed course abruptly and she ducked as the skis he carried just missed her head. Asher stepped protectively in front.

15

"This is worse than New York at rush hour," he remarked, the edge coming back into his voice.

They passed a building close to the parking lot and Elizabeth went to the door. "I'll just be a moment. I have a season locker."

He held the door for her and followed her inside. She went to a locker against a long wall and spun the combination lock. The worn metal door creaked open and she removed a pair of fur-trimmed boots; then she placed her skis and poles inside. As she bent over to change boots, Asher watched the fabric of her ski pants stretch across well-rounded, shapely buttocks. He had an urge to run his hands over them. She's a fine-looking woman, he thought.

Standing her ski boots on the floor of the locker, she spun the combination shut and turned to him. "All set."

"That's convenient," he observed. "I take it you live close by."

She smiled. "So close, I walked up."

"That's even more convenient," he said, grinning. "Now we need to clear snow from only one car."

When they stopped at his car in the first lot, Elizabeth said, "You must have arrived early."

"I was hoping to beat the crowd, but it caught up with me." He placed his skis and poles in the roof rack and locked them in place. With his jacketed arm he swept snow from the passenger door, unlocked it and held it for Elizabeth. Getting in, she reached across the console and opened the driver's door.

"Thank you," he said, easing into the low seat and starting the motor, which responded instantly. Reaching behind Elizabeth, he took out a boot bag and a snow brush. The movement brought him close to her face and he touched her cheek lightly with his lips.

"Stay where you are while I give us some visibility."

She ran her hand appreciatively along the burled walnut dash of the Mercedes. Too bad they're padding them now, she mused. Asher cleaned off the snow in long, sure strokes and the 350 SL's sleek silver color shone in the lights of the parking lot.

He changed boots and slid into the driver's seat. "And now, Elizabeth, what is your pleasure?" He shifted into

16

first, guiding the car through the snow and the skiers as easily as if he were on a clear, uncrowded freeway. "Where is this quiet place we can dine and converse without having to shout?"

"It's only a short drive, but, if you don't mind, I'd like to go home first and feed my animals. We can wash up and then phone for a reservation."

"Lead on," he said, accelerating. The Mercedes whipped through the snow like a whisk in cream.

"Turn left at the bottom of the hill. It's a dirt road, one lane and uphill all the way, but it's driveable."

Snow blanketed the windshield. Asher turned the wipers up to their fastest pitch.

"Are you sure you want to stop for dinner?" Elizabeth asked, peering through the frosted windows. "It might be difficult getting back to New York later on. You could just as well drop me at my house and . . ."

"And miss getting to know you? My dear Elizabeth, snow and I are old friends," Asher said calmly, his hands steady on the wheel as the car swerved slightly. "Besides, if it gets too tricky I can always pull into a motel."

She pointed to the turn and he eased the car into the narrow lane. The trees, weighted with snow, bent to form a bower. The headlights illuminated the drive, revealing such untracked, primitive beauty that he slowed, exclaiming, "It looks just like 'Sun Valley Serenade.' I expect to see Sonja Henie prance from behind a tree at any moment."

Elizabeth laughed. "You're dating yourself." She was pleased at his reaction. "The road is one of the reasons I bought my place. It's untouched, much like the Indian path it once was. There's only one other house besides mine and it's occupied only in summer and the occasional weekend."

He slowed again, enjoying the winding drive. The car slid, but he accelerated smoothly and his radials took hold.

"How do you get in and out in this kind of weather?"

Her answer was confident. "The state bought this road for fire access because we're surrounded by state game lands, and it's plowed whenever they plow the road to the ski area."

17

They came to a break in the trees. On their left a sheer cliff rose sharply. On the right the road fell away to a stream slashing through a narrow gorge.

"Beautiful, just beautiful," Asher breathed, stopping the car. "It's like Switzerland."

"I know," Elizabeth said softly. "I love it when it's like this. Whenever it snows, I grab my cross-country skis and try to get down here to the Gorge before the plow comes through. It's hard to believe we're only seventy-five miles from New York."

He turned to her. "Do you mean to say you ski at night on this road, alone?"

"It's not Manhattan," she said, smiling. "There's no one here but me, and there's nothing I'm afraid of in these woods. Besides, I'm not alone. Just wait until you see my companion."

He groaned. "None of this is real. You're not real, this road isn't real—it's all an illusion brought on by skiing on an empty stomach. I'm famished, dear lady. Please take us to the nearest table."

She laughed as he pressed the gas pedal and the powerful motor drove the car upward. They crossed a bridge, and beyond, to the right, Asher saw a circular driveway.

"That's it," Elizabeth said. "Be careful, there's a dip."

Asher pulled in. Too sharply. The car skidded on the ice under the snow and they drifted towards the trees. His reactions were swift and sure, she noted. He turned the wheel in the direction of the skid and the car straightened. But the low-slung Mercedes slid slowly into the dip, settling in deep snow.

Asher shut off the motor and turned to Elizabeth with a shrug. "Shovel time."

"Don't bother," Elizabeth said. "No restaurant is worth shovelling for. My handyman works at Cable and he'll come by to plow my driveway on his way home. His pickup will pull you out easily. We'll just dine chez Elizabeth." She inclined her head charmingly. "After all, it's the nearest table."

He smiled. "Thank you—that's very kind."

If she answered, he did not hear her words. Robust

18

barking broke the quiet, and the raucous sounds echoed off the hillside. A large, black shepherd loped towards the car. He wagged his tail in welcome when he saw Elizabeth; then he came around to Asher's side and growled threateningly.

"My companion," Elizabeth said, opening her door and getting out. Asher stayed in the car. The dog leapt to her side, licking her hands, his tail brushing a wide swath in the snow. She patted his massive head. He yelped at her touch, as if he were speaking to her. "Good boy, Blaze, good boy." Her voice was soft as she caressed him fondly. "We have company. Stay, Blaze, stay." The dog quieted.

She called to Asher. "It's all right. Come, meet Blaze."

Asher got out of the car and came around to her side. The dog cocked his head, his ears upright, his body tense. Elizabeth took Asher's arm and patted it. "Friend, Blaze, friend."

The dog circled the tall man. Asher stood still as the animal, his nose quivering, sniffed him thoroughly. When Asher touched the dog's head, Blaze licked his hand and pranced aside, his tail wagging once more.

Asher grinned at Elizabeth. "I see now why you have no fear. He's an extraordinary beast."

"That's no beast," Elizabeth declared. "That's my closest friend."

She went to a tree and threw a switch. Lights flooded the driveway and beyond. Asher judged the snow-covered form in the drive to be Elizabeth's car, but where was the house? He followed her through the trees and came to a rustic footbridge which traversed the rushing stream. The snow was inches deep and they stepped carefully, single file, across the narrow bridge. Then they made their way uphill through pine woods and Asher saw the house atop a knoll. The switch Elizabeth had activated across the stream had also turned on lights about the house. He stopped, surprised. The seclusion! No one could see the house until they had crossed the bridge.

Illuminated in the shadowy light was a rambling red-wood structure of angular shapes with glass walls, overlooking the creek. Wide, cantilevered decks jutted over the high bank, and a cut-stone chimney rose high above

19

the asymmetrical roofs. As they came onto the deck, two cats leapt from the roof, startling Asher. They brushed their bodies up against Blaze and mewed to get into the house.

Asher laughed, somewhat embarrassed by his reaction. "Seems they, too, are looking for the nearest table."

Elizabeth unlocked the door and Blaze barrelled through; the cats darted in under the dog's legs. Elizabeth and Asher stamped snow from their boots before stepping inside. She pressed a wall switch and Asher saw they were in a spacious, slate-floored entrance; plants hung from the ceiling and stood in stone containers before the full-length windows. An abstract marble sculpture, resembling a bird in flight, filled one corner. Asher ran his fingers along its smooth, polished white contours. He helped Elizabeth out of her parka, then hung their coats on a Bentwood clothes tree, and noting the art-filled walls, moved closer to study a favorite Escher print. It had never ceased to fascinate him. The sere black lines, the staircases angling, ascending, descending, an endless maze in which a lone figure trudged. *There is no exit,* Asher thought. *The future is only the past.*

Watching him, Elizabeth said, "Before I saw that print, I always thought of life as a circle—round, smooth, sheltering. Now I see it as all angles, knife-edged staircases winding cruelly, inviting you to stumble."

Slowly Asher smiled, feeling a rare comradeship towards this interesting woman. Following her into the large room which ran the length of the house, he felt an instant surge of warmth and color. She headed for a doorway, calling back: "There's a bathroom off the hallway. Make yourself comfortable. I'm off to the kitchen for something to hold us until dinner's ready."

"Thank you," Asher said, finding the small bathroom. It was painted a soft blue and the walls were filled with prints and original paintings scaled in size to complement the compact space. Like the art in the entryway, the pictures were an interesting choice.

He looked at his face in the mirror; it seemed more relaxed, less lined than it had been that morning. The sun early in the day had reddened his tan. He rubbed his hand

20

over the black and grey stubble beginning to show. Opening the pine cabinet, he found a packet of throwaway razors and shaved quickly, in short, precise strokes. He washed his face vigorously, feeling clean, refreshed, and splashed water until his skin shone. He ran long fingers through his hair and brushed it with a brush from the cabinet. When he finished, he went into the main part of the house.

He stood quietly in the center of the room, absorbing the essence of Elizabeth's home. This was not the simple country place he had expected. Browsing about, he recognized it as the creative expression of a sophisticated woman. Pine bookshelves lined one wall. He glanced at the titles. They were wide-ranging: classics, contemporary fiction and nonfiction, poetry, essays, art books, journals, magazines. One small section contained a collection of romance novels, many by Ellen Barclay. Ellen Barclay—she had been a favorite of Eleanore's.

The room was painted white, a perfect background, he thought, for the art and the colors which gave it life. Approaching the far end, he smiled as he noted the contents of the cabinets: it was a media center, and all the components were made by ICC: color television, video recorder, stereo, tape deck—all top of the line. The record on the turntable was Bruch's Violin Concerto in A Minor. The lady had taste. He pushed the red button; the record spun, the arm drifted lazily, and the melodic strains of Bruch's masterpiece filled the room.

He sank into a sofa flanking the stone fireplace, put his head back on the blue linen fabric, and looked up at the soaring cathedral ceiling. Those hand-hewn beams must have come from an old barn, he judged. A matching sofa faced him. In between was a round pine table polished to a tawny sheen and covered with newspapers, magazines, and books. He reached down and slipped out of his boots, stretching his toes on the soft pile of the rug beneath his feet and smiling inwardly. No rag rugs for Elizabeth! Scattered about the polished oak floors were Chinese and Persian rugs—lush, rich art objects in beautiful colors which she had skillfully repeated throughout the room in more muted tones. Blues, reds, and gold predominated.

From the sofa, Asher admired the art. He also admired whoever it was who had designed the ingenious lighting. Hidden lights formed an unbroken line in the bookshelves and outlined the niches on either side of the fireplace which contained small bronzes and other sculptures. The paintings and prints were also cleverly lighted. He got up to examine the far wall more closely. The quality of her collection intrigued him: Dali, Ben Shahn, Larry Rivers, Arshile Gorky, the Wyeths, Theodore Roszak! Either she had made a substantial income or she had begun collecting years ago.

He turned from the art to a grand piano which stood in front of the windows. It had intricately carved legs which arched gracefully, the sculpted designs replicated on the highly polished, burled walnut case. He ran his hand slowly along the bare, beautiful wood, feeling the smoothness, the outlines of the carvings; then his long fingers went to the gleaming ivory keys. He touched them lightly, picking out the notes of the Bruch. The piano was tuned. It had a deep, rich sound and was well taken care of. His regard for Elizabeth grew.

Beyond, backed by glass doors opening onto a wrap-around deck, was the dining area and to the side, a long hallway led to another wing of the house. In the corner, a spiral staircase wound upwards to other levels. Fresh eucalyptus leaves in a blue, Chinese urn next to the staircase made the room fragrant.

Elizabeth returned carrying a tray containing a bottle of white wine, two crystal glasses, fruit, cheeses on a wood board, and a basket of crackers. Asher took the tray from her and held it while she cleared the table between the sofas, putting the papers, magazines, and books underneath.

"I'm sorry to take so long," she said, sitting down opposite him. She began to slice the cheese. "But I had to feed the animals; otherwise they would give us no peace." She had also changed clothes. She wore a mauve cashmere sweater and a long, wool, burgundy skirt. Nor did she wear her wig. Her hair was brushed back and hung loosely to her shoulders. Her freshly washed face shone. How natural she is, Asher thought, comparing her with the

22

women he had recently dated. He reached over and filled the glasses with wine, handing one to her.

"Thank you," she said, "and thank you for turning on the Bruch." She handed him a cracker filled with cheese.

He raised his glass and smiled so engagingly she felt a quickening inside. "Here's to riding on lifts with ladies who lose their heads."

"And to the men who turn them." She raised her glass to his.

He laughed and sat back, looking at her appraisingly. "You have the most amazing complexion. Forgive me if I embarrass you, but I think it's charming that you blush so easily."

Her face reddened and they both laughed.

He sipped the wine. It was dry and light. He looked at the label on the bottle and then at Elizabeth. He twirled the wine in the glass, sniffing the bouquet. "My compliments. You have excellent taste in wine."

She accepted his praise with a gracious nod and then looked about, as if she had forgotten something. She rose, going to the fireplace. He jumped up and came around the sofa.

"Allow me," he said, taking the matches from her hand. Opening the glass doors of the hearth, he ignited the wood on the grate. Flames soon licked upward, sending warmth into the room.

"I'm afraid this isn't an energy-efficient house," she said, "but I love open fires and lots of windows. My handyman scolds me because he says so much heat goes up the chimney. I made a major concession when I had the glass doors installed."

The dog ambled into the room. He licked his lips lazily and began to make small circles in a corner near the window. Then he sank into his circle, his head between his paws. He turned wary amber eyes on Asher, who had returned to the sofa. Soon Blaze's heavy lids closed and he began to snore lightly. The cats padded in. One went to the dog and nestled close to his coarse black and tan coat. The other chose a warm spot near the fireplace.

"That's a contented crew. Do you share this house only with them?"

23

"To a degree," Elizabeth answered, cutting an apple and handing it to him. "My daughter visits frequently and then there are friends who come from time to time."

"How many children do you have?"

"Just the one. She lives in Manhattan." She sat back on the sofa and eyed him curiously. "I don't mean to pry," she apologized, "but I keep wondering why you're not in the Caribbean where you're supposed to be."

He gave her such an astonished look that she laughed outright.

"Don't worry, I'm not a stringer for the *National Enquirer,* but you were reported to be on a yacht somewhere near Barbados."

"I wonder if they report how many times a day I go to the bathroom." His tone was sardonic.

She shrugged. "To use an overworked cliché, that's the price of fame."

"It's the price of greed," he said emphatically. "But who am I to complain? My own network carries its share of gossips."

She met his gaze steadily. "That's a remarkably honest admission."

"Just don't tell my board of directors." He grinned, his teeth white against the tanned face. He ignored her initial question and asked instead, "Just what do you do out here in the woods? Earlier you mentioned your typewriter conking out, and with all these books about, I imagine you could be a writer, but there are many kinds of writers."

"There are, and I wish I could write like *they* do," she agreed, gesturing towards the bookcases. "I once dreamt of writing meaningful, important books that get front-page reviews in the *Times Book Review,* but I've finally accepted that I don't have that kind of mind, that kind of talent. So, I write for money—frothy, romantic novels that women enjoy reading."

He followed her eyes to the book-lined wall. Again he noted the quality of her collection. The small section devoted to a string of romances caught his eye. He got up and went over to the shelf. He turned and looked at her with surprise.

"You're Ellen Barclay!"

24

"Now you've blown my cover," she said, smiling.

"I wondered about those Barclays amongst all the heavyweights. Forgive me, I don't mean to imply that your work is unworthy."

Her laugh was open, without ego. "I stopped being sensitive about my work a long time ago. I enjoy what I do. I enjoy the letters I receive and most of all, I enjoy the freedom the money brings."

Asher took a title from the shelf and flipped its pages. When he spoke his voice held admiration. "My wife read your books. She would have enjoyed meeting you. I'm surprised we haven't met before. After all, ICC owns Transit, the company that publishes you in paperback. We should have run into each other in New York."

"Not really. I avoid parties; I hate the cocktail circuit," Elizabeth explained. "I had too much of that at one time. I'm very happy that I have to do little promotion nowadays. Most people around here don't even know that I'm Ellen Barclay."

A buzzer went off and she jumped. "That's our dinner!"

"Great!" Asher said, taking her by the arm. "I insist on helping. I'm a whiz in the kitchen."

"Oh no!" she giggled.

"What did I say?"

"You won't believe this." Her laughter rose. "It sounds so trite, but that's a line in my new book. The hero says to the heroine, the first night they meet . . . 'I insist on helping, Cassandra . . . I'm a whiz in the kitchen.'"

"Well then!" He arched his straight, thick eyebrows. "Lead on, Cassandra!"

Chapter Three

THE moment Asher stepped into Elizabeth's kitchen he knew he was in for a treat. From the stove came an aroma which tantalized his nostrils and warmed his heart. The scent brought memories of vegetables dug from his mother's root cellar and beef from his uncle's farm simmering on the enormous stove of the kitchen in Poland. He remembered his father ladling thick, pungent soup from a glazed pink and white tureen on a snowy day.

Asher lifted the cover of the pot on Elizabeth's stove to confirm his memory and turned to her.

"When did you get a chance to do this?"

She gave him a taste from a wooden spoon. "Like it?"

He rolled his eyes.

She laughed. "Thank Blaze. I buy huge bones for him and make up a stock of soup for winter; then I freeze it into small portions for people stranded in snowdrifts."

26

He asked for another spoonful, relishing the taste on his tongue: the richness of the stock, the pearls of barley, the mushrooms, the beef.

"That was my mother's favorite soup," he said quietly, his eyes deepening.

Elizabeth saw a flicker of sadness on his face and she handed him a maplewood bowl and a plastic bag filled with greens.

"You can help with the salad," she said.

They worked together well and soon dinner was on the table in the dining room. Asher held Elizabeth's chair, then stood by her side and uncorked a bottle of white Bordeaux. Pouring a small amount into her glass, he waited while she tasted it. When she nodded her approval, he filled her glass, then his own and sat down. He raised the slender crystal goblet:

"*A votre santé, madame, et merci, Dionysus.*"

She laughed gaily. "Dionysus my foot. Thank Izzie's Liquors."

Asher chuckled and they began to eat, appreciatively, hungry after the full day of skiing. They spoke little as they enjoyed the hot, hearty soup; the broiled chicken with spiced apples and chestnuts; the green salad tangy with anchovies, olives, and feta cheese, and Elizabeth's spicy herb dressing. Dessert was what she laughingly called the "world's fastest mousse," frozen strawberries whipped frothy with heavy cream, laced with Cointreau and served with delicious, wafer-thin almond cookies.

The glass walls made it seem as though they dined outside, protected from the storm like porcelain birds in a bell jar. The snow swirled, and the crystals caught in the lights glistened. Brahms' Fourth Symphony played softly and the glow of candles between them shone on their faces, smoothing the years. Asher poured the last of the wine into their glasses, pushed his empty plate aside, and sank back contentedly. He smiled at Elizabeth, his eyes mirroring the pleasure he felt.

She did not see the smile, so caught up was she in her thoughts. I write about men like him all the time, she reflected. Rich, beautiful, powerful men, men women

27

dream about, and I handle them so well on paper. Why do I feel so unsure, so insecure now?

The candlelight emphasized the green tints in her hazel eyes, the sheen of her skin. As she sat quietly studying Asher, she had no idea how lovely she looked.

"I think, Elizabeth, at this moment you've become Madame Barclay."

This time, when she looked at him, he knew she saw him.

"What makes you say that?"

"I feel I'm being examined like a character in one of your books."

She smiled self-consciously. "It's unusual to meet a man like Asher Jacobs at Cable Mountain."

He put down his glass and leaned forward. The smile curving his mouth was uncertain, as though he'd tasted wild fruit and was not sure it was edible.

"And who exactly is a man like Asher Jacobs? Am I not a man like any other man?"

Her laugh was spontaneous. "You sound as if we were at a Seder and you were asking the Passover questions. 'Why is this night different from any other night'?"

He paused. "I didn't realize you were Jewish."

"Why not?"

"Jewish women don't usually live alone in the woods, or ski in the dark hours of the night."

"That's an unfair generalization."

"Perhaps." There was no apology in his tone. "But you must admit, you're not the average woman."

"And you're not the average man, no more like other men than Passover was like other nights."

He threw back his head and laughed. "Are you comparing me to Moses?"

She gave him a mischievous look. "I hadn't thought about that, but now that you mention it . . ." Her eyes lit with fun and she leaned towards him, her elbows on the table. "Doesn't the power you have come from the same place? From up there in the sky? Electricity, radio, television, satellites? Maybe God hasn't handed you stone tablets, Asher, but something in today's context, as powerful."

28

The mood between them suddenly changed.

"That's a provocative thought," he said carefully.

"I didn't mean to become weighty," she said.

"Please go on. I've never been compared with Moses before," he said, trying to keep it light.

She rose. "This may sound like the fantasy of fiction, but bear with me."

She began to pace back and forth. Ideas came to Elizabeth readily; as with most writers, inchoate ideas sprang constantly into her imaginative mind, but she had learned to edit them so that she could express them clearly. She did this efficiently at the typewriter, but speaking off the top of her head, she feared sounding foolish. What she was about to say had bothered her for a long time, though, and when would she get another chance like this? Asher Jacobs was *here,* in her *home.* She plunged ahead.

"When you think of it, how much like Moses you are. You stand there on a mountaintop of power, and down below they worship false idols: 'One Day at a Time,' 'The Newlywed Game,' 'Johnny Carson.'" She took a deep breath. Asher listened, his eyes following her.

"What a contradiction television is!" She clasped her hands together. "On the one hand it brings us unbeatable on-the-spot news coverage, marvelous investigative reports, documentaries, drama, and comedy. On the other, it panders to the baser side of man with bosoms, backsides, and bullets. I'm not saying that television can solve the problems of man or bring world peace, but it certainly has the power to reveal truth!"

Her voice deepened. "Television showed us the truth in Vietnam, and people questioned the integrity of their government and for the first time truly protested." Emotion rose in her. "That is television's glory, the power to make us see, hear, feel, to make us care!"

Again she clasped her hands. She had not intended to flay him, to be so serious, so solemn, but she had picked at a scab of discontent and it bled. She could not staunch its flow.

"It's maddening! We're as stupidly territorial in a nuclear age as we were in prehistoric times. We kill to preserve

29

possessions, land, regimes; we enslave, imprison, torture, murder to protect ideologies, religion, ideas."

She stopped at the television set and touched it. Stroking the fine wood of the cabinet, she turned and looked at Asher.

"*This* can show it to us, much better than Moses could show his people." Her eyes challenged him as she spoke:

"Yet, most of what's on this miraculous machine dulls minds rather than nurtures. Television has created graven images and once more men worship them. And like it or not, Asher Jacobs, you are today's man on the mountain!" Her voice rang clear, her words resounding.

A small, appreciative smile formed around Asher's mouth. Her sincerity touched him, and she was absolutely lovely with the color high in her cheeks, her eyes afire. She was so *sure*. She almost made him believe, and she made him remember how *he* had once believed. Irony dulled his smile. The idealism of youth disintegrated too soon in the harsh demands of reality.

"Ah, Elizabeth," he began regretfully, "do you really think that I or any one man has that much power?"

Irony now touched her face. Her voice quieted.

"The problem, Asher, is that *men* have too *much* power, and they use it badly."

She came to him and took his hands, then squeezed them firmly.

"You have the power, Asher—you *can* do it!"

The phone rang shrilly.

They both jumped, then laughed.

Annoyed at the intrusion, Elizabeth went quickly to answer it.

A loud, twangy voice sounded across the room and Asher, standing nearby, heard it clearly.

"Miz Banks?"

"Yes, Mrs. Crouch, what is it?"

"Miz Banks?" the voice screeched again.

Elizabeth held the receiver away from her ear and shouted, "Yes, Mrs. Crouch, I'm here."

"Oh is that you, Miz Banks?"

"Yes, it is. What can I do for you?"

"Nuthin'. I jest called to tell ya that Jesse can't make it up to yer place t'night. He's stuck up on the mountain. They got troubles there 'cause of the wind, 'n he's gonna have ta work late, so he'll be by in the mornin' ter plow ya driveway.''

"Oh." Elizabeth looked at Asher. "All right. Just tell Jesse to come when he can. Thank you for calling."

"Ganight, Miz Banks," she yelled.

"Goodnight, Mrs. Crouch. Take care." Elizabeth hung up the phone.

"I take it Mrs. Crouch is slightly deaf," Asher said.

"No, she isn't, but she is old and doubts one can be heard. She's my handyman's mother. He can't get here until morning."

She felt uncomfortable. She went to the windows and peered outside at the deepening snow. Why did she hesitate to ask him to stay the night? Her home often sheltered acquaintances when weather turned nasty. She didn't want to admit it was because he awakened feelings she had held in check for so long. She turned and faced him, her eyes uncertain.

"You're welcome to stay here tonight."

There was just a suggestion of a smile on his face. "Was asking me really so difficult?"

Her eyes avoided his. "Yes, it was. You're a damned attractive man, and I don't like being in a situation in which I put my heroines."

He laughed heartily and came to her. Putting one hand on her shoulder, with the other he lifted her chin and looked down into her eyes. His own were amused.

"Elizabeth Banks, you're a very special woman and you've carved out the life you want to live. I'll do nothing to upset it. But I like you, and I want to know you better. I hope you will allow me that privilege."

Her eyes darkened and he saw uncertainty edge out the brightness. He bent his head and kissed her lids closed. Then he folded her in his arms.

"This is one novel in which there will be no sexual explicitness," he said laughingly, hugging her.

Her own laughter chimed as she returned his hug.

31

"If you stoke the fire, I'll clear up," she said, feeling comfortable once more.

"That's fair," he agreed, going to the fireplace. "After all, you can't expect Moses to do dishes."

Asher thought of Elizabeth's challenge as he stirred the flames and threw new logs on the fire. He could hear his own voice, years ago. He had just come to the United States and was arguing with Michael Cassidy.

"But Mike, there's no reason why we can't program one hour of news in prime time. All you have to do is say so."

Cassidy had laughed. "People don't want news, Asher, they want entertainment. Besides, if I were crazy enough to do as you ask, the other networks would throw Lucy and Uncle Miltie against us and we'd be clobbered." He had then become serious.

"Remember, Asher, television is a business, and like all business it must show a profit or go under. No one trusts losers. No one listens to losers. If you want to do any good at all, you've got to be a winner!"

Cassidy had been right. After Cassidy died, he had tested his own ideas and ICC lost in the ratings. He then grudgingly hired Barney Richmond away from NBC and now ICC led in prime time. He had busied himself with acquisitions and international markets, and since Eleanore's death, he had spent little time in the United States. Sitting cross-legged before the fire, Asher thought of what Elizabeth had said. Questions nagged at him: couldn't he have spent that time abroad more productively? In helping Third World countries set up television facilities, couldn't he have done more to encourage educational programs rather than tout popular programming?

Elizabeth returned carrying a small tray containing a teapot, cups, and saucers. She placed it on the table between the sofas and looked at Asher's back. She went to the stereo.

"Do you mind if I put on another album?"

He rose and turned to look at her. " 'The Unfinished Symphony' might be suitable," he said somewhat sardonically.

A light, teasing smile formed around her lips.

"No," she said, going to the machine and taking a record from the stack; she put it on the turntable, flicked the switch, and as the music flowed into the room, she went to the sofa and sat down.

"'The Pastorale' is far more suitable," she smiled, picking up the teapot and pouring a pungent brew into the two cups. "I hope you don't mind peppermint. I've run out of regular tea."

Asher sat down opposite her and she handed him a cup. He looked into the steaming liquid and a reminiscent smile eased his mouth. "I haven't had peppermint tea in years. We used to pick fresh peppermint near the house in Gstaad when we were kids."

"We?" Elizabeth asked.

"My wife Eleanore and I. We grew up together, in the same house—I was ten years older, and we were like brother and sister. When she died I lost more than a wife—I lost the only family I had left." He stared into the teacup.

"I used to read about the two of you," Elizabeth said, "and I envied you both. You seemed to have everything, even a happy marriage."

Asher raised his eyes to hers.

"No one has everything, Elizabeth, and few are privileged to know happiness. I think you are one of the privileged few. What makes you seem so happy?"

She shook her head and laughed, a light, saucy sound.

"This moment is lovely. This evening has been lovely. That's all one can expect—occasional moments. Maybe happiness is recognizing the moment and enjoying it. Surely, Asher, you've had your moments."

He laughed shortly, self-deprecatingly, and his eyebrows knitted.

"Yes, of course, but on balance, those moments are rare."

"Maybe you're used to too much," she said, sipping her tea.

He drank silently. When he had finished, he put down his cup and said, "Why aren't you writing more serious

33

books? Books that question, that challenge? You have the mind for it, Elizabeth, and a large, loyal following who'd buy whatever you wrote—that's power!"

"Ah, Asher," she parodied, a teasing glint in her eyes, "what makes you think I have that kind of ability?"

He ignored her paraphrasing. "Are you afraid to try?"

She met his eyes directly, uncompromisingly.

"I tried, and I was terrible. It's a God-given gift to write like Hellman, or Styron, or Faulkner. Serious thoughts spin in my head, but I can't translate them to paper. All I can do is entertain."

"And so you've become realistic about what you can and cannot write?"

She saw immediately where he had led her. "You mean the way you are realistic about what people will watch on television?"

"Exactly."

She flushed with embarrassment. "Was I really that pompous?"

"No." He smiled. "I've asked myself the same questions —although I never came up with the bold analogy you devised." His voice took on an authority that brooked no argument. "The idealist who refuses to accept the reality of a stark world is ineffectual. To do any good, one must be pragmatic. The bottom line is survival."

He stretched out his legs and put his head back on the plump pillows of the sofa. He looked at Elizabeth from under half-closed lids. The fire crackled, Beethoven's music surrounded them, and outside the snow still drifted.

"Why do you live alone?" he asked.

The question surprised her, as he had been surprised when she asked about the Caribbean. She put her cup on the table, sat back on the sofa, and pulled her feet under her. She thought of the question; there was no simple answer.

"It's comfortable." She hesitated. "I enjoy people and I can be gregarious, but I think I've reached a stage where what I want is more important than the give and take necessary to live with someone. I sleep when I want, work when I want, eat when and what I want—it's an easy, guilt-free life."

34

She leaned back, stretched her arms over her head, and let out a long sigh. "In fact, it's heaven." And then she looked at Asher and laughed self-consciously. "I think."

He laughed with her and said, "You have the most marvelous ability to make me feel good. You can't imagine how truculent I was this morning—I've been that way for weeks."

"Would you like to talk about it? Sometimes talking to someone you scarcely know is a great release."

His eyes roved her face, and the smile lingered at the corners of his mouth. "Not really." He got up and went to the fireplace. Taking a poker, he separated the burning logs, adding new wood which quickly caught the flaring sparks. He came back and sat down in the corner of the sofa on which she was seated. He placed his arms along its back and looked at her levelly.

"I'd much rather make love to you," he said quietly.

Elizabeth was caught totally off guard. She felt the flush begin in her chest and, helpless against its revealing sweep, she felt it spread to her temples.

Asher tried to assuage the discomfort he saw dawning in her eyes.

"You are a desirable woman, Elizabeth, and making love to you would be a joy."

Sensual thoughts rose in his eyes and Elizabeth read them clearly.

She got up abruptly, feelings tumbling in her like marbles. She went to the windows. He did not follow.

Elizabeth stood looking out at the snow. She felt like a glass jar placed carelessly on a hot stove. She could feel the beginnings of tiny cracks, but before they could spread and shatter, she gingerly moved the jar and set it on the sill to cool. She turned, went back to the sofa, and sat down.

When she faced him, Asher saw a clear, cool confidence in her eyes.

"Asher, that was a lovely compliment and I thank you." Her voice was soft and steady. "But I have been celibate for more than five years, and I have no desire to change."

The look he gave her was so incredulous, she almost laughed.

"Asher, is that really so unbelievable?"

35

He got up and stood facing her.

"Why would an intelligent, life-loving woman like you choose celibacy?"

His words resounded.

"Celibacy is the antithesis to life! It denies one's most natural instincts." His frustration of the morning returned. He strode to the bookcase, withdrew one of her books, and shook it at her.

"You are a fraud, Elizabeth Banks. Your novels are filled with sex, deliberately designed to stimulate. Oh yes, I know. Eleanore once read me one of your purple passages. And you have the gall to tell me you're celibate?"

His unexpected tirade astonished her. She felt as if she had been burned, and the fire in her drove her to her feet. How dare he!

"You have no right to criticize me for my position, so turn off that damned 'what-do-you-mean-we're-not-in-the-top-ten' look!"

The corners of his eyes began to crease, and the beginnings of a smile softened the tautness of his mouth.

"What a segue," he breathed. He put his hands on her shoulders to rivet her position. He leaned his face close to hers.

"Don't you realize, madame, how you keep tossing challenges at me as if we were playing ping-pong?"

She tried to turn from him, but his grip was sure.

"Don't you realize, Elizabeth, how seductive you are?"

He drew her closer.

"Don't you realize the sensuality of this house, the storm, the dinner, the music?" He bent his head, his eyes seeking hers. "Have you no idea, dear lovely lady, of the romance around us?"

Elizabeth stared at his lips a breath away. To taste warm lips again . . . No! She shoved hard, and Asher fell back onto the sofa. He sat there, startled.

Angry at herself, Elizabeth lashed out at him. "Jesus Christ, Asher! What if I'd said 'no' for any other reason? You'd accept it. Even if I said no because there was another man in my life—that you could understand. But

36

your outraged masculinity can't accept my denying you because I choose to be celibate."

She selected her next words carefully.

"Everything you've said is true. It's one of my romantic scenes come to life, and at the moment, we *are* caught up in each other, but it's my yesterdays and my tomorrows I must deal with as much as tonight." She lifted her shoulders in a slight shrug.

"I'm no good at casual sex. I don't have the emotional makeup to fall in and out of bed. I was raised in a time and in a tradition when love, sex, and marriage were indivisible. I don't want love or marriage, and since I can't accept sex without commitment, I've given up that which upsets my equilibrium."

As if to reassure herself, she walked about the room, savoring its beauty. "I enjoy my life. I love my work, and I have a freedom few people enjoy. How many others hopping from bed to bed can say the same?"

Asher rested his head back against the sofa pillow and watched her. He said so quietly she had to stop pacing to hear him:

"You've been hurt by love, Elizabeth, but do you think God counts only women's tears? Men suffer as much as women . . . and many men are even more romantic than women. Many of us dislike sex without love or commitment as much as you." His eyes held hers. "You and I are bound by many of the same traditions . . . but tradition can snare us as well as root us."

His eyes were solemn, and she sensed a deep sadness in him, a sadness like a sliver of steel hidden in such brilliantly cut crystal that one caught only the briefest glimpse beneath the glitter.

She stared at him and recognized in his eyes a kinship, a sense of loss she had known and which, even after all these years, surfaced and stung. Compassion rose in her and a stirring she had not allowed in a long time. Suddenly she wanted to hold him and kiss him until that slow, beautiful smile returned. Her eyes went to the strong mouth . . . she took a long breath . . . and then drew herself in tightly.

He saw her emotion, and her withdrawal, as clearly as if she pulled a drawstring around her feelings. He sat silently on the sofa. He wanted her, but only once before, many years ago, had he ever taken a woman against her wishes. The memory made him feel ashamed, and with the shame came weariness, edging through him, deepening the lines around his face and mouth.

Elizabeth saw the tiredness descend on him, stilling the strong features.

"Perhaps you'd like to turn in," she said softly. "There's a sauna adjacent to the bathroom—you might enjoy that."

"Thank you," he said, rising slowly. "It has been a long day. I'm too bushed for the sauna, but a shower will feel great—that way I can get an early start in the morning."

Chapter Four

AFTER she showed Asher to his room, Elizabeth went about her nightly chores. It was a ritual she enjoyed, and soon the house looked ready for an *Architectural Digest* photo session. When she finished she went into the foyer, slipped into her boots and parka, and whistled softly. The animals awakened immediately. The cats flew between her legs as she opened the door, and the dog shouldered her aside, plunging chest-deep into the drifts.

She had turned off the outside lights and she stood in the darkness, her head tossed back to catch the snow, which fell like iridescent mist. She wanted the crystalline chill to ice the emotion she had felt since first looking into those dark green eyes. She was acutely aware of the man who slept in the downstairs bedroom, and she closed her eyes to listen more keenly to all that was familiar, comforting: the rush of the stream, the movement of the wind in the

39

trees, the occasional stir of a nocturnal creature. Solitude was her sanctuary; she did not want the pain of caring.

She stood for a long while concentrating on the sounds and on the touch of the fragile snowflakes drifting and melting on her face, but then the animals charged from the woods, snow flying, eager to return to the warmth of the house. She went inside and put them into the mud room off the kitchen, turned off all the lights, and climbed the spiral staircase to her room. But she didn't feel tired; adrenaline raced through her—meeting Asher had been exciting.

Had Asher seen Elizabeth's bedroom, he would have instantly recognized the contradiction. It was a seductive room, to be shared with a man. A king-size bed, canopied like an Arabian princess's private pavilion with raw silk hangings in a subdued, blue floral print, sat on a cream-colored, carpeted platform angled to catch the view of woods and stream visible through floor-to-ceiling glass walls. The walls of the room were covered in the same fabric as the sheltering hangings, and the headboard was upholstered in pale blue ultrasuede. On either side of the bed were 19th-century burled walnut tables with slender brass lamps which cast a soft glow on three Matisse lithographs of voluptuous nudes and odalisques on a nearby wall. A Kirman rug in richly patterned tones lay on the creamy wall-to-wall carpeting, and near the glass doors leading to a balcony overlooking the stream was a Chippendale writing desk and chair. In a corner, set to catch the light and the view, was a chaise lounge luxuriously quilted in ivory silk. The wall opposite the sliding glass doors was mirrored, reflecting the night and the falling snow. Behind the mirrors were spacious closets in which was an eclectic collection of clothing: designer dresses and suits in fine, natural fabrics on scented, padded hangers; furs in protective cotton covers; casual clothes and sports-wear; dozens of shoes in plastic boxes. The built-in shelves and drawers held neatly folded sweaters, scarves, and lingerie; handbags and other accessories were arranged for easy selection—all was organized with the precision of a West Point cadet.

Elizabeth stood before the mirror, a flannel nightgown in her hands. She looked at herself, at the gown, and disdain touched her lips. Sliding the mirrored door open, she tossed the blue flannel on a shelf and rummaging through a drawer, took out a pale peach satin gown lavishly trimmed with ecru lace. Putting it on, she smiled at the woman in the mirror, pleased at how the gown clung to her body, pleased at the color in her face, the animation in her eyes. She had not felt this lovely in a long time. Looking through the mirror at the bed, she remembered how it had once held two lovers—how once a man had made her know what it was to be a woman in love. Shutting her eyes, she ran her hands slowly along the satin of her gown. How silky she felt. She thought of Asher sleeping downstairs and envisioned his hands on her. Her fingers closed on her breasts, caressing the hardened pink tips through the fragile lace. A deeply carnal feeling coursed through her; her head fell back.

She began to shiver. The iciness rising in her had nothing to do with the temperature of the room. "No!" she hissed aloud. "No! I won't think about him!"

Angrily, she strode into the bathroom, pulling the nightgown over her head, throwing it in a lump on the carpeted floor. Turning on the pulsating shower head, she stepped into stinging hot water and washed herself vigorously. When her head felt clear she turned the water off, wrapped herself in a large bath towel, and went back into the bedroom. Dropping the towel beside the bed, she quickly crawled between the covers.

If Bonnie were here, she thought, she'd say, "Go for it!" The thought of her daughter made her smile in the darkness. Bonnie! She had no false, romantic dreams— Bonnie knew what was real; she could handle anything, especially men. She closed her eyes to see her daughter better, and she remembered the night she realized Bonnie was no longer a child—the night after the big race. Bonnie had bounded in joyously, hair flying, her face shining as brightly as the medal around her neck.

"I won, Mom! I won!" She grabbed Elizabeth and hugged her hard. Elizabeth held her close, kissing her.

41

Bonnie was not demonstrative and it might be a long time before her daughter hugged her again.

"Terrific! I *knew* you could do it."

"You *always* know, but now *I* know it." Bonnie grinned, plopping onto the sofa. She took the medal from around her neck and held it out to her mother.

"It's yours."

"No, Bonnie, you worked for it."

"So did you, so take it. You know you're dying to show it off."

Elizabeth laughed, taking the gold disc on the long satin streamer.

"Thank you, I love having it. What was your time?"

"Doesn't matter. I won! That's all that counts." Bonnie got up and went to the bookcase. She opened a hinged lid, revealing a small bar. "Want a drink?"

"No, and you shouldn't have one either. What would Dave say?"

"Fuck Dave," Bonnie said, giggling, "and I have."

"Bonnie!"

"Are you shocked?"

"You bet I am!"

"What about? My saying 'fuck'? My drinking? Or giving my coach my *all?*"

"That's quite a choice!"

Bonnie half filled a glass with rye and added an equal amount of ginger ale. She came to where Elizabeth sat, easing herself onto the sofa opposite. Smiling sweetly at her mother, she spoke as if she were stroking a new-found kitten.

"I don't mean to hurt you, Mom. I know you hate dirty language. I know how you feel about booze, and I'm sure you hoped I'd be a virgin until I married. But I'm different from you, Mom. You're a romantic, an incurable idealist, and you believe in that world you write about. But the way I see it, life's a shit, and no pretty words will cover it up. And people fuck each other more than they make love. Love hurts, fucking feels good."

Bonnie was too young to be so old, Elizabeth thought.

"How could you possibly know that love hurts? You're only seventeen!"

42

"Are you kidding? Where do you think I've been, in a convent?"

"Oh, Bonnie," Elizabeth wailed. "It's terrible to be so cynical. You sound like a jaded old sot. What will you be like at my age?"

"Dead probably."

Elizabeth laughed outright. "You had me worried. Now you sound more like a teenager."

Bonnie had looked at her with a quizzical expression in her eyes. "Do you really think there'll be a twenty-first century?"

"Of course!" Elizabeth said. "I'm hoping to take a trip to the moon someday."

"You would." Bonnie grimaced. "I don't think either of us will be around for two thousand and one."

"Oh come on, Bonnie, you don't believe in doomsday."

"How can you *not* believe in it? Just look how we've messed up this planet—and in less than a hundred years! And what about all the nuclear weapons spread around—something's bound to happen! So I intend to enjoy myself. I told Dave I'm quitting."

"Bonnie!"

The girl looked at her, a regretful smile shading the shining face. "Sorry, Mom. I know how much it means to you, but think about it. I hate the training, I hate the grind, I hate the downhill. I race to make you happy."

She took off her boots and wiggled her toes. "What would you rather have? A miserable Olympic racer, or a happy ski bum who loves you?"

So Bonnie had quit racing, and before she entered Radcliffe, she took a year off, free-skiing every mountain she could find, glorying in the release from the rigidity of training and the demands of Elizabeth's expectations.

That evening had forever changed their relationship. Bonnie broke free from tradition, and from her mother. Now, ten years later, Elizabeth still felt a sense of loss, a sense of guilt, as if her daughter's lifestyle were somehow her fault. She wanted for her daughter what she had not known—a loving husband and a secure marriage. Instead, Bonnie, like her, was reluctant to commit herself to love and hostile to marriage. And what else should she have expected? Bonnie's father had left them before Bonnie was two—all the child had ever known was a woman who worked. *Damn you, Danny!* Elizabeth had cried silently through the years . . . *why couldn't you at least have seen Bonnie! Why did you desert her!* But she had come to understand why, and she could not hate the man she had married—he had been so touching, so in need of love.

When he was twelve, Danny's parents and two younger sisters had perished when the furnace in their house exploded. He had spent that night with a friend two houses down. Torn from bed by the blast, Danny had stood screaming in the street, unable to get near the house—screaming until the intern who arrived in the ambulance mercifully put a needle into the child's arm. After that, Danny lived in Catholic orphanages until he was old enough to join the Navy. Elizabeth had met him at a dance shortly before he was released from the service; he had been ten years older than she and had been stationed on an aircraft carrier in World War II. His surprising shyness attracted her; he was her first love, and when she became pregnant they married. She was not yet eighteen. But Danny feared marriage, he feared love, and when his fears became unmanageable, he simply walked out. Neither she nor Bonnie had seen him since.

Elizabeth pulled the quilt around her and turned on her side, seeking the softness, the solace, of sleep. But it did not come. Instead, drifting out of the past like a spectral dream came the man who once had made love to her in this bed. He came sometimes when she lay sleepless, and if she could not dispel the memory, she switched on the light and read or got up and went downstairs to browse in the reality of the refrigerator.

But tonight she lay and let the vision take shape. Why? Was it because she needed him to remind her of how painful caring for someone could be? To remind her that she simply couldn't go to bed with someone without becoming emotionally involved?

"Oh Lorne," she sighed aloud. "It was good between us."

She saw him now as she had ten years before, the year

Bonnie had quit racing, had gone out West, and Elizabeth had had to face that Bonnie was now a woman and that they must lead separate lives.

She had first met Lorne Fread in his New York office that exciting day they signed the contracts on the sale of her book to his movie production company. When Elizabeth and her agent walked into the sun-shaded office high above Fifth Avenue, she felt as if she had indeed gone through the Looking Glass. Mirrored walls reflected their movement across the thick grey carpet towards the remarkably young-looking, silver-haired man seated behind the chrome and marble-topped table that served as a desk.

He rose to greet them, his eyes traveling boldly upwards from Elizabeth's slim ankles shod in high-heeled pumps, along her rounded, seductive figure in the close-fitting, sheer wool dress. She could not see his eyes behind the grey-tinted, silver-rimmed glasses, but she *felt* them, and she felt also a strong sexuality exuding from his thousand-calories-a-day body sleek under the silver-grey suit. He was like a knife sheathed in silk. The collar of his white shirt shone, flawlessly ringing a slender neck that didn't dare to sag. His white-on-white foulard tie was tautly tied. He spoke in a carefully modulated voice, his manicured hands occasionally emphasizing his words. A wafer-thin silver watch showed beneath French cuffs fastened with sapphire and silver links. As he initialed clauses in the contract, the sun slitting through half-closed slats of the vertical blinds caught the star sapphire on his finger, sending prisms of light across the pages.

Elizabeth wondered if Fread had ever gone hungry, if he had ever slept in his clothes, if he had ever raised his voice, if he had ever raged—if he *felt* anything. All the silvered perfection bothered her, and a perverse vision rose in her mind, almost making her giggle. She envisioned an enormous elephant in this silvery room—a grey beast swathed in silver trappings, and as its trainer, dressed in silver sequins, smiled at Fread and signed their contract, the beast triumphantly raised its tail and shit on the silver-grey carpet.

Elizabeth knew the vision to be a defense. From the

45

moment she had walked into the room and shaken Fread's hand, she had felt an uncomfortable attraction for him. Whenever his eyes swept her, her pulse raced.

She had not seen him again until Los Angeles, and she was disappointed when he did not meet her plane. Instead a chauffeured Rolls Royce waited, a maroon, antique Rolls with crystal vases banded in silver. In the vases were single yellow roses. Right out of her book—she had to give him points.

Set into the padded partition separating the passenger compartment from the chauffeur was a polished rosewood bar, and against a crystal decanter, a note. Her name was on the outside. She withdrew the fine, deckle-edged paper from the envelope.

"My dear Elizabeth," she read. "Welcome. I could not meet you because of meetings. Please join me in the Polo Lounge at six. Penning and Edwards will join us for dinner in the Lanai Room at seven. You've been preregistered into Bungalow Ten. There's Pouilly-Fuisse in the decanter. Enjoy the drive to Beverly Hills—there's no smog in January. Until tonight . . . L.F." The script was so small, so pristine, it seemed the writer feared even these simple words revealed too much.

It was two-thirty in the afternoon when the Rolls drove up to the green and white striped porte cochere of the Beverly Hills Hotel.

The chauffeur had leapt from the car and opened her door. He said to the doorman:

"Miss Banks is preregistered into Bungalow Ten. Would you please see to her luggage."

Elizabeth recognized many well-known faces in the luncheon crowd waiting for their cars. People greeted each other warmly, smiling with their lips, their eyes busy, gauging each other's status by who they were with, how they dressed, what they drove. Those not working needed to be seen and to see who else was "at liberty." Cheeks turned to cheeks in casual embrace as car after car appeared, making the car jockeys hustle.

In a city where Rolls Royces are as common as station wagons, Lorne Fread's vintage Rolls with its right-hand drive and flower vases was instantly recognizable. That

46

Elizabeth was to be in Bungalow Ten added to her prestige. Many checked into the Beverly Hills Hotel, but few arrived in Fread's Rolls, and only very special guests were assigned to Bungalow Ten.

Elizabeth, therefore, was acknowledged with the half-smiles of the Polo Lounge crowd. Should she be truly important, the momentary smile could be built on later:

"Of course, darling. Don't you remember our meeting at the Beverly Hills Hotel the day you arrived?"

Should she prove unimportant, no real overture had been made on which she could presume acquaintance.

The alarm clock on the table next to the king-size bed in Bungalow Ten went off; its nagging buzz dragged Elizabeth from a deep sleep. She turned over in the darkened room and looked with one eye at the time: 5:15. With a groan she pulled the pillow over her head. No need to get up that early, she thought. She reached over to silence the alarm and then she realized where she was. It was not 5:15 *a.m.*, but 5:15 *p.m.* She had to meet Fread at six. She switched on the bedside lamp and lay back in the massive bed, her eyes wandering about the rococo room. She stretched, reached her arms above her head, feeling her body lengthen from toes to fingertips.

Her imagination reacted to where she was. My God! she thought, what went on in this bed! Clark Gable and Carole Lombard; Elizabeth Taylor and Richard Burton; Marilyn Monroe and Yves Montand; Warren Beatty and Leslie Caron; Lorne Fread and Elizabeth Banks! She sat bolt upright. *Why on earth had she thought of that!* It was bad business being involved with someone she would be working with so closely. Her father had always said that, soothing her mother, who had a strong streak of jealousy: "Lena, Lena, don't be silly, would I fool around with those girls? A foreman can never do that—it gives people a hold on you."

Her face saddened as she thought of her parents. If only they could see her now!

They had died too young, the Depression stealing their youth as surely as poverty steals all joy and makes one prematurely old. Elizabeth had no happy memories of

47

them; they were always tired, overworked, seldom smiling. She had been the only one of their four children to survive; the others died as infants. How her parents doted on her. Her father would stroke her hair and say to her mother:

"Wait, you'll see—Ellyah will be famous and we'll live on Park Avenue."

Park Avenue! That had been his dream; to take his family out of the fifth-floor walkup on Washington Avenue in the East Bronx, where tenement touched tenement. After trudging the five flights of stairs, Papa would gasp, his breaths short and raspy: "Someday we're going to live on Park Avenue with an elevator."

But he had died before his dream came true, and when Elizabeth made money and could afford to live anywhere, she could not bring herself to live on Park Avenue. They had found Papa on the third-floor landing. The bag of groceries he had picked up at Saltzman's on his way home from work lay split beside him: two cans of Heinz Vegetarian Beans, a can of Bumble Bee salmon, and a loaf of Silvercup Bread lay on the little black and white tiles. Elizabeth was eleven. Six years later Mama died, eaten by the cancer which Elizabeth felt was caused as much by her sorrow over Papa as by the tumor swelling unnoticed in her belly until it was too late.

With a sigh Elizabeth left the satiny sheets of the big bed in Bungalow Ten. No, she must not think of those sad times—she had to be bright and positive for her meeting with Fread.

Promptly at six, Elizabeth walked into the Polo Lounge, feeling like a silkened combatant in a gilded arena. Now that her book was to be a movie she wanted it to reflect her vision, and, refusing to accept the original offer, she had used the book's bestseller status to hold out for script approval.

Fread had been adamant. She had been immovable. Finally, he had phoned personally, and when he found Elizabeth logical and reasonable about his authority and the changes he deemed necessary, he agreed. After they met in New York, he had invited her to California.

The captain led her to his booth; Fread was on the

phone but he smiled and rose, still talking into the mouthpiece. He waited for her to be seated, his eyes following the folds of her green silk dress. It outlined her full breasts and accented the red tones in her hair.

A waiter poured Elizabeth a glass of wine from a bottle in a silver cooler. She sat back against the dark green leather, amused at the plug-in phones being hustled to the booths.

"Thank you, Francis, I'll be in touch," he said, hanging up the phone. "Sorry, Elizabeth, but that couldn't wait." Fread leaned towards her, a thin smile on the controlled face.

"Welcome to California, Elizabeth."

Carefully she subdued the excitement he aroused in her.

"Thank you for the elegant reception. It's very exciting and very Hollywood."

"And so it should be." Her appreciation pleased him. "We always treat our celebrities with care."

He saw little flecks of green light up in her eyes.

He sipped his wine, his beautifully groomed fingers graceful on the stem of the glass.

"Despite what people think about Hollywood, we are a businesslike town, and I hope you are an early riser. Our first story conference is Monday at nine."

"I'm happy to hear that," she responded. "I'm at my best in the mornings."

They then discussed her book, Fread explaining his ideas for the movie. She listened attentively, occasionally asking questions which he answered succinctly. She was surprised and impressed with how open he was. The man she had felt so wary about in New York seemed more genuine on his own turf. She began to relax.

He sat back and looked at her, and she was aware how closely he measured her. Her pulse picked up. She wished she could read his eyes more easily, but seeing through his eyeglasses was like looking through smoke. She glanced about the room and noted all the heavily tinted eyeglasses. Was it cosmetic affectation, she thought, or did these people feel safer behind their shades? But Lorne Fread was not the kind of man who needed ocular camouflage.

"Do you wear those glasses because you know it puts

49

people at a disadvantage," she asked, "or because you think it makes you more attractive?"

He laughed. It was a constrained laugh, like his handwriting. She realized she had never heard him laugh before. He took off his glasses and she saw his eyes were small, set close together. The grey eyes regarded her with calm amusement.

"You're right to wear them," she said with a smile. "They do a lot for you."

This time he laughed openly, genuinely.

"You had to be born in Brooklyn, and I'll bet it was Brownsville."

"No, the East Bronx. And you?"

"Flatbush. My father was a clothing manufacturer."

Teasingly, she slurred, New York style. "A rich kid, huh. Ya musta gone to Madison."

He answered with the same inflection, the same twang, "Ya guessed it—the Hollywood High of Brooklyn. Even in the Depression kids went to school in Packards."

They smiled at each other.

"How did you get to Hollywood?"

"After Madison, I went to Columbia and majored in journalism." Fread nodded to a group walking into the room, then continued. "My father hoped I would apply to the *New York Times,* but I had stars in my eyes. I joined Paramount's publicity department and, as they say, worked my way up."

"And up, and up," Elizabeth said, admiration in her voice. Fread had survived many changes in Hollywood and commanded financing whenever he needed it.

He glanced at his watch and rose, extending his hand to her. As they left the Polo Lounge, many waved to him; he returned the greetings with a nod. They turned right, going through the lobby with its two white plaster decorated fireplaces in which gas-burning logs flamed constantly. Beveled mirrors in white arches above the fireplaces reflected the soft lights in the green and pink carpeted lobby with its green and pink floral sofas.

Fread had chosen the green and white Lanai Room for their dinner meeting because it afforded a quiet, yet visible, setting. Aware of the public relations potential of every action, he knew that mention would be made of Elizabeth's meeting with Malcolm Penning, the director, and Bernard Edwards, the screenwriter.

He ate lightly and said little, listening to the lively conversation that skidded back and forth among the three. Elizabeth felt no inhibitions talking about her book, and Penning and Edwards expressed their opinions just as openly. The rapport was good, and the session was enhanced by the food, the wines, and the enthusiasm generated by creative people exchanging ideas.

Elizabeth was pleased that Fread had chosen seasoned men of her own generation for the film. It needed a sense of romance which she found lacking in younger filmmakers, and she voiced her confidence in both Penning and Edwards, pleasing them with her knowledge and her appreciation of their work.

When Fread, over coffee, offhandedly asked if she had any casting preferences, her answer not only amused them but indicated she was no novice to be taken lightly, for she was aware that Fread's query was made in a spirit of tact.

"Everyone I like is either dead or too old," she said wryly.

Fread smiled. "On that perceptive note, we can conclude."

He held Elizabeth's arm as he walked her through the lush, fragrant gardens and up the paved path to her bungalow. He stopped under one of the shaded garden lights and looked at her without smiling.

"You know I'm not happy about your having script approval," he said. "I'm relying on your good judgment. Writers and filmmakers create in different ways. Authors make autonomous decisions; movie people work in committee. Authors have a God-like power with paper and pencil—they create their own people, their own lands, and they set their own pace. And if things don't go right, they tear up what they've written. Paper is cheap. But for us every second costs thousands. For you, Elizabeth, words create character and plot. For us, words take second place—our milieu is visual, our stories are images, and we create those images with hundreds of technicians, with action, lights, camera, weather, and, God help us, *actors,* or even worse, *stars,* some of whom are so insecure they keep their agents on the set to check camera angles and every line of dialogue to make sure all emphasis is on them. Authors in Hollywood are like pesky fleas—to be swatted away. They must accept editing by committee, which is disjointed, chaotic, crazy, because everyone working on a movie thinks they're a writer, and the bottom line is not the written word. Believe me, no one thinks the play's the thing. What counts in Hollywood is how much will it make!"

They turned up the path. The night breezes blew in from the Pacific, stirring the leaves still on the trees but not one silver hair on the head of Lorne Fread. Elizabeth gathered her fur coat closely about her, glad that she had brought it. Silently, she thought of what he had said.

They reached her door. She extended her hand.

"Thank you, Lorne, for a truly lovely evening. And thank you also for being so honest."

He held her hand.

"Elizabeth, I respect your talent, and I think you've got enough Bronx moxie not to hassle us. I'll do my best to make this a good movie, but truthfully, if we're still speaking to each other when this is over, I'll be surprised. The car will be here Monday morning at eight to take you to the studio."

He turned and walked rapidly back to the hotel. Twenty years in Hollywood had not slowed his New York pace.

Elizabeth hated the movie, but she fell in love with Lorne Fread, and he with her.

It began one day when they argued over a scene and to make a point, Elizabeth quoted Shakespeare. Fread topped her with another Shakespearean quote. And she had to admit he was right. The next day he invited her to a production of *Hamlet* at the Pasadena Playhouse, and then to a Shakespeare reading at UCLA. Soon there were quiet picnics on Zuma Beach and in the hills above Malibu Canyon. They sat for hours reading aloud favorite passages from Shakespeare's plays and sonnets.

Fread was slow and cautious about revealing his feelings, but as they came to know each other, his reserve gave

52

way, and she saw a warmth in him which nourished her. After shooting ended on the film, they became lovers, and with the intimacy other changes occurred in Fread—he laughed more, he was less aloof, more flexible.

Elizabeth was aware of Fread's reputation as a ladies' man—he had been married only once, and divorced for many years. He had one child, a son, Steven, whom he doted on; the young man was in his twenties and an accomplished singer-composer-musician, whose first rock album promised fame. She was not so naive as to think Fread had stopped dating, and the knowledge hurt. One night they had an emotional argument and he stormed from the beachfront house she had rented in Malibu; he returned two days later and put a stunning sapphire and diamond ring on her finger, saying, "Elizabeth, I care deeply for you. I'll never marry—it's not for me—but neither shall I be unfaithful to you while we're together. Help me keep what we have."

For Elizabeth it was the best of two worlds: she had the freedom to which she had grown accustomed, and she had a love which cloaked her like a cashmere mantle—warm and light. Even their children, Steven and Bonnie, were woven into their lives—they all became friends. Elizabeth and Fread saw each other as much as possible, sharing the house in Malibu and her country home back East. The years were good to them all: Elizabeth did her best work, Fread had one success after another, Bonnie graduated from college and moved into Elizabeth's New York pied-à-terre to begin her career, and Steven's music made him a rock idol.

Elizabeth could not remember a more glorious time in her life.

When it shattered, it shattered so swiftly and with such pain, she was unprepared and defenseless.

Only in later years would she come to think that had Lorne been the same man she had first met, he might have managed to deal with his tragedy. But he had opened himself to love—not only hers, but the love of Steven and Bonnie—and he could not accept his loss.

Steven died in a senseless, tragic accident. He had driven down to Cheetah's in Venice, California, to hear a new group; after the performance he went backstage to offer his congratulations and walked in on an argument between the lead singer and the drummer. High on speed, the drummer drew a knife and lunged at the singer; he lost his footing and stumbled into Steven, the knife slicing into Steven's heart.

Lorne's reaction frightened her. He became like a stone, so cold she dared not touch him and barely spoke to him. She waited for him to cry, but the tears never came. Finally, she drove into Beverly Hills to consult with Lorne's doctor; she hoped he would prevail on Lorne to seek therapy. When she returned to Malibu later that afternoon, two police cars stood at her door.

Lorne Fread had drowned in the surf just a few hundred yards from the house. He had been an excellent swimmer.

Tears stole from under Elizabeth's lids as she lay in bed, remembering. She got up, put on a robe, and went down to the living room. Perhaps if she worked for a while, she might find it easier to sleep.

The fire flickered weakly behind glass doors; she opened them and threw kindling and logs onto the grate. Soon heat raced into the room. Going to the bar, she poured a glass of cream sherry and took a small tape recorder from a shelf. Returning to the fire, she piled pillows on the floor and settled down comfortably. Then she turned on the tape recorder and softly spoke into the microphone. It was with the characters in her books that she felt in control.

Chapter Five

Asher lay in the large, comfortable bed in Elizabeth's guest room at the end of the downstairs hall, staring into the darkness, unable to sleep. Damn that shower! He should have waited until morning, but he couldn't stand the smell of himself after stripping out of the clothes he had worn all day.

How peacefully he would be sleeping now, had he showered with Elizabeth, he thought. He turned on his side, closing his eyes to better conjure the two of them, warm water wetting their naked bodies. A pleasant, familiar stirring began in his loins as he concentrated on the images: he felt himself soaping her body, running his hands over her womanly breasts, down to the curve in her waist, gliding up her back, then down to the roundness of her behind. There was a throbbing between his legs as he

55

imagined the smoothness between her thighs, the softness of her hair as he parted it to find the hidden, moist pleasures within. He groaned in arousal, and, angry with himself for behaving like an adolescent, he kicked off the quilt and got out of bed, going to the window, wanting the chill of the room to still his desire. He shuddered as he stood naked, looking out into the night; with the outside lights off, the world no longer looked magical, only grey and cold. Damn it—it *was* cold! Too cold to stand naked! He got back into bed and turned on the bedside lamp. Reaching over, he took some paperbacks from the shelf below the nightstand . . . good . . . there were some Ludlams and Le Carrés, and here was a Graham Green he had missed: *Dr. Fischer and the Bomb Party.* He settled back against the pillows and began to read . . . soon his lids grew heavy, and the words on the page ran into each other. With a contented sigh, he rolled over, snapped off the light, and burrowed into the warmth of the down quilt. Sleep came quickly.

He had only a vague memory of the dream which awakened him. All he recalled was that he skied for miles and miles on some vast, windblown desert, the sand whipping into his face, his throat. God, he was thirsty—he wanted water with ice in it.

He got out of bed and shivered at the sudden cold; searching for something to cover and warm his nakedness, he found a robe in the closet. Putting it on, he went down the darkened hallway towards the kitchen. As he passed the living room, the glow in the fireplace surprised him— the fire flared in the grate, and the doors were open. Wouldn't Elizabeth have closed the doors, and wouldn't the fire be out by now?

He went to the fireplace and saw her sleeping on the floor, her arm outstretched on the pillows beneath her head. His steps were silent as he moved to close the doors, but she stirred, and her eyes flew open, startled.

"It's only me, Elizabeth," he whispered. "Don't be frightened."

Kneeling beside her, he saw the tape recorder—she had had trouble sleeping. The firelight illuminated her eyes

56

and he recognized a loneliness in their depths. It was a feeling he knew too well. He leaned towards her and brushed the hair from her cheek.

Her hands clenched.

He looked at the tightened fingers. Taking her hands in his, he gently opened each finger, one by one. Not moving his gaze from her, he kissed the open palm of one hand, then the other.

Elizabeth controlled the impulse to pull her hands from Asher's and run from the room. That was childish. Why deny herself the joy of this beautiful man?

He sensed her conflict. "Am I making it so difficult for you?"

She dropped her eyes, unable to find an honest answer. She needed distance between them so that she could think clearly, and she shrank away.

He let go of her hands and sat down, stretching his bare feet to the fire. He wanted her; he wanted to appease his loneliness; he wanted to share the thrill of sex with her. But she must want him as well.

Elizabeth looked at Asher's feet backlighted by the fire. The toes tapered evenly. He had high arches and strong-looking ankles. His legs were brawny and shadowed with black hair. The robe did not reveal his thighs, but she saw his chest where the folds parted. She saw its breadth, its muscularity. She saw the chest naked on hers, his toes curling around hers, and his legs pressing hers. Heat rose in her and she sat up quickly, facing the fire as he did.

She clasped her hands tightly in her lap, hoping to temper the feelings burning inside. Why not make love to this beautiful man and accept it for what it was . . . a moment to be enjoyed. Lorne had taught her to expect nothing more than moments; they'd had only one terrible quarrel before he stopped dating other women. The memory flashed unwanted in her brain.

"Don't lie to me!" she had screamed. "I've had it! I won't believe you anymore! 'When the blood burns, how prodigal lends the tongue vows!'"

Lorne had laughed mockingly: "Why cut me up with Hamlet, Liz, when your own words are razors?"

57

My God! It seemed like yesterday. She closed her eyes and exhaled a long sigh.

Asher turned his head from the fire. "Are you thinking of what you said earlier tonight?"

Her mind reeled back to the present. "I'm sorry, I was far away."

He asked again, "Is what you said this evening on your mind?"

She was puzzled. "We talked about so much. I don't know to what you refer."

"Celibacy, Elizabeth. What drove you to it?"

She sighed again. "I wasn't driven; it just happened. It was easier, more comfortable." Irony twisted her lips. "But I'm not comfortable now. Something I said years ago seems so apt at this moment . . . that is, if I just reverse the words."

Asher said nothing. His eyes held hers.

Her words came. They were slow, measured. "When the blood burns, how prodigal rends the vows tongued."

The fire highlighted the comprehension in his eyes. He took her face in his hands.

"Thank you for such an honest admission."

She tried to pull away, embarrassed by what she knew showed in her eyes.

"No! Don't back down now. Don't be ashamed of what you feel." His eyes were like magnets.

She couldn't face him; she closed her eyes.

"Look at me, Elizabeth."

She shook her head.

He lowered his face and barely brushed his lips on hers. Her mouth went taut. Slowly, his lips caressed hers, moving gently along the curve of her mouth, lingering at the corners, coming back to the center, pressing the twin peaks until her lips softened and parted under his. She felt the warm moistness of his mouth and her lips quivered; it had been so long since she'd known such tender warmth. His kisses were like a nourishing spring on parched earth, and she drank deeply, tasting his lips, his tongue, daring her lips and tongue to seek him voluptuously.

His fingers spread through her hair and he turned her

head from side to side, his lips closing her lids, tasting the flush of her cheeks, smoothing the uncertainty from her brow, and lingering long and hotly on her trembling mouth, delighting in her sensitivity. She moaned and surrendered to the exquisite sensations gilding her; all tenseness ebbed; she was a sail before the wind and her heart filled, her body reached, as wave after wave of sensuality swept her.

His lips grew hungrier and he kissed her neck, her ears, and the hollow in her throat. She felt herself grow moist, and low sounds of sheer pleasure came from her. She entwined her arms around his neck, pressing his head closer. Slowly, she ran her hands up under the sleeves of his robe, her fingers feathers as they floated along the fine hairs of his forearms; her hands closed around the strength in his muscles. Drawing his robe aside, her fingers curled into the soft hair on his chest, and, ever so lightly, skimmed across and around his nipples. His breath caught as she fondled and circled their growing hardness; she tweaked and caressed until they stood rigidly. His skin bristled with enjoyment and he chuckled deep from within, his voice husky with his pleasure.

With his mouth and lips following his hands, he slid the robe from her shoulders, kissing the glow of her skin, savoring the taste of its smoothness. The fire shone on her nakedness—she gleamed pink and silklike.

"What a lovely woman you are," he breathed, tracing her body with his hands and lips, kissing the curves of her thighs, raising her legs to kiss the warm glen behind her knees, trailing his lips down the slope of her calves to the shallows around her ankles and along the pale satin of her soles. She laughed joyfully and she reached out for him, tugging him upwards, sliding his robe from him. The firelight stroked him with amber, revealing a body young for its years. Her eyes feasted where her fingers touched.

She knew she wasn't beautiful, but he made her feel beautiful, and she settled against him, her lips enticing as they sought his flesh. The sensuality of her mouth enflamed him, and, his hands behind her back, feeling the arch where her waist flowed into seductive hips, he pressed

59

CHOICES

her back on the pillows, his body another skin on hers. He was highly aroused and, wanting to prolong the pleasure, he eased off her, sitting up, feasting his eyes on her soft, womanly beauty. The awakened sexuality in her face stirred his senses and he had to touch her. Like a Sumi artist painting with a slender Fude brush, he outlined delicate patterns on her skin, his fingers as light as the finest brush tip. Little goose bumps rose where he stroked. He traced the valley between her breasts, then wound his fingers around their rich fullness, encircling the warmth in his hands, teasing the pink-tipped nipples with his tongue. He raised his head and smiled rakishly at her:

"My cup runneth over."

Her laughter was young and happy. Enmeshing her hands in the thickness of his hair, she pulled his head to her lips, kissing him, darting her tongue in and out of his mouth. She couldn't get enough of him. Her hands groped for his. He teased her and moved out of her reach, his fingers relentless on the lush planes of her body; her skin responded with prickles of pleasure and his laugh was earthy as his fingers lured and tantalized.

Her stomach fluttered at his caresses and he bent to kiss the dell of her navel, rolling his tongue into its moist depth. Little cries came from her; he felt her every nuance and it excited him, quickened his stroking and kissing. His fingers, his lips, his tongue delved into her most secret places and her body swayed with desire; moistness gleamed on her skin as he drove her to an eroticism she had rejected. His touch became more fervent and demanding—her body flared. She could hold back no longer. Her breath came in quick, short gasps, and then with a long, low moan she succumbed to the utter joy he drew from her. She cried out in ecstatic pain, but he would not tear his mouth away from the wet, sweet-tasting lips of her womanhood. His passion joined hers as he kissed her into one climax after another.

He felt so turgid he thought he'd burst, but he could not tear his lips away. When he could contain himself no longer, he lifted his face and drew her legs high around his waist. He held back from plunging into her, forcing his

60

mind elsewhere—this was too wonderful to end. He stroked her gently, she quieted, and when he felt sure of himself once more, he slid his hands down the velvet of her thighs, his fingers entering a warmth so delicious he groaned. With a control that was almost painful, he slowly eased himself into her slowly . . . slowly. . . .

She tensed her muscles and tightened on him—then she let go. Her insides throbbed—then she tightened again. Her strength surprised him and he held still, closing his eyes to the incredible sensation. Her muscles pulsed, gripping him, releasing him—the joy of it made him cry out. He picked up her rhythm, thrusting into her, and she met his thrusts, throwing her hips against him, swirling her buttocks, making him plunge ever deeper. Her raw, unfettered desire drew from him cries dark with lust.

Her cries joined his, her body rose and swelled with his. She fired him with her passion and their minds and bodies exulted. She lost all inhibition, letting the jungle swallow her.

"Take me—take me!" she growled. "Take me *now!*" He felt her surge and the shudder of her body. He wanted more, but could not hold back. Her untamed ecstasy engulfed him and, drowning in the vortex, he plunged deep, feeling the marrow leave his bones with every throbbing spurt. His heart pounded, his legs stiffened, his back went weak. He slumped against her, breathing hard. Her own breath rasping, she held his head between her breasts. She felt his sweat on hers. Tenderly, she stroked his back, feeling a sweet surrender flow through her; she felt so warm, so wanted, so protected. Tears of fulfillment stole from under her closed lids. Asher moved to kiss her and felt their wetness.

"Why are you crying?" he asked, softly stroking the tears aside.

She shook her head, unable to speak.

"Is anything wrong?" Gently he kissed her hair, her cheeks, and when he moved to her lips she said, holding him tightly, "No, not at all, it's just that I feel so wonderful."

Gathering her close, he lay down beside her; he felt a

61

peace he had not known in a long time. She nestled into him, and soon, sleep came. The fire died; dawn creased the darkness and they slept, bodies entwined.

Insistent tapping, followed by the far-off sound of a dog barking, broke through the comforting blackness that cloaked Asher. He fought the sounds, refusing to awake, but the tapping, the barking would not stop. He dragged his mind from the depths of sleep and forced his eyes open. He was cold; he looked and saw his nakedness. Elizabeth slept in his arms, her body bare.

The barking came from afar, somewhere beyond the kitchen. But the tapping was close. He focused his eyes towards the disturbing sound; there was a man at the window, peering at him, at Elizabeth. Asher quickly threw her robe across her body and put on his own. Furiously, he went to the window and pulled the draperies closed, motioning the person to the door.

He cracked open the door. "What the hell do you want!" His voice was venomous: "How dare you spy like that!"

"Meant no harm." The man tried out a limp smile. Asher's look made the man's broad face settle into pink pudding. His wide lips swayed like a pendulum and his pale eyes receded behind lined pouches. Protruding ears held up his hat, a red, visored cap with a "TGA Feeds" insignia.

"I'm Jesse," he drawled, "and I jest plowed the driveway. There's a car there needs pullin' out. I need the keys."

"Why the hell didn't you knock on the door, instead of at the window?" Asher's anger would not lessen.

The man answered calmly, without apology. "Been doin' that fer a while. I heard the dog barkin' and when no one answered, thought I'd best look aroun'. Miz Banks is always up early. Thought somethin' mighta happened."

"Wait outside, till I get my clothes on." Asher was damned if he'd let him in the house.

"No need ter do that." Jesse's voice, like his face, was at one pitch. "Jest give me the keys. I'll pull yer car out and leave it in the driveway. The plow's already been through, and you'll have no trouble gettin' out. I'll bring yer keys back when I'm finished." He let out a sigh as if it was the longest he had ever spoken.

"I'll get them," Asher snapped, slamming the door shut.

Asher glanced into the living room. Elizabeth still slept. Good. No need for her to face Jesse at the moment. The nerve of the man! Asher followed the barking to the mud room off the kitchen; he let Blaze and the cats out the back door. He hoped the dog bit the man's goddamned pecker off. Getting his keys, he returned to the front door and flung them at Jesse. "I'll wait till you're finished."

"No need ter." Jesse smiled slyly. "Ya can go back ter sleep. I'll leave 'em in the bird feeder."

"No thanks, I'll wait." His malevolent look made Jesse turn quickly and plod through the snow towards the road. To add to Asher's fury, Blaze romped after Jesse, tail wagging.

Asher went into the kitchen and found the coffee pot. Soon an aromatic scent filled the room. He looked at the clock on the wall. 7:10! Damn! He'd been sleeping so peacefully. He sipped the coffee slowly, thinking of Elizabeth; the anger in him loosened as he remembered last night. He heard Jesse return and he went to the foyer.

Jesse handed him the keys with a knowing smile that made Asher want to punch him. "Yer car's out. Ya can leave whenever ya wants."

"Thanks." The word galled him.

"Tell Miz Banks, if she needs me ta call the house. We had more'n twelve inches last night, so I got lotsa plowin' ta do."

Asher nodded and shut the door. He didn't trust himself to talk with the man any further. The snow had stopped, but the day was grey, overcast. It was a morning for sleeping and Asher was grateful Elizabeth had not awakened. He went back into the living room and stood looking down at her.

She lay on her side, knees slightly drawn up, her hair across her cheek, her head on her arm. Her face was tanned, with a pink tinge that almost matched the soft robe covering her. How remarkably unlined her skin is,

63

Asher thought. She looked appealing, vulnerable, and he felt himself wanting her again. He smiled when he thought how good it had been.

He kneeled and picked her up in his arms. She stirred, her arms reaching around his neck. He kissed her forehead and she murmured, "Lorne, Lorne." He hesitated. "Ssh," he said. He carried her to his bedroom. The robe fell from her body as he put her into bed. He shed his own robe and got in beside her, pulling her close and the quilt over them both. She felt soft against him; her breath warmed his chest. His body urged him to awaken her, but her slow, even breathing lulled him back into sleep.

It was past noon when Elizabeth opened her eyes. She felt the heat of Asher's body and turned, startled to find him sleeping beside her. Then she remembered and wondered how she had gotten into the bedroom. She moved to get out of bed, but Asher threw a heavy arm around her. Gently she tried to maneuver free, and then she saw the half smile on his face.

"Good morning," she said.

"Hello, sleepyhead," he murmured, drawing her to him. "It's time you woke up."

"Time *I* woke up? Seems to me we're in this together." Even now, with stubble peppering his face, his skin creased from sleep, he was so handsome, she felt ugly. She didn't want him to look at her; only children looked lovely fresh from sleep.

She slipped out of his arms, needing to freshen up, to feel beautiful. "I'll be right back."

"You've got five minutes," he called after her.

"Be back sooner than that," she laughed, and she was.

"Come here," he grumbled, grabbing her, kissing her cheeks, her eyes, her mouth. "Mmmm, you smell delicious." His lips nipped at her. "You taste delicious." He closed his mouth on her breasts and laughed huskily as the nipples hardened under his tongue. Slowly he began to kiss her body, enjoying the response of her skin under his mouth, his fingers.

She reached for him, and gently he turned her so that she could kiss him as he kissed her. She lost all inhibition and surrendered to him with a desire she had thought was gone forever.

Later Elizabeth reached over to look at the clock on the bedside table. She began to giggle. Asher smiled as he felt the laughter in her body.

"What's so funny?"

"I haven't been in bed this late in a long time."

"Oh—so you did play around."

"I wish I had."

"Really? Why?"

"It would all be so much easier."

"What would?"

"This."

"This?" he teased, pulling at her nipples.

"Come on, you know what I mean."

He turned her face to his and looked in her eyes. "No, I don't. Tell me."

She kissed the stubble on his chin. "I'd bore you, Asher. If you get up, I'll make you a real country breakfast."

"You're on," he grinned. "But first, lovely lady, you will shower with me. It was my fantasy last night and now I want the real thing." He pinched her behind. "Let's go!"

He reached the bathroom first, in long, swift strides. He flicked the jet on high, and a sharp stream pulsed, filling the room with steam. He stepped in first and held out his hand to her. She sputtered as the water hit her face. She turned her back to him and to the deluge.

He pulled her to him and with slow, sensuous movements soaped her back, her arms, down the curve of her hips, around and around the swell of her buttocks. Massaging in a circular motion, his hands moved between and up the smoothness of her thighs. She gasped. Her hips began to move. Reaching around, he clasped her breasts, his fingers plucking gently at her nipples.

"Asher, Asher," she breathed, her voice deep, throaty. He pressed her close. She felt his excitement and bent forward, her body welcoming him.

When finally he turned her to face him, they were like saplings, languid after a torrential rain. They held each other as the water cascaded on them. He reached back and gentled the spray. They stood there, heads on each other's shoulders, letting the tepid drizzle revive them. As she watched the water circle into the drain beneath her feet, Elizabeth felt five years of discipline trickle out with the eddy. She knew she had lost the battle with her emotions.

Asher shut off the water, but did not release her; he brushed her wet hair back, and his expression was thoughtful. She met his eyes solemnly.

"I hope we can be friends," he said softly. Uncertainty rose in her eyes. "Why not?" he said, smiling.

She shivered. "I'm cold, Asher."

"I'm sorry." He grabbed a towel and dried her vigorously. She laughed as her skin turned pink.

"Now it's your turn!" She tossed a towel over him and tousled the thick hair on his head; then she roughly rubbed his back, his arms, and up and down his legs. He sighed in appreciation and wound a towel tightly around her.

"Get thee to the kitchen, wench, I'm starving!"

"With pleasure," she called, dashing from the room. "Breakfast will be ready by the time you've shaved and dressed."

When Asher walked into the main part of the house a half hour later, the delicious aroma of freshly brewed coffee and sizzling sausage came from the kitchen. The dining table was set, a fire blazed in the fireplace, and the room was filled with the melody of Grieg's Piano Concerto. He went into the kitchen, where Elizabeth, dressed in jeans and sweater, took hot rolls from the oven.

"You're just in time," she said, handing him a warming tray with food. "I'll bring the coffee and buns."

"You do that," he said, grabbing her rear.

She laughed and swatted him with a dish towel. They ate heartily, relishing the clean, sweet taste of the oranges, the spiced eggs and sausage, the rolls thick with cream cheese and jam. Asher wiped his plate clean with the last of the rolls and said, "Let's have coffee by the fire." He rose, took his mug and the coffee pot, and went into the living room. Elizabeth followed, cup in hand.

They settled onto the sofas and sipped their coffee. Neither spoke. The concerto ended sonorously and Asher let out a long sigh.

"Did you know Grieg wrote that on his honeymoon as a gift to his bride?"

"No, I didn't," Elizabeth said. "That explains why it's so romantic."

"He completed it in five weeks. Imagine creating a work so exquisite in so short a time." He glanced towards the piano. "Do you play?"

She shook her head. "I wish I did. I've always wanted to, but I never made time. My daughter plays."

He put his cup down and went to the piano.

"May I? I've been itching to try its tone since I first saw it."

"I'd be delighted," she said. "It's been so long since Bonnie's been home. I miss hearing it."

Asher propped open the top of the piano and sat down. His long fingers ran over the keys and then recreated the opening chromatic chords of Grieg's Piano Concerto. Elizabeth listened, astonished at the quality of his playing. He sat with his head back, his eyes closed—the late afternoon light behind him creating an aura around his face. She watched, entranced, envisioning Grieg himself at the piano. The last vestige of her reserve began to crumble, and she fought to conjure the Elizabeth she had been yesterday, the contained Elizabeth who worked hard at controlling her emotions.

This Elizabeth soothed her, made her feel comfortable, and now she reached for her, telling herself any woman would fall for Asher Jacobs. *Don't berate yourself. Enjoy this moment, and if you can't handle it, don't see him again. Just remember Cervantes, old girl: "Absence, that common cure of love."*

Elizabeth was so intent on her thoughts she did not realize Asher no longer played the Grieg until an unfamiliar melody echoed through to her. She listened intently, trying to place the pastoral theme, but she had never heard it before. The music was lovely—there was an eloquent caesura and then a rush of melody. Asher played with great tenderness. She looked at him and saw he was lost in the serenade, and when the music ended in a barely audible pianissimo, she felt an accompanying frisson edge up her spine.

He sat with his head bent. Again Elizabeth sensed that sadness in him. He left the piano and went to the window; the lowering light faded his presence.

He turned finally and said, "I'm sorry. It's been so long since I've played that—I'm afraid I was carried away. Would you mind if I poured myself a drink?"

"Not at all, I'll join you."

"What'll it be?"

"Scotch and water, please."

He went to pour the drinks.

"You play beautifully. You must have studied for years."

His reply was casual. "I had hoped to be a musician, but the war changed that. Now, I play for my own enjoyment and sometimes for special friends."

He seemed distant. He dropped his eyes and noticed the glasses in his hand. "Sorry." He handed Elizabeth her drink.

"Thank you." She went to the piano and sat down on the bench. With one finger she picked out a few of the notes she had heard him play. "It's lovely. Did you write it?"

He took a slow sip of his drink and came to where she was sitting. He stood looking down at her. "Yes, when I was seventeen and, like Grieg, I wrote it for my first love."

"But it's not at all like Grieg. It reminds me of Chopin."

The look he gave her was a mixture of surprise and admiration.

"At the time I was a Chopin scholar. I read all I could about him. I studied his scores—I identified with him, not only because I loved his music, but because of his affair with George Sand. You see, I was in the throes of my first passion, and she too was a married woman, older than I."

"And like Chopin, you died in her arms?"

His double take was so perfect, Elizabeth burst out laughing. The sadness on his face disintegrated and he laughed with her.

"Hail to thee, blithe spirit!" He raised his glass to her.

"Oh, to be a skylark!" She raised her own.

"Of course you'd know Shelley." He grinned, his eyes roving her face. "Elizabeth, you've made jumping ship in

68

CHOICES

Barbados worthwhile. I didn't mean to be rude last night when I avoided your questions about the Caribbean. I didn't want to talk about it, but now, I will tell you, if you're interested."

"I am."

"Well then," he replied, extending his hand to her, "come sit with me and I'll tell you all. You'll probably use the incident in one of your books," he teased.

"Of course!" She took his hand and went to sit with him on the sofa. She settled back onto the cushions. He leaned forward and began:

"I'm sure it's no surprise to learn that since my wife's death I've been fair game—and even before Eleanore died. We both were. But particularly since she died, I've been pursued with as much subtlety as a spread in *Hustler*. That was one of many reasons I went to Europe and Africa. But one can stay away only so long." He emptied his glass, put it down, and sat back.

"I dislike the visibility that's part of my life—you're a wise woman to have chosen to live away from the scrutiny which accompanies fame or achievement. You can appreciate the frustration when every aspect of your life is reported, exploited—violated; when every mistake you make is blown all out of proportion."

His voice became a whetstone for the knife-edge of his thoughts.

"We so-called 'celebrities' are lionized and Lennonized, and so to feel comfortable, and in some instances, *safe*, we withdraw into cliques, communicating only with others like us—naturally, this breeds resentment and criticism from those outside and we withdraw even more, distrusting everyone. Because of that withdrawal, we miss so much of what is truly *real*, truly meaningful." He got up and went to the bar. "Want a refill?"

"No, thank you."

He returned to the sofa, sat down, and stirred the ice in his glass with his fingers. After a time he said:

"All cliques are stifling—the same faces, the same places. We all seek the fresh, the untried, the unknown. We all want that special someone . . . and, as you so aptly put it . . . that special moment."

69

He drank slowly. "A group of us chartered a yacht for a Christmas cruise." His voice lightened. "I love the Caribbean. It's perhaps the most beautiful sailing in the world—unexplored coves, hidden beaches, crystal waters, and nights so clear you can see beyond the Milky Way. But the group I was with feared sailing beyond the safety of land. There's unrest in the Caribbean—political problems, hijackings by drug runners, and we were vulnerable. We sailed, but always close to port, and drank a lot; the conversations were endless and meaningless, the sex even more so. I left them in Barbados and flew back to New York on Thursday night. I wanted the sanity of my work, but even that did not ease the emptiness, which makes me restless and irascible."

He leaned towards Elizabeth.

"When I awakened yesterday, I was depressed, but thanks to you, Elizabeth, I feel better than I have in a long time." His voice became eager. "I'd like to see you again. Would you meet me in New York later this week?"

Elizabeth made a very quick decision. "I'm sorry. I promised friends in Palm Beach I'd fly down for Christmas." She kept her tone light.

"Oh?"

She felt herself flushing. She rose and went to the fire, where she brushed up wood scraps, tossing them into the flames. She added another log. Asher watched, but said nothing. She felt his eyes follow her retreat. She went to the window.

"Funny, I haven't seen Blaze or the cats all day. Well, they'll come home when they're hungry, that's for sure."

"Elizabeth." Asher's voice was placid. "Come here and sit down."

It was not an order—that she would have resented and refused. It was a request from someone who knew she was dissimulating and wanted to know why. She hesitated, hoping the phone would ring, hoping the animals would dash onto the deck begging to be let in, hoping for any interruption that would keep her from going to the sofa and facing Asher.

He sat there quietly with such assurance, she became annoyed. If she wanted to go to Palm Beach, why

70

shouldn't she? What did it matter when she made her decision? She approached the sofa, irritated that she felt defensive.

"Why did you decide suddenly to go away?" he asked easily. "If you don't care to see me again, why not say so?"

His directness disarmed her.

"You're right." She smiled slowly, self-deprecatingly. "I should have been more honest." She sat down and drew her feet up under her, as if by contracting her body she was less vulnerable to the lodestone of his attractiveness.

"Asher, I have a dear friend who recently made an agonizing decision. You probably know her since she is a celebrated actress. Well, she decided it was time for a face-lift. She's always been in films, has no stage experience to fall back on, and she is at that crucial stage when her appearance belies the still young woman inside. When she went for tests it was discovered she was allergic to anaesthesia, and she was also a latent diabetic. Surgery was possible, but risky. This was something she wanted; it was a boost not only to her career, but to her psyche. Every facet of her cried, 'Go—take a chance! Do it!' But she recognized the odds against her and she passed."

The only movement Elizabeth perceived in the eyes meeting hers was a momentary glint of green on green.

"And you are allergic to me." His voice was still so even-toned that it put her on edge.

"Asher, last night and today have been an interlude I shall always remember. You are a magnificent man and you make a woman feel very special, but I will not risk what happens to me. I've been there before."

"With Lorne?"

She looked at him sharply. "Lorne? What do you know of Lorne?"

"Nothing, except you whispered his name when I picked you up and took you to bed."

Her face turned crimson. "I'm sorry. I'm so damned sorry." Embarrassed, she got up and paced behind the sofa. He sat, waiting. She stopped and said, "What happened with Lorne has nothing to do with the woman I am now."

"That's not true, Elizabeth." The evenness was gone

71

from his tone. "Everything we do is a result of what's happened to us. When you whisper one man's name after another has made love to you, that man is in your heart and head, and you should do something about it."

She met his implacable gaze. "Memories erupt *unwanted*, and I think I'm handling mine very well!"

"By living here alone? By retiring from people? By refusing to accept sex as part of life?"

The look she gave him was sardonic. Her words came swiftly, flicking like flint on stone.

"If I were a *man*, you wouldn't say that to me! Isn't the solitary lifestyle when *men* do their best work? Write elegiac poems? Compose symphonies? Paint masterpieces? Why is it men who choose a monastic life are respected, honored, but women are considered neurotic?"

She plunged her hands into her jeans. "I'm so fed up with people telling me I need a man—I need love. I *have* what I need—uninterrupted time to work, to think, to read, to enjoy *me, myself!* It's a wonderful freedom, and I cherish it."

"And dating me means giving up this freedom—this joy?"

She sat down and faced him. "Asher, earlier you described a life of scrutiny, a life that offers little freedom, where the isolation of fame is a poor substitute for the serenity of solitude. Dating you exposes me to that."

A smile flickered on her lips.

"I'm sure if any of my readers heard me now, they'd think I was crazy . . . and my daughter . . . *well!*" Her smile turned droll. "On the other hand, she might think I've come a long way."

At the expression on his face, her smile sobered. She leaned towards him. "Asher, yesterday and today were beautiful . . . every moment so *special* it will nourish me for a long time. And now I want to get back to the life I feel most comfortable with."

The resentment he felt surprised him. Logically she had every right to say no, but her charm, her sincerity, her lovemaking had made him open himself to the warmth of a woman as he had not done in years. He felt strangely betrayed.

72

He got to his feet. "It's getting late, Elizabeth. I'd better head back to New York."

"Yes, it is getting late," she said, rising, extending her hand.

He looked at it, and annoyance hardened his jaw. "That's for strangers." He pulled her to him, kissing her hard and long.

She sensed his resentment, and she let herself be kissed. His mouth on hers softened. Her lips were giving, yet they did not promise more. She had made her choice.

When he let her go, he looked down into her eyes, and in his own, a small smile eased his irritation. His jaw relaxed. Lightly, he kissed the space between her eyes.

"We will meet again, Elizabeth, but in the meantime, if you change your mind—" the smile reached his lips, "—and many of us do—call me."

She laughed and gave him a friendly hug.

"Thank you. It's nice to know I can."

His arm around her shoulders, they went to the foyer.

"By the way, I had a little run-in with your handyman this morning when he came to plow out my car, but it's all settled." He decided to say nothing further. He put on his boots and slipped into his parka. Turning to her, he said, "Thank you, Elizabeth."

Quickly he went out the door, his shoulders almost filling the space.

Blaze bounded in from the woods, barking at him. Asher stopped and said, "Hello, fella." The dog came to him, wagging his tail. Without turning to look back at Elizabeth, Asher strode to his car, the dog trotting peacefully beside him. Elizabeth stood at the door, watching them, until they had disappeared across the bridge. She waited until she heard Asher's car go down the road. The dog dashed back across the bridge, up the hill, and into the house. Still looking towards the sound of Asher's car, she shut and locked the door.

73

Chapter Six

Driving down Elizabeth's road, Asher paused at the Gorge. The storm was over, but it had left behind a greyness which darkened the late afternoon. Yet there was more light than when they had stopped here yesterday. Sitting in the car, its motor idling smoothly, he gazed down at the stream rushing through the narrow walls, at the hemlock and pine on the high banks, and thought again how much it felt as if he were back in Gstaad. It was as though he were lost in time. Had it been only twenty-four hours since he had driven up this narrow, snow-covered trail? He felt he *belonged* in this place . . . and belonged in the house up the road.

Scorning his mood, Asher impatiently shifted into first and gunned the car; the wheels spun on the slick surface and he eased off, driving more gently. When he reached

74

the main road he inserted a cassette into the tape deck and began the drive back to Manhattan.

Entering his apartment, he handed his skis, poles, and boots to Charles, his butler. As he started up the stairs to his room, the man said, "I've made a fire in the study. I thought you'd enjoy having your dinner there."

"Thank you, Charles, that's very considerate."

Tossing his parka on the bed, Asher went directly to the phone; soon he had Elizabeth's number from directory assistance. As he dialed it, he pictured her coming to the phone. It rang three times before he heard: "Hello."

"Hi."

A pause.

"I'm home. The roads are fine." He chuckled. "Thought you'd like to know just in case you planned to come into the city in the next few days."

Her laughter echoed softly. "I plan to go where there's no snow."

"And miss all the great skiing?" In the background he heard the dog barking. "Is everything all right, Elizabeth?"

"Yes, fine . . . it's just some friends coming up the path. I'm joining them for dinner. We're going to the place I had planned to take you to last night."

"I see. Well then . . . I called, really, to thank you again for a truly beautiful evening. Have a splendid Christmas, and I hope the New Year brings you every blessing."

"Thank you, and thank you for calling—I'm glad to know you're home safely. Have a happy holiday, and may the New Year bring you happiness. Goodbye, Asher."

There was a finality in her words and in the silence of the line that he could not deny. He slowly got up off the bed and went to wash up and change out of the ski clothes he had been wearing since yesterday.

It was past ten when Asher tossed the last of the Sunday *Times* onto the heap of newspapers lying on the floor beside his chair in the study. Charles had long since removed his dinner tray. He put his palms over his eyes and rested them in the blackness. Lately his eyes grew tired from reading. He probably needed reading glasses—just one more sign of the years slipping by. The years slipping by . . . and yet, sitting in the car at the Gorge, it had seemed as if it were yesterday. Taking his hands from his eyes, Asher leaned his head back on the leather of the chair and stared into the fire . . . the fire . . . how inviting the fire had been in Elizabeth's house. He looked deep into the flames and other memories warmed him . . . how beautiful the fire had been those cold nights in Gstaad. He looked still deeper and saw the fire after supper in his mother's parlor when he was a boy. The flames leaping in sharp, serrated spasms lit the back of his mind and he saw his mother and father as clearly as if they stood before him. Tears rose in his eyes as they had that day he had last seen them . . .

Midsummer rain pelting on the high-arched roof of the Cracow railway station cooled the July heat. A huge black train spewed steam in short, hissing bursts. A tall, slender man with an olive complexion, high cheekbones, and a neatly trimmed black beard and moustache stood rigid, his eyes bright with tears held stoically in check. Next to him was a small woman with golden hair and green eyes; her tears fell like the rain. Her rapid words tumbled like pebbles on a slope:

"Don't cry, Asher, we've had such a wonderful celebration—such a Bar Mitzvah! We are so proud of you! It is something we will always remember, but Papa says you must go—God willing, only for a short time."

She hugged the young boy so tightly he felt the warmth of her body through the wool of his knickers. Sobbing and laughing, she continued: "The Cassidys are fine people. You will have a wonderful time in Switzerland, and before you know it, we will all be together again. Be good and write me every day!"

"Papa—*please!*" Asher cried, unashamed of the tears on his face. "I don't want to go—please don't make me! I want to stay home with you and Mama—I want to go to the farm for the harvest . . . Louie, Uncle Davie—they need me!"

76

The man's face crumpled as if the bones underneath gave way; the carefully checked tears flowed, wetting the black beard. He grabbed his son, holding him close, kissing him. Asher and his father clung to each other, unable to speak. Then his father thrust him away and in an unsteady voice, a voice Asher did not recognize, said, "You are a man now, Asher—act like one!"

Alone, aboard the train, Asher pressed himself against the window, waving to his parents long after he could see them no more. Morosely he sank back into the plush-covered seat. There was no joy, no excitement in this trip, not at all like the other trips when he and his father laughed and talked, or played word games while his mother knitted. There had always been a hamper filled with food and wine, and Irene, their cook, had never forgotten his favorite sweets. Asher looked at the box of food in his lap, but he wasn't hungry; he had had no appetite since his father told him he must leave home and go to Switzerland.

Asher glanced at the couple sitting opposite. There'd be no interesting conversations with them; the dour-faced man was engrossed in a newspaper, his mouth tight, his wire-rimmed eyeglasses on the edge of his nose. The pinched-faced woman beside him crocheted what looked like a shawl; occasionally she lifted washed-out eyes to look out the window.

Glumly, Asher rested his chin on his hand and gazed out the window. The green, lush countryside, misted with rain, sped by. He wondered if the sun shone at home. That's where he should be! Home! Home in Dzialoszyce. There was no need for him to be on this train! He was needed at home, and now that he was thirteen, he could really help with the harvest! He loved the summers on his uncle Dave's farm. There were many cousins there, while at home he was lonely; he had no brothers or sisters, and Papa was always busy in his laboratory. On the farm, at harvest, he was allowed to ride his uncle's prize white team. Standing barefoot astride their sweating, heavy backs, his toes gripping the coarse white hair, his hands steady on the reins, he would guide them as they pulled

77

the reaper. His cousin Louie would be astride the roans, and they'd laugh and call out to each other as the work horses moved through the golden grain.

He loved the farm even more than the stately brick house on the bank of the Zekie River in which he lived with his mother and father, and before she died, his grandmother. His father's laboratory, a steel and glass building, was in the rear, past the gardens. Here his father, a physicist, worked with two assistants. Often Asher stole away from piano practice to listen to his father and the assistants discuss what to him was a mystery: electronic scanning methods, velocity, the Doppler principle, calibration, high frequency pulses of electromagnetic energy, and other complicated ideas he wanted to understand.

The cavernous laboratory contained transmitters, receivers, cathode ray tubes, electron tubes, and even one of Zworykin's iconoscopic camera tubes. Dr. Jacobs specialized in electromagnetics; his work contributed to the development of radar, sonar, and television; he was a contemporary of the Scottish physicist Sir Robert Wilson-Watt, who first devised a radar installation in 1934–35. Asher vaguely remembered their frequent trips to Scotland and other places throughout Europe when he was very little. His father often met with colleagues and addressed symposia, and he and his mother always accompanied him; at an early age he had learned several languages. But the trips ended when Asher was ten. He had been privately tutored until then, and now his father wanted him to mingle with boys his own age and have a normal school life.

Scientists and businessmen came from all over the world to meet with his father, and Asher enjoyed these visits, for his mother entertained with delicious teas and lavish dinners. One of the visitors was Michael Cassidy of International Communications Corporation. Asher never forgot the conversation between his father and mother the night before Mr. Cassidy arrived for the first time. It was December, 1938.

They sat in the parlor after dinner. His father read a journal sent to him by a colleague at the University of Gothenburg, his mother worked on a needlepoint pillow cover, and Asher studied his Hebrew—his Bar Mitzvah would be in July. His father had been silent all evening; now he looked at his wife and said quietly, "Rachel, I've not told you the truth. Mr. Cassidy's visit is not a business call, nor is it a social visit, even though his wife and daughter will be with him." He hesitated, and looked at his wife and son solemnly. "He's coming because he wants us to leave Poland. He fears what's happening in Germany will happen here, and he's offered to fund a research facility for me in America."

His mother had looked up calmly when her husband first began to speak, but as his words sank in, her face tightened. Now she jabbed her needle in the air as though to emphasize the sharpness in her tone.

"Leave Dzialoszyce? Our families? Never!"

Her angry retort startled them both; she seldom spoke harshly.

His father rose and came to her. Kneeling by her side, he took her hands. She was such a small woman, it still amazed him that she had borne his child, but it was her fragility which had so attracted him. He ran his hand lovingly over her wheat-colored hair and looked deep into her green eyes.

"Rachel," he said softly, "times are bad for Jews. This madman in Germany is not to be taken lightly. You know how anti-Semitic Poland is, how bad it was for Jews when we were part of Russia—it can happen again."

There was nothing fragile about Rachel Jacobs' determination. She shot out feistily, "No! Not to us! Not in Dzialoszyce. Without the Jews, Dzialoszyce would be nothing! My God, Herman, there are only five thousand people in this town and almost four thousand are Jewish! Who would run the farms, the granaries, the flour mills, the brickworks? And without the Jacobs family, who would take care of the people?" Her voice rang with finality. "No! I will not leave all I love! And we have no *reason* to fear! They come to you from all over the world for your ideas. No one would be foolish enough to hurt us!"

What she said was true. Dzialoszyce was a haven for Jews in a Poland prone to outbursts of anti-Semitic violence, and Dr. Herman Jacobs, despite being a Jew, had achieved prominence throughout the academic and scientific community. Jews prospered in the town nestled in fertile farmland halfway between Warsaw and Cracow. The Jacobs family had made its fortune in grain and its sons went to universities in London and Paris, and before Hitler, to Berlin and Vienna. They returned as doctors, lawyers, and teachers, to become a dynasty in Dzialoszyce. Herman was the family's first physicist, and that he lived and worked among his close-knit family was no more than expected.

Rachel's outburst grieved Herman and he realized he could not desert his family. If he left he abandoned all he held dear. He could not leave the love, the religion, the customs which were their life: the Friday night services, and afterwards, the Sabbath dinner, when his large dining room was filled with those he loved and fragrant with the delicious aroma of the traditional meal; the conversations, the singing around the tables, the happiness they shared, shining in their faces lit by the Sabbath candles. And Asher would be thirteen in July! Rachel had planned his Bar Mitzvah from the day he was born. No. He could not consider Cassidy's offer.

The day the Cassidys arrived, Asher was ice-skating on the river behind the house with his cousins. December's early darkness broke up their games and, waving goodnight to them, he climbed the bank to the house, his skates still on. Pushing open the door to the mud room, he took off his skates and outerclothing and entered a large, well-scrubbed kitchen. His cheeks were rosy from the wind, the cold, the fun. He sniffed, his young boy's appetite responding instantly to the delicious smells in the room. Irene had made cookies. Wanda, his favorite amongst the servants with her shining black hair and high-cheekboned face, handed him a pair of slippers, kept in the kitchen so that dirty shoes did not smudge the shining floors. She helped her sister, Irene, with the cooking.

Asher leaned on the counter near the stove. "Got any icing pots I can lick?"

With her heavy hand Irene shooed him away as she always did when he tried to cajole her into giving him sweets before dinner. "They're all cleaned, Asher." A smile crossed her wide face. "But there's tea in the parlor, hot chocolate, too, and lots of sweets. Your parents are entertaining guests from America."

Asher ran down the red-carpeted hall towards the large, high-ceilinged drawing room that looked across sloping lawns to the town on the other side of the river. A bronze chandelier hung in the arched foyer, its tapered lights reflecting in the graceful, fan-shaped windows over the handsome set of carved oak doors with massive bronze hinges. Matching doors led into the parlor; they were closed, and beyond Asher heard soft laughter. Sliding the doors open, he entered a richly furnished room aglow with lights from crystal wall sconces and crystal table lamps. Lace curtains and heavy green velvet draperies with silk tassels adorned the tall French windows. Lustrous Persian rugs accented the dark, polished parquet floor. His father stood before the black marble fireplace, engrossed in conversation with a man as tall as he, but broader. He wore the dark suit he reserved for special guests, and the visitor was equally well dressed. They must be talking about something important, Asher thought, not to mind the fire blazing in the hearth.

His mother sat on a green velvet sofa before the fireplace with another lady whose back was to him. They were talking and laughing. On the low marble table before the sofa was a silver tea service. Under the grand piano which stood in the wide circle formed by large bow windows, a little girl played with a stuffed animal. She was about three years old, and long, honey-colored curls fell about her face as she alternately kissed and spanked her furry playmate.

His mother looked elegant. She wore a plum-colored silk dress and her shining hair was piled high like summer maize. She handed her guest a cup of tea in china so delicate Asher could see the golden color of the liquid through the flowered porcelain. Asher walked towards the sofa, his eyes on the sweet cakes.

81

"Ah, Asher." His mother smiled.

At that moment the woman turned and Asher stopped, staring. He had never seen such a beautiful woman!

Her hair was like hand-rubbed copper. It hung in soft waves below her shoulders, and the eyes which looked at him were exactly the same color. Copper-colored eyes! Asher could not pull his eyes from hers, and a soft flush began to diffuse her creamy skin.

The sound of his father's voice broke the grip she had on him.

"Asher, come and meet our guests. Mr. and Mrs. Cassidy, may I present my son, Asher."

Asher bowed from the waist.

"Asher, Mr. and Mrs. Michael Cassidy and their daughter, Eleanore."

Asher bowed again, his English, like his parents', charmingly accented.

"I am very pleased to make your acquaintance."

"How well you speak English," Mrs. Cassidy said, smiling. Asher felt himself flushing.

"Thank you, madame," he said with another slight bow.

"Here, Asher, a cup of chocolate. You must be hungry after so long outside." His mother handed him a steaming cup to which she had added heavy, sweet cream. He kissed her cheek and went to the sweet tray, where he surreptitiously piled three cakes on a small dish. He sat down in a corner where, unobserved, he could look at Mrs. Cassidy.

He watched as she chatted with his mother. She sat gracefully, her slender back straight, her long, shapely legs neatly crossed at the ankles. She wore a beige winter suit trimmed with red fox at the hem and at the collar of her jacket. She had removed the jacket and it lay about her shoulders, the fur forming a halo against the oval face with its small nose that flared slightly as she spoke. When she laughed, a dimple formed just below her lips.

Asher was used to beautiful women. His family was blessed with extraordinary genes. The Jacobs men were tall and darkly handsome, with clear, olive complexions and dark eyes. His mother's family was blonde, with ruddy skin and blue or green eyes.

As pretty as his mother was, though, as pretty as his

many aunts and cousins were, the stunning beauty of Mrs. Cassidy set her apart. Staring at her, Asher felt his penis harden. Mortified, he stuffed a sweet cake into his mouth and took a gulp of hot chocolate. He began to choke and his mother rose in alarm.

"Asher!"

He jumped up, coughing; the bone china cup, saucer, and cake dish crashed to the floor.

Seven months later, Dr. Jacobs was occupied in his laboratory when Michael Cassidy telephoned the Jacobs house. Asher, home from the farm to prepare for his Bar Mitzvah, just days away, answered the phone. Mr. Cassidy asked for Dr. Jacobs, and when Asher said he could not disturb his father, Cassidy thundered: "Go get him—*now!*"

"Will you wait, please? There's no telephone in the laboratory."

"Of course! Now, *run!*"

Asher ran out of the house, past the gardens, to the laboratory.

When his father heard how upset Mr. Cassidy was, he hurried to the house.

Asher stood and watched as his father listened to the voice on the phone—he tried to hear the conversation, but the words were just jumbled, staccato sounds. When, finally, his father put down the receiver, his eyes were so lifeless, Asher cried:

"Papa—what's wrong! Please—tell me!"

He let out a long, torturous breath. "I must go speak with your mother, but you must do as I say. I want you to call *everyone* in the family, *everyone,* do you understand? Tell them they are to come here *immediately*. They are to drop whatever they are doing and come *now*. It is very important."

When all the family had gathered, Asher's father began to speak. His face was grave and his voice quietly authoritative as he patiently explained why Mr. Cassidy had called. An invasion of Poland by the Germans was imminent. It was dangerous for them to stay.

The family erupted in protest. Cassidy had to be mistaken! And even if he wasn't, and the Germans did invade Poland, the family still would not leave—they would take their chances!

His words ringing, Dr. Jacobs insisted they must pack *now!* And leave as quickly as possible!

No! they shouted back. He had studied in Berlin! He *knew* the Germans! They were a fine, *cultured* people. Soon they would tire of Hitler, and these repressions of the Jews, if they truly existed, would end. Hadn't the Jews in Germany always thrived? They had the highest standard of living, the greatest opportunities . . . this would blow over. Jews had always been scapegoats, but they always survived! What he asked was impossible! Give up their homes . . . their land . . . pack up like peasants and run? They were people of *stature*—no one would dare to harm them! The Jacobs family? Impossible!

Even the Popers, Rachel's family, a hardy and affluent clan of farmers and horse breeders, announced they, too, would take their chances. With a heavy heart, Dr. Jacobs saw it was useless; he would not leave his family when they might need him most. But Asher must go! His only child—his son!—must not face such danger. With a cry, Asher protested, but his father silenced him with a "NO!" so stern, the room fell silent.

When Michael Cassidy called back to find out when he could expect Dr. Jacobs and his family to arrive in Switzerland, Herman thanked him for his concern and said only Asher was coming—the day after his Bar Mitzvah.

Asher closed his eyes, seeking to erase the memories the fire had lit in him, but instead, his lids became a screen, and he saw himself in the living room of the Cassidy chalet in Gstaad. Through the wide-open windows stretched high meadows dotted with Edelweiss, and beyond the lush foothills loomed the Bernese Alps. He stood awkwardly as the Cassidys, in tennis clothes, welcomed him. His wool knickers and jacket were uncomfortably warm in the summer heat.

"Come, Asher," Mrs. Cassidy said, putting her arm around his shoulders. "I'll show you your room and you can change and join us by the swimming pool."

He tried not to see the nipples showing through her thin tennis dress. He felt his heart thumping.

Marguerite and Michael Cassidy could not have been kinder to him, or more understanding, during those years he lived with them, first in Switzerland and then in England. It was as though he were their own son, and despite his longing for his family and his worry about their safety, they had made his days, especially in Gstaad before the war, beautiful.

There had been lazy picnics in the highlands overlooking the chalet, and one time Michael took him camping in the mountains. Just the two of them.

"Men need to be alone," Michael had said, "and men must know how to survive alone, because in the end, Asher, men must make their decisions alone." He taught Asher skills Dr. Jacobs had never learned and for which he had had no time. During that solitary week a bond developed between them that lasted a lifetime. But when war broke out, everything changed.

On September 1, 1939, when the German army invaded Poland, Asher stood anxiously at Michael's side, biting his lips, barely able to breathe, listening as Michael tried desperately to get through on the phone to his parents. Michael finally slammed down the receiver and turned to him, his broad Irish face, as changeable as Irish weather, stormy with frustration. Deep furrows creased the square forehead, red freckles stood out vividly on his short stub of a nose, and the wide mouth was grimly set. Normally youthful, he now looked every one of his forty-five years.

"It's no use, Asher."

Asher had cried then, long, bitter tears, and Michael had held him close.

"Don't give up hope, Asher. I know people. I'll do everything I can to get them out."

The day the radio crackled with the news war had been declared, Asher sat on the lawn beneath the windows of Michael's study, avidly reading every word of the invasion in the morning paper; the announcement interrupted a Mozart concerto. He jumped up so quickly to run to the study, the pages scattered. He rushed to gather them and then he heard Marguerite dash into the room, her heels like shot on the wood floor. He stood riveted and listened.

"Did you hear?" she cried. "And Duebendorf Airport in Zurich has closed down!"

"I heard," Michael snapped, and then turned contrite. "I'm sorry, I've been on the phone again trying to get through to Poland, but now we can forget about getting Jacobs and his family out."

"My God, Michael! Surely you don't think the Germans would harm a man as important as Dr. Jacobs—or his family. They're a civilized people!"

The chill in Michael's voice made Asher shiver, despite the sun on his back.

"You *saw* those fine 'civilized people,' Marge! You saw how they adore Hitler, how their faces light up when they speak of him, how they scream in adoration when he appears. They're no longer rational! This war will be a bloodbath! Hitler is a madman who doesn't intend for Jews or anyone else he thinks racially impure to survive. Jacobs may be important, but he is a Jew! Why do you think Einstein left? And why do you think Jacobs sent Asher to us? He *knew*—but he couldn't make the others see it."

The phone on the desk clanged. Asher jumped.

Michael leapt for it, urgency adding bite to his voice: "Cassidy here!"

Asher ran inside and into the study.

God, *please!* he prayed, *let it be my father!* When he heard Michael say, "Bill, old buddy—your voice is the first good thing I've heard today," Asher's heart sank.

He turned to leave, but with a wave of his hand, Michael indicated he stay. Asher watched the change of expression on Michael's face, from the first, cheery greeting, to solemn contemplation, and then, to a deep frown. His answers were clipped. Finally he said, "If you say so—of course."

When the conversation was finished Michael put the phone into its cradle slowly and, turning to Marguerite, said in a cool, flat voice:

"We'll not be going home, Marge. You'd best enter

Asher in school here. That was Bill Donovan on the phone—he's asked me to stay in Europe and take a leave of absence from ICC. I'm needed."

Approaching Asher, he said:

"That was a good friend, who's asked me to take on a job that might enable me to find out about your family and maybe even help them. But I can promise nothing other than that I will try. I'll be away most of the time, and while I'm gone, you'll be the man here." Michael held the young boy's eyes steadily. "You must *never* speak of this moment to *anyone*, or mention the name of the man to whom you heard me speak. Do you understand?"

Asher nodded, and in the boy's clear eyes, Michael saw an understanding he knew he could count on. Later, Asher came to know Michael's friend, Major General William Joseph "Wild Bill" Donovan, head of the Office of Strategic Services—the OSS.

For the next two years Michael Cassidy traveled to Paris, Berlin, Warsaw, and Moscow. In Poland, because of the delicacy of his assignments, he was unable to investigate the disappearance of Herman and Rachel Jacobs, or obtain any definite information about their whereabouts.

In late October, 1941, on one of Michael's rare visits home, the sound of the phone ringing startled Asher out of his sleep towards dawn. Michael came into his room, and seeing he was awake, said quietly:

"Get up, Asher, we have to leave."

Leaving their servants, Inge and Julian, to care for the chalet, the Cassidys with Asher entrained to the south of France. In Marseille, they boarded a freighter to Barcelona, and from there went by train to Lisbon. After waiting three hot, sticky days in a Lisbon teeming with refugees, they boarded a plane to London. Cassidy rented a thatched and timbered country cottage in Welford-on-Avon near Stratford for his family, then returned to London, where he was on assignment for the OSS until the war ended.

The wide, green lawns of St. Phillips Academy were crowded with smiling parents and laughing graduates. The young men wore sober tweed suits, too warm for the unseasonable heat that May of 1943. Their trousers were pressed with knife-edge precision.

"I'm proud of you, Asher," Michael said, pumping the tall young man's hand vigorously. "These years have not been easy, but now you'll have your chance—it's only a matter of weeks until you're seventeen—hang in as best you can."

"I knew you'd win the music medal!" Eleanore chanted, clapping her hands. She reached up and fingered the medallion hanging around his neck.

He smiled down at the seven-year-old child and ruffled the blonde curls on her head; she had become his true sister. "If you promise to practice piano every day, I'll give you the medal."

"I will! I will!" she cried, jumping up and down. Asher draped the blue and white satin ribbon with its golden disc over her head. She put her arms around his waist and hugged him.

Marguerite stepped close and kissed his cheek. "Congratulations."

Asher met her smiling gaze. He smiled briefly and looked quickly away lest she read the feelings her kiss and her closeness aroused. He turned to Michael. "How much longer must I wait? I've waited too long as it is."

Beneath his quiet, courteous manner, Asher seethed with impatience. He read every newspaper report of the conflict, listened intently to the BBC. The gains of the Nazis, the retreat of the French and British, and the thundering conquests of Holland, Belgium, and Poland depressed and angered him. He knew that back home boys his age were fighting, and he bitterly resented his safe, cloistered life. And this last year at school had been the worst. Since learning of the surrender of the German 6th Army at Stalingrad in February, and two weeks later, that the war in Africa had ended, he felt he couldn't wait any longer! Michael, as his guardian, had promised to sign the papers allowing him to enlist after he graduated.

"Michael," he began desperately.

The older man nodded. "I know, I know—but hear me out. It isn't only that I gave your father my word I'd always

88

look out for you. To allow you to enlist senselessly would be a waste. We need interpreters, men with your fluency in languages . . . and with your intelligence. I've arranged for you to join the OSS. The citizenship matter has all been taken care of, but we must wait until July, until your seventeenth birthday."

Marguerite put her arms through theirs, and tugging at them, she said, "Let's go home, and let's forget about the war this weekend. It's so good to have us all together."

Asher, too, was happy they were all together. Michael had been away too much, leaving him alone with Marguerite too often. He knew his feelings for the woman who had become a mother to him were more than a transference of filial love from one woman to another, and his passion for her ashamed and frightened him.

Blinking hard, Asher opened his eyes and got up out of his chair. The past was past—it was *over*. Only today mattered . . . and tomorrow.

And tomorrow he would check into getting reading glasses. And send Elizabeth two dozen roses.

Chapter Seven

BRONWYN O'Neill sat back and relaxed as the taxi sped south through slushy streets. Turning off Seventh Avenue, the cab hit a pothole and she grabbed the shopping bag on the seat next to her; it was filled with gaily wrapped gifts.

"Sorry, lady," the cabbie called back through the thick panel of plastic and wire screening, "but that's New York streets for ya."

"I'm not in a hurry, so take your time," she said. "Do you mind if I smoke?"

The man sitting fat and stolid in front of the protective plastic laughed hoarsely. "That's a hot one. With what I gotta breathe all day, the smoke'll smell good. Gawhead, enjoy yourself." He looked at her in the rear-view mirror. Some chick, he thought. Aloud he said, "Ya sure ya wanna go down to West Street? That's a bad neighborhood, 'specially this time a'night. No one's aroun', an' all that stuff you're totin' ain't gonna help any either. It certainly ain't no place for a good-lookin' girl like you."

Bronwyn smiled through the haze of blue smoke. "Thank you for your thoughtfulness, but someone's meeting me."

He shook his head sadly. "What this city's become," he moaned in a voice thickened by ten cigars a day. "When I wuz a kid, ya could go anywhere, anytime. New York wuz a dream, an' ya didn't need money either. We wuz all poor but there wuz movie houses open all night for a dime, ya could have coffee and donuts at Nedicks for a nickel, and ya could take a date to the Automat and have a full meal for seventy-five cents." The harshness went out of his voice as the memories came. "Cheez! I once saw Martin and Lewis at the Paramount for fifty cents, then later the same night I went to the Capitol and caught Lena Horne. One Sattaday I took my girl to see Tommy Dorsey 'n Frank Sinatra. She screamed an' screamed, but I couldn't see nothin' in him; he was just a skinny punk. Kids wuz on street corners all the time, an' they didn' make no trouble neitha; they just horsed aroun'. I never even had a key to the door, we never locked it. Who'd steal from us? We wuz all poor, an' everybody knew each other. Just look!" He gestured towards the deserted streets.

"Christmas Eve an' this city's a ghost town, an' it's only nine aclock. When I drop ya off, I'm goin' home. There ain't no business, not even uptown."

Bronwyn put her head back on the seat. "I'm glad it's now. It wasn't all that beautiful back then. People tend to forget the unpleasantness of the past. I make more money in one week than my mother made in six months, and I'd have had to be a man to get the job I have." She laughed. "Years from now, we'll be in vehicles manned by robots, and those of us left to remember will moan about the good old days when we rode in creaky New York cabs and schmoozed with the cabbies who drove them."

"Yeah, mebbe so." He turned and headed west on Houston Street. "Even though I make more money now, I wish it wuz then. Look at this coffin I gotta drive in. Ya got

91

any idea what it's like to drive in a cage all day? Do ya know how many cabbies get killed for a few bucks? We ain't safe even in a cage. Is that a way ta live?"

"I can't argue with that," Bronwyn soothed, "but let's forget it. It's Christmas Eve. I'm going to a party, and you're going home. Let's hope things get better for everyone."

"Fat chance! If Christ came back tanight an' took the subway to St. Pat's for Mass, they'd mug 'im." He pulled up before a darkened industrial building. "Here ya are, lady." He peered into the blackness. "Don't get out, I don't see anybody waitin'."

A light bulb encased in wire lit a metal doorway. To the side, another bulb lit the wide steel doors of an industrial elevator. It clanked open and a stocky man with a heavy black beard came out holding two Dobermans on a leash. They leapt towards the cab, barking fiercely. Their fangs glistened as they snarled and snapped.

"Jesus H. Christ!" the cabbie yelled, "don't let them sonsabitches near me!"

"Don't worry," Bronwyn said, rolling down her window slightly. "Hello, Zeus. Hello, Hera." The barking changed instantly; it became almost welcoming as the dogs recognized the young woman. Their clipped, stubby tails wagged wildly. With a smile, she handed the cab driver a twenty-dollar bill. "Keep the change, and Merry Christmas."

He grinned back. "Hey, lady, anyone ever tell ya you're a real doll? Thanks, an' Merry Christmas to you too. Be careful, don't go home alone."

"Why, Mr. Migliore," she said laughingly, reading his name off the hack license, "what a thing to say." She got out and handed the shopping bag to the man holding the dogs. The cabbie drove off quickly.

"Merry Christmas, Louis," she said, pulling her mink coat snugly about her. They went into the unheated, cavernous elevator, and the dogs sniffed her expectantly. She took two dog biscuits from the velvet-lined pocket of her coat. "Merry Christmas, monsters." She gave each a biscuit and they greedily licked her fingers.

"You spoil them, Miss O'Neill," Louis chided. The

92

elevator rose slowly towards the top floors, where her host, Willem Van Zuye, lived and worked in a unique four-story complex.

She smiled at the impassive man who stood like a martinet at the elevator controls. "Even guard dogs need affection, Louis." She indicated the shopping bag with a slight nod. "Those are for Mr. Van Zuye, for you and the rest of the staff. Have a happy holiday and a good New Year."

His reply was cordial, but spoken coldly. "Thank you, Miss O'Neill, I hope the New Year bodes well for you too."

How strange he is, she thought. *I've known him five years and I can't remember seeing him smile.* But Van Zuye was dour; why should she expect his majordomo to be any different? It was as if Van Zuye metamorphosed into his sculptures and paintings. A small, gnomelike man, his work was massive, the brusque, angular abstracts dominating plazas and buildings throughout the world. Bronwyn felt Van Zuye longed to be what he created, that his art was his persona: powerful, uncompromising. And those close to him were also big: his staff, his lovers—all were tall, beautiful people who clustered about him like chelae.

She thought Van Zuye temperamental, demanding, irascible, but it was his art which had catapulted her into the upper echelons of publishing. Five years ago, she had conceived the idea for a series of signed, limited edition art books with texts by famous contemporary authors. When friends brought Bronwyn to a Van Zuye party, she used the contact to advantage. That she was tall, uncommonly lovely, and young was also to her advantage, but still, it had taken a year before Van Zuye signed a contract. His book was the first; other artists and writers followed, and the series was extraordinarily successful. It made Bronwyn O'Neill Senior Editor and Vice-President of a major publishing house at twenty-seven.

Louis opened the elevator doors at the studio level and the dogs bounded to a blanket on the concrete floor beneath a metal worktable. They lay down, heads together, black bodies curled. The moment she entered the vast

93

workshop, Bronwyn felt its energy, its vitality. For her, coming to the studio was an artistic adventure. Work was always in progress in the high-ceilinged loft with its plaster models, clay maquettes, finished and unfinished shapes. Louis took her coat and boots as she changed into silver evening sandals. "Would you like me to take you to the aerie in the lift?" he asked, referring to the fanciful iron cage in the center of the studio. Van Zuye had found the Victorian elevator in London, a discard from a bombed-out hotel in Regent's Park. Its bird-cage look lent a fey, incongruous touch to the clutter of an artist's workshop.

"No thank you, I'd rather walk up," she said, going to a spiral staircase. Even though the lift gave a fine overview of the loft, Bronwyn preferred the iron and wood staircase Van Zuye had designed. Mounting the walnut treads, she ran her hand along the dark patina of the wood rail. She remembered ascending these stairs that first time and saying to Van Zuye, "I feel like Jack climbing the bean-stalk to face the Giant."

"How right you are," he had remarked, almost smiling.

Her aesthetic senses accelerated as she climbed up-wards. Below, near wire-paned windows, stood a four-figure plaster grouping nine feet high. Van Zuye's artisans had marked and studded it for bronzing. Bronwyn knew it was the Tyler Oil commission to be erected in the spring in the atrium of their Houston complex. Some feet away she saw a boulder of Leopoldo black granite under a tall gantry. It had been roughcut and would soon be turned over; the hoists and winches of the gantry would move the four-ton stone as if it were a pat of butter. This had not been there on her last visit, and Bronwyn made a mental note to ask the artist about it.

In an area at the far end, behind plastic sliding panels, in a place which seemed separate, more tranquil, stood easels of varying sizes, and on them were paintings in different stages of completion. Tables close by held paints and brushes; raw canvas hung neatly from a wall frame; finished paintings were stacked against a wall. Here Van Zuye relaxed, moving from easel to easel, working ran-domly. His small white painting jacket splashed with streaks of color hung from a peg. It was from her vantage point on the stairway that Bronwyn had had the studio photographed for the book.

She paused. What she saw was destined for immortality. Even if all else were destroyed, Van Zuye's art would survive. That she was close to its source, that she watched its creation, that she had been privileged to reveal it to others gave her a deep feeling of happiness and accomplishment.

She reached the landing to the living quarters. Here the concrete floors were planked with polished oak and accented with oriental rugs. A vaulted archway led into the apartment, where a maze of curved spaces flowed into living room, dining room, and bedroom. Paintings in bold brush strokes and vivid colors enlivened the stark white walls. Small bronzes and larger sculptures filled space with form, and concealed lights highlighted their shapes, their sheen. Near the full-length arched windows, plants grew lush and green, and in the bathrooms, plants hung in baskets.

But Bronwyn had been truly astonished when Van Zuye had shown her the grottolike swimming pool.

She had walked carefully around its tiled edge to the black lava waterfall at the far end, her slender high heels tapping rhythmically on the terrazzo floor. She had splashed her hands in the cascade tumbling over the rough rock; sunken lights made the water gleam like liquid emeralds. Beyond was a redwood deck with a smaller whirlpool, and in the wall, a redwood door led to the sauna.

"Come and swim whenever you like," Van Zuye had said, adding archly, "There is only one rule. No clothes allowed. Wearing clothes in water is unnatural."

She had walked slowly back to where he stood. She had no qualms about swimming nude, but she knew his reputation, his lusty appetite, and she did not plan to join his stable of long-limbed ladies.

"Thank you for the invitation," she had said, her voice as cool as the water still damp on her hands. "I'd love to swim here—it's stunning—but if I do, it will not precede my going to bed with you. If we are to work together, Mr. Van Zuye, it is important we maintain an objective relationship."

His black eyes had bored into hers, and then he had extended his small bony hand and grasped hers; the immense strength in his fingers had not surprised her.

"Agreed, Miss O'Neill. We shall work well together."

Bypassing the apartment, Bronwyn heard revelry above her; she ascended to the top floor, entering a glass penthouse which sat like a crystal prism in the midst of a garden overlooking the Hudson River. Here Van Zuye entertained in a manner as bold as his art.

He had bought the fourteen-story building in the fifties before the renovation of factories into lofts for living and working became fashionable. He rented the lower floors to other artists and remodeled the four upper floors for himself. Bronwyn had been to the celebrated aerie many times, but never before at Christmas. It blazed with the glitter of a festive party, and the sparkle of a handsome New York crowd.

She knew the aerie in daylight, when the city lay like a giant shoe, sprung with people, the tongue of Manhattan lapping into the protected harbor. Then the splendor, the shabbiness, the incongruity that is New York were clearly visible: sterile slabs of glass soaring over tenements where roach-infested apartments were being converted into eight hundred dollar a month studios; the rusted, corroded spine of the West River Drive rotting alongside the once active, but now deserted and dilapidated piers. In the harbor, Bartholdi's copper colossus, the Statue of Liberty, standing as neglected as the thousands of homeless who slept in parks, in subways, and in urine-drenched hallways. Arching from Brooklyn across the trim waist of the Narrows, looking like a priceless, bejeweled tiara, the Verrazzano Bridge descended into the clustered hills of Staten Island, once green, once country, but now concrete —an enclave of heavily mortgaged row houses.

But now, a scrim had dropped over the teeming city, and all Bronwyn saw was the dazzle of a skyline touching the stars with radiance: the gleam of the red-and-green-lighted spire of the Empire State Building reaching into the night; the diadem of the Chrysler Building, its silvered arches etched with neon; and the delicacy of the bridges sashing the rivers like strands of diamonds. How she loved New York, and how she loved seeing it from the aerie! She had thought the glass room most beautiful at sunset, when, hardly breathing, she had watched a lowering sun brush the city pink and orange—but now, lit for Christmas, as the city outside was lit for the holiday, the aerie was stunning!

A splendid, live Christmas tree towered at the far end, its fragrant branches glistening with glass ornaments. Hundreds of tiny, twinkling lights were laced through the green thickness. Everything shone: the extravagant fabrics on the supple young women, the patina of the handsomely groomed men, the green and gold canopies over the bars and buffet tables. Pots of poinsettias, Christmas cacti, and flowering Kolenchoe artfully screened groupings of banquettes and sofas.

Bronwyn made her way through the chattering, lively crowd, looking for Van Zuye. Snatches of conversation trailed her. "Listen, my friend had a gun shoved in his face in Central Park at high noon!" . . . "I haven't gone to an Altman movie since he destroyed *The Long Goodbye* . . . Imagine him trying to do Chandler!" . . . "My God, did you see that dress? She's wearing more on the inside of her skin than on the outside" . . . "Sure, I love Pavarotti, but what about the other great tenors?" . . . "Darling, I go to the Philharmonic mainly to watch Mehta—can you imagine tempoing with him or with Muti?" . . . "Movies are moving back to New York because talent is respected here. Broadway's what matters for an actor!"

Bronwyn heard Van Zuye before she saw him. His clipped, high-pitched voice rose from the circle girdling him. "Phil King is one of the finest sculptors working today! But hardly anyone in the United States knows him, because he's never had a retrospective here. He hasn't gotten the publicity Tony Caro has. King's an intellectual, and it's always difficult for an intellectual to accept publicity—but take it from me, the man's a monumental talent!"

"That may be true," interjected a rotund man in tight

97

green velvet pants. He reminded Bronwyn of a fat green worm she'd once found devouring her philodendron. "But how do you account for the grimness of his recent work?" he persisted. "Once he was so light, so pure, so pellucid . . ." The voice rose and the hands fluttered.

Van Zuye saw Bronwyn and cut the speaker short, saying curtly, "Unless an artist changes, he's a cookie cutter. King's gifted, and gifted people change, they experiment." He smiled thinly as Bronwyn came to him. As his lips stretched tightly across the small face, the skin wrinkled about his beady eyes. He was almost bald; just a fringe of coarse white hair ringed his small, perfectly round head. He stretched his five feet, two inches so that Bronwyn would not have to bend too far as she kissed his cheek.

"Merry Christmas," she said, smiling.

"So! You've finally come to one of my Christmas parties. To what do I owe the honor?"

Just like Van Zuye to chide instead of welcome her, Bronwyn thought, but she answered sweetly, "I've mountains of manuscripts to read, so I decided to stay in the city."

"Now you're civilized," he said tartly, taking her arm and leading her towards the bar. "Christmas in the country is for rustics, and for birds and animals. Cities are for people, especially those who have a sense of style. Cities are alive—the country sleeps, and so do the people who live there."

Bronwyn did not dispute Van Zuye on minor matters. She saved her disagreements with him for important encounters. "Bourbon and soda, please," she said to the bartender.

Van Zuye shook his head to indicate he wanted nothing. He drank little and ate sparingly. He was a fanatic about health, and no one was permitted to smoke in his presence. Consequently, the room was free of smoke, and those like Bronwyn who did smoke escaped to the garden outside.

"Bronwyn, I've heard of a young artist I'd like you to research for me," he said abruptly. "I understand he's done some exciting work in marble and that he's now carving a massive angel with wings so thin they'll be mostly translucent. He's unknown, and if he's as good as I've heard, I'd like to help him."

She looked at him quizzically. "Why me? I'm just an editor. You've a manager and an agent to handle assignments like that."

"Because, my dear, this young man is a rustic like you. He works in the wilderness and will see no one. But someone with your Irish charm and looks might get through to him."

"I'm sorry, Willem," she said, and there was no mistaking the decisiveness in her voice. "I just can't take the time. I must make final decisions on the fall books; we're about to be eaten up by a conglomerate, and if I survive the takeover there are sales meetings in January, and in the spring I hope to go to China and Japan. There's just no way I can hunt out your reclusive genius."

He looked at her slyly. "You'll be sorry when someone else discovers him and signs him to a contract."

"I can't win 'em all," she said laughingly, but Van Zuye was annoyed. He spun about without another word and joined a group who quickly drew him into their circle.

Bronwyn finished her drink and asked the bartender for a refill. It had been an endless day; her office had been filled with tension, not at all like a usual Christmas Eve, when people partied and left early. The imminent takeover generated animosity among the few who knew about it and nervous speculation among those who guessed some change was brewing.

She let the liquor slide slowly down her throat, enjoying its heat coursing through her. Her body began to relax, unwinding like a tightly coiled bud to the warmth of morning. She leaned against the backrest of the stool and closed her eyes, the slit skirt of her alabaster-colored dress parting to reveal her long, shapely legs.

Across the room a tall man with clear green eyes stood surrounded by a laughing, bantering group of people. He responded politely but his eyes restlessly swept the crowd. Suddenly his face froze. He looked so startled, someone said, "Come now, Asher, it can't be all that serious."

But Asher Jacobs did not hear. He felt as if he had been struck a strong blow. "Memories come unwanted," Elizabeth had said. Pain filled him. He stared at the girl sitting on the bar stool, her head back, her throat arching gracefully. Her hair! He had known hair like that only once before. Hair the color of copper, caught with amber, like the glimpse of gold in a hand-rubbed bronze . . .

He fought unsuccessfully against the déjà vu closing in on him . . .

Marguerite sat on the bar stool in the den, her legs crossed, her ivory-colored dress draping her long limbs, smiling up at the man who handed her a drink. The light from a silk-shaded lamp turned her copper hair amber, forming a nimbus around her oval face. Asher stood in the doorway, unable to tear his eyes from her. Michael saw him first.

"Come have a drink, Asher. If you're old enough to go to war, you're old enough to drink. What would you like?"

"I don't know, Mike. I've never tried liquor."

"Then start with Scotch. You'll dislike the first taste so much, you won't want a second . . . at least, not right away." Handing the drink to Asher, he raised his own glass and said, *"L'Chaim."*

Asher met his eyes with affection, knowing Michael used the toast to remind him not to give up hope for his family.

"Asher," Marguerite said, "please play your sonata. At school today, I was so excited when you won the medal, I'm sure I missed much of its beauty." She gave him a proud, loving smile.

His heart pounding, he took a quick swallow of his drink, ignoring the taste, grateful for the heat searing his throat and hoping the whiskey would subdue the beating in his chest. He couldn't speak. He nodded and went to the dark mahogany console against the wall. Marguerite and Michael went to sit on the sofa.

Afraid his feelings would show on his face, Asher was glad his back was to them. He had poured all his love, his desire for Marguerite into this composition. He began to play. In the low-ceilinged, beamed room with its white-washed walls and polished plank floors, the piano rang and reverberated. Every nuance the Cassidys had missed in the school auditorium now echoed until the last chord faded into a haunting *pianissimo*. No one spoke. Asher sat still, his head bent. Michael rose and went to him. Putting his hands on the young man's shoulders, he said, "You have real talent, Asher. Make music your career."

Asher looked up at him. "My parents wanted that, but if they're dead, I won't have the heart for it."

Eleanore dashed into the room, her curls bobbing. "Let's eat, I'm starved!"

Michael laughed as she tugged at his arm.

"Daddy, Daddy, could we go for a hike tomorrow?"

"Maybe very early. I've got to get back to London." Father and daughter went out the door.

Marguerite put her arm through Asher's and turned to follow her husband, but Asher stood fast.

"I wrote that for you, Marge. It's called 'Sonata for Marguerite.' "

She looked at him, surprised. "Why, Asher, how wonderful of you. Thank you. Someday, when I'm very old and you're very famous, I'll listen to that lovely music in some concert hall and remember this day. What a lovely memory that will be." She reached up and kissed his cheek.

He wanted so badly to say, "I love you." But he remained silent.

"Come along, dear," she said. "We're all hungry. It's been a long and marvelous day."

Chapter Eight

BRONWYN felt uneasy. She opened her eyes to face a man staring at her with such intensity, a strange sensation prickled the back of her neck. He came closer, his expression unchanged.

"Is there something wrong?" she asked. "You're staring at me, and it's very uncomfortable."

He blinked his eyes and then his face cleared. It was a handsome, distinguished face, she thought, not the face of someone she should fear.

"I'm sorry. You look so much like someone I knew, it's a shock."

"I'm not sure that's a compliment," she said, sitting up and adjusting her dress.

"It is," he said quickly, and then, to the bartender, "Scotch and water, please, and make it a double."

"She must have been quite a woman." Bronwyn smiled.

102

He turned and looked at her sharply. The resemblance was incredible. He knew he was staring, but he could not take his eyes from her face. He had to know more about her.

A lively group descended on the bar, and Asher's next words were drowned by their gaiety. With a hopeless shrug, he extended his hand to Bronwyn. She took it and followed as he led her to a banquette set relatively apart from the crowd.

He stopped at the small sofa and said with a half-smile, "Pardon me for acting so strangely. I'm Asher Jacobs."

Her head shot up and the startled look she gave him was filled with such annoyance he could not imagine how he had offended her.

"I don't believe it," she said stiffly.

"Why? What's wrong?"

"I'm Bronwyn O'Neill."

Surprise swept his face. He met her eyes, and after a long pause, said, "How ironic."

He fought the feeling of destiny creeping in on him; that was for Singer to write about, and for the farmers he'd known as a child in Poland to believe in. Asher trusted in reason, and yet there had been so much in his life he had been helpless to change, sometimes rationalization was difficult. He bowed slightly to the young woman before him, as much an obeisance, he felt, to the fates he denied, as an acknowledgement of their meeting.

"I had no idea my opponent would be so beautiful."

"Come now, Mr. Jacobs, I'd think a man of your stature could do better than such a chauvinistic cliché." Her eyes mocked him.

He laughed aloud, his mood lifting. "My dear Miss O'Neill, we're not in a boardroom, but at a party, and here you are indeed a beautiful woman."

His laughter and his engaging compliment made her feel foolish. It *was* a party; there was no need to turn a chance meeting into a confrontation.

"I did overreact," she admitted.

"Please sit down," he said. He noticed how lightly she moved and the way her silk dress moved with her; the plunging neckline shadowed young, upturned breasts, and

103

the nipples touched the soft folds of the creamy fabric. She wore no brassiere.

He sat down beside her and again searched her face. It was her hair that had first caught his attention, but now it was her eyes that held him: deep-set copper-colored eyes. He looked at her wide, elegantly curved mouth, her small nose with just a hint of a tilt. It was uncanny!

"Would you be related to a family named Nolan? Does the name Marguerite Nolan Cassidy mean anything to you?"

Bronwyn shook her head. "No, I don't think so. I'm Irish only on my father's side, and I barely knew him. My parents were divorced when I was a baby, and I know nothing of his family or his background."

Asher tore his eyes from her face and toyed with his glass. "It really isn't all that important." He took a long swallow of his drink and turned to her with a smile. "I'm glad we met tonight, Miss O'Neill. It's more pleasant than meeting at Mednam."

She observed him closely; evidently, seeing her had disturbed him. Was that why he preferred meeting her now? ICC's move to take over Mednam was still not common knowledge. Only Drew Mednam and two other executives besides herself had been informed, and her opposition was like pitting her Porsche against a bulldozer. Nevertheless, she had been adamant in her protest. She had seen many such sellouts in publishing and she knew the commitment to authors and good books suffered when independence was lost. Mednam was a prestigious firm and Bronwyn had enhanced their reputation by finding and nurturing new talent, by taking risks with new ideas. She was aware of the success of her division, and while she was not certain how many of her authors and artists would follow should she leave, she knew Mednam and ICC recognized the possibility.

A perverse thought struck her. At first she shunned it, but it took hold, rising in her mind, expanding in her brain, until she could not deny it. She saw the interest in his eyes and she smiled beguilingly.

"I, too, am glad we met," she said.

She held his eyes fast, and he felt a surge of excitement —a quickening inside, as if he were young again.

"I'd like another drink," she said, still smiling into his eyes.

He jumped up so quickly they both laughed. She handed him her glass. "Bourbon and soda, please."

"Done," he said, not wanting to leave her, but turning to the bar.

She watched him make his way across the room, his posture erect, his wide shoulders in the impeccable black silk tuxedo easing neatly through the crowd.

She sat back on the banquette and crossed her legs; her dress fell away again and her feet in the high-heeled silver sandals kept time to the music which sounded from across the room.

Asher returned, drinks in hand. He handed a glass to Bronwyn and laughed lightly.

"What's so funny?"

"Your eyes make me think of a bawdy toast."

"Bawdy? Somehow I can't equate you with bawdiness," she said, smiling.

"I can be."

"Well, let's hear it then."

He clinked his glass to hers:

> *"Here's to eyes, blue, brown, and brindle,*
> *The kind of eyes that make fires kindle,*
> *Not the fires that burn down shanties . . ."*

She interposed, laughing, *"But the kind of fires that pull down panties!"*

"You know it!" He laughed.

She nodded. "I learned it as a kid, and my mother had a fit every time I recited it at her parties. I mixed the meanest martinis when I was six."

Asher stared again. Marguerite had been just her age when he'd first seen her.

Bronwyn sensed his thoughts. "I feel you're comparing me to the woman I remind you of."

"Forgive me," he said lamely, "it's unintentional. My mind can't help reverting to the past when it's jogged so dramatically, but I am a realist, Miss O'Neill, and the

105

person sitting beside me is a lovely young woman I wish to know, and whom I would enjoy calling 'Bronwyn.' May I?"

He is smooth, Bronwyn thought. But then, one did not become an Asher Jacobs peddling potatoes. She sipped her drink and studied him. Her answer came slowly, the words measured. "I don't think that's appropriate at this time. We're at opposite ends of sensitive negotiations, and I would feel uncomfortable addressing you as 'Asher.' "

"I see," he said, and then with an easy smile, "There's no reason why we can't address each other socially by our first names and still be more formal in business. It makes for an interesting dichotomy, don't you agree?"

"No, I don't," she answered. "If I called you 'Asher' I could easily vent my temper and tell you how much I resent your swallowing up Mednam—but," she smiled teasingly, "I have to be polite to someone I call 'Mr. Jacobs.' "

He laughed heartily. "Well then, Miss O'Neill, it shall be as you wish." He rose and bowed with such patrician politesse, Bronwyn half-expected him to click his heels. "We shall be properly formal," he said, extending his hand to her with an insouciant smile. "Would you care to dance, Miss O'Neill? You do dance, don't you?"

She laughed, her mouth parting over small, even teeth. "I'd be delighted, Mr. Jacobs." She placed her hand in his and rose, allowing him to lead her towards the area cleared for dancing. As they approached, Van Zuye stopped them.

"So! You've met!" he said slyly. "Too bad, I wanted to be the one to introduce you to each other. I'm sorry to have missed that moment. It must have been interesting."

"It was, and it is," Asher smiled, not letting go of Bronwyn's hand.

"And you, Bronwyn?" Van Zuye was not one to be put off. "Tell me, how do you find our handsome Goliath?"

Bronwyn looked sharply at the artist. Did he know about the merger? she wondered. But how could he? With Van Zuye, anything was possible. What a nosy, contrary elf he was, always stirring up a brew, like some over-

106

worked witch. She leaned down and kissed the top of his head.

"Mr. Jacobs and I have a date on the dance floor."

"Step on his toes!" Van Zuye called as Asher led her away.

"He is wicked, but never dull," Asher said, stepping into the staccato of the three-piece band.

Bronwyn nodded but did not try to speak above the sound. Her body loosened as she danced; her hands came up and she snapped her fingers to the tempo; her taut breasts pushed against the folds of her dress, and Asher saw the outline of their surge and the thrust of her nipples. Her skirt clung to her thighs and the slit sides parted; her legs moved with animal grace. She tossed her head and her hair swung, its coppery lights flashing like exposed wire.

Asher felt his legs go weak. He struggled against the memory flooding him, but the flow of Bronwyn's hair was hypnotic, and he closed his eyes, seduced by the past.

The sensual strains of "Begin the Beguine" filled the room, coming from the radio in the corner. Artie Shaw's clarinet wove the music into an eloquent *glissando*, each note sounding with such rich darkness and sexual promise, Asher felt heat rise in his groin. He could not concentrate on the backgammon game he played with Marguerite. The music reached out in a rising *obbligato* and Marguerite began to hum along with the clarinet. Her body came alive, swaying to the music. She moved her head to its rhythms, and the firelight caught in her copper hair.

"Dance with me, Asher," she said, getting up.

He sat still, knowing what happened to him when she was in his arms.

"How shy you are." She smiled, taking his hand and pulling him up. Her body, liquid in the silk dress, flowed into his, and his muscles went taut, his hands trembled, and sweat dampened his brow. She smiled sadly up at him. "Don't let the war destroy all your innocence."

"Marge—Marge," he breathed huskily, pulling her body close to his, burying his face in her hair.

Drawing back, she looked at him, startled, and pulled away. He reached for her . . .

His hands encircled her waist. Lips parted, eyes closed, Bronwyn danced with abandon, enjoying the release she found in the loud, disjointed rhythms. The rush and the tenseness of her day left her body like a river. She slipped out of Asher's hands, following her own course, but he pursued her, dancing with such demanding physicality she found herself drifting back into his arms. His hands on her hips, he spun her around. The turn was swift, unexpected, but she did not falter. Her body moved like liquified light as he spun her.

Suddenly, then, he drew her solidly against him. He looked down at her, his eyes veiled, and said huskily, "I don't like dancing apart—this is dancing."

She bent her head back and gave him a long, cool look. He felt the curve in her waist, the arch of her back. He ran his hand from her waist to her neck. They were so close she did not have to raise her voice when she said: "No—it's vicarious sex."

Asher's face burned. He released her as if she were a comet, scorching, flaming. She danced back smoothly, her eyes fixed on his. He stood stolidly, surprise stilling his feet. And then anger propelled him. He grabbed her wrist and pulled her from among the dancers. She followed without resistance, not wanting Van Zuye or others to notice. Asher stopped behind a fern, its fronds shielding them from the room.

"That was a nasty thing to say," he snapped.

She looked down at her wrist still gripped in his hand. He followed her eyes but did not release her.

"Perhaps," she said curtly, "but what you were doing was just as nasty."

"What *I* was doing?" He let go of her wrist.

"Oh, come off it," she shot back scornfully. "You're no innocent. What do you *think* you were doing out there, grabbing me and holding me like that! You wanted me to feel your hardness—I hate hypocrisy and dance-floor come-ons!"

Asher's face became a mask, his lids hooding the

108

jade-green eyes. He spoke in a tone so brittle the words chipped like ice. "I shall not apologize for being a man and reacting as a man does to the stimulation of a woman as beautiful as you." He did not allow her time to reply. "We are physical beings, Miss O'Neill, and like it or not, our initial reactions to each other are physical—a matter of the laws of nature. Only later do we develop an appreciation for other attributes." His irritation increased. "Young women today are so uptight about being thought of as sex objects, they overlook an essential fact about human nature. We are *all* sex objects, men as much as women. Women react to men as avidly as any man responds to a woman. We are driven by physical attraction, Miss O'Neill, and if you deny that, you deny the essence of life."

Her copper eyes raked him. "Really?" She drew the word out as if it were rope she intended to bind him with.

"I think, Mr. Jacobs, you are the one who is uptight. It is exactly because I accept and respect my sexuality that I do not find it necessary to make love on the dance floor! Because I resent being considered a 'sex object,' as you put it, does not mean that I reject men, or sex. On the contrary, I enjoy them as nature intended—freely— without demands. It was men, Mr. Jacobs, who ringed sex with a band of gold and girdled women with false values and false expectations."

A smile began in Asher's eyes long before it reached his lips. The tightness in his face loosened.

"You're quite right, Miss O'Neill. I was ungentlemanly and I was churlish."

Bronwyn relaxed. "If that's an apology I accept it, Mr. Jacobs." A light smile touched her lips.

"Thank you," he said. And then he smiled. "I hope you're hungry, because I'm ravenous!"

She laughed. "I haven't eaten since lunch."

He took her by the elbow. "Let's see if Van Zuye's lived up to his reputation."

Van Zuye had.

Asher and Bronwyn wandered from buffet table to buffet table, heaping large plates with one delicacy after another: Beluga caviar spooned from a silver bowl, plump

109

Chincoteague oysters, jumbo shrimp, chunks of crab-meat, cold lobster, pungent Scotch salmon, pastry puffs filled with pâté, cold meats and salads. When their plates could hold no more, they found seats at a small candlelit table.

Asher looked at Bronwyn's plate and laughed. "How delightful to dine with someone who is not dieting."

"I come from a long line of food lovers," she said, smoothing caviar on a cracker.

"You're lucky it doesn't show." Asher deftly speared a chunk of lobster on a slender fork and held it out to her.

"Thank you." She smiled as she bent her head and closed her lips on the succulent pink flesh.

"My pleasure."

Bronwyn did not miss his glance scanning her figure.

"I diet at times—doesn't everyone?" She gave him a calculated look. Her eyes, like an abacus, tallied the body under the superbly tailored suit, cut, she estimated, without an inch to spare in the back rooms of Bond Street. "You can't tell me that build comes from bread, butter, and Godiva chocolates."

He nonchalantly popped a tender oyster into his mouth, wiped his lips, and said, "I admit nothing."

I'll bet you don't, Bronwyn thought. How must it feel, she wondered, to have all that money, all that power? To so easily say "yea" or "nay" to others' dreams?

They chatted as they ate, inconsequential small talk which revealed nothing. Asher observed Bronwyn closely. She seemed more accessible, yet she was elusive, mercurial. He wanted to know more about her, but each time he probed, she cleverly changed course.

"Do you play chess, Miss O'Neill?" he asked at one point.

"Yes, why?"

"I thought so."

Asher sat back against the gold spindles of the party chair. The food had been delicious, and he watched as Bronwyn finished a creamy pastry. "Miss O'Neill, I shall not be put off any longer. It's time to tell me about yourself. Where were you born?"

For a moment Bronwyn was caught off guard. She was

110

about to reply when she heard the tinkling of bells. She turned towards the sound.

Asher looked at his watch. "Willem is about to play Santa Claus. It's almost midnight."

"Midnight?" Bronwyn echoed. "I had no idea."

His smile was raffish. "It's the company."

"No doubt." Her smile was equally tantalizing.

"Let's see what Santa brings," he said, rising and coming around to hold her chair.

"Santa?" Bronwyn stood.

"You've not been to Van Zuye's before at Christmas?"

"No."

"Then you're in for a treat." He took her arm and steered her towards the crowd gathering at the tree. Someone dimmed the lights; only candles, the shining Christmas tree, and the skyline outside illuminated the room. The effect was magical.

Bronwyn heard a soft whirr, and she looked up. Her mouth opened in astonishment. The glass roof above her head slowly slid open! She squeezed Asher's arm, her eyes shining with anticipation.

"Oh, my!" she breathed as a small hot-air balloon drifted gracefully into view, its shrouds sparkling with hundreds of tiny lights twinkling like far-off stars. The red-green-and-gold-striped canopy glittered against the night sky.

"How lovely!" Bronwyn said, her fingers clutching Asher's arm. He felt a thrill run through him at her excitement. She was like an expectant child. He pressed her hand with his.

The satin balloon floated through the roof, its red gondola festooned with green and gold drapery studded with sequins. Inside the gondola a figure waved merrily to the applauding crowd. The balloon hovered above their heads; men on the roof secured it to a hook in the steel frame of the penthouse. The afterburner shut down and the roof panels slid shut. The grinning person in the gondola was dressed in a red suit, and a red peaked hat sat jauntily on a round, gnomelike head. It was Van Zuye!

"How ingenious!" Bronwyn laughed, clapping her hands with delight.

111

"Gelukkige Kerstmis! Gelukkige Kerstmis!" Van Zuye called. The Christmas greeting he'd cherished as a child in Holland echoed throughout the room. He bent down, then came up with a green and gold sack filled with gifts. He tossed small red packages tied with green and gold satin ribbon into the eager crowd, who shouted back happy greetings.

Van Zuye spotted Asher and Bronwyn, and with a devilish wink, aimed two presents in their direction. Asher reached up and caught one; the other slipped from his grasp, but Bronwyn caught it on the rebound, laughing so hard she almost missed it.

"What fun!" she exclaimed. "The giving is present enough. I don't even want to open it."

A teasing glint came into Asher's eyes. "Do you really have the discipline not to open a gift?"

"No more than I can give up chocolates." She laughed, ripping off the wrappings. For a moment she looked at Asher, her eyes alive with excitement as she opened a small, red velvet box.

"My goodness." Inside on a pouf of white satin lay an enameled miniature of the balloon from which Van Zuye still tossed presents.

"I've never seen Van Zuye like this," she said, lifting the tiny balloon from its bed. She turned it over. Engraved on the back was the famed WVZ logo and the date. "I thought he detested representational replicas."

"One never knows about Van Zuye." Asher opened his own identical package. "He's such a restless, multifaceted man, who can tell what direction he'll take? Even these Christmas parties—every year it's something new. I had no idea how much I missed them. I've not been to one for three years."

"Why not?" Bronwyn asked.

"Why haven't you come before?"

She laughed. "I asked first."

He tucked his gift into his pocket before he answered. "I've been away. And you?"

"I go home. Christmas is family-time."

"Then why not this year?"

She shrugged. "We all reach a point when tradition

112

gives way to other needs." Her eyes moved about the room. When she spoke, her words were thoughtful. "I understand now why Van Zuye resented my not accepting his Christmas invitations. When someone expends so much care and energy to entertain others, it's unworthy not to be there to share it."

"Ah, but don't let Willem know that, or he will exact his due."

She smiled. "He tries, but I've a thick hide, and little gets under it."

"Then why did you resent me so when we first met?"

She sighed. "I resent what will happen at Mednam, but most of all, I resent not having the power to stop it."

"But you know nothing about me," he said earnestly. "How can you be so certain that it won't be to Mednam's advantage? To your advantage?"

Her eyebrows arched and a cynical expression crossed her face. "I'm good at picking horses, Mr. Jacobs, and I often win at the races; my friends say it's Irish luck, but I know it's because I study my horses and their track records." She laughed dryly. "I wouldn't bet on ICC, based on its track record. When Mednam joins your stable, it will go to the post like all the other horses. It'll be in the race for the big book, that 'easily packaged' read that can be jockeyed into first place by talk shows, seven-figure paperback sales, TV miniseries, and movie tie-ins. There'll be no money on that track for thoroughbreds and yearlings to whom every word is like running in the mud."

She saw his eyes crinkle at the corners before she saw his smile.

"You're talking to a descendant of generations of horse breeders and traders, Miss O'Neill." He took her arm and led her to a sofa. "Let's discuss what's troubling you. First, would you join me in an after-dinner drink?"

"Thank you, I'd like a brandy."

"Good. I'll be right back."

Bronwyn sat down and waited for him. Asher soon returned, and handing a glass to her, he sat down, facing her.

Amusement showed in his eyes as he asked, "Wasn't it

Twain who said, 'It's a difference of opinion that makes horse races'?"

She met his eyes, her own sardonic. "You mean I shouldn't look a gift horse in the mouth?"

He laughed appreciatively and raised his glass to her.

"To your Irish wit, Miss O'Neill." He sipped his drink and, choosing his words with care, said, "It's not my intention to change Mednam's editorial policies. ICC is buying Mednam because it's good business. We can wrap up all rights on choice properties and assure maximum profits at the least cost. Now we bid against other houses whenever Transit, our paperback subsidiary, wants reprint rights. Our movie and television divisions then bid for performance rights, and our international associates bid for foreign rights. All this drives costs up and wastes energy. More important, it delays a work hitting the total market when both the market and the work are hot. With Mednam part of the ICC spectrum, all rights will be included in the initial contract. It's not only best for the company, it's preferable for the author—or the artist."

Bronwyn held the snifter to her nose, inhaling the pungent brandy. She savored its smoothness as it trickled down her throat. She swallowed it slowly and then turned to Asher. Her words came with certainty, as if she turned the pages in a book she had read many times.

"No, Mr. Jacobs, it is not preferable for the author or the artist to sign away all rights as part of one package, and you know it. The Author's Guild deplores such contracts and good agents will not negotiate them either. Naturally they're advantageous to a conglomerate, and that is what bothers me; creative projects and creative talents are treated as commercial commodities. Tell me, Mr. Jacobs, what if certain books, certain projects, though editorially exciting, don't show a profit? How long will you support Mednam's policies then?"

His answer was smoothly confident. "If editorial policies are sound, Miss O'Neill, Mednam will show a profit."

"That's absurd!" she shot back. "Hardcover houses can't even make money on lead titles, let alone mid-list books and first novels, without selling off those lucrative

114

subsidiary rights. If you take those sales away by wrapping all rights in one package, how can a hardcover division show a profit?"

His voice came quietly, trying to assuage her. "That's all being taken into account, and the management team, of which you are an important member, will solve those questions. I sincerely hope you will give us the benefit of your support and your experience."

Bronwyn returned his steady gaze. "How large will the editorial committee be?"

He hesitated. "That depends on Mednam's growth. Present plans call for two additions to the current committee: a vice-president for marketing and a vice-president for finance."

Her eyes filled with derision. "Then, of course, the bottom line will be the book's sales potential, rather than the ideas expressed."

"Not at all," he countered quickly. "Ideas are still paramount, but ideas without distribution and without profit are merely dreams no one is sharing. Give us a chance, Miss O'Neill. Trust me."

Bronwyn drained her glass and slowly she got up. He rose also.

She smiled thinly. "Maybe it's the brandy, maybe it's the excitement of the party, maybe it's just that I'm tired after a long week—but when you say 'Trust me' I think of some movie mogul coaxing a starlet to the casting couch."

His mouth hardened and she wondered if that was how he looked when he was outbid at Sotheby's.

She shrugged. "Perhaps you are sincere—I hope you are—but I find it difficult to cope with your corporate realities, your decisions by committee. I don't know if I can work that way, or if I want to. Now if you'll excuse me, I'm going to pay my respects to Van Zuye and call it a night."

She did not want to turn her back on him and walk away, so she waited for him to reply and by his answer release her. But he said nothing; he stood silent, looking at her, a frown between his eyes. Then his face relaxed.

"I've been a boor, Miss O'Neill, to discuss business. A

115

Christmas Eve party is no time for serious decisions. May I see you home? My car is more comfortable than a cold taxi."

His smile was so genuine she found she did not wish to refuse the invitation. "Thank you, Mr. Jacobs, I would like that."

"Good," he said, taking her by the arm. "Let's find Van Zuye."

116

Chapter Nine

Asher Jacobs was right, Bronwyn thought, settling deep into the grey plush of the sleek limousine; it was far more comfortable than a taxi.

Her head lay back on the seat, her eyes were half-closed, and she listened languidly to the music which floated about them softly—it seemed to come from all corners of the car.

Asher glanced at her profile, alternately shadowed and lit by the street lights filtering in as they drove through the deserted city streets. His fingers twitched as he remembered how once he had traced a face so like hers, touching, kissing the smooth forehead, the slightly tilted nose, the softly curving mouth. If he ran his fingertips along this young woman's face, would it feel the same? Folding his hands together, he suppressed the urge and sat quietly apart.

117

Her breathing deepened.

Smiling at her in the darkness, he said, "You'd best give me your address, Miss O'Neill. You'll be asleep before we reach Houston Street."

She sighed. "I could ride like this all night."

"Would you like to? I'm in no hurry to get home, and the city is beautiful when it's so dark and quiet."

"It's tempting, but thank you, no. My apartment is on Perry Street, just off Seventh Avenue. It's easiest if you drop me at the corner—it's a one-way street."

Young women! Asher thought, shaking his head to himself. It was nothing to them to be dropped on a deserted corner at 2 a.m. He'd never get used to it, nor did he want to. He pressed a button, and a microphone brought his voice to the man on the other side of the glass partition.

"Perry and Seventh please, Charles. Thank you."

"Yes, Mr. Jacobs," the man replied.

"Has he been waiting for you all evening?" Bronwyn asked, turning her face towards Asher.

He met her gaze. "No. Charles was at home with Ruth, his wife. She's my housekeeper and cook, and between them they run me. I phoned my apartment when I went to get our things, and the time we spent saying goodnight to Van Zuye and the others gave Charles time to get downtown. Why do you ask?"

"It bothers me to think of someone sitting outside in the cold all night while someone else parties. I know we all have jobs to do—and many are dreadful—but still . . ." Her voice trailed off.

"You don't like being waited on?"

"I hate it."

"Doesn't that make life difficult for you?"

"Sometimes."

"Ah, but don't you realize, Miss O'Neill, it gives people pleasure to wait on others. In Europe, to be in service is honorable. Unfortunately, in America, people equate service with servitude." He put his head back on the seat, and she turned again to look out the window.

"We're almost there," she said, sitting up. "Thank you, Mr. Jacobs, for taking me home. Frankly, I didn't look forward to meeting you, but it's been a lovely evening, and I've enjoyed your company."

Asher sat up also. "I, too, Miss O'Neill, and I'd like to see you again. Would you join me for lunch tomorrow? It's Christmas and a white Christmas at that. Central Park should be lovely. If you've been in your office all week, I'm sure you would enjoy walking in the park after lunch."

The car slowed and stopped. Bronwyn gathered her mink about her.

"I'm sorry. I stayed in the city so that I could work, and really, I must get the manuscripts out of the way before the January sales meetings."

His smile was droll. "Well, since I'm not in charge yet, there is little I can do—perhaps another time. I'll call you, that is, unless your phone is unlisted."

"No, I'm in the book."

"Fine," he said, getting out as Charles opened the door. He extended his hand to Bronwyn. "I'll walk you to your door."

"Thank you," she said, putting her hand in his, and turning to Charles, she thanked him as well.

Asher tucked her arm close to his; the fresh, dry snow crunched under their feet. The few, bare trees on the darkened street cast skeletal shadows across a whiteness which made the city look clean, almost untarnished. She stopped at a three-story brownstone and turned to him.

"Thank you again for seeing me home."

"But you're not there yet, Miss O'Neill. Security in these brownstones is nonexistent. I shall see you to your very door."

"If you insist," she said, going up the high stoop. Bronwyn unlocked the outside door and they entered a Victorian-style vestibule. A small bank of polished brass mailboxes gleamed in the red-papered walls, and double doors paneled with etched glass opened into a long hallway. Bronwyn unlocked the doors and turned to Asher. "All right?"

"No, to your very door."

She shrugged and went into the hallway. It was charmingly furnished; antique wall sconces and a bronze chandelier softly lit the red-carpeted area, with its papered walls

119

and white-painted stairs. Silk flowers sat in a blue porcelain bowl on a Chippendale table.

Asher followed Bronwyn up a long flight of stairs. On the first landing, she turned towards the rear of the house and stopped at a paneled door.

"Are you sure you don't want to check inside before I enter?" she asked, her copper eyes teasing.

His smile was roguish. "That's a good idea, Miss O'Neill."

She handed him her keys.

Asher unlocked the door and stepped inside, holding it open for her. She had left lights on and they revealed the cheerful clutter of one who doesn't care what her house looks like. Magazines, newspapers, books, clothes lay about the room, on tables, on chairs, on the floor. One entire wall held a fieldstone fireplace flanked by bookshelves which also overflowed. To the right, four steps led up to a glassed-in area which seemed to be for dining since it held a table and two chairs, but the plants crowding the small space made it more of a greenhouse. Off the main room, which was painted white, Asher spied a tiny kitchen. He judged the doorway in the wall led to other rooms.

Bronwyn waited at the door, a slight smile on her lips.

He turned, handing her the set of keys. "Everything seems to be fine." His green eyes lit with mischief. "Of course, if you prefer not to be alone on Christmas Eve, I can send Charles home."

She laughed lightly. "And spoil my rendezvous with Santa Claus?"

He shrugged. "That's formidable competition. Well—goodnight, Miss O'Neill. It's been a pleasure."

"Goodnight, Mr. Jacobs."

As he passed her at the door, he turned, a smile touching his lips. "Merry Christmas," he whispered.

Her coppery eyes danced with deviltry. "Merry Christmas to you too," she whispered back, shutting the door.

He waited until he heard her lock engage solidly in the wood, and then he went down the stairs.

Asher stood on the bare terrace, snow dusting his hair and shoulders, dusting Central Park below, transforming the blackness into a benign, beckoning beauty, veiling the dangerous no-man's-land the park became after dark.

The city slept, but there was no sleep in him. He blinked the snow from his lashes and thought of the past few days. He had not been moved by a woman in a long, long time, and now he'd met two: Elizabeth—and Bronwyn. He shook his head at the irony of it and looked across the park to the west. What a lovely woman Elizabeth was—he could still feel the warmth, the wonder of her. Was she asleep in her house by the stream—or had she indeed gone to Palm Beach? After their first phone conversation, only the mechanical rote of her voice on the message machine had answered his subsequent calls. Had she received the roses? He had wanted so to take her to Van Zuye's party. Perhaps if he had . . .

He took a deep breath and peered through the snow. It was not like him to flit from woman to woman. He had no respect for philanderers, yet here he was thinking of one woman and wanting another. But he and Elizabeth shared no real commitment, and it was *she* who had chosen not to see him again. But what if she hadn't? What if she *had* accompanied him to the party, and he had met Bronwyn?

Peering again into the snow-swept night, he squinted, trying to see beyond his eyes, trying to see the truth. In the ghostlike haze he saw Bronwyn as he had first seen her sitting at the bar. A throbbing began in the pit of his stomach. *So like Marge.* Like the phoenix—arisen. And he knew.

"Elizabeth," he murmured, "how wise you were."

Chapter Ten

It was past noon when Bronwyn opened her eyes. She loved sleeping late! She stretched lazily, reaching high above her head, extending her toes to the foot of the bed. Out of habit she reached to stroke her cat, and then she frowned. Poor Walter. What a funny cat he had been; she'd named him "Walter Cronkat" because he had looked so much like Walter Cronkite, his tawny cat's face calm, noncommittal. She would come home from work, switch on television, and be greeted by her two Walters: one rubbing against her legs, the other rubbing her nose in news which became more depressing each night. And then, Walter Cronkat ate her poinsettia plant and poisoned himself, and the poison of age soon retired Walter Cronkite.

She turned onto her stomach and thought about going back to sleep, but the manuscripts waiting for her pulled her from bed and into the bathroom. She took a long, hot shower, washed her hair, and put on her bathrobe. Reaching into the pocket, she found a crushed pack of cigarettes and lit one, inhaling deeply, closing her eyes with delight. She tried to cut back on her smoking and recently had been limiting herself to five a day, but it was this first drag in the morning she cherished.

Barefoot, she padded into the kitchen, went to the refrigerator, and poured herself a tall glass of apple juice to which she added ice cubes. Winter or summer, Bronwyn added ice to whatever she drank; she hated warm drinks and warm weather.

Cigarette and apple juice in hand, she went into the living room and sank into an easy chair next to a table piled with manuscripts. The lights from last night were still on; she seldom turned them off. Picking up a script, she began to read rapidly, her eyes swallowing complete sentences. Halfway through the thick sheaf of unbound pages the phone rang. Damn! She'd forgotten to pull the plug. With a sigh she put the two halves of the manuscript on the large hassock on which she rested her feet and went to answer the phone.

"Hello." Her voice was soft, pleasant, disguising the annoyance she felt.

A crisp masculine voice shot back at her. "How great that you're in the city! I thought you might be skiing. I'm *here*, in *New York!* I have to fly to Stuttgart tonight— Porsche is going to have the new 935 ready in time for Daytona! I can't wait to tell you all about it. I'll be right over!"

Just like MacCormack, she thought, scowling. She hadn't heard from him in weeks and presto! he was coming over. *Well, Douglas my boy*, she thought bitterly, *have I got news for you!*

Her voice was brittle, chilling.

"I won't be here. I'm on my way out and I won't be back until very late."

His tone quieted.

"Bronwyn, are you upset with me?"

She made her voice drip syrup. "Upset because you never showed up in Puerto Rico and I spent the god-

123

damned weekend alone? Upset because you've broken every date these past two months? Upset because the only way I know where you are is to read *Auto Week?* I can't imagine, Douglas, why you think I'm upset with you."

His laugh was low and sexual. Bronwyn could see his blue eyes narrowing in his tanned face. Damn him! He was the most exciting man she'd ever known, and he knew it! But she would no longer tolerate his selfishness, or her weakness for him. She was finished with him!

As if he undressed her, he purred into the phone. "Baby, I'm crazy about you, but my cars come first—just like your job. Would you give up that big office, that big salary for me? Aren't you the one who said she wanted no ties? Come on, honey, hang up the phone, open the door, and let's go to bed."

"Like *hell* I will," she shouted into the mouthpiece. "And don't you *ever* call me *baby!* I'm finished with you, MacCormack, so—*GO TO HELL!*" Slamming the receiver hard, she pulled the plug from the wall. Cursing at him, at the weakness in her for wanting him, she marched into the kitchen and poured a bourbon and soda into a wine glass and took it back to her chair.

She took a long sip of the drink and sank into the softness of the low chair, putting her head back on the pillow, thinking of Douglas MacCormack, and of herself. He turned her insides out as no other man could, and she was right not to see him again—it hurt, but so had other things in life, like not knowing her father. She had survived that, she could survive MacCormack. There were plenty of men around. She wasn't looking for a husband— all she wanted was a considerate, understanding relationship, and the more physical, the better. Then, why had she gotten so possessive of MacCormack? And why had she made a play for Asher Jacobs last night? Getting involved with him could be very complicated. Dammit! She was too busy to think of men—there was work to do! She emptied the wine glass and picked up a manuscript. She was still deeply engrossed two manuscripts later when the downstairs buzzer sounded.

"Damn you, Douglas!" she spat, going to the intercom in the wall and flicking the switch. "No one's home!"

There was no answer.

"Listen, Douglas, stop playing games. I told you—*GO TO HELL!*"

A throaty laugh crackled.

"Why, Miss O'Neill, you surprise me."

She stared at the wall unit. Recovering her composure, she redirected her anger.

"I don't remember inviting you over."

"You didn't." The voice was unperturbed. "When I couldn't reach you on the phone, I thought something might be amiss. Now that I know you're all right and don't wish to be disturbed, I'll be on my way."

Again, his courtesy made her feel foolish, defensive. "This is silly, talking like this. Please—come up." She pressed the buzzer, releasing the downstairs doors.

That she was still in her bathrobe did not bother her, just as the disarray of her apartment never concerned her. She opened the door and noted how much less formidable Asher Jacobs looked in casual clothes. He wore a down parka the color of a fine lapis, charcoal grey corduroy pants, and an Irish tweed cap in shades of grey and charcoal. Beads of mist clung to the cap and the shoulders of his jacket were dark with dampness.

He smiled at her engagingly. "I see, Miss O'Neill, you are not a woman of pretense." He liked the fact that she had made no quick attempt to dress and that she offered no apology for her appearance.

"Pretense is such a waste of time, Mr. Jacobs. Now, what can I do for you?"

"Miss O'Neill, if I were to answer that honestly, you would ask me to leave."

She smiled. "So, you are a *man* of pretense."

He liked her humor. "May I come in?"

She hesitated a moment and then opened the door fully. Asher stepped into the living room and noticed the open manuscript on the hassock. Turning, he said, "Since I've already disturbed you, why not chuck your work for the rest of the afternoon and join me for a walk? It will do you good and you can get back to it later, more refreshed."

She looked at him, a slight frown between her eyes. "What time is it?" she asked.

125

"A little after four."

"Have you eaten?"

He shook his head. "Not since morning, and I walked downtown. I'm hungry."

"Good," she said, smiling, "because I'm starved. I haven't eaten since last night. I have some chili in the fridge. I'll heat it up—it always tastes better the next day."

He held up his hand. "I wouldn't think of imposing on you. Please, Miss O'Neill, allow me to take you out to eat. It will make me feel less guilty about interrupting your work."

She gave him a quick, appraising look.

"Agreed, Mr. Jacobs. Clear a spot and make yourself comfortable. I'll be ready in a moment."

Asher took off his hat and jacket as Bronwyn left the room. He went to the chair in which she had been sitting; it was the only place without books, magazines, or clothes on it. The seat was still warm and he settled back into the soft pillow, feeling her presence. He picked up the manuscript she had been reading. Recognizing the author, he turned the pages, noting Bronwyn's pencilled comments on the margins; they were exacting, demanding—she was a tough editor.

He glanced about the room, smiling at the clutter; it made him realize the difference in their ages. She was still carefree.

She returned as quickly as she had promised, dressed for the outdoors in a beige cashmere sweater with a high cowl collar. Her brown wool pants were tucked into leather boots and Asher watched as she secured her hair under a brown tweed cap similar to his own. Tying a silk scarf around her throat, she put on a russet-colored down coat.

He rose and put on his hat and jacket, feeling a quiver inside him as he looked at her. She was even lovelier than she had seemed last night. She looked younger with no makeup; there was only a hint of gloss on her lips, and her skin gleamed.

"I'm glad you live in the Village," he said as they went down the stairs. "Almost everything uptown is closed on Christmas Day."

They descended to the street and Bronwyn saw that last

night's beautiful snowfall was now slush, ground into greyness by cars and people. A cold drizzle wet the air, and she glanced up at Asher.

"You walked downtown in this?"

"Weather never bothers me," he said, taking her arm as they crossed Seventh Avenue. The wide street was clear of the cars and trucks which normally thundered their way to the Holland Tunnel. Only a few scattered vehicles poked through the darkening dusk, their lights hazy in the wet mist.

"Do you mind walking in such weather?"

"Not at all," she said, her stride easily matching his. "I like cold, gloomy days. It's summer and sun I dislike."

"That's unusual."

"Not as unusual as a man like you, with all the cars he could summon, choosing to walk in freezing rain."

He gave her a teasing grin. "There's much about me that would surprise you."

Her smile matched his. "I've no doubt of that, Mr. Jacobs."

He looked at her and stopped. They stood in the middle of the sidewalk. He put his hands on her shoulders and smiled down at her, his green eyes cutting through the greyness.

"You will have to call me 'Asher.' I can't possibly make love to you, Bronwyn, if you insist on calling me 'Mr. Jacobs.' And I do intend to make love to you."

He laughed outright at the surprise which flooded her eyes. Without giving her a chance to reply, he took her arm again and turned her into Barrow Street. "I can't remember who said it—maybe it was Emerson, maybe not—but the phrase is: 'Mount to Paradise on the stairway of surprise!'"

He stopped her again as they came to an arched doorway which led into a dim courtyard. "Well?" he asked.

Bronwyn met his gaze, her coppery eyes noncommittal.

"I'm glad you know Chumley's, Asher. I love their hamburgers."

With a chuckle, he led her into the alleyway.

* * *

127

Bronwyn wiped the last vestiges of Chumley's exotic peanut sauce from her plate with what was left of her hamburger roll. She looked up to find Asher smiling at her and she grinned back.

"It seems I'm always eating when you're around."

He took pleasure in her enjoyment; she was so wonderfully young, so beautiful.

"It's refreshing to see someone eat so happily. People who love food, love life."

She wiped her mouth with the napkin and sat back. "Ironic, isn't it? All the experts tell us overeating shortens life."

"Does that worry you?"

"Overeating or dying?" she teased, scanning the dessert card on the table.

He laughed. "You've just answered my question."

"Do you mind if I smoke?" she asked.

"I'm not Van Zuye," he said, "but thank you for asking."

Bronwyn reached into her pocket for her cigarettes and by the time she had removed one from the pack, Asher held a lighted match.

"Thank you." She leaned against the dark wood paneling which rose halfway up the dingy walls of the wide room, which had been a speakeasy in the 1920s. There had been no attempt to update the premises; it was drab, seedy-looking, and that was its charm. They sat side-by-side on the worn wood bench which ran along the walls; the scarred wood tables were small and they sat, bodies touching.

Squinting through the smoke curling from her cigarette, Bronwyn asked, "Does dying worry you?"

"No," Asher said easily, "but I intend to put it off as long as I can."

"Is life that good for you?"

"Life is good, no matter what."

"You can't really believe that."

"I do."

She inhaled deeply, closing her eyes again to the delicious feeling nicotine always evoked in her. "I wonder sometimes if living is not death, and death, life."

128

Asher smiled. "When you're young and healthy, it's easy to be cavalier about death. You read about Joan of Arc, Sidney Carton, the Christians going to the lions, and death seems noble, but there is nothing noble about death. It is ugly, dirty, and heartbreaking, and the closer death comes, the more one sees its finality and clings to life."

"You'd get quite an argument from resurrectionists, reincarnationists, and all those in pain," Bronwyn said dryly. She searched his eyes and her tone softened. "How close were you to death?"

Asher stretched his legs under the table. He put his head back on the wainscoting and turned his face to her.

"Close enough to know how precious life is and how much I want to live." Grimacing, he leaned forward and took her hand in his. "How did we ever get on such a morbid subject?" He stroked her hand, running his fingers along her wrist to her fingertips. She had strong hands with long, tapering fingers and he envisioned her fingers like a willow in a summer breeze, caressing him. He closed his fingers tightly on hers to encapsulate the feeling.

"May I take you home, Bronwyn?"

She looked at him steadily. "I think not, Asher."

He raised her hand and kissed her fingertips. "Why not?" he asked, his eyes on hers.

"Because it's not *me* you want, it's the woman I remind you of."

His eyes studied her face.

"Yes, you are very much like her, but we want people for many reasons—many we don't even understand. Isn't it better I know *why* I'm so attracted to you?" The long look he gave her held no apology.

"But it isn't only your uncanny resemblance to a woman I once loved—I find you vibrantly intelligent . . . desirable . . . sexy. It is *you*, Bronwyn, I wish to make love to."

Her face was sober. "And Mednam?"

The fingers holding hers relaxed and a shadow crossed his face. She made no move to disengage her hand. Ordinarily she would enjoy making love to the stunning man sitting beside her. What better way to forget Douglas MacCormack? *But he is Asher Jacobs*, she warned herself.

129

If I become involved with him it can affect my career. But is that so bad? The closer the merger comes, the more I'm tempted to resign anyway. Perhaps being with Jacobs will help me make up my mind. Anyway, what's there to lose? A slow smile warmed her face.

Squeezing the hand still holding hers, she said softly, "Let's go home, Asher."

Chapter Eleven

ELIZABETH curled her toes in the hot sand and thought of refrigerators. Why were the refrigerators of the rich always empty? And rich WASPS were the worst! You were lucky if you found a can of diet ginger ale in their refrigerators. No matter how poor her own family had been, Mama's icebox had always been filled with something to eat: tuna salad, leftover chicken, pickles, bagels—*something* if you got up at night and couldn't sleep.

She sighed and stretched. Elizabeth lay on a beach lounge protected from the Florida sun by a striped umbrella. Beyond the sun-dappled breakers two men swam leisurely, backstroking parallel to the shoreline, their arms lifting and dropping in rhythm with the gentle swells. A light breeze stirred the white fringe of the green and yellow umbrella. Between the two sand chairs next to her,

131

on a small table, was a Scrabble set, its magnetic letters clinging to the well-worn board in angular patterns.

Glancing at the game, she smiled to herself. Never had she won against Paul or Arnold; in Scrabble, as in all else, they were unbeatable. She enjoyed them, and she was glad now she had flown down to Palm Beach for Christmas after all. But she had not been able to work since she had arrived. On other visits she would set up Paul's typewriter on the terrace under the banyan tree and work as comfortably as she did at home. This trip, she could not concentrate. She closed her eyes and, as she had for days, she relived the weekend before her departure. The memory of Asher making love to her sent shivers through her sunwarmed body. She had hoped the feelings he'd aroused would dull once she was surrounded by friends and warm sun, dull as sun dulls a color photo, but instead, her longing for him grew each day, making her restless, especially at night.

Not even the festive parties could make her forget him. And her friends had noticed. On their way to watch the Christmas Regatta from Michelle Landy's opulent 25th-floor penthouse overlooking Lake Worth, Arnold had said, "Elizabeth, I think you're in love."

"Don't pry," Paul had chided.

They had almost spent the evening on the Royal Palm Bridge; the white Rolls had cleared the span just seconds before the center section was raised for the passage of the brightly lit yachts and sailboats. They arrived at the party just as the lead boat, glimmering with Christmas lights, made its way down the Intercoastal Waterway. The extravagantly decorated apartment shone with color and colorfully dressed people. A vivacious woman in her seventies embraced Paul and Arnold. She wore grey lurex tights, snakeskin boots, a grey wool poncho, and strands of pearls. Heavy silver bracelets wound up her arms, and atop her silver hair was a grey fur hat. On someone with less panache the look would have been ludicrous; on her it was an expression of an ageless spirit.

Elizabeth went out to the wrap-around terrace to watch the flotilla sail by. Christmas lights outlined the rigging, hulls, superstructures, and bowsprits of the long line of

132

boats. Some masts had been turned into glowing, multicolored Christmas trees; other boats were all crystal—spidery, spun-glass vessels gliding on a black mirror sea.

Overhead, just above the terrace, the Goodyear blimp floated, its sides jazzy with psychedelic messages flashing in blazing technicolor as if a Christmas elf sat at its computer. Above it another shape, looking like a flying saucer, flew into view; it was an airplane, its fuselage invisible against the stars, the underside of its wings an electronic billboard spelling out greetings. Soon the sound of fireworks thundered and shafts of light lit the sky, starburst upon starburst.

Elizabeth did not know what made her suddenly turn to look through the wide glass walls into the white-tiled, mirrored living room. She froze. A man and woman had just arrived; they stood with their backs to her, greeting Michelle, who was vibrant in a red silk chiffon blouse and black satin harlequin trousers. Elizabeth's heart turned in her chest as her eyes bored into the back of the tall, broad-shouldered man. And then a large woman stepped in front of her, obscuring her view, and when she moved aside, the couple was gone. Elizabeth wandered slowly around the terrace, looking casually into the many rooms of the apartment. People were everywhere: talking, drinking, eating Chinese food spooned from silver warming trays onto red, gold-banded plates.

There he was! He sat with his back half turned to her, his handsome head almost touching the beak of an enormous papier-mâché toucan perched behind the red and turquoise printed sofa. His long legs stretched across the zebra-skin rug and he bent close to the exquisitely dressed woman beside him. Elizabeth felt her pulse race. He reached for his drink on the mirrored cocktail table, and she saw his profile. Her heart sank. It was not Asher. The disappointment flooding through her made her dizzy and she sat down dolefully on a plump, red satin pouf.

"My, you're lazy today," Paul said, breaking into her reverie.

"Mmmmm." She stretched again, opening her eyes,

133

looking through the dark sunglasses as he dried himself vigorously with a boldly patterned beach towel.

"Where's Arnold?" she asked.

"Still in the surf. I don't like his swimming alone. Perhaps you'd spell me."

"Of course." She doffed her sunglasses, picked up her swim mask, and ran gingerly across the hot sand to the water. *How considerate they are of each other,* she thought, *even after all these years.* Arnold loved to swim; Paul hated even getting wet, but after Arnold's heart attack, Paul never permitted Arnold to swim alone. She knew of few relationships between men and women which were so caring.

Elizabeth stroked towards the white-haired man floating with his arms and legs spread wide atop a rising swell. "Hi!" she called. He turned over and waved as she came close.

"Paul send you out to ride shotgun?"

She smiled. "It's time I got off my duff and took a swim."

"You look like a grinning sea monster in that mask. You'll scare the fish!"

Pushing the mask atop her head, she turned onto her back. How good the water felt! It was unusually calm for the last day of December. Her body rose and fell, light as a bobbing cork.

"Take your swim," Arnold said. "The water is so loving today, I could float all afternoon."

Loving. Elizabeth turned her head to look at him. What a perfect word for the smooth sea. Sighing with pleasure, she closed her eyes against the bright sun.

"Wouldn't it be lovely to float like this forever? No cares, no memories—just to be a fish?"

Arnold looked at her. "What about the sharks?"

She met his eyes. "At least in the sea, they kill quickly."

His grey eyes gleamed like a gull's. "No kill is painless, Elizabeth. We're alive, kid, that's all that counts. Come on, I'll race you to the seawall." Turning onto his stomach, he swam in long, even strokes. Elizabeth pulled on her mask and followed.

* * *

134

Paul eased the Rolls through the traffic on Worth Avenue and into the alley behind the Garner-Eglin Gallery. "I'll only be a minute," he said.

Browsers thronged the street of costly, elegant shops although it was the afternoon of New Year's Eve. Paul, disdainful of the tourist trade, had left his clerks in charge and they had gone to the beach, driving past the lavish homes on South Ocean Boulevard, parking in Lily Pierson's cobbled drive behind the high stone walls and neatly clipped ficus hedge, crossing on foot to the manicured, scalloped lawn and hedges of sea grape, through the cedar gate, down to the cabana on the private strip of sand bordering the Atlantic Ocean.

Tired from the sun and swimming, Elizabeth rested her head back on the blue leather seat, her eyes closed. Paul returned and, looking at her as he got into the car, said: "Don't fall asleep, Elizabeth. We'll all take a nap when we get home, for I doubt we'll see our beds again before dawn."

Later, resting on her white wicker bed, Elizabeth reviewed the ritual she knew would follow. New Year's Eve began with cocktails on the torchlit terraces of the Pantheon of Palm Beach, Lily Pierson's Moorish estate overlooking the Atlantic. Black men, dressed in red livery and wearing white gloves, served drinks and hors d'oeuvres from silver trays. Later there was a candlelit supper in the high-ceilinged dining room surrounded by tropical gardens meandering to the shores of Lake Worth. Hidden lights softly illuminated the plantings, silhouetting the magnificent palm trees against a night sky thick with stars. After dinner there was dancing in the tiled-floor ballroom festooned with swags of evergreen and holly. The Lester Lanin Orchestra were all dressed in white jackets with red carnations in their lapels. Towards dawn they moved on to Dolly Brewer's pink Mediterranean villa on the Atlantic beachfront, north of the Breakers Hotel. There a breakfast was served, and they welcomed the sunrise drinking champagne and orange juice Mimosas.

Urbane, elegant men, Paul Garner and Arnold Eglin were popular guests, and their own parties were creative and sophisticated, but, unlike many in Palm Beach, they

135

were serious working men, men who had earned their fortune and who accepted the Palm Beach scene with a healthy cynicism. They knew success, money, and celebrity were what opened doors, and consequently, when Elizabeth first visited, they made sure to introduce her as "Ellen Barclay."

Elizabeth, however, always felt more a spectator than a participant. She found Palm Beach conversation as glossy as glass; people avoided the scratch of discussion and controversy as carefully as they avoided synthetics. Because of her friends, Elizabeth curbed her outspoken tendencies, and at parties she amused herself by watching how men and women eyed each other, how women eyed women, and how men measured men, appraising appearances, judging worth, as though they were all under a jeweler's loupe.

Cicadas chirping in the branches of the giant banyan tree outside her window awakened Elizabeth. A soft breeze from the lake wafted through the partially open French doors. Voices came from the far end of the screened gallery linking the upstairs bedrooms of the French-style chateau on the eastern shore of Lake Worth. Taking her peignoir from the foot of the bed, Elizabeth went out on the balcony, where her friends reclined on rattan chaises.

"Did you sleep?" she asked.

"Delightfully," Paul said. "We came out to see the clouds at sunset; it's what I love most about Florida—the cloud formations make up for the paucity of the landscape, as if nature, contrite at how uninteresting and flat she made Florida, tossed mountains into the heavens in recompense. Ah, if Turner could have seen *these* skys!"

Elizabeth nestled onto an adjacent chaise and watched the setting sun stretch long, languorous fingers, lighting mass upon mass of clouds, tinging one smoky puff atop another with dichromatic color. Slowly the sun sank from view but its color lingered, turning the cloud towers topaz. They watched the spectacle in silence, and as the light dimmed Arnold said:

"Talk to us, Elizabeth."

She sighed lazily. "I'd rather listen to night coming on."

He sat up and arranged the folds of his silk caftan.

"You mean you'd rather listen to us gossip; it gives you fodder for your books. I found all that dirt about Buffy and Pug thinly disguised in your last masterpiece."

She chuckled. "You've no faith in me."

"None at all," he said, smiling.

How sweet they were, Elizabeth thought. She had first walked into their 57th Street gallery years back with thirty dollars she had managed to save. Bonnie was a year old and she had wanted to buy a special gift for her baby, one which would grow in value as the child grew. *What can I give my child that is as precious as she is, that will bring her as much joy as she brings me?* she had thought as she walked the few blocks from the Hearst Building on Eighth Avenue, where she worked as an editorial assistant on *Good Housekeeping* magazine. She had stood, entranced by a Ben Shahn print in the window, caught up in the exciting blues and yellows, in the strength of the brush strokes and the absolute perfection of the composition. Timidly she had walked inside, and although the thirty dollars was just enough for a down payment on the print, Paul and Arnold had treated her like a valued client. Each year on Bonnie's birthday Elizabeth had added to the collection, Paul and Arnold teaching her about art, directing her purchases, and becoming her friends.

With Paul the friendship grew slowly, but with Arnold it was instant. Paul was private, aristocratic; Arnold was volatile, a time bomb of emotions. They were as disparate physically: Paul looked like a majestic Indian carved from rare potash granite; he was tall and slender, with dark, greying hair, deep brown eyes, and a perpetually tanned, hawklike face with a prominent nose and high cheekbones. Arnold was short, rotund, with a pink and white skin, and a heavy shock of coarse white hair atop a face so smooth and pleasant, you wanted to hug him.

Paul broke into Elizabeth's thoughts, his tone imperious. "It's time we talked, Elizabeth. Something's bothering you."

"I thought you said not to pry," Arnold laughed.

"I'm not prying, I'm concerned," Paul said haughtily.

Elizabeth looked from one to the other. She had never inquired into their personal lives. All she knew of them was what she observed and what she assumed, but they knew everything about her. They were almost like the parents she had lost. There was so much about them she wanted to know, but never dared mention. How could she ask: what chemistry between you brings such contentment? Why don't you bicker brutally like men and women? What makes your love so strong—so kind? And why can't love be so kind for me?

She sighed, knowing she could never pose such questions. Instead, she told them of herself and before she knew it, of Asher, confiding in them, speaking softly as dusk descended on the balcony. When she finished, Arnold whistled long and low.

"Asher Jacobs! That's quite a catch, Elizabeth."

Annoyance rose in her. "I *hate* that word! I'm not interested in *catching* any man! As far as I'm concerned it was a lovely interlude, and now it's over. I'm perfectly content with my work; that's what gives meaning to my life. I have a rare happiness. What more could I possibly need?"

"Really?" Paul drew the word out slyly. " 'The lady doth protest too much, methinks.' "

"And methinks," Arnold laughed, "that you're bananas over him, Elizabeth, and it scares you to death."

"No, on both counts!" she said hotly.

"I don't believe you." Paul languidly stretched his long limbs, and then he sat up, fastening his eaglelike eyes on her. "You're afraid of Asher Jacobs, Elizabeth, because he is a successful, sought-after man, and that makes you uncomfortable. Any woman in Palm Beach would cut off her right arm to get him. But you, my dear, are afraid to step into the arena. It's so much easier for you to retreat into your typewriter and spin fantasies that have little resemblance to real life."

"Oh, stop being bitchy," Elizabeth said shortly.

"Aha! So I have hit a nerve," Paul gloated. Elegantly, with his long and tapering fingers, he turned the bowl of hibiscus on the table next to his chaise so that the velvety red petals faced him. When he spoke next, his clipped, cultured voice was made even more authoritative by the quietness of his tone.

"Sit back and buckle your seat belt, my dear, because as La Davis, the one and only Bette, divinely put it, 'it's going to be a *bumpy* night!' "

Elizabeth had never known anyone so thoroughly intimidating as Paul Garner. She gathered her defenses as she listened.

"The worst of it is, Elizabeth, you are beginning to believe what you write, and mere mortals with all their humanness and their frailties hold no attraction for you—you expect Nirvana. And since Lorne died you've shied away from real men—men who would challenge you. Oh, how I'd love to see a strong man take you in hand! Strong, secure men make the best lovers! They *give* as much as they take! Why must it be you who always gives? We've watched you through the years, and you make the men in your life weak, because you give too much! To give and not take is selfish—it deprives the other of the pleasure of giving. Why are you afraid to make demands of men? Don't you know *expecting* the best, and asking for it, makes others strong?"

Elizabeth stared at him, disturbed by a view of herself she did not like.

"You know we love you, darling," Arnold said kindly, "but sometimes we could really kick your ass. Asher Jacobs needs a woman like you. The more powerful someone is, the more he needs a sincere, loving person to share the loneliness power brings. The average person makes all his mistakes in private, but those in visible positions do not have that privilege, and they become cautious, to the point that loving freely, *believing* fully in someone else is difficult. We all need love, Elizabeth. Work without love is only half a life—it upsets the balance of nature. Don't be a fool, Elizabeth. You made a good start with a fine man—*now, go after him!*" Arnold's voice rang with emotion.

"Easy, Arnold, easy." Paul reached out and touched his friend.

But Arnold went on. "It takes practice to love, and you're out of practice, Elizabeth. You exercise regularly to keep in shape. Well, what about shaping up your love life? You gotta get in the bullpen and pitch, kiddo. You can be young alone, but you don't want to be old alone, and once a woman passes fifty, it's the minor leagues."

"Oh, Arnold," Elizabeth protested, "I don't want the pain of love again!"

"Bullshit!" Arnold exploded. "You'd rather have the pain of loneliness? At least with love, pain is *memorable!* Even when it tears your heart out, you know you're *alive!* The pain of loneliness is like *death!*"

"That's *enough,* Arnold!" Paul uncoiled himself from the chaise. "I don't want the pain of you in the hospital again. It's time we got dressed. I want you both in high spirits and looking wonderful—not one more word of pain tonight!"

Rising, Elizabeth went to Arnold and kissed his cheek. "Thank you, darling. I'll think about what you said."

She turned to Paul and hugged him warmly. "And thank you too. How can I have gotten to this age and know so little about myself?"

He kissed her forehead. "Join the club."

As she dressed, Elizabeth thought of what Paul and Arnold had said. Paul's words particularly haunted her, and she filed them in the back of her mind to be studied and thought about. And Arnold's words, too, had come frighteningly close. Lately, despite her denials, voiced and unvoiced, the aloneness she cherished was becoming suspect. At first the feeling was fleeting, like a word flashed on a screen, registering only subliminally, but since she had met Asher, the word had lingered until it could be read: *loneliness.* She had not been able to face the holidays alone after Asher had left. Wasn't that the *real* reason she had left for Palm Beach? Bonnie's not being home for Christmas was just an excuse. And what had she been thinking about constantly since she arrived? Her face grew warm at the memory. How she wanted him!

She looked at the woman staring back at her in the mirror, a handsome woman wearing a black chiffon evening dress with large, hand-painted poppies splashed asymmetrically along the hem. The sheer blackness of the gown complemented the clarity of her skin; her auburn

140

hair was brushed sleekly back and secured with a diamond clip. Her face glowed from the sun and the warmth of her thoughts, and her hazel eyes shone with the memory of the man who made her feel this beautiful.

Arnold and Paul were right—she should go for it! She deserved a man like Asher Jacobs.

Chapter Twelve

ASHER ran his fingers slowly along the curve of the hip nestled naked against his thigh. In the darkness he could not see the rounded shape, but his fingers, lovingly tracing the smooth skin, knew every inch. Turning on his side, he drew the sleeping woman closer, fitting himself tightly against the swell, the warmth of her buttocks. She slept soundlessly, her breathing so soft that though he lay close, he heard nothing.

Soon he would waken her, but for now he just wanted to hold her. Hold her. He sighed. Could one hold firelight? Perhaps in this quiet moment before sunrise, in her sleep, she might reveal more than she had since they met four days ago. How private she was; he longed to know her feelings as he had come to know her body, but Bronwyn remained elusive, as though her heart and mind were a cloister he could not enter.

142

He buried his face in her hair and entwined his fingers in its silkened thickness. Slowly, from the deep recesses of his mind, like the shadow of a lost painting under another, he saw his fingers entwined in another's hair.

He saw Marguerite before she saw him. She stood in the doorway of the Ritz Bar, an expectant look on her beautiful face. As she scanned the room, her face sobered and a frown creased her smooth forehead. Turning towards the crowded bar, her eyes swept its length. They met Asher's astonished look and widened in surprise; an unbelieving smile crossed her face. She waved happily and Asher shouldered his way towards her through the throng of soldiers.

"I can't believe it! How wonderful to see you!" Marguerite exclaimed as he hugged her, lifting her off her feet. "Why didn't you write you were coming home? Michael said nothing about you meeting us!"

Grinning with pleasure, he put her down. "Michael? Here? Where?"

"He's to meet me. Didn't you know?"

He shook his head. "I haven't seen Mike in months." He couldn't take his eyes off her. She was lovelier than he remembered. She wore a grey suit with a matching hat whose upturned brim swept across her wide forehead; her hair was pulled back over her ears and coiled into a chignon. He held tightly to her hands in grey kid gloves, proudly aware of how the men around him looked at her.

She stepped back to see him better. Her face sobered, and she reached up to touch his cheek. "It's been more than a year," she said softly. "We've missed you. Your last letter came weeks ago."

War had touched him; he could not tell her where he'd been or what he'd been doing, but the drawn look around his eyes and mouth spoke for him. He had grown taller and in his uniform he looked older than his eighteen years.

"You're no longer a boy," she said sadly.

He laughed. "I hoped you'd think that."

She looked around the smoke-filled room. "Let's find a table. You can buy me a drink and we'll wait for Mike."

"There hasn't been an empty table in this room since the

143

war started, especially on a Friday night," Asher said, putting his glass back on the bar.

"Well, let's wait upstairs then. I hate standing at crowded bars." She took his arm. "Mike pulled strings and got us a suite for the weekend. We can have a cot set up in the living room for you."

Asher settled into a large wing chair and watched Marguerite phone downstairs for drinks. He wondered why Michael had allowed her to come to London. Since the landings in Normandy the Germans had stepped up the bombing and the buzz bombs came without warning.

A waiter arrived with bottles and glasses on a tray. Marguerite poured their drinks. She handed one to Asher, then raised her glass. "May God keep you safe. And may God protect Mike and end this war soon."

She looked at Asher as they sat sipping their drinks, and he could feel her impatience. Finally she got up and paced restlessly about the room.

"He'll be here soon, Marge," Asher said quietly.

"Yes, yes, of course." Her voice held no conviction. She wandered to the window, but stopped short when she saw the drawn blackout drapes. She laughed nervously.

"I really gave Mike a hard time about coming this weekend."

"I wondered why you were here," Asher said. "Mike's right. London's as dangerous now as the front."

"And you've been there?" The moment she uttered the words she knew she should not have. "I'm sorry, don't answer that." She sank into the wing chair opposite him and laughed again, a short, nervous sound. "Did I ever tell you one of Mike's most classic remarks?" She didn't wait for Asher's answer but hurried on.

"I met Mike at an opening night party. It was my first show—I was in the chorus. He invited me to an early dinner the next night, before the performance. He was late so I grabbed a sandwich. Just before the curtain went up I was called to the stage door. Mike stood there with dozens of roses, smiling as if nothing had happened. 'I'm sorry, Marge,' he said, 'I'm always on time. I'm never more than an hour late.'"

144

They laughed, her laugh becoming more natural, more relaxed. She had taken off her suit jacket and her silk blouse was a light green shade that made her skin look like cream. He tried not to notice how the blouse clung and how her nipples showed when she moved. Her hair was still in the coiled chignon and without the hat it shone, the hairline framing her flawless face. Her copper-colored eyebrows were perfect ellipses over the wide-set eyes, and her wide, curving mouth made him hunger to kiss her. He knew he should leave, but like a tiger moth mesmerized by flame, he found it impossible to move.

Abruptly she got up again. Suddenly from the lips he fantasized kissing came a torrent of words that startled him.

"Asher, I'm going crazy out there in the country! It's as bad as it was in Switzerland! My God, Asher, you can't know how I hated being in Gstaad those first years of the war! People were dying all over Europe, and the Swiss could care less. I couldn't stand their callous righteousness, their arrogance, their cruel disregard for suffering. If we hadn't come to England, I would have gone mad! But then, even here, I'm left out of it! Michael keeps me in the country and all I can do is *wait*. I have nothing but empty hours with an eight-year-old child who resents me—God knows why. Of course, I can't really blame her. What fun can she have with a mother who's so bored, she drinks most of the time? I must get into *something!* I can't just sit and worry about him, about you. I can't just keep waiting and waiting."

She went to the tray and poured herself a double Scotch.

"It's gotten so bad, I don't even care if the V-2's come over tonight. At least I'd feel my adrenaline pumping and know I'm alive. At least I'd feel part of this goddamned war!" She threw her head back and drained her glass.

Asher sat in shocked silence. This was someone he didn't know. It was Marguerite who held *them* together, who was always there for them, smiling, strong, dependable. *My God*, he thought, *how we've taken her for granted*.

The phone rang. They both looked at it, and then at each other.

145

At least it isn't a telegram, Asher thought.

It continued to ring, and Marguerite stared at the black instrument, refusing to answer it.

"I hate phones," she said bitterly. "It's always some colonel telling me Mike will be in touch eventually."

Asher tried to set her at ease. "Come on, Marge, it's probably the desk telling us Mike's on his way up."

She gave him a sardonic look. "Want to bet?"

The ringing persisted and finally, with a sigh, she went to the table and picked up the receiver.

"Yes?" Her voice was subdued, without emotion. "No, that won't be necessary. Yes, yes, I understand. Thank you for calling."

Asher waited. Marguerite stood with her back to him. When she turned, her face was as expressionless as her voice on the phone.

"Anything wrong?"

She gave him a strange look. "No. Isn't it terrible? I almost wish there was. Maybe then I wouldn't feel so dead." She saw the concern in his face. "I'm sorry. That was Colonel Scott—he must be new—anyway, Mike's on assignment. I'm to go home and wait for him to contact me."

Asher saw the tautness in her head, her shoulders, her hands, and then she crumpled, sobbing, her beautiful features spilling together, frustration breaking through her reserve. Her shoulders shook and she put her hands over her eyes, angry at herself for losing control, angry with Michael for disappointing her, and angry that she felt so helpless.

Asher got up quickly and took her in his arms. "Don't, Marge, don't," he said huskily. He kissed the top of her head and felt a pulse begin to beat deep within him. He stroked her shoulders, trying to soothe her, and then his hands touched her hair. He began to shake inside. Trembling, he undid the coiled knot at the back of her neck, and her loosened hair tumbled over his fingers.

As he laced his hands through the thickness of her hair, the years of wanting her, of dreaming of her closed in on him. Instinct that began in steaming, prehistoric bogs engulfed him. Passion locked his mind as passion had

146

locked the minds of men for eons, driving them to desperate acts over women. And with Asher the drive was overdue, for until this moment he had never known a woman. His breath came hoarsely.

"Marge, Marge, let me make you feel alive!"

His hands in her hair, he pulled her head back and kissed her. There was no mistaking the meaning of that kiss, and she stiffened, trying to pull away, but he held her fast, his lips, his hands demanding.

She pushed hard against him and tried to turn her mouth from his, but his lips held hers fast, and his arms tightened. Her lips moved under his, trying to form the word "No!" but Asher was adamant. His fingers found her breasts, and through the silk he stroked her nipples until they hardened under his touch. He felt her shudder, and his tongue darted between her teeth. He edged his thigh between her legs, and his hands closed on her buttocks.

Marguerite had coped with the love of the boy, but she was no match for the primitive passion of the man. She struggled, but Asher was unrelenting, and his fierceness fed her own anger, her own frustration—and answered her need. With a moan born long before Eve, her body settled against his, her lips parted under the strength of his lips, and her arms came up around his neck, pulling him closer. His heart thudded at her response and, not taking his mouth from her, he picked her up in his arms and carried her into the bedroom.

Only a shaft of grey light filtered into the room, a light so dark and dull, it was as if dawn did not wish to wake to such a cold, dank day. In bed for the past hour, they made love, such heated love that the room seemed filled with the warmth of summer.

Bronwyn flung her legs high around his hips and tightened her thighs like a vise, pulling him closer, deeper. Arching her body to meet his thrusts, she pumped her hips wildly. He felt her wetness, her heat and he closed his eyes, breathing deeply—he wanted it to last and last, but she wanted it *now!* She cried out, a long, wailing sound, and surged beneath him, the climax she had withheld coming—drowning her. He felt her surge and with a guttural groan he grabbed her, circling her round, firm rump on the hardness of his erection. She screamed then and climaxed again. Inside, her muscles flexed, pulsed, and he could hold back no longer. With a primeval cry, his ejaculation coming from the well of his being, he erupted in her.

She reached up and drew his sweating body down on hers. He lay against her softness, hearing her heart, like his, slow down. Tears of release burned behind his eyes, and lovingly he smoothed back the hair fallen across her face. *This* is the essence of life, he thought; all else means nothing. *This* is creation, as much the beginning of life as the birth of a star. He kissed her face tenderly. He would never let her go again.

"You're in terrific shape, Asher Jacobs," she said, smiling up at him in the dim light. "You make love like a boy of eighteen. I can't keep up with you."

"Good." He chuckled, nipping at her ear. "I like a woman who knows her limits."

She punched him playfully. "For an old man, Jacobs, you're quite a stud."

He looked down at her. "Am I too old for you, Bronwyn?"

She searched his eyes and said quietly, "I was only teasing."

"I know," he said, smiling, "but I'm not. I want you, Bronwyn, and I don't mean just once in a while, here in bed. I want you for the rest of my life." He stroked the copper-colored eyebrows and touched his lips to her forehead. When he spoke his voice was so soft, had his lips not been close to her ear she could not have made out the words.

"I love you, Bronwyn. Will you marry me?"

Her body beneath him went rigid. He raised himself up on his elbows. "I'm sorry. I'm too heavy on you."

She slid smoothly from underneath him, and wrapping the sheet around her she sat up and looked at him squarely, a slight frown between her eyes. He drew the blanket over him and watched her, his eyes drawn to her lips and the words she carefully measured.

"What a beautiful thing to say, Asher, and I thank

you." She ran her fingers along his hairline. "And it's not because I've known you less than a week that I cannot accept. It's because I don't plan to marry—*ever.*"

He sat up, amusement in his eyes.

"Ever? What makes you say that?"

She laughed easily. "I dislike the idea of marriage. It destroys one's privacy, it dilutes one's independence, and—" She gave him a saucy look. "It makes one answer telephones."

He leaned against the headboard and laughed happily. Drawing her to him, he put her head on his shoulder and stroked her hair.

"And what about love, Bronwyn? Do you dislike love also?"

The head under his hand nodded. "Yes," she said.

"How could anyone as responsive as you not want love?" He kissed the top of her head.

"Do you mean love? Or do you mean possession?"

He turned her to face him. "Both," he said firmly. "By nature, they are inseparable."

"Baloney!" she shot back. "That's a male concept. In nature, animals mate and go their own way."

"Not all." He grinned. "Birds are mostly monogamous, lions have their pride . . ."

"And Asher Jacobs his woman," she smiled back.

"You can bet on that."

"I'm sorry to disappoint you, but it won't be this woman."

"Why not?"

"Do you know how tough it is to find an apartment in Greenwich Village?"

"Come on, Bronwyn, be serious."

"I've never been more serious."

His eyes met hers. "You can keep your apartment."

She laughed again. "I don't believe you. You're so sure of yourself. You've never even asked how I feel about you. How can you be so sure that I don't dislike you, that I'm not using you?"

He took her hands and kissed them and he looked at her levelly. "Because you could never make love to me as you have."

149

"Oh come on, Asher. I've made love like that since I was seventeen. No, that's not quite true. I'm better than I was at seventeen, and I hope to be better when I'm forty. Do you think it's only men who can make love and not get emotionally involved?"

"And what makes you think men don't become emotionally involved? Christ!" he said shortly, leaping out of bed, wrapping the blanket around himself to ward off the chill of the room. "You've got feminist tunnel vision, Bronwyn. Men and women are *human,* with the same drives, the same emotions. I've never made love to a woman and not felt *something.* We may not choose to marry every woman we sleep with, but that doesn't mean we don't *care."*

"But you hardly know me. How can you know that you love me, or that you want to marry me?"

He stopped moving about the room and looked down at her. "I know—as surely as I know this room is too damn cold." Keeping the emotions welling in him under control, he asked evenly, "And you, do you care for me, Bronwyn, or am I just a body you desire?"

Without taking her eyes from his she said, "No, Asher, you're not just a body I desire. But I don't know if I love you. We've had a great time these past few days, but . . ." Three sharp lines broke the smoothness of her brow. "It's just too soon—I've recently broken off with someone I've known for a long time . . . I'm not sure, even, if I know what love is . . ."

He sat down on the edge of the bed and took her hand. And then he wrapped the blanket around both of them. "Once when I was a little boy, I came down the hall and heard my grandmother speaking to my cousin Jenny. I loved Jenny. She was ten years older, and I had a terrific crush on her. It was the night before her wedding and the women in our family went to the *mikveh* before they married. It's a ritual bath in which women cleanse not only their bodies, but their souls as well, for marriage. And they spent the night with my grandmother, who instructed them in what it meant to become a wife." His voice softened and he pulled Bronwyn close.

"Our family was religious and the marriages were

150

arranged. Jenny had probably been betrothed when she was born, and as I came down the hall, I heard her crying. I stopped to listen. I heard her tell my grandmother she hardly knew her husband-to-be—how could she love him? She didn't even know what love meant. I can still hear my grandmother:

" 'The love you dream of, Jenny, is like a storm—beautiful, breathtaking, exciting—but like all storms it can hurt you, and like all storms it passes. In the Talmud it says of Isaac and Rebekah . . . *she became his wife, and he loved her* not *he loved Rebekah and she became his wife.* The order of those words, Jenny, is very important, because our Jewish tradition tells us that while romantic love before marriage is beautiful, it is far more important *after marriage* to be devoted and affectionate, to be kind to each other and do for each other. This then becomes *true love*—a love you will learn as surely as you learned to walk and talk, for if you walk and talk together and give to each other, your love will become cement binding you together forever, and this no wind, no storm can blow away. Besides, for a woman it is much better if the man she marries loves her just a little bit more than she loves him.' "

Bronwyn laughed at the little accent and shrug Asher used for the last sentence. "Did Jenny live happily ever after?"

"She died in a concentration camp along with most of my family."

Bronwyn reached out for him. "Oh, Asher, forgive me for being flip."

He kissed the top of her head.

"It's okay. I've learned to live with it."

"You're incredibly understanding."

"Am I?"

"Of course you are! It's what I like most about you. I can say *anything* to you. We talk about so much, and no matter how we differ, you listen to me, you don't judge me. You're not stuffy about sex, you don't mind my untidiness, you don't even blink when I'm brutally frank. You're really a wonderful man, and if I were more like Little Mary Sunshine, I'd marry you tomorrow, but I'm a

151

willful, impatient, self-indulgent person, and I would hurt you."

He put his fingers on her lips.

"Let me worry about that. You see, Bronwyn, my grandmother was right. I love you—more than you love me, and I will be very good to you. You will learn to love."

"Do you really believe that?" Her eyes searched his.

He smiled. "With all my heart."

Chapter Thirteen

Iт was early evening when Asher took a cab uptown from Bronwyn's apartment. Traffic was heavy for a Sunday night, and Asher sank back into the scarred seat, looking thoughtfully out the window. Never had he been this impulsive with a woman. Bronwyn was right in her hesitation. It *was* too soon, and yet he knew it could be no other way. And she had been right to shoo him out.

"I want to be in my office first thing tomorrow, alert and snappy," she had said. "I need sleep with no one beside me."

Was she also right when she insisted his feelings for her were because he was still in love with a memory? He sighed. Since he'd met her, the past had become the present. Even now, he saw himself in another cab, threading its way through a darkened city . . .

* * *

153

"Sit back, mate. I'll make Charin' Cross with minutes to spare."

A cigarette dangled from the thin lips of the Cockney cabbie as he sped through narrow streets shadowed with dawn, turning sharply, detouring around bombed-out buildings and roads filled with rubble.

Bounced around in the back seat, a drawn-faced Asher did not answer. God! He'd slunk from the warmth of her bed like a criminal, afraid Marguerite would waken and find him there. How could he have done such a thing! And now, like the cad he was, he couldn't face her! Remorse choked him.

Three days later he was in France, and for the rest of the war, he posted only brief, occasional letters to assure her he was safe, tearing up the other letters in which he asked her forgiveness. Some weeks before the Armistice he met Michael at SHAEF headquarters in Paris.

They sat in an anteroom. Michael's hands were tightly clasped. His right shoulder, injured in a bomb blast two years before, was an inch or more lower than the left. His voice constrained, Michael said, "We've finally gotten confirmation on your parents."

Asher sucked in his breath. Michael's face said it all.

"How? Where?" Asher croaked.

"In Germany. Your parents were taken somewhere secret right after Poland was invaded. That's why I could never draw a line on them. They tried to get your father to cooperate, and when he wouldn't they shot him—and your mother."

Bile rose in Asher, turning his mouth acid. "And the others?"

"We're not sure. When the Russians liberated Maidanek, they found a young boy, Morris Poper. Others may have survived elsewhere. When this is over, maybe we'll find them. I've got friends in Moscow and I'll try to get the Russians to release Morris to us."

One day shortly after the Armistice, a painfully thin boy stood in the doorway of Asher's office. Twisting his hands nervously, his voice trembling, he said in Polish, "Asher Jacobs?"

154

Asher, still wearing his American uniform, looked up from behind his desk. And then he peered closely at the boy; the youngster's green eyes shifted anxiously. Asher felt every muscle in him contract. He got up slowly, his heart a jackhammer.

"Moishele?" he whispered.

When the boy heard the name his father had always called him, he sobbed. With a low moan Asher went to him, grabbing him close. They clung to each other and wept.

It was days before Morris, who had been only seven years old when Asher left Poland, told his cousin what he could remember. Each word tore into Asher's heart; Asher vowed to make up to Morris for all that he had suffered, but the boy wanted nothing other than to go to Palestine.

"Asher, please. I don't want to live with Gentiles. I want to be with Jews, in a Jewish land."

"Moishele." Asher spoke in Polish. "You're little more than a *Bar Mitzvah bucher*. You can't go off alone where you have no one."

"I became a man a long time ago," Morris said bitterly. "I became a man in a cemetery in July, 1942." And Morris told Asher what had happened to him and the Jews of Dzialoszyce that July morning.

It was a morning so beautiful people would speak of it for years. Morris awakened before dawn. He sat up, wondering why he awoke so early. All was quiet. Only Mama and Papa slept in the other room; his brothers and sister had been sent to labor camps. Papa worked in the flour mill, and he and Mama worked in the fields. Now he remembered—he wanted to get up early to go to the cemetery: just a year ago his sister Rosie had been run down by a truck carrying German soldiers. He wanted to put a stone on her grave, and some wild flowers. How Rosie had loved flowers! He ran out of the house, as silent as a moth.

The first golden strokes of daylight brushed the cobalt sky, gilding the wheat moving gently in the early breeze.

155

Birds swooped down to feast on the fat grain. Morris hurried; he had to be back in time to go to the fields with Mama.

Behind him, towards town, Morris heard noises and the sound of trucks breaking the sweet stillness of dawn. Stopping only to pick the flowers, he soon reached the cemetery. The sun rose, and every flower reaching for life from amongst the tombstones opened its petals. It was a day to work the fields, to feel the fullness of the kernal, to thank God for a fine harvest—all around, God gave life!

Tired from running, Morris lay on his back in the soft grass of Rosie's grave and watched two birds fly about busily. And then he heard it! Trucks rumbling, and beneath the rumble, a sound he would never forget. The low moans of hundreds of people! Turning over, he peered through the dust kicked up by trucks on the road, now sun-baked and hot. He saw soldiers and a long line of people carrying shovels—many were barefoot and dressed in nightclothes. He pressed his body into the earth of Rosie's grave, hiding behind the tombstone, but unable to keep himself from peeking. What he saw filled his ten-year-old eyes with acid, etching a horror he could never erase. The line halted, and the digging began.

Twenty-five hundred Jews of Dzialoszyce, tears coursing through the sweat and dirt on their faces, dug a long, shallow trench, while the soldiers beat them whenever their shovels slowed. Time inched torturously. Now even the sun had no mercy, blistering them with heat. Finally the black ditch stretched two hundred yards.

"Achtung!" shouted a fat, red-faced officer with the pale eyes of a fox. *"ACHTUNG!"* Leaping away from the ditch, the soldiers raised their rifles. The canvas sides of the trucks flew upwards. Machine guns clicked into place. A long, terrible cry came from the Jews—a wailing prayer no one answered. Surely God could not forsake them! Some fell to their knees, others huddled screaming, still others broke and ran.

"FEUER!" barked the officer. Rifles and machine guns roared. Bullets ripped into flesh, tearing, exploding. Screaming, sobbing, scattering, stumbling, men, women,

and children fell on top of each other like scythed wheat. The black earth reddened with their blood.

Morris's lungs screamed. Shoving a fist into his mouth, he buried his face into the grass of Rosie's grave, vowing revenge. He lay for a long time, his tears turning to stone. When there were no more voices, no more sounds, he lifted his head and peered from behind the tombstone. He saw nothing—only a long black mound. Shivering, gulping for air, he crawled on his hands and knees from tombstone to tombstone; then, hunched over, he ran from tree to tree. Reaching his house, his screams tore at the air.

"Mama! Papa! Mama! Papa!" Birds nesting in the eaves flew wildly, screaming with him.

There were no other sounds.

The next day, the remaining Jews of Dzialoszyce, Morris among them, were herded into cattle cars and sent to Maidenek, Treblinka, and Auschwitz.

Asher made precise and careful arrangements to get Morris into Palestine. It was not easy, for thousands of Jews waited in detention camps on Cyprus.

Michael returned to the United States and to ICC, but Asher stayed in Europe and reenlisted, serving as an interpreter with the Army of Occupation. He interviewed death camp survivors, translated testimony at the Nuremburg trials, and helped resettle refugees. Everywhere, he sought his family, but other than Morris, no one else survived. When his reenlistment was up, he accepted his discharge and returned to London; he entered Cambridge in 1949.

Asher and Michael corresponded regularly through the years; at times Michael's letters included a short postscript from Marguerite. Asher read and reread her finely penned handwriting, trying to sense the true feelings behind the casual words. Not once had he forgotten her. And the women he had had while in the Army in Europe and the others he had known during his four years at Cambridge had not erased her memory. At night, when he closed his eyes, he felt the silken warmth of her skin.

The Cassidys did not return to the chalet in Gstaad after

157

the war, and the house was rented to an English actor whose movie contract stipulated he could not be engaged during ski season. Marguerite refused to return to Switzerland. Her dislike of the Swiss for their callousness during the war had not diminished. The Cassidys built a chalet in Sun Valley, a mile east of Ernest Hemingway's house on the mountain road outside Ketchum.

Michael attended Asher's graduation from Cambridge in 1953 and later, as they sat and talked in Asher's room, Michael said, "I'd like you to join ICC, Asher. We've all missed you, and we want you to come home and live with us again. Eleanore keeps talking about you, and Marguerite—well, she hasn't been the same since she lost this last baby. She so much wants another child, but God hasn't blessed us for such a long time." He paused, and a shadow darkened the ruddy face.

"And Eleanore—well, she's a typical teenager. I guess all young girls have differences with their mother at that age. Anyway, you'd bring a needed presence."

Asher looked away, out through the multipaned leaded windows. He longed to see Marguerite, but he said, "I don't think so, Mike, not right now. I'd like to go back to Poland. I'd like to see our house and my father's laboratory. I'd like to go out to my uncle's farm and walk through the fields . . ." His words trailed.

Michael leaned over and touched his arm.

"Don't do it, Asher. Your home is with us. We're your family now. Come back to America with me."

Asher shook his head. "Not just yet. But thank you for asking."

"Then let me make a spot for you in the international division," Michael persisted. "You like London, you can work out of our offices in Chelsea."

Asher fell silent. He looked out into the late afternoon sun slanting in through the windows, casting diamond patterns on the bare wood floor. He spoke finally, his words coming slowly as if he thought aloud.

"My father always used to get so excited when he spoke of television—how important it would be some day, how every home, all over the world, would have it, like the telephone. He saw television as the one way to bring

158

people together—to make one world, where there would be no war, or hatred. Isn't it ironic that I, who am no scientist, should have an opportunity to work in an industry in which he would have been so important?"

He looked at Michael. "Can you really use me, or are you just keeping your promise to my father?"

Michael squeezed Asher's shoulder.

"I can use you, and I need you. You're the son I've never had. I don't want to leave this business to strangers, and television is going to be a young man's world. I'd rather have you in New York where the action is—and the backbiting. But, I'll wait until you're ready to come. In the meantime, you'll learn a lot over here."

The big Lockheed had been circling for an hour, its four propellers a mighty drone. Traffic over Idlewild, socked in by fog, was stacked in layers, a thousand feet apart. Asher looked at his watch impatiently and then at the impenetrable grey shroud outside the oval window. He saw only his reflection in the glass. He hadn't expected fog over New York. Fog was for London and Newfoundland. In his mind New York shimmered and glittered; skyscrapers reached into a sky made bright by their lights. He'd been disappointed not to see the shoreline of America when they'd swung south after refueling at Gander, but fog had followed all the way and now it clouded his first view of New York. He had tried to read on the long trip over, choosing Dos Passos', *USA*, hoping to lose himself in the thickness of the book so that he would not think of Marguerite. But the book lay open in his hands, unread.

It was *ten* years!

What would she look like?

What would she say?

What could *he* say?

The no smoking sign lit up and Asher's pulse accelerated with the engines.

He had only one suitcase and cleared Customs quickly. As he came through the wide swinging doors a young woman rushed up to him. She threw her arms around his neck and kissed him full on the mouth.

159

"Welcome *home,* Asher—my God, how I've waited for you!"

He stepped back, startled. *Eleanore?* This tall, grown-up young woman? He touched her short, blunt-cut hair. Where had the bobbing curls gone? But her blue eyes still held mischief. He hugged her soundly, kissing the top of her head.

"How did you know me?" he laughed. "I would never have recognized you."

She put her arm through his. "You haven't changed, you're just bigger, and Daddy showed us the photos taken of you for the company files. I hope you think I'm as beautiful as I think you are. Come on—the car's outside. Daddy's hung up in a meeting, and Marge decided to wait at home. I've got you all to myself, so we can talk, talk, talk!"

Eleanore led him towards a dark green Cadillac limousine. The uniformed chauffeur standing beside it quickly took Asher's suitcase.

"Is that all you brought with you?" Eleanore asked, noticing his luggage for the first time.

"It's enough for two weeks," Asher said.

She stood stock-still, her happy look gone.

"You can't *mean* that! Daddy said you were coming *home.*"

"And so I am," Asher smiled, "but only for a visit, and only to talk with Mike about a deal I've worked out with the BBC."

Her square jaw set stubbornly and Asher thought how much Michael's daughter she truly was. He took her arm and said gently, "Let's go home and talk."

Her eyes lit up hopefully and she smiled back at him. "Take the Belt, Joseph," she said, getting into the car. "This is Mr. Jacobs' first trip to the United States. We might be able to see something of Coney Island, the Narrows, and the skyline. It looks as if the fog's lifting a bit."

"Yes, Miss Cassidy," the chauffeur replied, shutting their door. He pulled out of the airport and turned west on the Belt Parkway.

Eleanore settled back into the seat and took Asher's

hand. "I want to hear everything of what you've been doing all these years, and that's going to take a lot longer than two weeks. And right now I'm going to tell you all about this beautiful city." As they drove into Manhattan she began a travelogue that ended only when they reached the doors of River House, where the Cassidys lived in a duplex penthouse overlooking the East River.

Julian opened the door. He was older and greyer, but his carriage was as rigidly erect and his manner as formal as ever.

"Julian! It's so good to see you!" Asher shook the butler's hand warmly.

"Good evening, Mr. Jacobs," the man said with his customary reserve.

"I'm still Asher to you."

"No, it would not be proper."

European formality, Asher thought. Somehow he hadn't expected that in America and certainly not in the Cassidys' house. He glanced casually about the spacious, marble-floored entrance hall, trying to prepare himself for his first glimpse of Marguerite. *Where was she?*

"Inge will be so pleased to see you, Mr. Jacobs. She's made a special dinner, just for you."

"Thank you," Asher replied. He heard a stirring down the hall and turned quickly, his pulse racing. A small, fluffy dog whose lineage was as mixed as most Americans' flew towards Eleanore, its brown tail wagging furiously. It leapt expectantly around her feet until she picked it up, laughing as the dog tried to lick her face.

"Meet Begger," she said to Asher. "Daddy found it wandering on Third Avenue and he made the mistake of buying it a hamburger. It's been ours ever since."

"Mrs. Cassidy is in the library," Julian said, telling Asher what he longed to ask.

Hoping his voice didn't reveal the quiver inside him, Asher said to Eleanore, "Lead on."

She gave him a long, measuring look. "I'll see you later. I've some things I must do before dinner." She ran quickly up the stairs, the little dog still in her arms. Asher stared after her, surprised by her quick change of mood.

161

"This way, Mr. Jacobs," Julian said, going down the hallway.

Asher followed, wishing his feet were silent on the marble, wanting to see her before she saw him, needing a few private moments to put his heart and mind in neutral. They entered the library.

"Mrs. Cassidy?" Julian said.

There was no answer.

Asher keenly felt the disappointment rise in him. He looked about the room; it seemed occupied. The lights were lit, casting a soft glow on the dark paneled walls; the draperies were opened wide across the paned windows looking out on the river, and a fire flared in the green onyx fireplace. But the room was empty.

"May I mix you a drink, Mr. Jacobs?" Julian asked. "I'm sure Mrs. Cassidy will be here directly. Perhaps she's gone to check with Inge about dinner."

"No, Julian, don't bother. Don't let me keep you."

The man left and Asher wandered over to the windows. The fog was now wet mist and the lights of homeward-bound traffic on the streets below were hazy halos.

Asher looked out at the city, seeing its splendor for the first time. The mist made New York even more magical than he had imagined it could be. What energy there was! A pace he had never known! Even here, high above the street, in the quiet comfort of this beautiful room with its warming fire, the city's vitality touched him, dispelling the tiredness of the long flight and the hours without sleep. It would not be easy to leave New York, he thought, but he had known the moment he stepped into the apartment that he would have to make his visit as brief as possible.

A fleeting movement in the glass drew his eyes upwards from the river drive, and behind him, reflected in the window, stood Marguerite. Their eyes met in the reflection.

"Hello, Asher."

Her voice was cool, detached, as though they'd seen each other daily these past ten years.

He turned around, unable to speak, her name caught in his throat.

Averting her eyes, she moved to a small table very much

like the little serving table he remembered at the cottage outside Stratford. On it were the same two Waterford decanters. He felt strangely comforted. Some things had not changed.

"Shall I make you a Scotch?" she asked, pouring herself a drink.

His eyes followed her every move. "No, thank you, I've been drinking on the plane."

"Was it a good flight?"

"Interminable." *How could she be so cold?*

"I wish you wouldn't stare at me that way," she said uneasily, moving away towards the far side of the room.

He followed her, a bemused smile curving his lips. "I can't help it. You were always so beautiful. You're even more beautiful now. I like your hair braided around your head—it looks like a crown—but I'm not sure I like how thin you are."

She managed a dry laugh. "Dior would disagree."

"Marge?"

She raised wary eyes to his. "Yes?"

For years he had imagined this moment and had wondered if, on seeing her, he would still feel the same way. He did.

She mistook his silence and said crisply, "Don't be embarrassed, Asher. What happened in London was simply a casualty of war. It meant nothing."

Her face tinged with color, her eyes skidded away from his, and Asher knew she lied. It had meant as much to her as it had to him.

She took a quick drink and said with false lightness, "I thought surely we would have seen you before this." Asher heard the slight edge of accusation in her voice. Her eyes caught his briefly, and his pulse quickened.

She was not at all as distant as she pretended.

He came to her and, taking the glass from her hand, he put it down on a nearby table; then, his eyes never leaving her face, he drew her into his arms, resting his cheek against her hair.

With a sob, she held him close.

It was moments before he spoke.

"I couldn't come back, Marge, because for me, that

163

night was not a casualty of war. It meant *everything*. I've tried loving other women, but all I do is compare them with you. I came now, because I couldn't stay away any longer, and I hoped the reality of seeing you might erase the fantasy—but the moment I walked in the door, I knew nothing could. I love you, Marge. I have since the first day I saw you. I want you more than ever."

She shuddered and Asher stroked her back, pressing his lips to the crown of her hair. "Marge—Marge," he breathed, "I've waited so long to hold you like this."

She gripped him and whispered, "Don't leave us, Asher. God forgive me, I need you."

The cab pulled up to the blue-canopied entrance of the white limestone apartment building on Fifth Avenue. A uniformed doorman quickly stepped to the curb and opened the door, but the person sitting inside made no move to get out. Leaning his ruddy face into the cab, the doorman recognized the passenger.

"Are you all right, Mr. Jacobs?"

Memory still gripped Asher, and it took him a moment to realize where he was. With an effort, he got out of the cab.

"Fine, Gus. I was lost in thought." Rummaging in the pocket of his jeans, Asher paid the driver.

Gus held open the beveled glass door, but he knew he might as well have been a robot to the withdrawn tenant who occupied the penthouse. He had often wondered what one man did with so many rooms.

"Thank you," Asher said, going to the elevator. He leaned back against the heavy mahogany paneling. He was drained—drained by days of lovemaking, and drained emotionally.

"Goodnight, Mr. Jacobs," the elevator operator said as they reached the top floor. Asher merely nodded. Charles, buzzed by the doorman, held open the apartment door. He saw the tiredness in his employer's face and, helping Asher out of his parka, he said quietly, "Would you like supper in your room, sir?"

Asher shook his head and went to the winding stairway.

"No, thank you, Charles. I just want to sleep until

morning. Why don't you and Ruth take the night off? I won't be needing you."

"Thank you, sir. The missus has been wanting to see the holiday show at Radio City."

"Enjoy yourselves," Asher said, mounting the stairs. Ten minutes later he was asleep.

He was caught up in a sun-fed thermal, floating with the clouds, his arms spread like wings as he drifted lazily over the copper-colored canyon. Catching an updraft, he rolled over and over in leisurely Immelmann turns, his body a fuselage, weightless in the vast blue sky. He looked below at the mile-deep canyon spreading wide its rims, beckoning him, its chasm glowing with light, the colors bouncing off the striated sides changing from gold to orange to red to rust. He soared high, high above the endless mesas, circling, circling. It was so beautiful! He felt so free! And then, suddenly, the sky darkened . . . thunder rumbled . . . the clouds pressed in . . . pressed down . . . His arms, his body, weighted with ice . . . He spun dizzily, nose-diving towards the muddy river deep in the canyon's floor. He screamed—but no sound came from his frozen throat. He fell faster, faster . . . He closed his eyes against the impact!

He awoke—trembling, wet, as if he had been de-iced.

"Oh my God," he groaned, sitting up, smelling his sweat.

Asher leaned back against the headboard, trying to bring his breathing under control. He had done well these past twenty-five years in pushing that day into a void in his mind where it no longer seared him, but tonight the memory had flared and trapped him, as fire traps the sleeping . . .

"We're leaving today, Asher," Marguerite said on the phone. "Mike's closed the deal on the Zukor holdings. He feels the future for television is here in Los Angeles. We'll be in New York by five—on TWA. See you then."

Her voice was light, unworried, not at all what Asher expected.

"I know," he said guardedly. "Mike phoned me from the studio. Marge—is that all you have to tell me?" She

165

did not answer. Barely controlling his impatience, he pressed on. "Did you speak to him—did you tell Mike? Marge? Did you hear me? Did you tell him?"

And still there was silence.

"Marge, please—answer me."

"I can't, Asher."

"Can't what? Answer me? Or tell him?"

"Both."

"That's ridiculous!"

"Asher, please! We can't discuss this on the phone."

"When, then? You keep putting it off! *When* will you discuss it? We've got to settle this now!"

Again that silence. How helpless the phone in his hand made him feel. He hated phones! They made it too easy to evade the truth, to conceal one's feelings. He wanted to face her and have her tell him with her eyes.

Finally she spoke. "Asher, we can't settle this now, or *ever*. I can't do this to Mike—he's a sick man. And we're Catholics. Divorce is impossible, and if Mike knew of our relationship, it would kill him."

He didn't want to hear what she was saying. "Marge, I can't go on like this. Either you speak to Mike, or I will. He's bound to find out and it's better if he finds out from us."

"*NO!*" she said sharply. "He won't find out, because there'll no longer be anything for him to *find* out. Asher, it's over, because it *has* to be over. There's no other way." Her voice broke, and Asher knew her harshness hurt her as much as it did him. His tone softened.

"And what about the baby?"

Her silence lasted so long this time, Asher feared she had put the phone down and walked away. He held the receiver to his ear, hoping—hoping for what? What could they hope for?

When she spoke her voice held such sadness, he knew there was no hope.

"Mike will think the child a gift from God, a blessing to us both after so many years."

"Oh my God, Marge, Mike is no fool."

"No, Asher, he isn't, but Mike loves us both, and he will want to believe whatever I can make him believe."

166

"And us?"

She sighed, and with an irony that lately had become part of her, she said, "We get exactly what we deserve, Asher. We've sinned, and this is God's punishment—our retribution."

"No, Marge!" he hissed into the phone. "You can't write us off so easily. You can't tell me love is a sin, or that your God thinks love is a sin, or that our child growing in you is a sin! I don't accept it, and I don't think in your heart you believe it either!"

She sobbed. "Asher, please! Love *is* sinful when it hurts others. I'm sorry—I must say goodbye." She hung up, leaving him with the receiver still pressed to his ear.

Asher stared into the darkness, trying as he had for years to see her as she must have looked, sitting in the plane next to Michael. They would have been forward, in the first-class cabin of the big Super Constellation, Michael at the window. No matter how often he flew coast-to-coast, Michael loved to look out at the countryside and never missed the view of the Grand Canyon on a clear day. And that day the weather was beautiful. A shuddering sigh escaped Asher's lips.

Oh how he hoped she had said nothing! How he hoped they had been chatting happily over cocktails, and that they never saw the United plane.

No one could explain why two eastbound planes, the United DC-7 and the TWA Super Constellation, collided in such perfect visibility that June 30 over the Grand Canyon.

Asher closed his eyes against the pain. He took deep breaths to relieve the constriction in his throat. From the back of his mind, unwanted, unsought, came a guilt he thought he had long since buried. *Eleanore!*

His eyes narrowed as he told himself it was his despair at losing Marguerite and his unborn child, and the maelstrom into which he had been plunged at ICC after the accident, which made him unaware of how deeply disturbed Eleanore was at the death of her parents. Only when she was hospitalized did he realize the enormity of her breakdown and how much she loved him. And during her therapy he learned that she knew of his affair with her mother and that jealousy had festered in her for years; that when Marguerite died, Eleanore saw it as a wish fulfillment and was crushed by her love and guilt. He had never expected Eleanore to shatter—she was so like Michael. Strong, positive, outgoing. Her collapse, and especially the reasons for it, were another terrible blow, but her need pulled him from a despondency so deep, it affected him even more than the deaths of his own family.

After her release from the Menninger Clinic they were married. To him she had always been a dear sister; he loved her, but not as a man loves a woman, and in bed with her, he was uncomfortable. Only sheer physical need drove him. Her pious upbringing had not prepared her for the nuptial bed, and she accepted his cool, pedestrian lovemaking because she knew no other. They were kind to each other, and he had remained faithful more in absolution than in love. They longed for children to bring warmth into their home, but when, at last, Eleanore knew she was barren and he proposed they adopt a child, she refused. Seeing her barrenness as retribution, she did not want to tempt fate.

Eleanore never mentioned her mother, and he said nothing when all photographs of Marguerite disappeared. But she enshrined Michael and grieved deeply for him. They had been comrades as well as father and daughter, and Michael had lovingly encouraged Eleanore's considerable athletic skills. After his death she became a driven participant in one daring sport after another, recklessly winning championships, breaking records, driving herself as if Michael stood in the stands cheering her on.

She raced speedboats, jumped horses, flew hot-air balloons, scuba dived. At forty she discovered what she called "the ultimate high"—hang gliding—and pursued it with such mad impetuosity that for the first time he had tried to discourage her, fearing her compulsion was a death wish. Knowing she did not have enough experience, he forbade her to compete in the California championships. Angrily she accused him of not wanting her accomplishments to overshadow his.

The bleak day the call came from Yosemite telling him

Eleanore had crashed in a downdraft as she leapt from El Capitan, he hung up silently. He had known before he picked up the receiver.

Sitting up against the pillows, Asher wept now as he had not wept the day Michael and Marguerite were killed, the day Eleanore died, or the day he knew his parents were gone forever. Now, he did not fight the tears inside him. They wet his face, his pajamas, the sheets on his bed. He gave in to them as he should have long ago. When the sobs shaking him stopped, he got out of bed. Without turning on the lights, he went into the bathroom and shed his nightclothes. Stepping into the shower, he turned on the jet. He threw his head back and let the water cleanse him, closing his eyes to the cascading torrent, willing it to wash the past away. He stood for a long time under the hot, thundering, pulsing stream, and then he turned the shower head until a fine spray washed over him. He felt its gentle warmth douse his grief, his guilt.

He thought of Bronwyn and said her name aloud.

"Bronwyn . . . Bronwyn." He rolled her name on his tongue. It sounded like "Byron," and a passage from his favorite poet came to mind:

> *"What is the worst of woes that wait on age?*
> *What stamps the wrinkle deeper on the brow?*
> *To view each loved one blotted from life's page,*
> *And be alone on earth, as I am now."*

"Bronwyn," he crooned, turning his face up into the spray. "I'm no longer alone."

Three days later, on New Year's Eve, in a modest white clapboard house on the Connecticut shore near Darien, Justice of the Peace Donald Millbrand, with only his wife and daughter as witnesses, married Asher Jacobs and Bronwyn O'Neill.

Chapter Fourteen

ASHER and Bronwyn strolled along the deserted beach. The sands were heavy, grey with sooty snow and wind-swept with winter. The slate-colored swells of Long Island Sound heaved in loneliness. Gulls, their shrill, raucous cries the only sound other than the sea, swooped low, hoping for a handout from the two lone people walking the abandoned spit of land.

"How beautiful it is," Bronwyn said, and Asher, his arm about her, squeezed her shoulder in agreement. "I hate beaches in summer," she continued, kicking the sand ahead of her as she walked. "They're hot, crowded, and ugly, but this—this is divine." She lifted her face into the wind coming off the Sound.

With mock solemnity Asher said, "Mrs. Jacobs, all we've done since we got married is walk, talk, eat, and make love."

Mrs. Jacobs, Bronwyn thought. It sounded so strange.

"If you set that to music," she said, "you'll have a hit."

"No doubt."

"Are you complaining?" she teased.

"Not at all." He grinned, and she saw the pleasure in his eyes. "But someone as special as you should have a special honeymoon." His tone turned wry. "Even if it's only for three days. Are you sure you won't change your mind about going in on Monday?"

"No," she said firmly. "It's going to be tough enough, Asher, without my throwing in their faces that I'm the boss's wife."

"They're going to resent it no matter what you do, Bronwyn." His face brightened. "What about catching the Concorde tomorrow morning? We'd get to Paris in time for dinner, catch the late show at Le Bilbouquet—it's a marvelous jazz club on the Left Bank—spend Saturday at the Louvre, take a Sunday morning walk in the Tuileries Gardens, and then the Concorde home. We'd have you back in the office Monday morning."

She giggled. "Talk about life in the fast lane." The wind picked up her laughter and tossed it across the bay to the Connecticut coast from where they'd come.

"Well, are you game?"

"No," she said, smiling. "That's too fast for me. I like to sink into a city, to stew in its juices, and I love Paris too much for a 72-hour hors d'oeuvre." She stopped and looked up at him. "Do you like to ski?"

He hugged her. "Love it, but after this week with you, there's no strength in my legs."

She gave him an oblique look. "I'll never believe that, but in deference to your advanced age, we could just sit around an open fire . . ."

". . . and make love," he said with a laugh.

"No," she said quietly. "We could read, do the *Times* crossword, listen to music, walk in the woods . . ." She hesitated. "Maybe we could even talk about Mednam. There are questions I'll have to face Monday, and I also must make some decisions for the board meeting."

Asher took her chin in his hand and looked down into

171

her eyes. "Does that make you uncomfortable, Mrs. Jacobs?"

She met his gaze steadily. "Yes, it does."

"Then we'll talk about it." His eyes lit mischievously. "Your place or mine?"

She laughed. "Neither. Mine's too sloppy for a honeymoon, yours is probably too pristine. I know the perfect spot."

"Where?"

She folded her arm in his. "That's my surprise."

They turned back, towards Darien.

"Whither thou goest, Mrs. Jacobs," Asher said.

Elizabeth had been home only three hours, but she had cleared the deck outside of snow, wood was stacked in the niche near the fireplace, and inside, logs blazed and crackled. She plumped pillows, straightened pictures, and dusted while her mind raced with plans. As always the house comforted her, but this time there was an excitement in coming home that she had not felt in a long time. Adding to the excitement was the message from the local florist on the answering machine. They had held an order for two dozen roses since the Monday before Christmas—they would deliver them as soon as she returned the call. The deep red roses now stood in a crystal vase in the center of the round table between the sofas. She smiled whenever she looked at them. There had been no note, but she knew who had sent them.

She looked about the room and still felt his presence.

Perhaps she should have stayed out the holiday weekend in Palm Beach, but she had been too restless, too eager to return. Paul and Arnold had taken her to the airport for her early morning flight, and as they kissed her goodbye, Paul said dryly, "Even if nothing works out, Elizabeth, at least you will avoid the insanity of all those bodies flying north on Sunday."

She dusted the phone and stopped, the receiver in her hand. Should she call him now? But where? She looked at her watch. Four-thirty—his office was probably closed for the long weekend. And she was sure his home phone was unlisted. No, Elizabeth, she cautioned herself, putting the

172

phone down. Wait. Wait until Monday, then call casually, late in the day. Say you're coming into New York on Wednesday or Thursday to shop, perhaps he'd have time for lunch.

Looking at the phone again, compulsion drove her. But if she called anyone, she told herself sternly, it should be Bonnie. Wouldn't Bonnie be surprised at *why* she had cut her visit short, even more surprised than she had been the morning Elizabeth phoned from the airport to say she was leaving for Palm Beach. Maybe Bonnie would drive up for the weekend. Elizabeth smiled at the prospect. There was so much she wanted to tell her. How pleased Bonnie would be to learn about Asher and to know that after so long, her mother was in love.

In love! Elizabeth stood still, startled by the words her mind had just pulled from her heart. She sank down on the sofa, the dustrag in her hands. Again she heard the words in her head, and she closed her eyes and saw them—words like the colors of a magical scarf, spiraling in the hands of a sorcerer.

In love! Yes, she was in love with Asher Jacobs.

She got up and went to the phone and dialed her daughter's number. The phone echoed hollowly as if it rang in an endless, vaulted hallway. *Is there any sound lonelier than a phone that rings and rings and rings?* Elizabeth thought. She replaced the receiver with a sigh and, going into the kitchen, put away her cleaning supplies. Then she went into the powder room, washed her hands and face, and brushed her hair. Back in the living room she put a record on the stereo. She paused, listening. A car was pulling into the driveway. *Here comes Jesse with the animals,* she thought, going to the door.

Bronwyn accelerated and the low-slung yellow Porsche sped west on the broad concrete stretch of Route 80. "You look mighty pleased with yourself," she said, glancing briefly at Asher as they drove past the Meadowlands complex. Traffic was unusually light for a Friday afternoon.

"I am." He smiled, leaning back against the headrest and stretching his legs. "We've been married forty-eight

173

hours and not even my own newshawks have found out. Connecticut was a great idea."

"I'm glad," Bronwyn nodded, her eyes on the road ahead. "I dread publicity. It's going to make that board meeting even more complicated."

He patted her knee briefly. "I know, darling, but we'll work it out. We'll make an official announcement of our marriage Monday and take it from there." Asher's tone was authoritative, assured, and Bronwyn realized this must be his chairman-of-the-board voice. It gave her a confident, cared-for feeling she was not used to. She was surprised to find she liked it.

He looked out the window at the monotony of the Jersey flatlands. "Won't you even give me a hint as to where we're going?"

"No," she said, her own voice authoritative.

"Well, so far, your surprises have not disappointed me."

"I haven't surprised you with very much."

He smiled and reached over to tenderly push her hair behind her ear so that he could see her profile better. "You're a constant surprise, and wonderfully mysterious. This car, and the way you drive—few women drive so skillfully, and even fewer drive a Porsche Targa. You drive it like a racer—this is a racing machine!"

"Careful, your chauvinism is showing," she said, laughing.

He laughed back. "I am a chauvinist and you may as well get used to it. All men are, just as all women are feminists."

"I don't accept such broad generalities," she scoffed.

"I didn't expect you to. Where did you learn to drive like this, Indianapolis?"

"Sorry." She gentled her foot on the accelerator.

"Don't slow down for me, darling," Asher said, adjusting his seat belt to a more comfortable position. He looked at her proudly. "You're a terrific driver. You don't take your eyes off the road, you go into a curve slowly and out fast, and you fasten your seat belt—all the marks of a professional driver. I feel like I'm in the jump seat with Andretti. Whoever taught you did a good job."

"Thank you." She glanced into the rear-view mirror and

sensitively depressed the gas pedal. Instantly the high-performance auto sped forward, the needle on the speedometer inching upwards until it hovered steadily at 120.

Asher exclaimed, "It's as quiet as a Rolls! I had no idea Targas raced this quietly. And your tach is only at fifty. You have a mighty fine engine."

The trees on the side of the highway blurred past, and Asher felt excitement churn inside. It had been months since he'd felt so alive. His adrenaline pumped. When the fuzz buster on the visor above Bronwyn's head flashed, its green digital lights glowing, disappointment made Asher grimace.

Bronwyn eased off the gas gently, down-shifting expertly as the needle sank back into the legal range.

His eyes scanned the road, but he saw nothing. "Ever get caught?"

"No, but I've been lucky." Her eyes quickly checked the mirror, the median, the road ahead, and the side roads leading onto the highway. "He's out there somewhere. Guess we'll have to Model-T it."

"Where'd you ever get that expression?"

"I just made it up." She caught his eyes briefly and smiled at him. It was a warm, fond smile, and it made Asher reach over and kiss her cheek.

She laughed lightly. "The only time I've ever been stopped for speeding was on a ski slope out West."

He chuckled. She was like a good book; every page held more adventure. "Then you ski as fast as you drive."

"Not anymore. Maybe that's why I like driving fast. Most ski racers are fast drivers, and ex-ski racers even more so. We're trying to recapture the high we used to get racing."

Asher studied her speculatively. "Were you a serious racer?"

"Serious enough to make the U.S. Ski Team, but not obsessed enough with winning to stick with it."

He whistled softly. "I better start making a list of your surprises." He turned fully in his seat to look at her. "It's hard to think of you as a jock, but you must have gone through years of rugged training to make the team. What made you give it up?"

175

She shrugged slightly. The fuzz buster above her head stayed docile. "I'm not competitive. In fact, I dislike competition intensely. I raced for the fun of it, the thrill of the run. I loved pitting myself against the snow, against the gates, even against the clock, but I hated competing against my teammates, even against members of other teams. Once in a race I loaned my helmet to a racer who'd had hers ripped off while she was in the ladies' room. That really blew my coach's mind because I had to wait until she finished her run and came back up the mountain, and by then I'd been put six or seven skiers back, the course was more rutted, icier, and I did badly. He ranted and raved. It was more important to him that I won, than that a teammate be safe. Christ! *Nothing* is that important! *Nothing* means that much to me."

There was such finality in her voice that he wondered, would anything mean so much to her that she'd fight for it? Could she ever build a deep attachment to him? Not wanting to think further, he concentrated on the scenery. It seemed so familiar. Of course! It was the same road he'd taken by mistake the weekend before Christmas. Was it only two weeks ago? It didn't seem possible. Never had so much change taken place in his life in so short a time.

Aware that the road west of Hackettstown was a speed trap, Bronwyn switched on a tape and settled back to drive within the speed limit.

"Ah, Mendelssohn," Asher said, pulling a lever and reclining his seat. He put his head back and closed his eyes; the familiar strains of the Scotch Symphony slowed his thoughts as the dancing digitals above the visor had slowed Bronwyn. Soon he slept.

A gnawing premonition ate into the tranquility of Asher's nap. He awakened, annoyed at the apprehension growing in his mind. He kept his eyes closed, consciously rejecting the irrationality of the unforeseen. The feeling persisted, and he opened his eyes to look at Bronwyn.

Nothing had changed. She sat as before, her hands lightly on the wheel, her eyes straight ahead. The car purred, cruising just below 65, and Mendelssohn's Scotch Symphony rose to its melodic close. But there was a dread

CHOICES

in him that made his neck ache. He looked outside and instantly understood. He pulled the lever beneath the seat hard. It shot up, bucking him forward.

Bronwyn turned, her eyebrows arching. She gave him a playful grin. "No use trying to eject. I traded my James Bond model for this car."

He tried to seem nonchalant but dismay corroded in him. Quietly he said, "I'd really like to know where you're taking me."

She heard the uneasiness in his voice, and with a soft smile she said, "I know it's a touristy area, but we're going to my home, and you'll love it. It's wonderfully secluded, quiet—absolutely perfect for a honeymoon."

The stiffness in his neck stretched long, long talons, reaching, reaching, until his body ached all over. His voice constricted, he asked, "But won't your family be there?"

"My only family is my mother, and she's away. We'll have the place to ourselves."

He knew.

He sank back, hoping she could not discern the turmoil shredding him, hoping he was wrong, hoping it was a crazy idea foisted on him by a familiar road, hoping Bronwyn's mother was fat, with stout, sturdy legs, a wonderfully warm, motherly woman instead of the wonderfully warm, spirited woman with whom he had made such enjoyable love.

He searched Bronwyn's profile. He saw no resemblance, and hope flared in him. After all, hundreds of people lived near Cable Mountain.

Bronwyn turned off the highway and they were on the two-lane winding road to the ski area.

"Isn't it lovely!" she exclaimed. "Look at all the snow. Cable will be crowded because of the holidays, but if you wish, we can cross-country ski in the hills behind the house. We've got loads of extra equipment you can use."

Her face shone with joy as she guided the car up the mountain, shifting, down-shifting, the sleek sports coupe clinging to the road, cornering beautifully. Ordinarily Asher would have enjoyed watching how skillfully she drove, but his mind raced ahead of the car.

"How I miss all this," she said. "Each time I come home

177

I swear I'm going to chuck New York and work from here. I could set up a consulting service and go into Manhattan once a week to meet with clients."

They neared the switchback and Asher held his breath, his eyes darting from Bronwyn's hands on the wheel to her foot on the gas pedal. Gun it! Gun it! his mind cried. Don't clutch! Accelerate up that damn hill! Pass the curve, pass, *pass* that damn curve. Don't turn into it!

But like a pilot controlling the rudders of a fast jet, Bronwyn's feet in fine leather boots moved in unison, lifting off the accelerator, pressing down on the clutch as she shifted into second, her gloved hands gently easing the wheel so that the car turned gracefully, smoothly into the snow-covered, pine-bordered lane on the curve.

Every nerve in him taut, Asher's mind snapped into action. He made quick, precise plans. Since Elizabeth was not at home, he could easily explain to Bronwyn that while it was a marvelous idea, and the house was utterly charming, it reminded him too much of the house in Gstaad and he preferred they did not stay. They could drive further west or even north into the Adirondacks. He would allow nothing to spoil this all-important time between them, and later, much later, when their relationship had solidified, he would agree to meet Bronwyn's mother. Bronwyn need never know. He was certain Elizabeth would agree.

They came to the steep, rock-strewn gorge, and Bronwyn slowed the car as he had done that first night.

"Take a look at that," she said, her eyes shining.

He looked at her, his eyes as dark as the hemlocks shadowing the rugged slope. "It's beautiful, Bronwyn."

"Wait, just wait till you see the house," she breathed happily.

Asher felt as if he were shrouded in stone.

Bronwyn rolled the window down and took deep breaths of the clear, cold air. A frown knifed between her eyes.

"That's funny," she said, "I smell a wood fire." She looked at Asher. "Probably Jesse's at the house taking care of the animals. We have a dog and two cats, and Jesse's our handyman and sometime caretaker. Unfortunately, he's also a product of generations of backwoods inbreeding."

They came to the bridge, and beyond, Asher saw the driveway into which he had skidded. Bronwyn pulled in, avoiding the dip.

"This is it!" she exclaimed, leaping out of the car.

Asher got out slowly, unwillingly, wishing he could coax Bronwyn back into the car and head back to New York.

"Well, my mother's car is still covered with snow, so it must be Jesse who started the fire," Bronwyn said. The low shape looked to Asher exactly as it had looked the night he had first driven in. Bronwyn paused, the frown returning. "I wonder where his truck is?" It was as though she spoke to herself. She shrugged and took Asher's arm, pulling him towards the footbridge.

"Probably someone dropped him off. Don't worry, I'll get rid of him quickly. I can't stand him, but he is helpful to my mother."

Asher followed as though his feet were pillars of ice.

"Come on, slow poke!" Bronwyn called. "I can't wait to show you the house!"

As they crossed the bridge they heard a door open, and a woman came out onto the deck, waving, smiling.

Bronwyn looked up and stopped dead, the joy draining from her face.

"Oh dammit!" She was so disappointed at seeing her mother that she never noticed the stricken look on Asher's face.

Chapter Fifteen

ELIZABETH peered through the glass door, trying to determine who had driven into her driveway. Had it been Jesse, Blaze would have been across the bridge by now, bounding, barking, happy to be home. How dark it was! Up on the mountain at four-thirty it was still light, the sun skidding towards the horizon beyond the ski slopes, but here in the hollow, the heavy forest held constant night.

Hearing faint sounds of a woman's voice, Elizabeth squinted into the shadows, trying to make out who trudged across the bridge. It seemed there were two people. The dark shape of a woman emerged from under the branches, and Elizabeth's heart warmed with surprise.

"*Bonnie!*" she exclaimed. "*Bonnie!*" She laughed, opening the door wide and going out onto the deck, waving, smiling.

"Bonnie! I was just calling you!"

"Oh dammit!" Bronwyn said under her breath. What the hell was Elizabeth doing home? She stopped and waited for Asher.

When he heard Elizabeth's voice, Asher could go no further. His feet felt frozen to the rough planks of the bridge. He looked down at the water swirling below, feeling caught in the same vortex. Bronwyn came back to him, an apologetic smile on her face.

"Well, this is one surprise that backfired. I'm sorry. I had no idea my mother was home." She looked at his drawn face and took his arm. "Cheer up, we don't have to stay. I'll just introduce you two, call some inns, and we'll leave." She sighed. "At least my mother won't have to read about our marriage in the papers."

The thought stopped her, carving deep lines into the corners of her mouth. Regret and embarrassment rose in her. She should have called Elizabeth and told her! Now her mother would be hurt, and rightly so. Why had she been so loath to make that call? Why did she feel so reluctant to tell her mother she had married?

Asher said nothing, angry at the incredible coincidence, angry with himself for not knowing more about Bronwyn.

Elizabeth wondered why Bonnie did not return her wave, why she stood so still, why she did not call back. And then, as if looking through a flickering kinescope, she saw the other person come out of the dappled shade of the hemlocks. Her eyes narrowed in disbelief, and she began to shiver. The man standing beside Bonnie was *Asher Jacobs!*

Asher? Bonnie? How? Where? The questions in her rushed and tumbled as the stream below rushed and tumbled over the rocks. Her eyes searched their faces as they came up on the deck. The delight Elizabeth first felt on seeing her daughter was quenched by the lack of joy on Bronwyn's face. The quietness of her demeanor and Asher's solemn look made Elizabeth wary of her words, wary of her welcome.

She did not move to embrace Bronwyn as she would have. With Elizabeth and Bronwyn there was a rare understanding and respect that made them close friends, but Bronwyn's reserved, private nature made it difficult

181

for her to be demonstrative, and Elizabeth, more ebullient, always made the first move. Bronwyn was grateful now that her mother did not rush to her.

"This is a surprise," Elizabeth said, her voice shaking as she shivered. Her remark was directed more at Asher than at her daughter, and he met her eyes with such embarrassment she held her breath.

"Let's go inside, Mother, you're freezing. Why did you rush out without a jacket?" It was an admonition, not a greeting, and Elizabeth heard the edge in Bronwyn's voice. She turned and hurried into the house, going directly to the fireplace, hoping its warmth would stop her trembling.

Asher helped Bronwyn out of her coat and as they shed their boots she looked at him. His face was hard, grim, and she took his silence to be the same disappointment, the same frustration she felt. She knew he had to be as tired as she . . . the last few days had been an emotional tour-de-force for both of them, and she had brought him to the quiet place she cherished because it was here she always came when she needed solitude, peace. She had hoped the soothing privacy would enable them to plan for the reality of Monday. What a foul-up! she thought bitterly.

Trying to cheer Asher up and lighten her own mood, Bronwyn pasted a smile on her face. Taking his hand, she tugged him towards the living room. "Let's have a drink, break the news to my mother, and I'll make some phone calls."

"Wait a minute," Asher said, staying her.

"Yes?" She stopped and looked at him.

He met her eyes squarely. Why not tell her now? Not everything, of course . . . keep it light . . . keep it casual. But the deeper he delved into the coppery eyes holding his, the more he realized how fragile, how tenuous their marriage really was. They needed time . . . the cement had not yet begun to set.

"Never mind," he said, lifting her hand and kissing it. Releasing her hand, he ran his fingers through his hair, pretending it needed brushing back. He did not want to walk into the living room and face Elizabeth holding Bronwyn's hand.

CHOICES

Elizabeth stood before the fire, her arms clasped about her, trying to bring warmth back into her body. She stared into the flames, slowing her tumbling thoughts, focusing in on the facts. Unless Bonnie had phoned Paul and Arnold's house, she had no way of knowing Elizabeth had returned from Florida—she had brought Asher here thinking they'd be alone. Asher! *Bonnie and Asher! How could he come here with her!* Jealousy kindled in Elizabeth, leaping like the tongues of flame in the fireplace. Again she saw them come up on the deck together and the harried look on Asher's face. *He hadn't known!* Of course! That's why he looked so stunned. He had had no idea she was Bonnie's mother! Then, he couldn't have known where he was going. And, if he had not known *that,* he could not know Bonnie very well. Elizabeth felt foolish at her resentment. After all, Bonnie met many men and often brought them home. When she heard them come into the room, Elizabeth turned and said with a composed smile, "What brings you home, Bonnie?"

Bronwyn's lips curved ironically. "I could ask you the same question."

Elizabeth laughed dryly, but did not answer.

What the hell, Bronwyn thought. *I was stupid not to call and check first. I should know by now how she changes her mind. This wasn't her mother's fault.*

When Bronwyn spoke, her tone was kinder.

"Mother, this is Asher Jacobs. Asher, my mother . . . Elizabeth Banks."

Their eyes met across the flowers. Elizabeth saw a dark flush diffuse his face as he looked at the roses on the table. She didn't feel sorry for him in the least. She wondered if he would reveal that they knew each other.

Not moving from where he stood at the end of the sofa, Asher said formally, "How do you do."

Disappointment tightened in Elizabeth like twisting steel. Not trusting her voice, she nodded.

"Mother—what lovely roses!" Bronwyn exclaimed. Her mood was now relaxed, friendly. "You've been holding out on me. Well, whoever he is he has terrific taste."

This time the color rose in Elizabeth's face, and Bronwyn laughed.

183

"Same old Mom. Well, let's have a drink. Scotch for you, Asher?"

"Please." And to Elizabeth he said, "May I sit down?"

"Of course," Elizabeth replied quickly. "Forgive me for seeming inhospitable, but it was such a sho—" She caught herself. "It was such a surprise seeing you both."

She moved to the sofa, but Asher, unable to face Elizabeth at close range, quickly looked away to Bronwyn at the bar. Seeing his discomfort, Elizabeth turned away and joined Bronwyn there. Asher sank back against the pillows.

"Wine for you, Mother?"

"No, thank you, I'd prefer this." Elizabeth picked up a bottle of Crown Royal and poured half a tumbler. She did not add soda or water.

Bronwyn raised her eyebrows. "Straight, Mother? Are you sure that's what you want?"

"Very sure," Elizabeth said, not meeting Bronwyn's eyes. "Don't keep your friend waiting, Bonnie, he looks like he could use a drink."

Bronwyn glanced to the sofa where Asher sat, his head back, his eyes closed.

Elizabeth followed Bronwyn's eyes, but she saw Asher as he had sat that first night when he had said, "I'd much rather make love to you." She closed her eyes against the longing surging in her and took a long swallow of her drink.

Bronwyn watched her mother drain half the glass; she had never seen her drink neat like that. *This is as good a time as any,* she thought, and softly, Bronwyn said:

"Asher's not my friend, Mother, he's my husband."

Slowly Elizabeth opened her eyes and looked at Bronwyn. She felt a carousel start up in her brain; it began to spin crazily, and demented, mirrored images—Bonnie, Asher, herself, all naked and entwined—careened madly. She had to get off! She gripped Bronwyn's arm.

"No!" she hissed. *"No, he's not!"* Her whisper hardened accusingly. "You'd never marry someone without first discussing it with me. You'd never marry someone without inviting me! I don't believe it! You said you'd never marry at all!"

184

Bronwyn stared at Elizabeth; she had never seen such acrimony in her mother, and a wave of guilt swept her. She tightened her hand on Elizabeth's, but her mother pulled away, fighting a jealousy so painful, it was physical.

Lowering her voice so that Asher, resting on the sofa, could not hear, Bronwyn said, "I can't believe it either, and I wouldn't have hurt you for the world, but all this happened so quickly—I was swept up, intrigued . . . I'm sorry to tell you after the fact, Mother, and you're right, I never planned to marry, but I've never known such a compelling man. Maybe the reason I never phoned was because I was unsure and somewhat embarrassed to admit I was marrying someone I had met only a week before, someone, even now, I'm not sure I love."

The carousel in Elizabeth began again and to still it, her voice became the brake on its wheel. "When? How? You couldn't! I spoke to you the afternoon of Christmas Eve—you would have said *something!*"

Bronwyn shook her head, and a rueful expression crossed her face.

"No, I hadn't even met him then. We met Christmas Eve and we were married New Year's Eve."

Was it the drink which caused her head to spin so? Elizabeth wondered, or was it Bonnie's words which set her churning? A memory flashed in the mirrored carousel; once, long ago, she'd known this jealousy, and it had shamed her then as it did now—it was the day Bonnie came out to the pool wearing her first bikini. Lorne had looked at her and let out a long, low whistle, and Elizabeth had hated what she saw in his eyes—she'd been grateful when Bonnie had left for summer training in Bariloche. Angry with herself, she went abruptly to the bar and picked up the bottle of Crown Royal, but her hands betrayed her and the bottle slipped from her palsied grasp, smashing loudly onto the marble counter, splintering crystal shards to the floor. The amber liquid spilled, gurgling towards the richly colored oriental rug. Her tears broke loose, spilling as the liquor spilled.

The smashing sound jolted Asher and he leapt up, hurrying to help. He grabbed napkins from the bar and bent, staunching the flow of liquor before it reached the carpet.

"Thank you," Bronwyn said, bending beside him, carefully, delicately picking up slivers of glass.

Elizabeth looked down at the two of them, their heads together. How recently she had run her fingers through that silvered, coal-black hair. How proudly she once brushed the beautiful coppery head bent so close to his. The memory was too much. Sobbing, she ran from the room.

"I never thought she'd be so upset," Bronwyn said to Asher as they cleaned up.

His head pounded. Was it demons of destiny dancing on his nerves, taunting him? Not wanting to think, he busied himself picking up bits and pieces of glass, but his mind raced. He hoped fervently Bronwyn would think Elizabeth's reaction was merely shock at the news of their marriage, the normal disappointment of a mother who had not seen her daughter walk down the aisle. And Elizabeth. How sorry he was!

With a deep sigh he rose heavily, the broken glass in his hands. Turning towards the kitchen, he caught himself and stopped.

"Where shall I take this?"

Getting up, Bronwyn said, "Follow me. I'll get a mop and some detergent to kill the smell of the liquor."

Upstairs Elizabeth splashed cold water on her face. But as she bathed her swollen eyes and felt the water sliding on her skin, she remembered the water sliding all over her as Asher held her, bathed her, and slid into her. She cried out, her sobs coming in angry bursts. And then another vision spun madly in her mind—*Asher and Bonnie;* the image of the two of them, naked in the shower, naked in bed, naked together caused her to grip the countertop with an agony so painful, she sobbed again. She never heard Jesse's truck or even Blaze barking furiously.

The dog had picked up Bronwyn's scent even before Jesse pulled into the driveway, and the animal leapt from the open pickup yelping in expectation, charging across the bridge, up onto the deck, his tail wagging wildly.

186

Bronwyn ran to the door and for the first time since she arrived, a wide, happy smile lit her face. When the dog saw her, he pranced excitedly, his high-pitched yelps echoing off the hill behind the house.

"Down, Blaze, down!" Bronwyn said sternly, opening the door.

The dog responded instantly, with a guttural, protesting moan that came from deep within his belly. He slunk to the floor, his tail thumping loudly, and he cocked his head, his large brown eyes pleading for Bronwyn's touch.

"All right, you scoundrel." She laughed, patting her chest. "Give me a kiss, and then to the kitchen you go!"

The massive shepherd sprang up and with incredible gentleness he placed his front paws on her shoulders and licked her face. She hugged him tightly and kissed his cold, wet nose.

"This is Blaze, Asher," Bronwyn said, taking the dog by his collar and leading him to the back of the house. The dog, elated by Bronwyn's show of affection, ignored Asher and followed her docilely.

Asher paid little attention, his eyes moving to the heavy shadow trudging up the hill, a cat carrier in each hand. How stupid he had been! How could he have forgotten about the dog and the man who would be bringing him home! Feeling as though he were caught in some crazy charade, Asher went to the fireplace and angrily stoked the flames.

He heard Bronwyn open the door and say, "Come in, Jesse, my mother is busy. Thank you for taking care of the animals. Wait here and I'll write out a check."

Jesse bent and released the cats, who scampered towards the kitchen, and as if he hadn't heard her, he followed Bronwyn into the living room.

"Sure's a surprise ta see ya, Bonnie." He strung her name out childishly. "Happy New Year. Yer mom sure came home unexpectedly. Lucky I wasn't too busy." He saw Asher at the fireplace and a sheepish grin crossed his face. "How do," he said.

Asher did not acknowledge the greeting, and animosity filled Jesse's pale, porcine eyes.

Bronwyn wrote out a check, ignoring Jesse as she

usually did. Her dislike for him went back to when she was fifteen, to a sun-filled summer day when Prince, the shepherd before Blaze, flushed Jesse from the woods near the deep pool upstream where she swam naked. It was then she realized Jesse spied on her. She had never told her mother, but instead had called Mrs. Crouch. The old woman had beaten her son with a rug swatter and Jesse had never bothered her again. But Bronwyn knew he disliked her as much as she disliked him, and she did not trust him.

"Does this cover it?" she asked, handing him the check, dismissal evident in her tone.

"Sure, okay." Jesse took the check and stepped towards Asher.

"I'm sorry I dented yer car," he said, "but them Mercedes are built so low, it's tough ta get a good hold."

Like hell! Asher thought. You dented that car on purpose, you bastard. But he said nothing, staring at Jesse implacably.

Bronwyn looked from Jesse to Asher. "What on earth are you talking about, Jesse?"

The puttylike face moved into an apologetic grimace. "I shoulda said somethin' ta him when I gave him the keys, but I'd already woken him 'n Miz Banks up, 'n I didn' wanna bother 'em no more, seein's how they wanted ta be alone, but them Mercedes are so low, it's hard ta get a good grip 'n my winch slipped an' dented his bumper."

Bronwyn's eyes flew to Asher's. A deliberate, blank look crossed his face. *He was hiding something!*

"What bumper, Jesse? Whose?"

Jesse nodded towards Asher. "His, it wuz his Mercedes I pulled outta the dip that Sunday before Christmas when we had the big storm."

Elizabeth came out onto the upstairs landing, and Jesse whipped the red TGA Feeds cap off his head.

"Hello, Miz Banks, I came soon's I could, 'n Bonnie jest gave me a check. I jest been apologizin' fer dentin' this man's car when I pulled it out that Sunday."

Elizabeth's eyes darted from one to the other as she came down the spiral stairs. When she looked at Asher the back of her neck tightened. His tenseness reached across the room to her, and she stopped partway, gripping the handrail.

Bronwyn caught the eye contact between her mother and Asher. A pulse throbbed in her stomach. She turned to Jesse, her face a facade, her voice cool. She hated what she was about to say, but she had to *know!*

"You're mistaken, Jesse. This is my husband, Asher Jacobs. We were married New Year's Eve, and Mr. Jacobs has not been here before."

Jesse's mouth slackened and his head swung from Asher to Elizabeth. Bronwyn saw how clearly startled he was.

"But . . ." he began. Elizabeth's quick, meaningful look cut him off.

Bronwyn's eyes instantly encircled her mother and Asher. It *had* been his car! They *did* know each other! But why keep it a secret? Why pretend to be strangers?

Asher turned his back and went to the window.

Embarrassment swept Bronwyn. She felt like a fool in front of Jesse. Angrily she went to the bar and, picking up the glass of Bourbon she had left sitting there, she drank it all.

Elizabeth descended the stairs and escorted Jesse to the door.

"Thank you for coming by with the animals. I'm sorry to have disturbed you so unexpectedly."

Jesse held back, twisting his cap in his hands.

"Meant no harm, Miz Banks. Hope I didn't let any cats outta the bag." He laughed slyly, pleased with his own joke.

"Goodnight, Jesse," Elizabeth said firmly. Still he did not move. He looked towards Asher and then at Bronwyn, unable to hide his glee.

"Goodnight, Bonnie, good luck to you 'n—yer *husband.*" Bronwyn heard the emphasis and the insidious intent in his tone. She knew he took joy in getting back at her, but what had happened between Asher and her mother to give him such satisfaction? What did he know? She turned her back on him and poured another shot of Bourbon into her glass. She went to the sofa and sat down.

"Goodnight, Jesse," Elizabeth said, moving to the door, but Jesse did not follow.

189

Nothing so interesting had happened to him before, and his slow mind enjoyed every moment. A cunning smile stretched the loose skin around his mouth. How he'd like to spit the truth in that bitch Bonnie's face, but her mother paid him well and he needed the money. His eyes slitted behind the puffy bags. Taking them all in, he said knowingly, "Well, goodnight. It's real nice to see a family that gets on so well tagether."

Elizabeth took his arm and pulled him to the door. What made him so insinuating? she wondered. Her mind sped back to the weekend with Asher. What had Jesse seen? When? She watched Jesse plod to the bridge, and reluctantly she turned back towards the living room. Taking a deep breath, forcing herself to appear casual, she went in to face her daughter and Asher.

Bronwyn sat stonily, and Asher stood at the window, his back to the room. Elizabeth was not sure what she should do, what she should say.

Bronwyn broke the silence.

"Why didn't you tell me you'd met before?"

Asher turned and looked at Elizabeth; his face seemed remarkably calm. The remark was addressed to both of them, and each hesitated. Such a simple, candid question deserved a direct reply, but both were loath to give it.

Fear swept through Elizabeth, holding her lips fast. The truth now, she realized, could be a blade that might forever cleave them, and yet what answer could she give her daughter?

Seeing the dread in Elizabeth's eyes, Asher wished he could assuage her fears, but his concern was for his relationship with Bronwyn, and he came to the sofa and stood looking down at his wife. He said with quiet resolve:

"Because the proper moment did not present itself. We did not intend to conceal that we knew each other, but the complete and utter shock of learning that you were Elizabeth's daughter prevented me from acting as openly as I should, and your mother, taking her cue from me, acquiesced. Before we turned off the highway I had a premonition where you were taking me, and when you turned into the lane, I planned then to tell you. At the bridge, at the door, I hesitated. Do you remember?"

190

Bronwyn met his eyes accusingly.

"Yes, I do remember, and I also remember how unhappy you looked, how uncomfortable you seemed." Her voice became bitter as suspicion seeped through her, its acid rising in her throat. "If you just knew each other casually, you would have laughed at the wild coincidence —we would all have had a jolly good time. Instead you look grim, my mother breaks a bottle of liquor she rarely touches, dissolves into tears, and runs upstairs."

Bronwyn rose abruptly and began to pace as her mother had paced that first night. Asher saw a resemblance now that had escaped him. She stopped finally and faced them, her face, her body as taut as the strings on the piano she stood next to.

Trying to make her voice calmer than she felt, she said, "Simple minds tend to spew out just what they see, and evidently Jesse saw more than a car caught in a dip."

Elizabeth's breath caught, and she reached out to hold onto the back of a chair. Bonnie had never sounded so distant, and she held on tightly as if to keep her daughter from slipping away.

Asher sighed. He had had enough of lying, of concealment, during those years with Marguerite, but would he lose Bronwyn if he told her the truth?

She forced his decision.

"I'm your *wife,* Asher," she said, her eyes square on his. "I want to *know,* and I have a right to know how long and how well you've known my mother."

His answer was firm, unapologetic. "We met on the chairlift the Saturday before Christmas."

"And that's all?" Bronwyn hated the sarcasm in her tone.

Stoically, Asher held her eyes. "I've not asked you about any men before me."

"This is different!" she snapped. *"We're talking about you and my mother!"* Her eyes shot to Elizabeth, and Elizabeth's chest tightened at the coldness in her daughter's face.

Asher moved to Bronwyn but stopped when he saw her step back. His voice softened. "Bronwyn, please try to understand. This is all an unforeseen, regrettable coinci-

CHOICES

dence, something none of us wanted, and a woman of your intelligence should recognize how horrible your mother and I feel, but can't you accept a cruel twist of fate? Can't you understand how we both love you, and be kind?"

"Be *kind?*" Bronwyn's voice cracked. "It's not as simple as that! You send my mother roses and marry me? And your love only makes it worse! How the hell do you think I *feel,* thinking that you've made love to my *mother!* I feel as if you're my father, that I'm caught up in some mad, incestuous relationship! Do you think I can sleep with you and not see what Jesse must have seen?"

"Bonnie!" Elizabeth cried. "That's not fair!"

"Truth isn't fair, Mother!" Bronwyn spat. "It's the way I *feel,* and you both may as well face it!" Her voice broke and angry tears flooded her eyes. "Oh, Christ! I've got to get the hell out of here!"

Asher quickly stepped forward, blocking her way. He put his hands on her shoulders and forced her to meet his eyes. The despair behind her tears made him say with great care, "Not without *me,* Bronwyn! As you said, you're my *wife,* and the 'for better or worse' begins *right now!* I love you—you must believe that—and you must also believe we'll work this out. Together."

At his words, Elizabeth felt as though he twisted a knife in her heart. *He loved Bronwyn.* Jealousy, like bile, rose in her.

Bronwyn shrugged loose from his grasp. "I brought you here, I'll take you back, but I *must* be alone. I need to be alone." Not looking at her mother, she went to the foyer.

"Bonnie!" Elizabeth's voice was filled with such pain that Bronwyn stopped and turned. She looked haltingly at her mother, confusion and anger lancing through her. How she loved her—but how she hated her right now!

Elizabeth reached out, needing to touch her daughter.

"Please," Bronwyn said, moving back. "Don't." Swiftly she grabbed her coat and boots. "I'll wait by the car—I need a smoke."

She ran out the door.

Elizabeth put her face in her hands and sobbed, knowing that at that moment she had forever lost a rare and precious closeness with her daughter.

192

Asher stood dejectedly and then, hesitating only a moment, he went to Elizabeth and put his arms around her, holding her as he had the day he had left. She buried her face in his shoulder and knew she still wanted him—would always want him. He stroked her hair, saying, "Forgive me, Elizabeth. I had no way of knowing, but I love your Bonnie as I've not loved in a long time. I loved her from the moment I saw her, and I'll do what I can to set this right."

Elizabeth's body tensed, his words cutting her more than he could have imagined.

Pushing him away and bringing her tears under control, she said in a strangely detached tone, "Thank you, Asher. Please see that Bonnie gets back safely."

Asher searched her face, puzzled at her coldness. "Have I said something to hurt you?"

She felt tears threaten again and shook her head. "Forget it. It's been a miserable evening, and now I, too, need to be alone."

He took her hand. "I wish I could say 'till we meet again,' but under the circumstances it may be a long time before we do. I hope to take Bronwyn away, abroad perhaps. It's our only chance, Elizabeth. I don't intend to lose her again." He raised her hand and kissed it, and Elizabeth's heart turned over.

"I wish to hell you weren't my mother-in-law."

Quickly he got into his coat and boots and strode out the door, and Elizabeth watched the night close in on him.

"I don't intend to lose her again" rang in her mind. What could he have meant? Bonnie had said they'd been married New Year's Eve. Only forty-eight hours! She listened intently for the sound of the car. When she heard it pull out of the drive and head down the road, desolation coursed through her. Blaze whined and scratched loudly in the room off the kitchen, and dejectedly Elizabeth went towards the sounds. As she entered, the animal nuzzled her, nipping her affectionately. She sank down beside the dog and hugged him close. He licked her face, her ears, and she began to cry in long, heaving sobs that wet his thick, lustrous coat. She had never felt so totally alone.

193

Chapter Sixteen

WHEN Asher reached the car Bronwyn was in the driver's seat with the engine running. Opening the door, he leaned down and asked, "Would you like me to drive?"

She shook her head. "No, thank you. It's better for me to drive."

He nodded and got in.

She put the car in gear and turned out of the driveway. "If you don't mind, I'd prefer to go back to New York." Her words were polite but Asher heard a finality he chose not to argue with; it would be futile to tell her he would rather they check into some small country inn.

"If you wish," he said, leaning back. He longed to talk with her but he would give her the time, the space she needed.

The cigarette had helped Bronwyn slow the feelings that raged through her as she ran from her mother's home.

194

Now, driving helped her even more. She concentrated on the road, steadying her mind as she steadied the high-powered car.

Only she knew how tenuous was the tether which checked her emotions. Her true nature was like a forest sprouting with spring, her passions as swift as the snow-fed streams. She wanted to be more like summer—relaxed, easygoing—but she was the child of an impetuous mother whose enthusiasms blazed like maples in autumn, whose false hopes tumbled about her like dried winter leaves. Bronwyn hated emotional scenes. Now, as ferment rose in her, she forced herself to think logically. It was a tiring, draining effort, and finally she pulled over to the side of the road, shifting into neutral and pulling on the brake.

"Please take over, Asher. I'm beat." Without waiting for his answer, she got out and came around to the passenger side.

"Of course," he said, grateful for any break in the silence between them. He held the door as she got in and said, "Try and take a nap."

Avoiding his gaze, she put her head back against the seat and closed her eyes. Asher maneuvered the auto back onto the road. He was glad to drive, hoping it would alleviate his brooding. Soon Bronwyn's soft, regular breathing told him she slept. His mind began to click off plans as the digital clock on the dash clicked off minutes. He knew that when they reached New York she would want to retreat alone to her apartment, and every instinct cautioned him against this. They needed to be together; silence, apartness, might divide them further.

And their position made it even more difficult. Complicating their personal trauma was the need for an announcement of their marriage. If the media sensed a rift between them it would be magnified into a rupture. They had to talk, not only of their feelings, but of a practical plan which would protect them from the hurt of public speculation. His mouth hardened as he realized how vulnerable they were.

As they approached New York, he turned on the radio, tuning in his favorite classical station. Keeping the music low so as not to awaken Bronwyn, he let his mind relax.

195

Soon the lighted towers of the George Washington Bridge shimmered in the distance. He down-shifted as they came to the toll gates, and once across the arching span, he turned south onto the Henry Hudson Parkway.

The river lay wide and peaceful, its swift current invisible in the darkness. Across the Hudson, atop the bluffs of the Palisades, an unbroken line of monolithic high-rises shadowed the sky, their lighted windows like concrete checkerboards. On the New York side, lining Riverside Drive, were stands of serried architectural splendor: houses of varied design and height with curving bow windows that shot back the lights of the city like iridescent rainbows; houses with heavily carved facades and curving shapes; houses of wide stoops, intricate iron banisters, and bold balustrades; houses built by proud craftsmen in an age when style and skill were blended in with the mortar mix. No longer the mansions of the privileged, but sliced into apartments, the houses still reigned over the river like the elegant doyennes who once resided in them. Asher drove slowly in the lane closest to the water, soothed by the beauty of the river and the silence of the parklike shoreline winding from the Cloisters north of the bridge to 72nd Street.

At 72nd, the parkway disintegrated into the West Side Highway and Asher drove by enclaves of boxlike, boxed-in housing projects and then past a gloomy concatenation of a city's down-by-the-river necessities: docks, warehouses, factories, garages. He turned off at 23rd Street, heading east towards Seventh Avenue. Bronwyn still slept but Asher knew the pulse of the city would soon awaken her. At 18th Street, a cab rushing the light cut him off and he braked hard. Bronwyn sat up abruptly and looked around.

"We're in New York already."

Asher nodded, stopping at the light. He turned to her with a hopeful smile. "I'm famished. There's an Italian restaurant I like on MacDougal. How about it?"

"Monte's?" Her voice reflected her surprise. It was unpretentious, inexpensive—not the type of restaurant men like Asher generally frequented.

He laughed. "Do you think I dine only at Le Cirque and '21'?"

She looked at him without smiling. "It's Friday night and Monte's is sure to be packed. We might have to wait an hour or more for a table."

"You're right," he said, starting up again as the light turned green. "I've lost track of the days. And any other good restaurant down here will be just as bad. Well— what about my place? Ruth always keeps a full refrigerator."

Bronwyn looked out the window. "I'd rather not."

Asher felt his stomach tighten at her refusal and he knew it had nothing to do with his being hungry. At West 4th Street, she turned to him.

"I know you want to talk, and I guess we should discuss how we announce our marriage, but I'd feel very uncomfortable in your apartment, especially with servants around. If you don't mind the mess in my place and if you don't mind sandwiches, there's a great deli nearby; if you drop me there I'll get us something to eat."

He pulled over and stopped. "Thank you," he said, holding her eyes with his.

"What for?"

"I appreciate your having dinner with me and agreeing to talk. I never mind the state of your apartment. I find it charmingly free." His lips curved into a slow, ingratiating smile. "I'll take hot pastrami on rye with potato salad, cole slaw, and beer. And I'll have a fire going by the time you get home. It's bitterly cold tonight and your place is chilly. We can eat before the fireplace."

"All right," she said, her face still solemn. "But I expect you to leave afterwards. I need time for myself."

"Agreed." He pulled back into traffic.

She rummaged in her purse, coming up with a set of keys, and handed them to him. "Please, don't move too much. If you clean up, I'll never find a thing."

Asher chuckled. He wished he were not behind the wheel so that he could kiss her, but he cautioned himself not to make any such move, now or in her apartment.

He stopped at the delicatessen and as she got out he said, "Don't forget sour pickles and Lido cookies."

She turned to look at him, and he saw how she strove to suppress the smile that almost flickered on her lips.

197

"Don't be afraid to smile, Bronwyn," he said softly. "You'll solve nothing by being dour."

Quickly she shut the car door and went into the crowded store.

"Nothing smells as good as hot pastrami when you're hungry," Asher said, eagerly unwrapping the thick, pungent sandwich. They sat on the floor in front of the fireplace, eating from the delicatessen cartons on the low table between them, drinking beer directly from chilled bottles. They ate hungrily, saying little.

Asher had managed to create a comfortable setting by gathering pillows and arranging them on the floor and selecting records which played softly. A Tiffany lamp on a side table cast amber shadows, and the light of candles he'd found on the mantle muted the strewn-about look of the cartons and sandwich wrappings. Bronwyn kept a supply of wood tossed in a corner and a bright fire blazed, lighting their faces, warming them.

When they finished eating, Bronwyn stuffed the crumpled paper into the cartons and threw them into the fire. She got up and took the empty beer bottles into the kitchen.

"Would you like coffee?" she asked, standing at the kitchen door.

Asher leaned back against the side of an easy chair and stretched his stockinged feet towards the fire. He unscrewed the cap off another bottle of beer. "No thanks."

She came back into the room and, shoving aside books and magazines, sank into a chair near the fire, curling her feet under her.

"Is it okay if I smoke?"

He smiled gently. "Why do ask me that, Bronwyn? It's your home."

Her hair fell over her face as she bent to open the drawer in the table next to her. The firelight caught its movement and Asher longed to pull her to him and bury his face in its glowing thickness.

"Most people who don't smoke mind when others do," she said, taking a crushed pack of cigarettes from the drawer.

"And do you always acquiesce to them?"

"If they object, yes."

"Why should you subjugate yourself to another?"

"Because it's not that important."

"What you want *is important,* Bronwyn!"

A frown deepened between her eyes.

He laughed. "Light up and enjoy yourself, Bronwyn. I've an entire package of Pepperidge Farm cookies to enjoy." Opening the package, he asked, "Want one?"

Smiling, she reached out her hand. "Not one, but a paper cup full. They're my favorites. You can have the rest."

He placed the crinkled paper cup in her hand, his fingers closing on hers. Slowly he drew her towards him, his eyes never leaving her face. "Bronwyn," he said longingly.

She sat rigid. "Asher, you promised."

He stroked her hand, his fingers moving across her wrist, up under the sleeve of her sweater. Moving closer, he said, "I also promised to love, honor, and cherish you."

She pulled away abruptly. "When did you really meet my mother?" she asked sardonically.

It was as if she had slapped him. He sat back on the pillows and said in a clipped voice, "As I told you, the weekend before Christmas." Bleakly, he stared into the fire.

Bronwyn lit a cigarette and inhaled deeply. Letting the smoke out slowly, she watched the wisps curl upwards in the draft from the fireplace. She began to speak, choosing her words carefully.

"All night I've been trying to control what I feel. I keep telling myself that whatever happened between you and my mother doesn't concern me, but it does. It bothers me terribly, and I can't get it out of my mind."

She laughed shortly, without humor. "I can't believe myself. I detest self-righteousness—I accept almost anything. Once someone called me decadent and I thought it was a compliment, but now, I can't seem to accept so human a situation as you and my mother. My mind tells me what I feel is childish, but it is what I *feel* that matters!"

He turned to face her, but he said nothing, grateful that finally, she was talking.

Clasping her hands tightly, she continued. "I've never felt so confused, so overwhelmed—and so hemmed in. Ever since I was little I've had to feel I was in control. I don't feel that now. Despite my mother's overprotective nature, she never really restricted me. I've always loved her for that." Her voice broke, and she quickly lit another cigarette, inhaling deeply. "If I'd had an authoritarian father, I don't know what might have happened. Probably I'd have run away. I'm willful, temperamental, impatient, and somehow my mother accepted that, and the more freedom she gave me, the less I needed. Oh, we've fought and said nasty things to each other—most mothers and daughters do—but we've always managed to work it out."

She stopped and a thoughtful expression crossed her face.

"You have no idea what a brat I was! But when you think about it, kids aren't really being bratty, they're just fighting for survival, for self-expression, to grow the way they want. Kids are selfish. I certainly was, but I think it's part of growing, part of surviving in an adult world, and the selfishness tends to disappear as we mature, as we learn to compromise." Her voice drifted, as if she were speaking to herself. "I've always thought I was mature, but I find it difficult to compromise. Maybe you were right when you said I feared marriage. I've never thought of it as fear; I just dislike sharing my life, but maybe dislike *is* fear."

Leaning towards him, she shook her head ruefully.

"Asher, I'll never fit into this merger, and I'm not going to make it as your wife, either. I'm no good at compromising, and I'm not a corporation person, and marriage is like working for a corporation. I'm a loner, and loners must live and work independently." She held his eyes solemnly, and her voice softened. "Loners also hurt those who love them. We don't want to, but we do, and if you let us, you must share our guilt. I tried to tell you about me, but you wouldn't listen, and I drank too deeply the aphrodisiacs you offered." She hesitated, and her eyes lit with determination.

"I want out, Asher. I'm going to resign from Mednam. I thought about it long before I met you, and now there's no question in my mind. And, if you will permit me, I also wish to resign from our marriage."

Asher had listened carefully to every word, his eyes never leaving her face. He marveled at the deeper facets of this beautiful, mercurial woman he had married. He had not been unprepared for her decision; he had sensed her withdrawal when they left her mother's house.

He smiled gently, with such unperturbed calm that she became uncomfortable.

"Bronwyn, have you any idea how many people regret marrying almost immediately after the ceremony, and how many more wish to back out as they voice their vows?" His voice was low, unruffled. "Your reaction is natural and only proves what a deeply serious and caring person you are. I love you, Bronwyn, but that's irrelevant, for while my love created the climate for our marriage, only under-standing and reason will weather it and make it endure. You can't resign from marriage as you would from your position at Mednam. Your career concerns only you, but our marriage includes me. I will not consent to dissolve this marriage any more than I would consent to dismiss an idea that's not been given a chance.

"We've both been hit hard tonight, and we're too tired to make decisions. I appreciate your choice of words. 'If you will permit me,' you said, and now I ask the same consideration. If you will permit me, I propose a tempo-rary expedient. Let's say it's like laying down a primer on a canvas that has yet to be sketched in. I will announce our marriage on Monday and say that until negotiations for the acquisition of Mednam are completed, because of our personal relationship you are taking a leave of absence. Because of our business commitments we are postponing a honeymoon and the decision as to where we shall live."

He looked at her for a long moment. She made no move to rebut him, and he continued.

"This will give you time to reconsider your feelings about staying on at Mednam and to finish what you're currently working on with no interruptions. And—you can also think about us. You won't feel pressed to explain why we're not together, and if you choose to see me, we can be with each other without the gossips making it all ugly."

She leaned back in her chair and studied him. Was he always so sure, so logical? Slowly her brow unfurrowed, and she sighed tiredly.

"If you intended to deflate me with such clear-headedness, you have, and I agree, but only in part. Your leave of absence idea is splendid and I thank you for that, but I don't want to be in New York when you announce our marriage. I hate being interviewed and questioned, and if I stay in the city, it's inevitable. And even if I don't go into the office, Drew Mednam and others I work with are sure to call me. They won't be able to contain their questions or their speculations. Since we have a few weeks before the board meeting, I'm going to steal away and get out where the fresh mountain air will clear my head. Skiing and working have always been the best prescription for me, so I'm going to pack up this pile of manuscripts and catch a flight to Salt Lake City on Sunday. I wish I could go tomorrow, but all I want to do for the next twenty-four hours is sleep." She smiled lightly. "I know you'll handle everything beautifully—after all, the media is your milieu—but if they give you a hard time, just remind them that Fannie Hurst and her husband maintained separate apartments throughout their marriage."

Asher had not expected her to leave the city. He had made his proposal coolly, but inside he seethed with emotion. He knew they both needed rest, but he had planned to see her tomorrow and be with her. He hoped that by Monday they would be together. Now she had maneuvered him into a position from which his refusal would seem dictatorial. But if he had been more firm with her, he thought bitterly, they would be in Paris right now, asleep in each other's arms in a suite in the Plaza Athénée. Frustration rose in him.

"I don't agree to your leaving New York." Vexation sharpened his tone. "You're running away! From me, from Mednam, and from yourself."

Her mouth set stubbornly. "I don't see it that way! If I am running, it's *to* myself, to make sure of what *I* want!"

He rose impatiently. He wanted to grab her, shake her, and hold her until there was no question of her leaving him. He clenched his fists to hold himself back. She sat coiled like a cougar, a beautiful, tawny feline too volatile to touch. God, how he wanted her, but he'd be damned if he forced himself on her! He brought his voice under control and said shortly, "If you insist, but let me know where you are."

She sensed his anger, and as though it were *she* soothing a restive animal, said quietly, "Of course. Please call me tomorrow and I'll tell you just where I'll be."

He stood silently looking down at her. Her eyes were the same color as the firelight reflected on her face. Leaning down, he kissed her cheek lightly.

"Sleep well," he said. Turning quickly, he went into the small hallway, put on his boots and coat, and let himself out.

Chapter Seventeen

A small cry of erotic pleasure escaped Bronwyn's parted lips and she stretched languidly in her sleep, opening her legs for the man making love to her in her dream. She reached out to him, trying to see his face, but he drew back, pulling his body from hers. She groaned and groped for her elusive lover, wanting him close again, but her fingers found only the empty pillow beside her. Her brow tightened, and reluctantly she opened her eyes. The warmth her dream had brought vanished. For days Asher's lovemaking had awakened her, and her body tingled with the memory of her dream. Wanting the vision to return, she curled her legs, burying herself in the quilt and in the pillows, seeking the darkness, the delight of the dream. And then the face of the man making love to her materialized. It was not Asher.

She sat bolt upright. *Damn! Screw you, MacCormack!*

Nervously she began to giggle. That was just what she had been doing!

The alarm buzzed and Bronwyn stumbled out of bed, across the room, to shut it off. It was a ploy she'd long ago adopted, putting the clock out of reach. Her head felt as though she had slept in a sawmill; the dream had come only towards morning, after a restless night. Naked, she groped her way to the bathroom and turned on the shower, hot and full force, filling the room with heat and steam. Cooling the water, she stepped into the spray and began to soap her body briskly. As she lathered her breasts and the thickness of red hair between her thighs, the sensitivity brought on by the dream returned, and trying to dispel her guilt, she made herself think of Asher, and how he had washed her and fondled her as the water tumbled on them. She turned her face up, closing her eyes as though for his kiss, but water splashed her face, making her sputter, dousing her deception.

"Forget it!" she cried, throwing her head back, letting the water soak her hair. She took the shampoo from the caddy and washed her hair until it squeaked.

Later, wrapped in a terry robe, Bronwyn sat in the chair near the fireplace, a pad and pencil in her lap. An empty coffee cup was on the table next to her, and she stubbed out her cigarette. Picking up the pad, she went over the long list she had made, her brow knitting in concentration as she underlined some notes and circled others. When she had finished she reviewed her jottings, and the frown between her eyes deepened. Leaning back against the pillow, she closed her eyes. After a while she opened them and with a long, drawn-out breath, wrote down at the end of the list: "Call Mother."

Reaching under a pile of magazines, she pulled the phone onto her lap and dialed the airlines, booking a flight early the next morning to Salt Lake City. Then she called the Alta Lodge and made a reservation. Looking at her watch, she grimaced. Now she would have to make all the calls on her list. She had to speak with Drew Mednam, with Van Zuye and those artists and authors with whom she was currently working. She would try and keep explanations short, putting them all off until she returned.

Returned? When? She hadn't thought about that. She would have to be at the board meeting, and she could not leave Mednam until after the sales meetings at least. She owed her authors that. Only she knew enough about the books scheduled for publication to make a proper sales presentation. She would have to come back in a week—there was too much to do to stay away longer.

For the next two hours Bronwyn was on the telephone. Finally she took a break and was about to go to the kitchen for a cup of fresh coffee when the phone rang. She wanted to ignore it, but then, realizing it might be Asher, she picked up the receiver and answered more pleasantly than she felt.

"Hello." His voice was lazy, enticing. "You sound so sweet. I wish you were here with me. I want you."

"Are you still in bed?" she asked, surprised.

"Ummhmm," he murmured. "Come and join me. I miss you. It's terrible waking up and not finding you beside me."

Bronwyn sat silent, thinking of how she had awakened.

Her silence encouraged him. "If you won't come here, darling, let me come to you." His voice was a caress, as though he drew a feather along her spine. "Bronwyn, I love you, I want to hold you. Don't shut me out. Life's too short to throw love away."

She couldn't listen anymore. "Asher, please, you're making it difficult for both of us." She ran on hurriedly. "I'll be at the Alta Lodge, but I'd appreciate it if you wouldn't phone me. I'll be back next Saturday night. I've called Drew Mednam. He can't believe we're married, or that I'm leaving. I told him I had to have this week to myself, and he finally agreed, but I'm to meet him next Sunday. He wants to talk, away from the office. I also spoke to Van Zuye—he's even more astounded. I have a meeting with him after I see Drew, and later I'll meet with two of my authors."

Her words fell like weights, crushing his hopes. "And just when do you plan to meet with me?" He made no effort to soften his sarcasm. There would be no dissembling between them. Sitting up abruptly in his bed, he said heatedly, "I resent your asking me not to phone you in

Alta, I resent your leaving the city at this time, and I deeply resent all your meetings next Sunday! I should think you would reserve that time for *us!* My God, Bronwyn! Doesn't our future mean *anything* to you?"

She said nothing, and like an attorney who asks a question without first knowing the answer, Asher regretted his outburst.

Finally her voice came over the wire—it was quiet, hesitant.

"I really don't know how to answer you, Asher. All I know is that if I let myself brood over my impulsiveness in marrying you—and over what happened between you and my mother—we have no chance at all."

She sighed. "Isn't it better that I concentrate on work right now? So much has happened to me so quickly—I need time to sort things out. I have to feel that *I* am making my *own* decisions. If you don't push me, maybe I'll discover how I feel about you. Right now . . . I just don't know. I need time for myself. I'm all confused."

Asher held the receiver for a long time. He couldn't deny the logic in her plea, or the pain in her voice.

Bronwyn waited for him to speak, but there was only silence.

"Asher, I'm dying for a cup of coffee. May I say goodbye?"

"What time is your flight tomorrow?"

"Shortly after ten. I get into Salt Lake about 3:30. I should be at the lodge in time for supper."

"Will you call me if there are any problems—if you need anything?"

She smiled into the phone. "You are such a sweet, loving man, Asher Jacobs. I wish I could live up to you."

"Take care skiing. Call me when you get back." He hung up quickly, fighting the emotion in him.

By ten p.m. Bronwyn's suitcase stood in the hallway beside a bulging boot bag and a double ski bag crammed with two pairs of skis, poles, and miscellaneous gear. Manuscripts were stuffed into a large tote bag she would carry onboard. All was set for her to leave tomorrow morning. She looked about her in satisfaction. She'd even managed to tidy the apartment, and she stood for a moment admiring her work. She'd really have to be more disciplined and keep it like this all the time.

She went into the kitchen and poured herself a Bourbon and soda, then came back to sit near the fireplace. She took the list from her pocket and slowly crossed out the chores she had completed. Her pencil poised above the last item. Taking slow sips of her drink, Bronwyn drew circle over circle over circle on the note until it was illegible. It would have to wait. She couldn't handle talking to Elizabeth just yet.

Asher leaned back in the cordovan leather chair and put his feet up on the nineteenth-century walnut desk which had been in the office of the President of International Communications Corporation since the days of Michael Cassidy's father. He gazed up at the Waterford chandelier which hung in the center of the paneled ceiling. His chin rested on the pyramid his hands formed. The circular office was richly paneled in walnut; Persian rugs accented the dark parquet flooring, and cordovan leather furniture formed comfortable conversation groupings. A door in one wall led to a well-stocked bar, a compact kitchen, a handsome dining room, a smaller room with a sleeping sofa, and a bathroom.

On another wall, a Flemish tapestry concealed a sophisticated media center which Asher activated from an electronic panel built into a drawer of his massive desk. The spacious suite with its tall, arched windows overlooking Fifth Avenue sat dead center on the fifty-fourth floor of the towering Art Deco ICC building. Double doors in heavy, carved walnut opened into the private office of his executive secretary, Claire Lanstrom; beyond, paneled doors led to a reception area in which two additional secretaries worked, and past them were glass doors to the complex of offices making up the ICC executive suite. The linen-covered walls of the beige-carpeted hallways were hung with a colorful collection of abstract and surrealistic art, illuminated by recessed ceiling lights.

Asher enjoyed the antique ambience of his office; it offered a quiet respite from the high-tech pace beyond the double doors. Now, after hours, he sat, pleased with himself. The announcement Monday of his marriage had been easier than expected. No real issue had been made of its effect on the coming merger, and there had been only brief mentions on the evening news and in the wire service stories. There was more extensive coverage in the financial pages and the daily *Times,* but not enough to cause embarrassment; this was not going to be another Bendix.

Bronwyn had not called, nor had he tried to reach her. But today, he'd had a long conversation with Drew Mednam, and that gave him the excuse he had been seeking to phone her. He glanced at the ormolu clock on his desk. It was almost six—in Alta, almost four. She should be back from skiing by now. He picked up the phone and then, hesitated. Slowly he put it down. No. It could wait until she returned.

He lowered his feet from the desk and sat up. Damn! He was restless. Opening a drawer he pushed some buttons. The tapestry slid silently aside, revealing an electronic complex. Images emerged instantly on the multiple screen, and the local newscasts of the three major television networks sounded. He got up, went to the bar and poured Scotch into a glass, then moved to the window and looked down into the street.

The city glistened like patent leather in the sleeting rain. Through the wet haze, lights twinkled like man-made stars. Far below all seemed Lilliputian—he could barely make out the people hurrying home and the toy cars, speeding and honking crazily.

He felt strangely apart—as though he looked down from another planet, a far-off, lonely planet. How damn lonely he felt! And going home alone each night heightened his longing for Bronwyn. He did not want to dine out without her; it would only cause talk. And so he had eaten at home in front of the television and later worked at his desk, trying to fill his empty hours. At least he had caught up on his work. Now he'd be free to take her away right after the sales meetings. He hadn't spoken to her in four days! To hell with it! He'd call her! He took a long swallow of his drink and strode quickly back to his desk. Just as he reached it, his private line rang. It startled him, and the liquor in his glass spun. He stopped and looked quizzically at the sleek instrument in the cordovan leather case. Very few people had that number. Could it be Bronwyn? He'd given her the number shortly after they met. Expectantly he picked up the receiver, and a pleased smile crossed his face as he heard her voice.

"Hi," she said doubtfully. "I wasn't sure you'd be in this late."

He pushed a button to silence the television. He laughed huskily. "This is early for me, darling. I don't generally leave until after the network newscasts."

"Oh, I'm sorry, I'm disturbing you. I'll call back later."

"No, you won't! Your call is the best news I could have. Nothing is more important!"

He heard only silence, and then she said very quietly, "How can you always be so sweet to me when I'm such a bitch?"

Asher sat down in his chair and, pushing buttons, shut off the TV and all the lights in the room. He swiveled the chair so that it faced the city gleaming outside. He closed his eyes, trying to feel her across the miles.

"Bronwyn, you're a wonderfully sensitive woman, and I love you. I don't think there's anything you could say or do that would make me feel otherwise."

He heard her take a deep breath, and when she spoke her voice was casual, noncommittal. "I feel much better. I had two days of glorious skiing and I've also worked and accomplished a good deal. That always makes me feel good."

Asher, hearing her coolness, controlled the emotions which coursed through him. "I'm glad," he said evenly.

"Today was rotten, though," she continued. "There's been more than two feet of snow and the mountain's shut down. We've had Inter-Lodge—no one is permitted outside because of avalanche danger. Little Cottonwood Canyon is closed, and the only way in or out is by helicopter. They've been shooting avalanches all day so I've just stayed in my room and worked."

Her voice took on a lighter note. "They say it'll be clear

tomorrow, and I plan to get out early and ski the chutes before the powder freaks track them up."

Asher wished her enthusiasm was for him.

"Those Baldy chutes can be tricky, Bronwyn, especially after a heavy snowfall. Don't ski them alone."

She laughed gaily. "You've skied them?"

He hadn't heard her laugh in so long. It lifted his spirits.

"When you were just out of diapers," he said, smiling into the phone. "I can still give you a run for your money. Why don't you wait and we'll ski them together? The ICC plane can get me there before the lifts open tomorrow."

The line went silent. He waited, feeling her withdrawal. After what seemed an eternity, she said, "I'd rather not. And don't worry, I won't be alone. If they open the chutes, every good skier in Alta will be hiking the ridge to them. But I didn't call to talk about skiing. I called to thank you."

"What for?"

"For being so understanding, and for making the announcement alone. How did things go?"

"Fine. Better than I expected. But Drew Mednam is certainly on edge."

"Oh?"

"He phoned today and insisted I meet him for lunch tomorrow." He paused. "He doesn't want to lose you, Bronwyn." He took a deep breath and thought, *Neither do I.* Aloud he said, "I'm going to discuss some ideas with him that should be very attractive to you."

"I'd rather not hear about it now," she said quickly.

Asher felt his stomach tense. "As you wish." He was about to change the subject back to skiing, anything to keep her on the phone, keep her close, but she said, "I'll call you when I get back to New York Saturday night. Take care."

"Bronwyn."

"Yes?"

He wanted to say so much, but said only, "Goodnight, darling. Think of me."

Again that silence, that breathing, but when she spoke his heart filled with hope.

211

Her voice was low, hesitant: "I have. I will."
He held the phone to his ear long after she hung up.

Bronwyn let the phone settle slowly into its cradle. She turned over on the wide bed, resting her chin on her hands. Why had she called him? she wondered. She hadn't planned to. When she first picked up the phone it was to call Elizabeth—she had been putting that off since she had arrived—but instead she found herself dialing Asher. And she had told him the truth; she had been thinking of him. She turned on her back and looked up at the ceiling. His voice, warm, loving, still sounded in her ears. He was so *damn* sweet. Had she overreacted? He'd had every right to be with whomever he chose. But her *mother!* So what? reason pounded.

"Shit!," she said aloud, getting up and going to the mirror. Looking sternly at her reflection, she said: "Forget it. Go downstairs, have a drink, and relax. *Stop thinking!"*

The bar at the Alta Lodge sat in a pit before a stone fireplace centered between wide windows facing the mountain, which loomed like a ghostly giant in the greyness of twilight. Outside lights brightened the hill which sloped gently down to the lifts, where a rope tow pulled skiers up from the lift area to the lodge. The ropes lay still now, moving only to the occasional gust of wind. Benches flanked the fireplace, and candles lit the wood tables. Old photographs depicting Alta when it was a mining town hung on the walls. A small window at the side looked up the canyon.

Bronwyn entered, carrying a bottle of Bourbon in a brown paper sack. The crowd inside the bar surprised her; there weren't that many guests in the lodge. She guessed the alert was over and people could once more move about freely. Few chanced the five hundred dollar fine levied if one went outside during "Inter-Lodge"—a ban imposed by the U.S. Avalanche and Control Center, headquartered in Little Cottonwood Canyon.

"Hi there, Miss O'Neill." The deeply tanned young bartender greeted her with a broad smile; his ski goggles

212

had left white circles around his eyes and he looked like a strange, grinning owl. His brown hair was streaked blond from the sun and premature lines etched his pleasant face. *Too many hours in high altitude and strong sun,* Bronwyn thought, returning his smile. She sat down and he put her set-up on the bar.

"Thank you, Jed. Looks like you've got a lively crowd tonight."

"Inter-Lodge. People get crazy when they've been cooped up all day, but they just called it off." He leaned close, whispering. "Some Florida ski club—long on drinking, short on skiing. The patrol told me they measured over three feet of new snow, and these turkeys can't ski powder. If the road's closed tomorrow even the townies won't be able to get in, and we'll have the mountain to ourselves!"

Bronwyn raised her glass in a toast. "To a terrific day of skiing." Jed moved down the bar, and when he returned to place another set-up before her she said, "Do me a favor and stow this bottle when I go in to dinner."

He shook his head. "Sorry, Miss O'Neill, we're not allowed to keep liquor."

"I wish Alta weren't in Utah." She sighed, taking a cigarette from her pack on the bartop.

"Know what you mean. I'm from California myself." He flipped his lighter and lit her cigarette.

"Why would you want to work in Utah?" she asked.

He nodded towards the windows. "Best snow in the world. You know why? The clouds coming off the Pacific dump on the Sierras first—big, wet flakes. Then the air cuts across the Nevada desert. It's real dry, but it picks up just enough moisture, especially when it crosses Great Salt Lake, so that when the clouds hit the Wasatch"—he smacked his hands together—"they spill the finest, driest powder you can find anywhere."

Bronwyn smiled. "That's what I love about bars; you never know what you might learn."

"Or who you might meet." He grinned, moving away to serve two couples who had just entered.

Looking around at the crowd, Bronwyn felt a pang of

213

nostalgia. She didn't know a soul. Just a few years ago she could not have walked into any bar in a western ski town and not run into someone she knew.

Suddenly hands were over her eyes, blocking out the light. She felt moist lips behind her ear, closing on her lobe, sucking it. A tongue shot into her ear cavity. Only one man had ever kissed her in just that way. She leaned back against the hardness of his chest, remembering how it felt. He had not changed. He even smelled the same.

"Dave, you son-of-a-bitch!" She giggled. "What the hell are you doing in Alta with the team in Europe?"

The man took his hands from her eyes and spun her around. Without saying a word, he leaned down and kissed her full on the mouth, his lips parting hers, his tongue darting between her teeth. Someone at the bar whistled and Bronwyn tried to disengage herself, but Dave Bradley held her fast. When he finally let go, he stepped back.

"Just wanted to make sure you'd remember who's in charge."

His brown eyes swept her, and a smile deepened the lines around his wide, full mouth. She wore a dark green velour pant suit; her russet hair was held back with a green silk scarf coiled into a band around her forehead. Bradley curled a strand of her hair around his finger. "You've grown into a beautiful woman, Bon."

"I should hope so." She laughed uneasily, shaken by the intensity of his kiss. "I was an awkward, gangly kid."

He touched her cheek fondly. "No, you were a lonely kid and too damn smart for your own good."

She watched him ease his compact, athlete's body onto the seat next to her. Dave Bradley was not much taller than Bronwyn. He had an attractive, boyish face that had aged little. A deep tan darkened his naturally fair skin, and his coarse, sandy hair was streaked with grey. Bronwyn noted the grey and the lines in his face. *But he's still a stud,* she thought.

Raising his glass, he bent close. "To my virgin."

Embarrassed, she laughed self-consciously. "Come on, Dave, you must have had hundreds."

He sipped his beer, examining her face as if he were

checking gates on a slalom course. "No, Bonnie, you were one of the rare ones. Maybe that's why I could never forget you. You were my Galatea."

She dropped her eyes and stirred the ice in her glass. "How come you're not with the team?"

Bradley smiled briefly. "So you're no longer reading *Racing News.* That's good. I quit coaching two years ago because Rossignol made me an offer I couldn't refuse. Skiing doesn't pay like football, you know, and I was pushing forty, so now I'm a vice-president. I travel around the country, meet with racers, coaches, reps, writers, whoever. It's a good life, no heartaches." He moved his glass around slowly, making five rings with the wet bottom on the polished wood—the Olympics symbol. He grinned crookedly. "But racing's still in my blood. At Sarajevo I sweated every gate—I yelled myself hoarse." He drained his glass, motioned to the bartender for a refill, and turned to Bronwyn accusingly. "How come you didn't go to the championships in Placid? Everyone was there—Becky, Vickie, Mary, Bruce, Phil. We had a ball. Holly asked if I ever see you. She said she hadn't heard from you in a long time. I don't get it. Your own back yard and you don't even show!"

She put her arm around his shoulder and bent her head to his. "You're such a romantic, Dave—you always were. That's so long ago for me. I have no regrets. Besides, I had a much better view on television, and if it makes you feel better, I, too, yelled myself hoarse, especially for Holly." She smiled at him. "What about you, Dave? Are you married? I heard you were going hot and heavy with Mary."

"I was," he said wryly, "but the circuit is no place for love and marriage. The sex is too free and easy, and it's the same for the women. They've got to unwind just like the men, and all those tight-assed racers are hot to trot. We called it off after three years, and now I'm too spoiled and too demanding to settle down."

Bronwyn picked up her glass and his eyes went to her hands.

"When did this happen?" He took the glass from her hand and stroked the gold band on her third finger.

215

"New Year's Eve."

"This New Year's Eve?"

"Uh huh."

"Where's your husband?"

"In New York."

"New York?"

She laughed. "We sound like an old comedy team."

"It's no joke."

"What's no joke?" She laughed again.

"Come on, Bonnie," he said impatiently. "What gives?"

"Nothing."

"Don't give me that crap! Nobody gets married New Year's Eve and a week later is off alone, miles away."

Leaning towards him, she put her finger on his lips. "Sorry, Dave, I don't want to talk about it. Besides, it's really none of your business."

His dark brown eyes bored into her. "I know, but I'm asking anyway. You know, Bonnie, I really cared about you. I took chances with you I'd never taken before"—he hesitated—"or since. But you were such a *woman* for an untried kid, and you had the makings of a great racer. I never knew if you quit because you hated racing, or if you ran away from me." He ran his finger along the furrow in her brow. "Men don't really forget their virgins, any more than they forget the woman with whom they first had sex."

She had not forgotten either, but it meant nothing to her now. Her brow cleared and a small smile lifted the corners of her mouth. "Don't beat yourself, Dave. I did what I did because at the time, it was what I wanted. When we're young, we don't think about *why* we do things. We're like puppies making a mess on the carpet. Even when we're older it's tough to be sensible. We give in to whatever makes us feel good, so as long as we live we have to walk around with pooper-scoopers."

His eyes gripped hers, and then he leaned over and kissed her forehead. "How long you staying?"

"Till Saturday morning."

He nodded. "I'm leaving Saturday, too. I'm on my way to Mammoth and Tahoe. I hope to see Jonesy."

"He can't still be coaching!"

216

Bradley chuckled. "Are you kidding? Jonesy'll be at the finish line in the year 2000!"

He swung around, gazing out the windows towards the mountain, now hidden in darkness. The lights caught the dazzle of the dry powder falling so fine it looked like frosted mist. People played in the drifts, trying to make snowballs, but it was like shaping goosedown. The snow blew apart in their hands. Others sped down the hill on whatever they could find—sleds, trays, plastic garbage bags. A few novice skiers tried their first taste of powder but didn't get far; they fell laughing—disappearing into fluff they had never known.

His eyes aglow, Bradley turned to Bronwyn and said eagerly: "If this mist keeps up, it'll cover the crud the avalanche boys blew up. They might even open the chutes tomorrow. If they do, no one'll come to any meeting after the lifts open—lucky I met with Alf and Max today. Everyone'll be out making tracks. How about it, Bon? The Baldy chutes—High Rustler—Eagle's Nest! It'll be like old times." His smile dared her. "Think you can still keep up with me?"

She hesitated. She wanted to be alone—to ski alone—but the prospect of tracking with him was too enticing. With a laugh she said, "You bet I can!"

"It's settled then!" He got up and tossed some bills on the bar. Taking her bottle and tucking it under his arm, he said, "You're in training now, kid. No more booze till tomorrow night. Let's get some dinner and you can tell me all about this mysterious man you've married." He took her arm firmly and led her towards the dining room. She knew it was useless to argue. Dave Bradley was too accustomed to giving orders, and she had been one of his soldiers for five years.

217

Chapter Eighteen

Elizabeth made her way up the path late Wednesday night, her arms filled with materials from her computer class. Blaze pranced about her legs, welcoming her and looking, in the shadows cast by the lights, like a playful bear. As she came up on the deck she heard the phone ringing. She paused, puzzled by the persistent sound. Then she remembered she had forgotten to switch on the answering machine. It might be Bonnie! She hurried to unlock the door, balancing the books and pamphlets in one arm. For five days she had been hoping for a call! She rushed inside, the dog at her heels, dumped her armful on the sofa, and picked up the phone.

"Lizzie!" The voice was sharp, impatient. "Where the hell have you been? I don't mind getting your damn machine because then I know you're out, but when your phone rings and rings after eleven o'clock at night and you don't answer, then I worry."

"Hello, Tom." Her voice sank with disappointment. "I'm sorry, I forgot to turn on the machine. What's up?"

He let out a long breath. He hadn't meant to jump at her but he'd had little sleep the last few days. There was no life, no welcome in her voice. Was she so depressed because of Bronwyn's marriage? He'd first heard the announcement Monday night when he'd been in the doctor's lounge at the hospital, drinking coffee, beat after hours of operating. The television news droned meaninglessly. Since New Year's he had heard too many cries of anguish, seen too many broken bodies to care about what passed for news on the screen.

Death and Calhoun were close associates—adversaries mostly, but at times, reluctant colleagues. For the hopeless, he accepted death as a natural extension of life, but for those in whom the smallest life force shimmered, he fought death with formidable determination and skill. What he could not accept was senseless carnage, and just an hour before, the last teenager cut from the wreckage of a station wagon crushed by a train on New Year's Eve died—eight young people killed because the driver, intoxicated, had tried to beat a train to a crossing.

Tom Calhoun had finished his coffee, washed up, and walked home to his apartment overlooking the East River, too angry to stop for dinner. Glancing through an accumulation of unread newspapers at breakfast the next morning, what he'd vaguely heard on television became fact. A photo of Asher Jacobs caught his eye, and Calhoun scanned the story. He put his fork down. How the hell had *that* happened? He reread the story carefully, but it told him nothing.

Elizabeth's silence told him more. She always phoned when she had happy news, and what should have been happier than her daughter's marriage? It was then he'd made plans to come out and see her.

Now, on the telephone, he softened his tone. "Liz, I'm sorry, I didn't mean to snap at you, but it's been a hellish two weeks. I'm in a foul mood. Remember when I said I

219

might be up for New Year's? Well, my partner had the flu and I've been on call. I haven't been out of the hospital in days, but now I'm free until Monday. I need a break. How about it? Interested in some skiing and dancing?"

Elizabeth hesitated. Calhoun rarely sounded so strained. Perhaps they could soothe each other. "Come on up, Tom. I should be able to meet you at the mountain by eleven. They're delivering a word processor tomorrow morning. That's where I've been nights. I've been taking computer classes and I've been teaching skiing again."

So—Bonnie's marriage had hit her hard. "I'll call when I get to Cable," he said, and then, making his voice lighter than he felt, "Get a good night's sleep because I hope to ski and dance your legs off."

A flickering brightness forced Elizabeth to open her eyes. Sunlight danced on the wall, the colors chasing each other as the spectrum filtering through the windows collided with the mirror. Pulling a pillow over her head to black out the brightness, she turned over, not wanting to wake up. Again it had been a bad night. For days she had tried to keep busy, hoping tiredness would help her sleep, but at night her mind exploded, reliving the moments with Asher. And eating into those memories came a bitter jealousy as she imagined her daughter in bed with him. The first terrible night after Bronwyn and Asher had left, Elizabeth fled from the silence of the house, driving into town, desperate for the sound of people.

But even then, thoughts of her daughter followed. In Andy's Tavern, a dark, cavernous, candlelit hangout crowded with skiers and red-jacketed instructors, she ran into Joe Adrinas, Director of the Cable Ski School, and his wife, Blue. Adrinas insisted she have dinner with them, and with a pang she remembered the day they had first met.

Bronwyn had been only six when Elizabeth heard herself paged on the ski area loudspeaker. Alarmed, she had hurried to the office to find a glaring Adrinas and a defiant little girl.

"This your daughter?"

"Yes . . . what's wrong?"

"I caught her *schussing* Corkscrew! If she's going to ski that fast, put her in training!"

Adrinas was the first to coach Bronwyn, and one season, caught shorthanded, he asked Elizabeth if she would teach part-time. Surprised, Elizabeth laughingly declined, but Adrinas persisted.

"Why not? You don't have to be a super skier to be a good teacher."

Bronwyn's delight and proud encouragement prompted Elizabeth to accept the offer, and through the years she had worked for Adrinas during peak times. And that night in Andy's when Adrinas again asked her to help out, Elizabeth agreed readily, hoping to forget herself in the teaching.

The days on the mountain lightened her mood, but at night, depression closed in, black as the darkened peaks. One night, unable to face an empty house and even more unable to face the young, pleasure-loving crowd in Andy's, Elizabeth drove directly from the ski area to a shopping mall and wandered aimlessly. She stopped at a computer store and looked in the window. How long was it since her fingers had touched typewriter keys? She hadn't even called the shop to find out if her typewriter had been repaired. Idly she entered the store.

A personable young salesman greeted her. Noting her uniform, he said with a smile, "You're the first ski instructor we've had in here."

"I only teach part-time," she replied, running her fingers over the black keys of a nearby machine.

"And I only ski part-time." The salesman pulled back a chair and switched on a lever. "Make yourself comfortable, give it a try—it's remarkably easy," he said as the screen lit up.

Elizabeth sat down and tapped out a few meaningless phrases. The salesman began to speak softly, supportively. By the time the store closed at nine, Elizabeth had purchased the computer, a printer, and word-processing software. And she signed up for three nights of instruction at the store. Driving home last night after her final class, a pleasant sense of accomplishment had begun to ease the heaviness weighting her heart and mind. For the first time in days, she had felt *good*. She had even managed to make sense of what had at first seemed so incomprehensible! Ideas had begun to light up the screen of her mind, feeding byte after byte into her brain. As the desire to write again stirred in her, a smile had softened her lips.

The alarm went off and she groaned, this time coming fully awake. Why did the best sleep come only towards morning? Slowly she got out of bed and made her way to the shower; the stinging hot spray bit into her and her pores flew open, shedding her sleepiness. She washed briskly, rubbing her skin pink, and then let the water drench the soapy lather from her body. Turning off the shower, she stepped into a big, thick towel, moving quickly, not wanting to remember how Asher had once dried her. At her closet she chose a one-piece suit and dressed as though she were a fireman on call. The full-length zipper slid up easily. At least, I've lost weight, she thought.

The computer was delivered soon after nine and within the hour it was set up in her office, ready to function. She fed the cats, released Blaze to guard the house, and walked up to the ski area. By eleven-thirty she was skiing with Calhoun, and two hours later they sat in the warm sunshine, eating lunch. Elizabeth ate a sandwich, Calhoun drank a Bloody Mary.

Calhoun leaned back against the wall of the building, his large legs propped on the rail of the deck. His face, ruddy under the red beard, was turned up to the sun. He breathed heavily, dozing like a hibernating grizzly. He had drunk more than he had eaten and Elizabeth reached over to take the glass from his hand.

His fingers tightened on the drink. "I'm awake, Liz."

Putting her feet up on the rail, Elizabeth took a small tube from her pocket and smoothed an orange gel on her face and lips. She closed her eyes, releasing her senses to the fragrance of the mountain air and the soft breeze on her face.

After a while the big man beside her stirred and murmured, "Did you ever wonder, Liz, why I never married?"

Opening her eyes, she looked at him quizzically. "What brought that on?"

"Who knows? But answer me anyway." He opened his eyes slightly and rolled his head to look at her.

She smiled. "Yes, I wondered at first, but then I thought I knew, so I've never asked."

He laughed. "What do you think you know?"

"That you like too many women to settle for one."

He nodded. "That's part of it, but not the real reason."

"Why then?"

He took a long swallow of his drink. "I never wanted children."

She sat up and faced him. "That's so strange. You're wonderful with children."

"Perhaps, but they grow up to race motorcycles and joyride in cars." He turned away and, raising the glass to his lips, he finished all of the tall drink.

Elizabeth knew the liquor was beginning to depress him and she wondered how she could tactfully get him to eat, but Calhoun had already signalled the waitress working the outdoor deck for another round.

"Tom, I'm full," Elizabeth said. "Why don't you finish my sandwich."

"The birds need it more than I do, Liz. Give 'em a treat."

She directed a scolding look at him, and, breaking the food into bits, she tossed the remains of her sandwich onto the snow. Instantly sparrows and belligerent starlings dove from under the eaves, and within seconds no trace of food remained. The waitress returned with his drink, and Calhoun tipped the young girl generously.

"That's a nice kid," he said, a deep frown knifing between his brows. "I lost a kid just like her on Monday. You'd think I'd be used to it by now, but this kid survived a crash New Year's Eve that killed seven others. It was a miracle she ever got to the operating table. How I wanted her to live! We worked on this kid for five hours, and I was sure I'd chalked one up for our side—but Monday night, she died of pneumonia."

Elizabeth didn't know what to say. Calhoun seldom

spoke of his work, and never of the tragedies, but she knew what a brooding, sensitive man he was under the bluster.

He kneaded his brow as though he sought to rub away his depression.

"I remember once my father broke down and cried over a horse that died of pneumonia. It was a shock to me. I'd never seen a man cry before, least of all my father—he never even cried when my sister Nora died. He was a hard-living, hard-drinking blacksmith—moved from track to track in the racing season—and I realized then, he loved horses more than people."

Calhoun sat up, speaking with an energy more familiar to Elizabeth than his dejection. It was as though speaking of the past helped him block out the present. A nostalgic smile crossed his face. "Pop always said he fell in love with my mum because she looked like a horse and had stronger withers. Once I caught him pinching her as she walked by. Whenever he came home we'd stay up till all hours listening to his stories. One night he picked up my hands and said, 'Ye got the hands of a blacksmith, Tom, but if ye become a doctor ye can own a string o' horses, 'stead o'workin' like one.' I never forgot that."

Elizabeth listened quietly. When he said nothing more she remarked, "You've never mentioned your family before."

"That's because they're dead," he said shortly. "Paddy —that's my oldest brother—enlisted in the Navy when he was seventeen and died when the *Arizona* was sunk at Pearl Harbor. Jimmy didn't have to go, but he wanted to avenge his big brother—he was killed at Remagen shortly before the war ended. Nora died of leukemia. Losing them all was too much for Mum and Pop. They never lived to see me practice. I never got a chance to buy my father a string of horses." He got up abruptly. "Come on, Lizzie, let's ski. I've talked too much."

Calhoun skied relentlessly and Elizabeth drove herself to keep up with him. Despite the liquor, or maybe because of it, he skied without effort and when at four he turned to go back up the lift, Elizabeth said, "I've had it, Tom. I'll wait for you in the lodge."

"You're right," he said. "We should have quit earlier. Come on, let's get a drink."

They sat at a small table in front of the full-length windows overlooking the slopes. There were few people in the lounge, and Elizabeth was pleased it was so quiet. Tomorrow night there would be a band blaring near where they sat, and the room would be mobbed with skiers up for the weekend.

"Why haven't you told me Bonnie married Asher Jacobs?" Calhoun said, biting into the stalk of celery from his Bloody Mary.

Elizabeth looked at him in surprise. "How did you know?"

He shrugged. "It was in the papers."

Sipping her wine, she avoided the eyes which watched her.

"I'd rather not talk about it."

"It's better if you do."

"Like hell it is!"

"Come on, Liz. Talking helps."

Leaning back, she looked at him levelly. "Don't worry about me, Tom. I'm a strong lady, I'll manage."

"How? By crawling back into that goddamned typewriter? Excuse me," he mocked, "now it's a word processor, you can grind out copy even faster! Dammit, Liz! You gave up living when Lorne died, and all that crap you write is as much an escape for you as it is for the women who read it. It's about time you woke up to the *real world* and live life the way it *is!* Bonnie knows more about life and living than you do!"

"Drop it, Tom!"

"I'm not going to drop it!" he said gruffly. "Tell me—why aren't we lovers? We like the same things. How come we've never made it together?"

He laughed shortly at the astonished look on her face.

"I'll tell you why, Liz, and it's not the drinks talking, it's *me*. I never got that signal from you that women give out. Why? Don't tell me there's no chemistry between us. We couldn't be the friends we are without feeling *something*. It's not natural for a man and a woman who like each other as we do, not to wind up in bed. You're afraid of me,

Liz—you're afraid of men who have it together, men who make demands. You were comfortable with Lorne because he asked for so little, but men who want little, give even less, and—God knows why—you think very little is due you. You have no confidence with a strong man—you're afraid even to go to bed with him! I'll bet Jacobs made a pass at you—I could see it coming—and I'll bet it scared the hell out of you. You probably sent him packing."

She gripped her glass of wine. The familiarity of his words stung her. Paul and Arnold had said almost the same. *It had to be true!* If she could not see what they saw, was it because she was afraid to look? Was that why she sought friendship instead of love? What was that line of Byron's? *"Friendship is love without his wings."*

Maybe it was time to learn how to fly.

Her voice very small, she said, "I did send Asher away, and then in Palm Beach, I realized how much I wanted him. That's why I came home. I was going after him, as a woman would, but he and Bonnie walked in Friday night—she thought I was still in Florida, he didn't know she was my daughter—and I had no idea they'd just been married."

With great effort Elizabeth controlled herself; she would *not* break down and cry! "Bonnie didn't know we knew each other, that we'd been together, but whoever it is that controls our destinies made sure she found out. I won't go into how, but it was dreadful! She ran out of the house, and Asher followed her. I haven't heard from her since. I don't know where she is, I don't know what to do, and worst of all, *I hate her!* I hate my own daughter for taking the man I want, and I hate myself for hating her!"

Her control snapped, and she sobbed, long, racking sobs.

The few people in the lounge looked their way.

"Jesus Christ!" Calhoun whispered, annoyed with himself for being so harsh. He pulled his chair close and put his arms around Elizabeth. "Stop crying, Liz. Come on, let's go back to the house, heat up the sauna, and sweat out our sorrows."

She got up and he leaned heavily on her.

226

"You'll have to drive, old girl; I've had too much to drink."

Elizabeth was in the shower when the phone rang.

"I'll get it," Calhoun called from downstairs. The sauna and the shower had sobered him, and he lay relaxed on the sofa. Reaching lazily, he picked up the receiver. "Calhoun speaking."

His shaggy red eyebrows rose at the voice in his ear. "Just a minute," he said. "Elizabeth's in the shower."

"Wait! Don't call her. God, I'm glad you're there! Listen to me first!"

As he listened Calhoun went rigid. Slowly, painfully, he got to his feet. Deep lines again etched his face. When the person finished speaking, Calhoun said hoarsely, "We'll leave immediately. Wait for us—you might need me."

Elizabeth came out onto the upstairs landing, a bath towel wrapped around her. Eagerly she said, "If it's Bonnie, tell her to hold on."

Slowly Calhoun hung up the phone.

She looked at him questioningly. "Tom, who was it?"

The look he gave her was filled with such sorrow she cried, "My God, Tom! What is it?"

Chapter Nineteen

BRONWYN waited for Dave Bradley at the Collins lift on Thursday morning. He was to join her after his breakfast meeting at Goldminer's Daughter with ski shop personnel and instructors. Skiers milled about, waiting for the lifts to open at nine-thirty. A long line had already formed, and Bronwyn was edging towards the maze when she heard Bradley call her name.

Stepping aside, she watched admiringly as he skied towards her in a jaunty skating step, poles tucked under one arm, powder gaiters zipped to his knees. He wore a navy blue one-piece stretch suit with red and white striped padding at the shoulders, elbows, and knees, blue leather gloves, and a white knit hat and turtleneck shirt with "Rossignol" emblazoned in blue. She couldn't help grinning; she remembered how carelessly he used to dress. Now he looked like a fashion page in *Ski* magazine.

Understanding her grin, he smiled, eyeing her figure in a skin-tight teal-blue suit. "And when did you start wearing *Ellesse?* I remember how tough it was to get you out of baggy warmups and into racing clothes."

"I've become shallow and self-indulgent," she said laughingly, falling in beside him.

"Can you imagine how mobbed this place would be if the road was open?" he remarked, looking around at the crowd. "Alf told me they had a slide down below Snowbird." Reaching into his fanny pack, he took out two beepers used when skiing in avalanche country and handed one to Bronwyn. "Here, put this on."

"Good old careful coach," she said with a sigh.

"Don't argue, Bon, just wear it."

They put the beepers on and taking her by the arm, Bradley steered her to the adjacent lift.

"Let's take Wildcat up, the line's shorter. We'll take a quick run down Warmup and cut through the trees above the Watson Shelter to Germania."

"Good idea," she agreed. The lifts began loading as they stepped into line, and soon they were in the chair moving up the face of the mountain.

"We couldn't ask for a more beautiful day," Bronwyn said, hunching forward, elbows on her knees, poles dangling.

Amusement touched Bradley's face as he looked at her. How eager she was to hit the powder. She had her goggles on, and her hair was tied back in a bright scarf. He remembered that hunched over, at-the-ready stance from when she was a young racer and they had ridden the lifts together to the starting gate. He could swear he was back ten years.

She's hardly changed, he thought, but then people never change. Their natures, their habits just become more set, like clay hardening. She'd been an aloof, private kid; now she was an even more reserved woman. He had learned little last night about her marriage, but he had ferreted out that her husband was Asher Jacobs, President of ICC. That was a bit of all right—but was *she* all right? Something was wrong; she was all pulled into herself. *Forget it, Bradley!* he told himself. *Enjoy the day.*

229

He ran his hand down her back. She sat up at his touch and leaned against his arm. His goggles atop his head, Bradley closed his eyes to the sun, breathing deeply the sweet fragrance of a mountain morning.

"Is there anything in life more beautiful than right now?" he mused.

Bronwyn raised her goggles, turning her face up into the sun.

"You know, Dave," she said quietly, "every time I ride a chair-lift on a morning like this, I feel that if everything ended right now, it would be okay. I've had enough."

He squeezed her shoulder. "Not me! I want to ski and hump until I'm ninety. And then I'll be happy to sit in the timing shack." He opened his eyes and ran his fingers along her smooth cheek. "How can you tie yourself to a desk, when all this is out here? Jesus, Bon, life's so damn short."

She looked around at the mountains. "I've been thinking about that." They rode along a hillside thick with stands of blue spruce, their branches bent with snow, shading steep, winding trails. The trees came so close Bronwyn reached out, trying to flick snow from a branch with the tip of her ski pole. She loved skiing these shadowy ravines—they were like a mysterious, bowered sanctuary. Below them, two instructors, knee-deep in the powder, threaded expertly through the trees. Recognizing them, Bradley called out, "Hey Gene—Nick—keep those hands square!"

Without breaking their speed, they waved, one calling back, "Hey, turkey!"

Rattling over the pulleys, the chair cleared mid-station. As they approached the top, the Wildcat ridge came into view, and the lofty Wasatch wilderness unfolded in a vast cyclorama, its beauty as chaste as a Victorian bride, white peak topping white peak, reaching primly into a flawless blue sky. Directly above loomed the north face of Mount Baldy, but few climbed this long route to the chutes. Their own climb would be along Baldy's shorter but craggier eastern ridge, reached from the top of the Germania lift.

They looked westward, across the ridge, down the deep valley towards Snowbird. Bradley nudged her. "If the

Keyhole access is open, what about cutting over the ridge tomorrow to Snowbird? We'll ski the bumps, have lunch, and take a shuttle back."

"Let me think about that," Bronwyn said, touching her skis to the ramp. They skied off to the side, stopping to tighten their boots and pull their gaiters up high. They lowered their goggles and nodded to each other.

"Let's go!" Bradley yelled, leaping over the edge and onto the steep. Instantly he was thigh-deep in fluffy powder, his body moving up and down, his hands square, making smooth, wide S-turns. Bronwyn followed, her weight slightly back, her turns as beautifully even. She crossed his tracks with such precision, they left a long pattern of perfect eights behind. The light, dry powder flew above their heads. It was like skiing in a sun storm, before the snow crystals had time to set. Rhythmically they moved down the slope, their bodies in graceful unison cutting a trail so clean, skiers riding the Collins lift nudged each other, pointing at their tracks.

Exhilaration raced through Bronwyn as they picked up speed. Bradley's trail scattered snow on her face, misting her goggles. She couldn't see or hear her skis and she felt as though she floated in cool, soft clouds. The steep gully bottomed out just above the trees, but Bradley did not slow down, and Bronwyn stayed on his heels. She watched him hit the rise with a spread-eagle jump. Laughing, she did the same. Her arms spread wide, her feet kicked out high, and her hair, tied in the green and blue scarf, streamed behind her. As she soared, she let out a joyous yell, her body in the tight teal suit, sleek as a bird in flight.

Dropping into a thickly forested slope, they snaked through the tall spruce in short, quick, slalom turns, slowing only when the hill joined Main Street, a trafficked trail leading to the Germania lift. At the lift line, Bradley stopped in a turn that spewed snow. He pushed his goggles back and grinned at Bronwyn right behind him.

"You've still got it, kid. I felt your breath on my ass."

"You bastard," she giggled. "You never let us jump like that, and here you are, spread-eagling it at high speed."

Pulling a kerchief from his pocket, he raised her goggles and wiped the wetness from her face. "That's because I'm now a Vice President. I no longer have to set a good example." His eyebrow arched wickedly.

Her eyes shone with a happiness he had not seen in them the night before. Now she looked like the girl he had known, her face full of life and joy.

"Really turns you on, doesn't it?" he said softly.

"Like nothing else." She smiled, taking the kerchief from him and drying his face. "Come on, coach, let's go to the top."

In the chairlift Bradley pointed across the wide valley between Sugarloaf and Baldy to Wildcat, where their tracks were still visible. "Not bad for an old woman. You must have had a good teacher."

She kicked his thigh with hers and snorted. "And a modest one. In the chutes, Dave, I go first. Let's see if you can cross my tracks as pretty as that."

"That depends on whether you can still climb. All that damn smoking doesn't do your wind any good. I never thought you'd be dumb enough to smoke."

"We can't all be pure and perfect." She'd let nothing spoil this day for her. Until Saturday, when she returned to New York, all she wanted to think about was how the sun felt on her face, how the breeze tugged at her hair, and how silently her skis floated, as though she levitated through some ethereal cosmos. It was why she had not phoned Elizabeth, nor would she call Asher again until she got back to her apartment.

Beneath the chair powerful, orange-colored Cats lumbered, dragging wide, steel meshes, packing the main trails for those who could not ski powder. Some skiers gave the unpacked hillsides a good try, sitting back awkwardly, managing to make a turn or two before they tumbled, snow filling their mouths. Others struggled, trying to keep their skis from spreading, and when they fell, struggled to put their skis back on in the deep fluff. A young woman careened down a gentle slope, yelling, "Oooooh, it's just like bubble bath!" She lost control and sat down, laughing. Bradley and Bronwyn laughed with her.

From the Germania lift they had a perfect view across

the vast, treeless slopes of Ballroom, a white-crested, icy sea on which skiers, like surfers, rode undulating, frozen waves. Above towered Mount Baldy, over 11,000 feet high, its sloping ridge a series of craggy pockets which held snow throughout the year. When gorged with snow, as they were now, the rockbound ravines became smooth, powdery chutes challenging the best of skiers.

"Look!" Bronwyn exclaimed, pointing to a group of skiers approaching the chutes.

Bradley whistled in surprise. "Must be the ski patrol. No one else could get up there so early. The climb takes at least forty minutes and the lifts just opened."

"If it is the patrol, I don't mind," Bronwyn said. "They've earned first run."

"It looks like they're only taking two chutes," observed Bradley. The skiers began their descent through the sheer, narrow gorges, skiing expertly, four to a chute, dead center, straight down the fall line, laying two sets of smooth eights in each course.

"Isn't that beautiful?" Bronwyn breathed, her eyes skiing with them, making every turn, her body feeling the flow of their methodical movements.

Bradley peered across the valley. "I think they doubled up because number three's got crud at the top."

She followed his eyes. "You may be right, but below the cliff it looks fantastic. If the top is bad we can ski down the ridge and cut over into the chute lower down."

"That's it!" he agreed. "We'll know more when we get close."

They were on their feet the moment the chair reached the ramp, and forty minutes later they sat in the sun on top of Baldy, cleaning their goggles, resting after the arduous climb.

Bronwyn breathed heavily. "My wind sure isn't what it used to be."

"What did you expect? Fill your body with garbage and it becomes garbage."

"Okay, Mr. Clean, knock it off. Look around you." She waved her arm in a sweeping arc. To the south the snow-capped range reached endlessly towards the Arizona

233

border; to the east the Uinta Mountains spread tor on tor into Colorado, and far below, the tiny, cloistered town of Alta huddled in the cul-de-sac of the canyon.

Bradley turned and looked at her. "What is it about being on top of a mountain that makes you want to whisper? It's like being in church." He leaned back on his elbow. "Can you imagine, some people live all their lives and die without ever seeing the view from the top of a mountain?"

Bronwyn squinted into the horizon, her brow creased against the sun. She sighed and spoke so softly Bradley bent close to hear her. "What about those who see nothing but the view from a slum window, a jail cell, or a hospital bed?" She shuddered. "I couldn't handle that. I'm not sure I can even handle going back to New York."

Bradley tried to read her eyes behind her narrowed lids. Even as a young girl she had had a dark side he could never fathom. As he had done whenever her moodiness erupted, he fondly tugged the end of her hair tied in a pony tail. "You can handle anything, Bon." He got up and extended his hand. "Come on, nicotine Nellie, let's see if you've still got steel in those legs."

Ignoring his hand, she got up lithely.

"When we bottom out, Dave, let's track all through Ballroom and then race to the lift. Loser buys lunch. Okay?"

He grinned. "You're on!"

They tightened their boots, put on their goggles, and tested their beepers. Bronwyn leading, they moved single file along the ridge, past the steep cornices rimming the first two chutes, to the last and steepest channel. It was the most treacherous of the ravines narrowing into a one-skier run just before the steep dropped into the open terrain of Ballroom. The jagged cliffs at this point fall sharply one hundred feet or more.

Bronwyn stopped, disappointed. The ski patrol had posted a "Closed" sign at the top. She looked down the chute; it was like looking down the wall of a giant teacup.

"Damn it, Dave, let's ski it anyway."

He came to her side, and supporting himself on his poles he leaned out, checking the slope.

He shook his head. "No way. There's real garbage where they shot down the overhang. But down below it's clean. Let's ski the ridge and cut back into the chute above the cliff—that's where it's steepest anyway. But be careful. It's a sharp right turn back into the chute. One false move and you're a bird in thin air. I better go first."

She stopped him, reaching over and kissing his cheek lightly.

"Don't worry, coach, I'm a big girl. Follow me."

She pushed off onto the *arête;* a hundred yards down she turned into the fall line, the same excitement rising in her as when she had been a racer breaking out of the starting gate. The snowfield fell at a fifty degree incline, getting steeper as it funneled into the chute. She tucked a joyous yell deep inside her; in an avalanche-prone chute, all she dared was a sibilant "WHOOSH!" sliding between her teeth. She carved graceful S-turns and Bradley followed, timing his rhythm to hers.

The run was so vertical that standing up, they could reach out and touch the snow. If inadvertently they did that, they'd lose it—the slightest weight shift uphill, into the mountain, would make them crash. She looked ahead, estimating where she'd have to turn sharply into the chute. She picked up speed as the steep increased. Deep powder billowed around her shoulders—she skied in a cloud, whiteness fogging her goggles. Was it that which distorted her vision?

She missed the turn.

Horrified, Bradley saw her hurtle towards the cliff. Breaking the silence he screamed hoarsely, *"THE CLIFF! JUMP! TURN! TURN!"*

She heard and tried lifting her feet, but momentum had her, catapulting her forward as though she were a rocket, flinging her over the cliff, screaming, *"DAVE! DAVE!"*

She flew through the air like a wounded bird, terrified, her poles dangling from her flailing arms, her hair a vivid plume streaming behind her. The whiteness blinded her, but as her body twisted, she saw blue sky. Her mind reacted. *How far am I falling—how much will it hurt?* flashed through her. And then memory screamed, *FLIP! FLIP!*

235

CHOICES

Instinctively her legs curled, her head tucked, her arms spread wide, and like some wonderfully colorful bird of paradise, her body soared, and almost as though she were in slow motion, she turned completely over, her knees tucked to her chest. *Let me make it! Let me make it!* Her head pounded. Snow came at her, enveloping her . . . so soft . . . so cool. Hope swept her and she relaxed slightly, but then she struck rock beneath the snow. Her legs crunched, her head snapped back—hard! Her goggles and scarf flew off at the impact—her hair tumbled, spilling copper across the whiteness of the snow, across the whiteness of her face. Excruciating pain pitched through her, a poison-tipped shaft stabbing her feet, shooting up her spine, into her brain. She wailed and knew no more.

Chapter Twenty

ASHER was in a happy mood as he left the Palm on Second Avenue, where he had just lunched with Drew Mednam. Their discussions and the memory of Bronwyn's call the night before added lightness to his step as he strolled west towards Fifth Avenue. Bronwyn would be pleased with their offer—her own imprint, total autonomy. He could hardly wait to tell her, but he would not phone her in Utah; he wanted to watch the expression in her eyes when he surprised her with his news. He would meet her plane Saturday; even though she had not said when she would arrive, finding out was no problem. Expectation flooded him as he envisioned himself greeting her, holding her in his arms. He lifted his face to the sun streaming through the narrow side street. It was a shining day, the kind of crisp winter day when New York is

237

glorious, when even the grey pavements seem clean and the city crackles with energy.

Picking up his pace to the excitement in his heart, he turned north on Fifth Avenue, passing store windows filled with colorful, lavish displays. Slowing, he began to judge what he saw by how it would look on Bronwyn. Becoming intrigued with his thoughts, he perused one seductive display after another. At Saks he stopped, his senses snared by the costume in the window. The high-cheekboned, titian-haired mannequin stood against a cerulean background, her delicate, molded hands holding an Afghan hound so real-looking, Asher could almost hear it pant. She was dressed in a creamy leather suit, so buttery soft it draped in silk-like folds. The jacket had an opulent red fox collar. He had seen a suit just like that once, long ago. He went inside.

Never had he enjoyed shopping so much. He bought the suit and then wandered through the store searching for the special, the unique, delighting the salesgirls with his purchases. They eyed him invitingly, envying the woman for whom he bought such exquisite, tasteful gifts.

Leaving Saks he continued up Fifth Avenue, past St. Patrick's Cathedral, its Gothic spires lit bluish-pink by the setting sun. He waited at the light on 52nd Street and as it changed, he changed his mind. Turning back, he went into Cartiers. It was near closing time but the clerk responded warmly, his practiced eye recognizing a man of wealth, eager to buy. Asher asked to see an emerald ring. After carefully examining several, he chose a superb round stone set in gold, circled with small diamonds. Proffering his identification, Asher told the salesman to send the bill to his office—he would take the ring with him. With a pleased smile the clerk watched him sign the receipt, aware he had not asked the price. Asher tucked the green velvet box into his breast pocket and turned to leave. Surprised, he saw the store had closed. He glanced at the ornate overhead clock. He had completely lost track of time. The guard at the door smiled and tipped his hat as he let him out.

The streets were thronged with people hurrying home. Asher flowed with the traffic, caught up in a feeling of euphoria. He entered the lobby of the ICC building, and a uniformed man hurried to him.

"Good evening, Mr. Jacobs. Mrs. Lanstrom said to tell you she's waiting with an important message."

Still thinking of Bronwyn, Asher said offhandedly, "Thank you, Karl." The man accompanied him to the executive elevator.

Claire Lanstrom paced impatiently. Where could he be? In the twelve years she had worked for Asher Jacobs she could not remember a time as unsettling as the past two weeks. Even when his wife had been killed, he had been predictable. But since Christmas he had been a different man, cancelling appointments, making unexpected changes in her precise scheduling, and then, last Monday, announcing he had been married New Year's Eve! And where was his wife? Was that what the phone calls from Utah were all about? The man she had spoken to would give no details but her instincts told her something was very wrong, and so she had waited even though Axel hated it when she got home late. Axel expected her to prepare their dinner—he was so European, but it was exactly his European traits which had attracted her, prompting her to marry the young shipwright when she'd met him in Sweden on her vacation last year. And she was surprised to find how much she loved him. For so long she'd thought the only man for her was Asher Jacobs.

The door opened and Asher came in. She rushed to him.

"I tried calling you at the Palm, but you'd left. Then I phoned Mr. Mednam. He told me you were on your way back. It's not like you to go off without telling me where I can reach you."

"Hold on, Claire," he said, laughing. "Nothing's that important. I've been out shopping. It's been a long time since I've had such fun. What's all the fuss about?"

Looking at him, his hair blown by the wind, his face glowing with happiness, she felt a familiar twinge, but she buried it quickly. Axel Lanstrom was no Asher Jacobs, but he was a placid cove in which she gladly anchored after five, when once she had drifted rudderless through singles bars.

She took his coat as he shrugged out of it. "A David Bradley has been calling from Utah. He wouldn't tell me what it was about, but he said it was urgent and I was to contact you immediately. When I couldn't reach you I became concerned—it sounded personal."

All Asher heard was "Utah." He looked at her sharply. "Did he leave a number?"

"Several times. Do you want me to get it for you?"

"No, I'll call. Thank you for staying."

She handed him the memo and he hurried into his office, calling back, "I'll leave a message on the Dictaphone if there's any problem." He closed the doors behind him, went to his desk and picked up his private line, punching in the area code and number Claire Lanstrom had typed on the note, where she had also indicated the time of each call. There had been five calls since 3:30. Damn!

He waited impatiently as the phone rang and rang. Finally a voice rattled: "LDS . . . one moment, please."

Asher fumed as he was put on hold. *LDS?* he wondered. *What the hell is LDS?*

The voice came back on and he said quickly, "One moment—don't put me on hold again. I'm calling from New York. First, what is LDS? And then I want extension two-three-three."

"I'm sorry," the operator drawled, "but we're very busy. LDS is the Hospital of Latter Day Saints. Hold on, I'm ringing extension two-three-three."

Asher went cold.

The phone rang in his ear. It seemed minutes before someone answered, "Waiting room."

"David Bradley, please."

"One moment."

Asher drummed his fingers on the desk.

"Mr. Jacobs?" The man's voice was unfamiliar. "We've never met. I was Bonnie's racing coach and I ran into her at the lodge last night. Today we skied together." He hesitated briefly. "There's been an accident, but she's getting the best of treatment."

Asher sucked in his breath. It was serious; otherwise Bronwyn would have called herself. "How bad is it?"

240

The momentary silence at the other end of the line sent Asher's heart pounding.

"I'm not sure. I was with her when she fell, and I accompanied her to the hospital." He didn't want to tell him on the phone that Bonnie had been brought in by helicopter.

"Who's the doctor treating her?"

"Anthony Andresen, but you won't be able to reach him."

"Why not?"

Again silence, and Asher felt an unreasonable anger surge through him. "Damn it, what are you hiding? I want to know everything, and I want to know it *now!*"

Bradley phrased his next words carefully. "She's hurt her back and she has leg fractures. She was in shock when she reached the hospital, and she had to be stabilized. That's why you can't speak to Andresen. They won't put calls through to the emergency room or the operating room. They've got a fine trauma team here, experienced in handling ski injuries."

Asher quieted. He had no right to vent his feelings on Bradley. "Thank you for calling. I couldn't return your calls earlier. I was out of my office all afternoon." Emotion welled in him. All that time he'd felt so close to her, she'd . . . he put his hand over his eyes, pulling her closer. He saw her in his arms those wonderful mornings . . . he walked with her on a deserted beach . . . and now . . .

Bradley interrupted his thoughts. "Mr. Jacobs, would you call Bonnie's mother? I can't bring myself to do that. They're so close, I can't tell her about this."

Fear choked Asher. It *was* more serious than Bradley would admit. Foreboding gripped him. "I'll take care of it. We'll fly out there tonight."

"Are you sure there are flights out of New York into Salt Lake this late?"

"It doesn't matter. I have a plane. Thank you again, Mr. Bradley." Fighting the worry in him, Asher pressed the button disconnecting Bradley. He then phoned Jeff Gordon, his pilot, and tersely made the necessary arrangements. When he had finished, he sat, the receiver still in his hand. He had to call Elizabeth; even if Bradley had not

241

asked him to, it was something he had to do. He began to place the call, and then he put the phone down.

He sank back into his chair, despondency taking hold of him. Closing his eyes, he saw Elizabeth that first night on the mountain—how vulnerable she had been, battered by the wind, desperately trying to hold on to her dignity, and then laughing in wild, wonderful abandon. Would she ever laugh that way again? A pulse pounded in his head. Because of him Bronwyn had gone off to Utah—how could he now face Elizabeth? All he ever brought to women was sadness and tragedy.

He sat up, and with a hand as heavy as iron he pressed the buttons on the phone, listening to tones echoing across a void so vast it seemed to join trillions of like tones echoing at the same time. When he heard Calhoun's voice, he breathed gratefully.

Elizabeth sped at eighty miles an hour towards Newark Airport. A deadening coldness, as though she raced death on a darkened track, gripped her, and she handled Calhoun's heavy Continental with a steady relentlessness that belied her anxiety. Calhoun had told her *so little*. Only that Bonnie had been hurt skiing and that Asher waited at Newark to fly them to Salt Lake City. But why was Bonnie in Alta and Asher in New York? She had heard Calhoun call the hospital as she dressed, but when she had questioned him he said it was too early to know anything definite. She glanced at Calhoun out of the corner of her eye. He slouched in the big seat, his head against the headrest, his eyes closed. He had asked her to drive, telling her he still had too much alcohol in his blood, but she knew it was a ruse—if she drove, he could pretend to be sleeping, cutting off her questions.

Under heavy-lidded eyes Calhoun tried to shroud himself with professional detachment. To break bad news was terrible. With strangers, at least, unfamiliarity stood like protective glass, but he had known Bonnie since she was a baby, and only the raw gut of affection and love stood between his words and Elizabeth. He opened his eyes only when he heard the noises of the airport.

Pulling into the parking lot opposite the baggage claim

242

area, Elizabeth saw Asher pacing the curb, his hands plunged into the pockets of his trench coat. Motioning her to a reserved parking space, he had her door open even before she stopped. He was pallid under his tan, his mouth a grim slash in his stony face, but he still looked so attractive, an unwanted tremor hit her when he helped her from the car. She withdrew her hand, but he grasped her arm as he shook hands with Calhoun. Then he hurried them through the arrivals section, into a door marked "No Admittance," and out onto the tarmac, where a Lear jet looking like a silver bullet idled smoothly.

They ran up the stairs and once inside, an attendant slammed the door shut and the aircraft began to back out. The young man took their coats and they sank into seats facing each other, buckling their seat belts as the plane taxied to the runway. Soon, with a powerful thrust, the jet lifted off steeply.

Elizabeth took a deep breath, a numbing weariness filling her. She looked at Asher sitting opposite and saw the worry in his face. The same questions which had crowded her mind as she had driven to the airport now tumbled in her. Why was Bonnie in Utah? Why weren't they together? He had said he'd be taking Bonnie abroad. What had happened? Who told him Bonnie'd been hurt? How had she been hurt?

The attendant interrupted her thoughts. Would they like a drink? Drink? Elizabeth had difficulty sorting out the question from the others in her head. Asher leaned towards her and said gently, "Would you like anything, Elizabeth? Wine—Scotch—juice?"

"It doesn't matter, whatever you're drinking."

He ordered Scotch for both of them. Calhoun asked for ginger ale and they drank silently. Elizabeth glanced furtively at Asher, guilt heavy in her. Bonnie lay hurt, and here she sat remembering him as he had made love to her. She tore her eyes away and caught Calhoun watching her. The blood rose in her face. Turning abruptly to the window, she stared unseeing into the blackness.

When the plane reached cruising altitude the young man returned, gleaming white dinner napkins in his hand. "Are you ready for dinner?" he asked.

243

Calhoun's eyes shot open and for the first time that evening, he smiled. "Whatever it is, I'll take doubles."

The attendant returned with plates of steaming roast beef, buttered carrots, and browned potatoes. There was also a crisp green salad with Belgian endive.

"You have ESP, Jacobs," Calhoun said appreciatively, cutting into the tender, rare beef. "I haven't eaten all day."

The young man poured a robust red Bordeaux into their wine glasses.

"I hoped a heavy meal might help us sleep," Asher said. "There are usually strong head winds this time of year. The flight will take at least five hours, so the rear seats have been made up into beds."

For dessert there were Anjou pears, a creamy Brie, and a fine Auselese wine. Twirling his wine glass to the light, Calhoun looked at Asher. No wonder Elizabeth had fallen for him. Wryly he said, "You can't tell me this is aircraft catering—you must have called in Lutece."

"It helps to know people," Asher replied, and then he leaned towards the big man. "Dr. Calhoun, I can't tell you how grateful I am that you're accompanying us. I hope you'll allow me to make it up to you."

Their eyes met. "I will, Jacobs."

Asher knew Calhoun meant not for himself.

Elizabeth's eyes grew heavy even before the trays were cleared. Thanking Asher and squeezing Calhoun's hand, she got up and followed the steward aft, where she drowsily fell onto the bed. Later, Asher and Calhoun also lay down; the lights were turned off and they slept, helped by the food, the wine, and the drone of the engines.

They arrived at the hospital after midnight, and Calhoun went immediately to consult with the doctors treating Bronwyn. Elizabeth and Asher found David Bradley still in the waiting room. He rose quickly as they came in and went to embrace Elizabeth.

"I regret seeing you again under these circumstances," he said.

Her eyes filled with tears, and she held onto him.

"Oh Dave, thank God you were with her. Thank you so

244

much for waiting. Please tell me what happened. I know so little."

Asher stood silent. He knew he should be grateful, but it rankled that someone else had been with Bronwyn when she needed him most. And this man and Bronwyn had to have been close: why else would he have waited all these hours and gone to so much trouble? A thought he hated crossed his mind. Had they been together last night? With difficulty, he said, "How do you do, Mr. Bradley. I'm Bronwyn's husband. We spoke on the phone." He did not extend his hand.

With the quickness brought on by years of keenly observing the most minute movements in a person's body, Bradley saw the stiffness in Asher and sensed his resentment. He felt an unfamiliar and unwelcome jealousy rise in him as he measured the man she'd married. Was it because way, way in the back of his mind he still wanted her? Jacobs looked young for someone in his fifties, he had to give him that, but there was an authoritarian manner in the man that he recognized in himself, and for someone as independent as Bonnie, coping with dominance would be difficult—he knew that from all too personal experience.

Bradley nodded briefly, acknowledging Asher, and then he turned his attention to Elizabeth, trying to soothe her fears as gently as possible. He knew he had to keep her from asking questions he did not want to answer; he had seen too many ski injuries not to know Bonnie had been badly hurt, so he went into minutiae that would keep Elizabeth's mind busy.

"The fall wasn't Bonnie's fault. The powder was deep, we were skiing fast, and you know, Elizabeth, how fresh fluff flies all around and obscures your vision. Bonnie missed a turn and she landed in deep snow." He couldn't tell her Bonnie had gone off a hundred-foot cliff. "Someone on the chair-lift must have seen her fall and called the patrol because they were there in minutes. They put her into a KED. It's like a backboard with a padded blanket— it keeps a skier rigid and prevents further injury on the rescue sled. The patrol eased that sled down as though she were glass, and when we reached Ballroom, a Life-Flight helicopter was already there. It's wonderful

245

how quickly and efficiently the rescue operations are coordinated here—nothing like that happens in Europe. I went with her in the chopper, and the air medics treated her for shock on the way in; when we arrived at the hospital the trauma team took over. She couldn't be in better hands, Elizabeth." He looked at Asher. "I'd like to wait until there's definite word on her condition."

Asher nodded. "If you wish."

They were escorted to the doctors' lounge, and Asher knew the preferential treatment was because of Calhoun. He sank into an easy chair and put his hands over his eyes, trying to contain the despondency which had risen in him as Bradley spoke; he had perceived the real truth behind the carefully chosen words.

After what seemed hours, the door swung open. They all jumped up nervously. Calhoun came in, accompanied by two men dressed in green surgical robes. Asher searched their expressionless faces, and the apprehension in him became electric. Doctors' faces are like molded plastic when news is not good.

Calhoun introduced the two physicians. The shorter, older man sat down and motioned for them to do the same. He inclined his head towards Calhoun, and Elizabeth's friend began to speak.

"Bonnie was lucky. The ski patrol got to her quickly, the air medics knew just what to do, and the team here is skilled at handling ski injuries." Asher tried hard to hear beyond the precision in Calhoun's voice—he wanted to shout, *Get on with it! How bad is it?* Had he known how Calhoun fought to keep himself objective, he would have felt a deep sorrow for this man who had never inured himself to the tragedy of being a doctor, to the helplessness of human feelings.

Calhoun continued. "She was in neurogenic shock when she reached the hospital. This was stabilized before anything else could be done." He paused and looked at Elizabeth and then at Asher. Asher felt his heart turn over as Calhoun said, "Her injuries are severe."

A sob escaped Elizabeth's tightly drawn lips.

Indicating his colleagues, Calhoun became increasingly

clinical, as if he were describing smashed china being pieced together. "Dr. Andresen is a neurosurgeon; Dr. Nichols, an orthopedic surgeon. Bronwyn has fractured heels, compound tibia fractures, and a fractured pelvis." He cleared his throat, trying to delay what he had to say next. Elizabeth's eyes were fastened on him, and he had to look away.

The blood drained from her face. "Tom!" she cried chokingly, "what are you trying to tell me?"

He leaned across the table and took her hands in his. How cold they were! He rubbed the back of her hands with his large thumbs.

Asher's head began to pound and a lump rose in his throat.

Calhoun tried a strange, hopeful smile, but it disintegrated on his face. "God stretched out his hand and caught her, Elizabeth, because she survived a fall that should have been fatal—but she has a C6-C7 cervical fracture. We don't know yet whether it's a complete or incomplete injury because she's in spinal shock with the resultant edema; there is compression on the cord, but this could be the swelling. The shock can last for several days, in rare cases for several weeks, and until it subsides we can't make any definite prognosis."

Asher felt a numbness like death take hold of him.

Elizabeth wrested her hands from Calhoun and stared at him with eyes so dark they seemed all black pupil. She stumbled to her feet.

"No! Oh no! Don't tell me that! A fractured neck! Please don't say that. Even when Bonnie raced I never thought of that! She'll never walk again—never move again! Oh my God!" Her face contorted with grief, and tears spilled down her cheeks.

Calhoun got up heavily and enclosed her in his arms. He put his head on hers and said, so quietly she had to stop crying to hear him, "Elizabeth, listen to me and listen carefully. People recover from fractured necks as they recover from other fractures, provided there is no transection of the cord, or other complete injuries. It's too early to make any judgments, *or to make any promises,* but

247

Bonnie is young, strong, with good muscularity, and there is no transection, so if the injury is *not complete*, there is *hope*, do you understand me? *Hope."*

She clung to him as she clung to his words.

"Come," he said. "We're all very, very tired."

Asher sat, unable to move. He bowed his head; he did not want Elizabeth to see the tears in his eyes.

Bradley let out a silent sigh of relief. He had suspected a neck injury the moment he had seen Bonnie sprawled in the snow, and as he had helped the ski patrol carefully immobilize her in a neck brace and the KED, all he could think of was another skier he had seen with a similar injury. But that fracture *had* transected the cord, and the man was paralyzed for life. Calhoun was right. Bonnie was lucky. Lucky? My God! She faced months of confinement and pain. And what if it was a complete injury? She would be paralyzed—she could never take that! His throat tightened as he thought of her waking up and finding out. Slowly he got up and followed the doctors and Elizabeth out of the room.

Asher sat alone.

It was Saturday before Asher and Elizabeth were permitted to visit Bronwyn. Calhoun left for the hospital early after convincing them at breakfast to take a long walk, perhaps down to Temple Square. He did not want them at the hospital before eleven. Their first sight of Bronwyn would be traumatic enough without their witnessing the extensive and complicated nursing routine.

Dave Bradley waited for Calhoun in the lobby of the hospital. Calhoun almost walked by without recognizing him. Bradley was dressed in a tweed business suit and carried an overcoat on his arm.

"Good morning, Dr. Calhoun," he said. "My plane leaves at ten. Might I see Bonnie before I take off?"

"Of course, come with me."

Bradley fell into step beside him.

"Have you ever seen someone with a cervical injury?" Calhoun asked.

"Yes, once—a racer. Bonnie knew him—we were there

when he crashed—but he had head injuries. He didn't make it."

"He was lucky."

Bradley stopped. Calhoun did not break his stride, and Bradley caught up with him at the elevator. "That's strange for you to say."

Pressing the elevator button, Calhoun looked at him. "Mr. Bradley, that racer knew nothing but the peace death brings."

Silently they rode up to the intensive care floor.

Bronwyn was being catherized when they arrived. Calhoun went to check her charts at the nurses' station, and Bradley walked down the long hallway to the windows. Morning sun was gentle on the neatly laid out grid of the city, tinging the snowy peaks to the east with soft pastels shading from peach to pink to orange. How fragrant it had been driving in from Alta! He'd rolled down the windows to catch the brisk alpine air. He looked towards the mountains and saw Bronwyn that morning atop Baldy, her eyes narrowed to the sun, her face glistening with the sweat they had raised in their climb. He remembered her words and shuddered. He looked back down the corridor. Blank walls, blank doorways, the smell of disinfectant.

An aching sadness consumed him, and he knew he could not bear to see her bolted into traction—a poor, crippled bird. He had remembered her all these years like the beautiful swallow she had been. He turned back to the windows, to the mountains ringing the flat, arid valley. That was how he wanted to see her, as she rode the lifts, hunched over in her eagerness to hit the course, flying—her copper hair streaming, her body free, alive with joy.

He walked back to the nurses' station and said to Calhoun:

"I can't miss my plane—please tell Bonnie I was here. Maybe later, on my way back East . . ." He couldn't meet Calhoun's eyes.

"I understand," Calhoun said quietly.

Bradley looked at him then. *No, you can't understand,* he thought. *You can't know what injury means to those whose bodies bring them joy—who glory in the thrill of challenging the clock, breaking the tape, of pitting their will, their muscle against all odds. For someone raised like that, and for those of us who nurture that perfection, crippling is a horror we sometimes can't face.*

Bradley turned to the elevator and Calhoun walked with him.

"Mr. Bradley, what you're feeling is natural, so don't let guilt get to you. Actually it's better for Bonnie right now if you don't see her. The less she's reminded of the past, the quicker she'll adjust."

He stuck his hand out. "Thank you for all you did."

Bradley grasped the hand. What strength, what life he felt in its freckled grip! "Tell Elizabeth I'll be in touch."

The elevator came and he was gone.

Calhoun had tried to prepare Elizabeth and Asher for what to expect when they saw Bronwyn, but when she walked into the room and saw her daughter, the shock was too much for Elizabeth. She clung weakly to Calhoun, sobbing quietly, tears blinding her. Sternly he took her outside, into the corridor. His voice was a whip.

"Elizabeth! I don't want her to hear you cry or see your tears! You must get hold of yourself!"

"I'm sorry." Elizabeth wept, taking gulping breaths. She brought herself under control. "I'm all right now, Tom. I promise."

They went back into the room. Asher stood by the bed, his face dark, deep circles under his eyes. A pulse ticked in his jaw as he looked down at Bronwyn.

The beautiful oval face was remarkably untouched—her skin tawny with the sheen of a winter tan. Were it not for the stainless steel traction around her head, Asher would have thought she merely slept. But her copper hair was shaved at the sides, and in the ugly white patches, bolts had been driven into her skull to hold the halo traction; bracing the cage was a rigid steel frame attached to her shoulders. Her legs, encased in long leg casts, hung suspended in a maze of pulleys.

Gazing at his wife, a painful and guilty realization drove a bolt into his own skull. Never had he seen the shadow of death on one he loved. His parents' agony he could only

250

imagine; he had not witnessed their suffering, or kissed their cold lips. What they had found of Michael and Marguerite had been sent back East in sealed caskets. And even Eleanore—her remains had been cremated and strewn over the wilderness she loved. Never had he witnessed their agony, and now as he tenderly took Bronwyn's hand, all those agonies tightened in him. Her hand lay limp in his. He squeezed her fingers, but they did not respond. He remembered the ring still in his pocket, and unshed tears clouded his eyes as he bent to kiss the gold wedding band on her left hand. There was no response in her at all. He kissed her gently on the cheek. "Hello," he said, his voice thick.

Her eyes opened briefly.

"Hello, darling," he said again, moving so that his face was directly in front of her.

She looked at him. "I'm sorry," she whispered and closed her eyes.

"Keep talking to her," Calhoun said.

"Bronwyn . . . Bronwyn, open your eyes." When she did, Asher smiled into them. "Even here, darling, you've arranged for the coldest room in the place."

Her lips curved slightly, a smile almost appearing. "Told you I was strange," she said sleepily.

Taking Elizabeth by the arm, Calhoun went to the foot of the bed.

"Hi, Bonnie," he said lightly. "Do you know who I am?"

Slowly Bronwyn focused her eyes on him, and again a semblance of a smile softened her lips. "You taking care of me, Tom?" And then she saw Elizabeth. A slight frown edged between her brows. "Hello, Mother." She closed her eyes. "I was going to call you. I'm sorry—I screwed up." She drifted off.

Elizabeth made a move to her, but Calhoun held her back. He did not like Bronwyn's reaction to her mother. "That's enough for now," he said.

Reluctantly Asher let go of Bronwyn's hand. Bending over again, he kissed her lips. Her eyelids fluttered and he kissed them softly, carefully maneuvering his head past the traction.

Elizabeth watched, pain stabbing her, a pain that brought guilt. Was it the pain of seeing Bonnie like this—or was it the pain of seeing the depth of Asher's love? Calhoun steered her outside. In the corridor he turned to them.

"After a while she won't be this heavily sedated. I know how you feel about drugs, Elizabeth, and don't worry, there's little danger she'll become addicted. We don't use morphine in cervical injuries because it has a depressive effect on respiratory function. She's getting only mild analgesics such as aspirin compounds and codeine."

"Why is the room so cold?" Asher asked.

Leading them into the lounge, Calhoun explained. "Patients in spinal shock can't sweat below the level of their injury, and when the body can't lose heat they become feverish. Bonnie must be kept cool, but not too cold, because pneumonia is always a danger."

"How long before she can be moved back to New York?"

"That depends." Calhoun saw Asher's grimace. "I know that sounds like a medical cop-out, but it's hard to tell at this time. I'd guess anywhere from three to six months. And I'm going to tell you something else you won't like."

"I won't go back without her," Asher said quietly.

Sweet Jesus! Calhoun thought. *If only all we had to deal with were patients.* He faced Asher grimly. "The last thing Bonnie needs now is you. What were her first words? *'I'm sorry.'* She's *sorry!* She doesn't know yet how badly she's hurt, but she feels guilty. Damn it, Asher! Guilt is a terribly debilitating side effect, and sympathy is a terrible burden for a patient. They hate themselves for what happened to them, and they hate the pity they see directed at them. Eventually they come to accept their suffering, but it's the suffering they feel they've inflicted on others which drives them up the wall! For Bonnie's sake, return to New York with me. Give her a chance to face what's happened without her having to face you."

"My God, Tom! Do you know what you're asking? I can't leave her!"

Calhoun's look was bleak. "I know, but you must. She

252

needs impersonal, unemotional, professional care. You'd only be in the way, especially now, when her care is constant. She has to be turned frequently, she'll be catherized, fed intravenously—she would detest having either of you witness the indignity to which she will be subjected. She'll be grateful she won't have to put on a cheerful act—she can vent her anger, her misery. She won't think you've deserted her. In fact, she'll bless the slightest bit of privacy. Call her, send flowers, write letters—and try to make her laugh. You're in the right business, Asher. Get her a VCR and a supply of old comedies, the crazy stuff that makes you laugh even when you hurt. Later, when the spinal shock subsides and she's more stable, I'll return with you and you can fly her home."

Elizabeth glared at Calhoun and shook her head stubbornly. "No, Tom, there's no way I'm going back right now and leave her."

Calhoun sighed regretfully. He had hoped to spare her. He didn't want to be cruel, but she left him no choice. No matter her intelligence, at this moment she was a pawn of her emotions, unable to think clearly. The intensity in his eyes underlined his words.

"If you stay, Elizabeth, you will harm her. She can't cope with additional trauma. You know how she reacted when she saw you. Do you have any idea what it will be like for her when she realizes how long and how tough a struggle it's going to be just to *move* again? And with nerve pressure, she might *never* do that! Do you know what that means to a woman like Bonnie? She must face the possibility of paralysis *alone*, and come to terms with it. If it happens, you can't help her, and you can't fill yourself or her with false hopes! Every small step she takes will be because she's struggled to bring life back into that body. She'll become ultrasensitive to every word, every nuance. God! How perceptive people become when they've been hurt! She will see how you feel, Elizabeth— *about everything.*" He looked from her to Asher. "How the hell can she handle *that*, along with her own tragedy?"

Chapter Twenty-one

BRONWYN had long ago learned about injury. Once after crashing in a practice run, she had insisted on racing and won, despite the agony in her boot. Later, X-rays revealed her ankle was broken. Another time, competing in Cortina, she had dislocated her shoulder and skied off the course, refusing the sled. Elizabeth had weaned her on "Invictus" and Bradley had trained her for toughness, infusing her with the power of mind over body.

She comforted herself with positive thoughts, knowing that the healing of bones was as miraculous as life itself. An almost religious trinity, she thought: the bone's vascularity making it bleed—the very blood of bone, its birth, collecting, fastening the break; the blood then organizing into a hematoma—like a wafer, uniting the broken ends with fibrous soft tissue; finally, she imagined the mineral salts depositing, like invading osteoblasts, building, shap-

254

ing her hard bone, forming a healing callus. She was sure of how her bones would knit, but she was uncertain of how fragile might be the slender cord that runs the length of one's back, the sheath of life, the only conducting spiral of nerve impulses to and from the brain.

Try as she might, she could not will her hands to move.

And yet, she knew of many miraculous recoveries: Gene Rankowski, a coach, coming out of a months-long coma after Bobby Downs hit him head-on as Gene reset a gate during the Can-Am trials. Penny Richman winning a Silver with knees so pieced together, inside they looked like crochet. And hadn't Phil Mahre won the World Cup the year after his ankle had been shattered? Her numbness had to be the spinal shock she heard the doctors discuss. Soon, soon, she would move again. And once the damn traction was removed, she'd work at getting well.

But her emotions were not so easily disciplined, and her feelings pitched like a sloop in a heavy sea, some days riding high on the crest of hope, others swamped in depression. A week after the accident, Dr. Andresen phoned Asher and suggested a psychiatrist visit Bronwyn regularly. Asher agreed. And Dr. Wilbur Novatt, a thin-haired, slender man with a weathered sportsman's face, came to see Bronwyn each day. One afternoon he said, "Why not get back to work?"

Her laugh was derisive. "How? Where?"

"Here and right now."

"You've got to be kidding."

"We can have a speaker phone installed and you can dictate to your office in New York. You can even record your recommendations for that sales meeting you're so concerned about. We'll set up a slanted table for reading, and you can dictate your notes and manuscript changes." He paused, lit a cigarette, and took a deep puff. Seeing the hunger in her eyes, he leaned over and put the end between her lips.

"Why didn't you tell me you enjoy smoking?" he asked.

She gave him a surprised look and gratefully took a long drag, savoring the taste of the tobacco. When he took the cigarette from her, she said, "Thank you, but I'm not allowed to smoke."

255

"I know." He smiled. "Neither should I, but what are they going to do—take away your urine bag and throw me out?"

She laughed and he was pleased. They became friends.

One day, delayed by a conference with Bronwyn's doctors concerning her slow nerve recovery, Dr. Novatt walked in late and heard the end of a phone conversation between Bronwyn and her mother. He noted the strain in the young woman's voice and the tightness of her face. After a smoke, casually, lightly, with the deftness of the fly fisherman he was, he cast out a line. Like a skittish trout, Bronwyn evaded him, but he saw resentment in the aqueous movements of her eyes. He was patient and days later, when the setting sun filtering through the windows made a rainbow of her hair, Novatt cast his line again, and lured by the quicksilver turn in their conversation, Bronwyn bit—taking the hook whole. Her eyes flashed angrily with realization. She struggled against the feelings surfacing in her, but Novatt would not ease up, and finally she screamed out her rage: How could she have been so *stupid* to miss the turn! How could she have been so *weak* to marry someone she hardly *knew!* And then *blame* him for knowing her mother! And her mother! How could she be so *hateful* to her? She *hated* her—no—she *loved* her—oh Christ!—she didn't know how the hell she felt. She felt like *shit!*

Afterwards, exhausted, Bronwyn lay limp in the eddy of her emotions.

Dr. Novatt got up quietly. He went to the bed, took Bronwyn's hand, and squeezed it; there was no response. Bending over, he kissed her lightly on the forehead. She closed her eyes.

"Try to sleep," he said. "I'll see you tomorrow."

Bronwyn slept into the night. Her nurse did not wake her for supper. It was the first sleep without medication her patient had known.

Asher kept her room filled with flowers and phoned Bronwyn every night. She was grateful to him for the speaker phone, the worktable, the video and tape recorders, the comedy tapes. Most of all she was grateful to him

256

for acquiescing when she asked him not to visit. And her appreciation grew as the days passed with still no response in her limbs. She could not cope with Asher's pity—or his love. Novatt had helped her realize these weeks were like those moments before plunging out of the starting gate— she had to concentrate only on the course! If she wanted to walk again, all else had to be edited out—like too many adjectives. She would get well—she would!

After the board meeting Asher sent her a videotape of the proceedings and she watched it with mixed feelings. She yearned for the pulse, the excitement of her work, but she remembered the peace, the serenity atop the mountain that morning. Would she ever know either again? She watched the merger put to a vote. Drew Mednam read her ballot—it was the only "nay." The merger was finalized, and although she had known the outcome, she moaned in disappointment. There was additional business to which she paid little attention. Just before the meeting adjourned Mednam looked into the camera and addressed her personally. It was as if he were in the room with her and, surprised, she said, "Yes?"

His next words came as if he heard her. Holding up an attractively designed logo, he announced a new imprint to be distributed by Mednam. *(So, they were keeping the name—good.)* The new imprint was to be called "BRON-JAC." Bronwyn stared, puzzled, until suddenly she realized it was *her imprint!* And she was to have editorial and financial autonomy! The board applauded and unanimously agreed, the camera panning to each of them as they smiled into the lens and wished her well. The tape concluded with Asher. She had forgotten how stunning he was. Smiling into the camera, he said, "I love you, darling. Get well soon."

Bronwyn looked at the screen long after the tape flickered off. Positive and negative feelings flashed in her like the positive and negative lines flashing on the empty screen. It was as though she had been given the key to a candy shop and told to eat whatever she liked—how could she turn down the sweetness of that offer? And yet, how soon too much sweet turned sour. *BRONJAC*. The name rankled, but shame dispelled her vexation. She was being an ungrateful bitch. Still, it would have been nice to choose the name for her imprint. She would have preferred not to use her married name. Why? It was a logical choice . . . still . . . oh, it was too much to think about now . . . there was just too much to think about . . .

Closing her eyes, silently she began to repeat a mantra. Novatt had suggested meditating, and after a while, lulled by her deep breathing, she napped.

Douglas MacCormack entered the lobby of the Hospital of Latter Day Saints carrying three dozen yellow roses and a sculptured cruse of Chloé perfume. His gait was so light, the young woman at the receptionist's desk did not hear his step on the hard floor until the fragrance of roses drew her eyes upwards.

Her mouth dropped open and she stared into dark blue eyes exuding such sexual vitality she felt a sudden pang in the pit of her stomach. His black hair glistened like coal, curling tightly around his bony, rugged face; it was a face, she determined, that could earn millions posing for cigarette ads. He was right out of the romance novel lying open in her desk drawer. Her thin-lipped mouth softened into an inviting smile.

"May I help you?" she almost sang.

"Yes, thank you. In what room will I find Bronwyn O'Neill? Excuse me, I mean Bronwyn Jacobs." Her married name stuck in his throat.

"Nine forty-five," the young woman replied, before realizing visitors were restricted. Flustered, she said: "But you can't go up. You're not a member of the immediate family, are you?"

Breaking off a rose, MacCormack leaned over and slid the flower into her hair. "I'm closer than that," he whispered and turning, he went to the elevator.

She stared after him, but made no attempt to stop him, thinking, *If I'm ever hurt—oh God, send a man like that to me!*

The elevator rose in fits and starts and MacCormack moved into the far corner of the cheerless metal box, trying not to look at the pallid patient on a stretcher, his wrists taped where tubes fed intravenous solution from a

258

bottle of clear fluid dangling on a metal holder that trundled alongside. But one's eyes are always drawn to tragedy. Even in a race, accelerating past crackups, MacCormack caught them out of the corners of his eyes. He felt a pulse beat in his stomach. Bronwyn, with her bones broken? Irony filled him. Never had he expected *he* would be the visitor and *she* the patient. In all the years he had raced, he had never known a serious injury. Guilt gnawed at him, compounded by a deeper guilt he had felt ever since he had heard of her marriage, and of her accident.

If only—if only. The words clamped on his head like a vise. If only *I'd made more time for her* . . . if only *I'd gone after her, when she hung up on me Christmas Day* . . . if only *I hadn't caught the plane to Stuttgart. But I had to! There was no time! Falke waited in Weissach. He'd even called the staff in on a holiday to make sure the 935 was ready for the Daytona Race. I couldn't keep Helmuth Falke and the entire Porsche Racing Division waiting because I had a fight with my woman!* If only . . . *Damn,* he thought angrily. Such stupid words.

The car clunked to a stop at the ninth floor; the attendant moved the stretcher slightly so that MacCormack could get out. MacCormack's legs felt suddenly heavy, and avoiding the nurses' station he walked slowly down the hall, looking for 945. At the far end, from a corner room, came an unmistakeable sound. Laughter. *Her laughter!* The same laugh that had caught his attention that first night at the party—a lilting, uninhibited laugh, soaring without reserve into a room and making others smile. What on earth could she be laughing at *now?* His steps quickened and as he came closer he heard voices and stopped. *The Three Stooges?*

His face, which had grown so serious the moment he stepped into the elevator, relaxed, and a smile turned up the corners of his sensual mouth. Clearly, he heard the antics of Larry, Moe, and Curly. Without knocking, he walked into the room. Bronwyn was watching television. Her bed was angled to face the windows and she did not see him, nor did she hear him as she laughed at the zaniness on the screen. But he saw her clearly and the

259

smile faded from his face. His solar plexus tightened as if he had been struck a hard blow, and sudden sharp tears stung his eyes. Good God! He hadn't expected this!

This poor creature, her legs suspended in pulleys, her head encircled in steel, couldn't be Bronwyn! His Bronwyn was like a gazelle, matching his pace. He thought of the spring days when they would stride side-by-side from the Guggenheim all the way back to her apartment in the Village. Those legs had wrapped like silk around his hips, and that head had lain in his groin, filling him with a splendor he had not thought possible. He shut his eyes tight, trying to stem the memories and the tears. He turned aside, fighting the emotions flooding him. But his heart was no machine and it flared, forcing him to face what he tried to deny. *So this is what it feels like!* he thought. *This is what* they *feel when they see us hurt.* He didn't want to think of the women who loved men like him, who rushed in relief to the pits when the race was over. He didn't want to look behind the cheers, the high-pitched lifestyle of the race course, and see the fears, the heartbreak. He had never allowed real contact with any one woman; instead he planed as if he were on an oil-slick road in a light drizzle.

The three funny men on the screen erupted into crazy, shouting exaggerations which brought the film to a close. Giggling, Bronwyn pressed her shoulders, activating a switch on her pillow which shut off the tape. It was then she sensed his presence.

"Who's there?" It wasn't like her nurse, or anyone else on the staff, to stand outside her vision. "Is that you, Maude?"

Forcing a smile, MacCormack moved so that she could see him.

She gasped. Her eyes darkened and before she knew it, they brimmed with tears. "No!" she cried. "No! Please don't look at me! I don't want you to see me this way!"

He caught his breath and his heart seemed to turn in his chest.

"Don't!" he said sharply. "Don't you dare think so *little* of me, that you can't face me as you are! I came *because*

you're hurt, and because I can't believe you'd marry someone and not tell me about it!"

His vehemence startled her and she stopped crying. His expression softened at the frown edging between her brows; it was such a giveaway—even in poker she couldn't control that frown.

He went to the bed and was just about to lay the flowers in her arms, when an instinct (from years of sensing what was just behind or just ahead on the track?) made him hold the roses close to her face. She inhaled the fragrance of the petals, enjoying the satin touch against her skin.

"Thank you," she said, smiling up at him. "They're beautiful."

As he'd done earlier, he broke off a rose and placed it over her ear, just below the bolts which held her traction. "If I'd known you were wearing a halo," he joked, "I'd have had the roses woven into a proper crown of thorns."

She laughed and the tension between them eased.

"What's that?" she asked, referring to the gold foil package tied with silver ribbon, still in his hand.

"Oh, just a little something I picked up in Paris," he teased.

Surprise crossed her face. "When did you get there? I thought you had to go directly from Weissach to Daytona."

His eyes shifted uneasily. "I heard about your marriage and I needed Paris."

"You heard about my marriage in Germany?"

"It was on German television. Your husband is an important man in Europe. I was at Falke's house for dinner—you remember him, don't you?"

"The heavy man you introduced me to at Le Mans?"

"Yes."

"Strange, I didn't think you were that friendly. He wasn't too happy you beat the factory team."

MacCormack shrugged, and the close-fitting Italian suit flexed across his muscular shoulders. "I beat them at Daytona again last week. But they're friendly. It doesn't matter as long as a Porsche wins."

A smile brightened her face. "You won at Daytona? I

261

haven't kept up with racing very much—I've been kind of out of it. I'm happy for you. Congratulations."

"Thank you." His voice took on a familiar excitement. "Bronwyn, just wait until you see this new nine-three-five —it's like a big, quiet cat. It purrs, and purrs, and then *ZOOOOM*—it takes off like a panther! It just floats around the track. I hardly felt the twenty-four hours at Daytona. I can't wait for Sebring. Twelve hours won't seem an endurance race at all."

He fastened warmly encouraging eyes on hers. "When you're better, you can try her out, take her around the track."

Bronwyn dropped her eyes. "I don't think so, Doug." And then she looked at him challengingly. "Why did you come now?"

His face turned grave. "You know why."

Her eyes blazed. "No, I don't! You've never told me!"

"I don't have to. Just being here is enough."

"It's never *enough!* It has to be *said!*"

"Then why didn't *you* ever tell *me?*"

She closed her eyes in frustration. Why? Why hadn't she simply said, *I love you, Doug.* But what did it matter now? It was over. She opened her eyes and looked again at the package. "Is it what I think it is?"

"Of course."

"Thank you." She sighed sardonically. "I really need it. Maybe it will help kill the antiseptic stink. Please—open it. Put it on me."

MacCormack unwrapped the package and removed the perfume. He released the delicate sculptured stopper and dabbed the essence on the pulses in Bronwyn's wrists and behind the lobes of her ears. Then he touched it to the hollow in her throat and to the pulses in her temples. Moistening the crystal again, he slipped aside the satin of her gown and brushed the fragrance on the warmth between her breasts. Bronwyn's lids closed as she inhaled the exotic scent distilled from the most perfect petals. Behind the blackness of her eyes she envisioned him caressing her with the Chloé, caressing her as he always had.

The same visions rose in MacCormack, and abruptly he

262

replaced the stopper, twisting it, sealing in the fragrance as if to seal in the memories. He picked up the roses from Bronwyn's lap and went across the room to where vases of flowers broke the starkness of a formica hospital dresser. He took one vase and tossed its flowers into a plastic trash can, then refilled the vase with fresh water and inserted the roses, fanning the buds out so that they stood proudly on their long stems. The small tasks quieted the feelings racing in him and he stood with his back to Bronwyn, looking out the windows towards the mountains, but not seeing any of it. What he saw was inside himself—a void she had filled without his ever realizing it. *Hold on, Mac,* an inner voice cautioned. *She's married now. Let it lay, she's made her choice.* But the forces driving him were more powerful than any machine he had ever handled. Sucking in his breath, he turned to her, narrowing his eyes as though to sharpen the focus of the insight taking hold of him. What he said next surprised him as much as it did her.

"I love you, Bronwyn, and I don't care about this damn marriage of yours—it means nothing. You hardly know the man, so how could you love him? It's *me* you love! And if you don't use that love to make yourself well and marry me, you're a bigger fool than either of us has been these past five years!"

Bronwyn stared at him, her throat going dry. "You say that to me *now?*" she croaked. "Why? What suddenly makes you care enough? Don't you realize I might be crippled?" A thought stopped her, but she couldn't help what came out next. "Or is it my *helplessness* that attracts you? Am I a bunch of poor parts you want to make whole?"

"It could have been me, you know," he said quietly. "Could you have walked away if I was lying there?"

She looked at him wordlessly. "That's different," she said finally.

"How?"

"It wouldn't have been pity."

"And you think that's what I feel?"

Anger began to scald her. She felt an unbearable tautness as if the traction holding her head, her legs, drew so tightly her body bowed. The pressure became intolera-

263

ble and she screamed out in pain, her words arrows, propelled by a rage she couldn't even begin to understand.

"Damn you, Douglas! How dare you tell me you love me now! How dare you tear me apart like this! Oh Christ! Leave me alone! Leave me alone!"

He stood startled, impaled by her fury.

She began to sob—deep, painful sobs.

A nurse came rushing into the room. "Mrs. Jacobs! What's wrong?"

Quickly the woman checked the traction, her hands flying along the apparatus. Satisfied all was right, she lifted the covers to examine the elimination bags. Then she took her patient's pulse. With a frown she glanced at MacCormack and with a sharp shake of her head, she indicated he leave.

But he did not move . . . he wanted to hold Bronwyn and soothe her; he wanted to tear the bolts from her body and heal her with his own hands; he wanted to protect her always. A feeling that was totally alien, a loathsome impotence, choked him as he watched her weep.

The nurse hurried from the room, her stocky legs driving like pistons. She soon returned with a hypodermic needle which she swiftly inserted into Bronwyn's arm. Then, with a crispness that made her uniform rustle and her starched cap bob, she took MacCormack's arm and led him outside.

"She'll sleep for a while," the woman said coldly, her grey eyes accusing behind the wire-rimmed glasses. "You've upset her, and I can't permit that."

"Are you Maude?" he asked.

"Yes."

"How bad is she really?"

"You'll have to ask her doctors that."

"Come on, Maude, I'm asking *you*. I care for her. I want to *know!*"

The nurse gave him a long, searching look. She was uneasy with handsome men; they made her painfully aware of her own plainness. "I suggest you ask Mr. Jacobs whatever you'd like to know about his wife," she said stiffly.

"That might be a problem," MacCormack said with a teasing smile.

"Only if you make it one!" She glared at him. "What happened before is none of my business, but what happens *now, is!* That girl in there has it tough enough and I won't let *anything* upset her, so if you care for her, think about *her* before you see her again." She turned to go, and another thought stopped her. "And think about it, too, before you call her."

She strode away, her rubber-soled shoes silent on the shining floor. Her head was high, her shoulders square, and her wide hips rolled as she sailed down the corridor like a battleship after a foray. MacCormack couldn't help but smile.

He went to the elevator and pressed the button. *Bronwyn's in good hands*, he thought. *I can wait.*

Chapter Twenty-two

Dᴜʀɪɴɢ the first depressing days after the accident, Asher phoned Elizabeth for reassurance that it was indeed Bronwyn's nature to be laconic on the telephone. Elizabeth gave him the comfort he sought, assuring him Bronwyn disliked talking on the phone with *anyone,* and sharing with him her own brief conversations with her daughter, even though there was little to tell.

They fell into a comfortable pattern; Asher continued to call, and they exchanged whatever each felt was not personal or hurtful. Initially Elizabeth found it difficult to concentrate on what Asher said, so caught up was she in just the sound of his voice. She listened to him as she listened to music, hearing the telephone amplifying the masculine timbre in his tone, the cadence of his words. That first night he called, they talked for more than an hour, and after they said goodnight, Elizabeth lay sleepless.

One night he asked if she had gone back to writing; she told him no, she could not write, but that she was teaching skiing; she had asked the school for the most timid, fearful students, and the patience they required drove all else from her mind. At night she was too tired to think. Another night he asked about Bronwyn as a child, and she began to reminisce, remembrances of her daughter falling from her lips. She stopped, embarrassed, but Asher said eagerly, "Please go on. I know so little about her." Just before they hung up he said, "Elizabeth, will you meet me in New York tomorrow? I want to surprise Bronwyn, and I'll need your help."

She fell silent. She clung to these conversations with him, but seeing him was another matter. And yet, how could she refuse anything that had to do with Bonnie? "I teach tomorrow, but I can take Thursday off. I'll come in then."

"Good!" He was so engrossed in his thoughts, he did not hear the reluctance in her voice. "Meet me at my apartment for lunch, and I'll tell you what I propose." He gave her the address on Fifth Avenue, telling her to leave her car with the doorman.

His apartment surprised her. She had expected a handsomely furnished manse. What she saw was depressing, as if sheets had been hastily removed from furniture just taken out of storage.

"Thank you for coming," Asher said, "but keep your coat on."

She gave him a puzzled look. He laughed and took her arm, leading her throughout the high-ceilinged rooms as though they were on an inspection tour. She had not heard him laugh or seen him in such good spirits since their first meeting. Her pulse raced. She could barely keep her mind on what he showed her.

The fifteen-room duplex contained many fine antiques and several good paintings, but there was no cohesive design, no attempt to create an aesthetic whole. They ended the tour on a large wrap-around terrace.

Thirty stories below lay Central Park, a treasured fossil, a remnant of the natural beauty Manhattan had once had in abundance. Through the trees bared by winter she could see the reservoir, the Delacorte Theatre, and the luxury apartments on Central Park West. Nostalgia pricked at her as she remembered long-ago Saturdays when she and a young Bonnie ice-skated on the Wollman Rink. She sighed, and turning around, looked to the east and the river, a glimpse of slate through breaks in the architectural colossi which reflected the richness that is New York, and then to the north, where the park ended at 125th Street and the greyness of the Harlem ghetto began.

Her gaze wandered downtown, towards 59th Street, where the park opened onto the lavish elegance of Central Park South. *Only sixty-six blocks,* she thought; *sixty-six blocks—a buffer zone between rich and poor.* It was absurd that in such a short distance, in the richest city in the world, life could be so cruelly unequal. Yes, life was cruel. Her eyes again sought the more familiar south edge of the park; she saw the Plaza Hotel and the fountain, dormant and deserted now in the chill of February. She thought instead of lively spring days when water danced in the Plaza fountain. When a grown Bonnie, who hated shopping, sat on the fountain's rim in the warm sunshine, waiting for her while she browsed in Bergdorf's. When she came out with packages Bonnie smiled and said, "Just browsing, huh?" They laughed and walked up the street to Rumplemayer's for ice cream sodas.

A blast of icy air blew in from the East River, and Elizabeth drew the collar of her coat to her face.

"It's a magnificent view, Asher."

He smiled down at her. "It may not be your mountain, but it's the next best thing. Bronwyn should like it out here. She'll be home by spring, and by then I want this terrace to look like a forest—trees, shrubs, flowers—as verdant as it is around your house. I want to make this beautiful for her. I remember how eager her face was the day she drove me . . ." He stopped, embarrassed.

"It's all right, Asher. Neither of us could have known."

He took her hand. His green eyes were dark and somber.

268

"Elizabeth, I'd do anything if I could blot that day from our lives. It's why Bronwyn fled to Utah—she ran from me, from you, and I can't help but feel responsible for what happened."

She saw how tightly his jaw was clenched. How she wanted to run her fingertips along his face and ease that clenching; how she'd like to bring the smile back to his eyes. Their eyes met, and he suddenly saw in her face what he had not recognized before. He let go of her hand, troubled by the feelings he saw in her, and troubled even more by his own response to those feelings. No, he could not involve her in what he planned.

Elizabeth sensed his withdrawal, and the struggle in him. She hoped fervently her face had not given her away. She had to make sure!

In a light, casual voice she said, "Asher, you would not have asked me to come all this way without good reason, but now, suddenly, I feel you've changed your mind. If it's because of what happened between us, don't be concerned. We're both adults, and remember also—it was *my* decision not to see you again." Thank God she hadn't called him from Florida as Arnold had urged! "I won't deny that you're an attractive man, and any woman would respond to you. But you are my daughter's husband, and I, if you'll recall, have chosen to live alone, so please, let's be friends, and whatever is on your mind, let's discuss it as friends do. I'm sure it's for Bonnie's benefit."

He turned to her with a grateful smile and then he began to walk around the terrace. Elizabeth followed him.

"Yes, I did ask you to come for a reason," he said. "And if I'm asking too much, please say so, and I'll understand." He would leave it to her to accept or refuse.

"It's ironic," he continued. "Bronwyn didn't want to come here. She thought my home was too 'pristine.' She apologized for her clutter, not knowing I've been living much the same way. After my wife died I sold our apartment and put everything in storage; when I returned from Europe I bought all this space because I didn't have the heart or the time to cull what generations of Cassidys had accumulated. But now, having all these rooms is perfect for what Bronwyn will need, and yet, I can't expect

269

her to take the time to supervise what needs to be done. And she would not have the energy. It will be many months before she's well enough to do much. Besides, I have a feeling she doesn't really care about doing over a house. But I want to make this into a home she'll grow to love, and it needs the touch of those who love her." Enthusiasm built in him and he looked eagerly at Elizabeth.

"You know more than anyone else what she likes. When we talked the other night about what she'd been like as a girl, the idea came to me. I don't want her home to have the glossy, impersonal look of the professional decorator. I want it to be as warm, as beautiful as the home in which she grew up. She's an unpretentious person and that's what she'll feel most comfortable with. No designer can do what you will do. Elizabeth, will you help put this house together for her?"

Elizabeth stared at him, and then a pain ran through her so intense she had to turn away. Put the house together for Bonnie! Bonnie could not care less what her home looked like. This home should be for *her!* She tasted the bitterness of jealousy in her mouth and felt ashamed. Her daughter lay crippled and she was *envious!* She should be thankful he cared so much, that despite Bonnie's accident he loved her so and wanted the best for her. *Oh, Elizabeth!* she castigated herself, *how can you be so selfish!* Without facing him she said, "Yes, Asher, I'll help you."

The cynicism with which Bronwyn had protected herself in her relationship with Douglas MacCormack did not help her after he left. She felt a profound sense of loss, as if her youth, the exuberant, reckless daring that so often silvered her days with him, walked out when he did. She found herself sinking back on dangerous ground, hoping as she had hoped in their early days that perhaps he *had* changed. But no, she cautioned herself, people *don't* change; they are what they are, and either you lived with it, or you stepped away. Stepped away? Was that what she had done when she married Asher? Had she subconsciously taken advantage of him to help herself forget MacCormack? No!

270

She had accepted long before she met Asher that her situation with Douglas was self-destructive and had made up her mind to end it. But why had she married Asher so impulsively? Was it the power he exuded? No, she detested men who flaunted power, and despite his position, Asher was sincere and candid. She liked his lack of pretense, his sense of fairness. He made her feel she could trust him. And there was something more—his love was so encompassing, it made her feel as though it was her own. And what was wrong with that? Certainly he had shown her more consideration in the short time she had known him than Douglas ever had! Wasn't kindness and understanding most important?

She sighed deeply as if her very breath could extinguish the chemistry that attracts one to another. The incandescence she felt whenever she was with MacCormack, the incredible excitement they brought to each other—*How do I still that?* she wondered. *What do I do about what happens* inside *me—that quickness, that sharp upbeat—the tingling warmth he fires in me?* Would this torment in her heal as her bones healed? *It would!* she vowed. She would make sure she forgot MacCormack! And so, after his visit, more and more she opened up to Dr. Novatt, hoping to come to terms with her feelings not only towards MacCormack, but towards Asher and her mother.

Although she disliked talking on telephones, Bronwyn's conversations with Asher grew lengthier and warmer. She told him of her sessions with Novatt, she described her consultations with Andresen and Nichols and went into details concerning her physical therapy ("Yes, I am getting sensations, but there's still no movement"). She made Asher chuckle with her stories about Maude. But she told him nothing of MacCormack's visit.

Asher was delighted with the change in Bronwyn and in turn, he told her everything he did during the day, filling her in on the news in publishing, in acquisitions, in whatever she asked. And he made her laugh, coming out with one funny line after another until she accused him of hiring a network of comedy writers. Like quiet fog cozying in on a rocky coast, a camaraderie developed between them, and she felt sheltered. Asher did not tell her of the apartment or that Elizabeth was redoing it. He wanted it to be a surprise.

Spring softened the snows on the Wasatch, warming the dry powder into heavy, knee-wrenching wetness. The locals waxed and stored their skis, but snow-parched Easterners thronged the Salt Lake airport, filling the buses to Alta, Snowbird, and Park City. The staff at LDS made ready for an influx of injuries, and among themselves, discussed the patient in 945, the bright-haired young woman they had all come to know. They worried about the day her traction would be removed.

One night late in April, Asher phoned and said with a happy eagerness, "I'll see you Friday."

Trepidation raced through Bronwyn. "No! I'm not ready!"

"You are, darling." He smiled into the phone. "Dr. Nichols called me. They're taking off your traction tomorrow. Dr. Calhoun and I are flying out to bring you back to New York."

Bronwyn watched with baited breath as Dr. Nichols and three of his residents gathered around her bed.

She smiled tremulously at him, trying to keep calm, but her heart pounded. He returned her smile, but she saw caution corral it, keeping it within the confines of his narrow lips. She hoped she could contain her impatience during the usual amenities. If she heard another "Well, how are we today?" she'd scream.

Nichols sensed her nervousness and got right down to business.

"Bronwyn, we're going to remove these long leg casts and put you into something lighter. Your legs still need to be in casts for a few more weeks, but you'll find these more comfortable, and they'll make your trip back East easier, because you'll be able to sit up in a wheelchair."

Her heart soared. "Are they walking casts?"

He hesitated and then answered carefully. "They can be used for walking, but it's much too soon for you to be thinking of that."

Too soon? It was *always* too soon! When would *soon* be *now?* But she kept silent.

Nichols went to the foot of the bed. "Please close your eyes and keep them closed until I tell you." He took the toes of her feet in his hands. "What am I doing?"

"You're holding my toes."

He bent the big toe of her right foot forward and backward. "And now?"

A frown creased her forehead. "You're bending my toe."

"Which foot and which toe?"

"The right, and it's my big toe."

He nodded and repeated the exercise with her other foot. Again she answered correctly. Then he applied pressure behind her metatarsals. "Do you feel anything?"

"Yes, you're pressing my feet."

"Both feet or just one?" he said, letting go of her right foot.

"At first it was both. Now you're pressing my left foot."

"Good." Swiftly he pricked the skin in back of her toes with a pin.

"Hey, that stings," she said, elation filling her.

"I hoped it would," he said and nodded to Maude, who handed him a small plastic bag filled with ice. Holding the ice against Bronwyn's feet, he asked. "What's this?"

"If it's what I think it is, I'd like it better if you'd drop it into a glass filled with Bourbon and soda."

They all laughed lightly.

"Are your eyes still closed?" he asked, coming to the head of the bed.

"Would I disobey you, Dr. Nichols?"

He repeated his tests with her hands, and each time she recognized the movement and correctly identified it. "Press my fingers," he instructed. She tried, concentrating hard, but there was only the smallest movement, as if cotton had brushed against his hand.

"You can open your eyes now, Bronwyn."

She looked at him imploringly. "Does this mean I'll walk again, have free use of my arms again?"

His gaze was unblinking, but she saw a noncommittal

273

look descend like a protective shade across the keen intelligence of his brown eyes. It was the same look she saw when she watched presidential press conferences.

"You're a fortunate young woman, Bronwyn, but I must caution you to be patient and take one day at a time. Recovery in cervical injuries such as yours is never total, and we can never be sure just how much full recovery there will be, and there will always be a certain spasticity. I can't make you any promises, but since you can feel sensations, and since now we know your injury is incomplete, there is a good chance that given time, and therapy, you will regain movement."

Movement? What did he mean by *movement?* But before she could ask, a technician came forward holding a vestlike apparatus.

"What's that?" Her voice was unnaturally high.

"Tell you when we get it on," Nichols said, beginning to undo the traction which had secured her head for over three months. "Hold perfectly still. Don't make a move of any kind."

For a moment her head felt wonderfully light, and she longed to just *feel* it turn, but she held still. Soon she felt a tightness again as a new circle of steel was attached. Nichols and one of the residents picked up her arms, slipping them into the armholes of the vest.

"Now you can be mobile," Nichols smiled, his skin drawing tightly over his prominent cheekbones. "That's a halo vest you're wearing. It should feel a lot lighter. You'll have to wear it another month or two, until the fracture has healed totally. You'll be able to move your head and shoulders, and also by then the casts will be off your legs. But now that you can get around in a wheelchair, you won't be so confined. That's why we've had you doing so many shoulder exercises—these new wheelchairs can be activated by your shoulder muscles."

"My shoulder muscles?" she screeched. "What about my arms, my legs? I thought once the spinal shock was gone—how long? *How long?"* She gasped as a terrible thought engulfed her. Her eyes flew to Nichols. *He was lying!* He was trying to be kind, to break it to her gently! She'd never walk again, never move her arms again.

274

"You're lying to me!" she screamed. *"You're lying! I'll never walk again!"*

Nichols signaled to the young men and quietly they left the room.

He pulled up a chair and sat down. Maude hovered close by, wondering if she should call Dr. Novatt. In a steady voice which was not impersonal, Nichols said, "I'm *not* lying to you, Bronwyn. I didn't say you'll *never* walk again; many patients *have*. What I'm saying is I can't *promise* you will. I *think* you will, I *hope* you will, but I can't go further than that."

She closed her eyes tightly, wanting to believe him. With an effort she tried hard to open and close her fingers—with a greater effort she tried to wiggle her toes. Tears of frustration oozed from her tight lids when they did not move. *This* was what she believed—*this* reality!

"Damn it, *move, move!*" she screamed at her flaccid fingers, her still toes.

Nichols rose and went to Maude.

"Give her ten milligrams of Valium."

For the next two days Bronwyn raged, her curses caroming off the blank walls of her room, echoing down the corridor, ceasing only after tranquilizers were needled into her arms. She welcomed the oblivion they brought. Even Dr. Novatt could not break beyond the barrier of her despondency. By Friday she lay in a quiet cauldron of despair, determined to keep the cauldron from tilting; she must rage no more, she must not spill the molten steel of her anguish. If her plans were to be successful, she had to maintain a semblance of ironclad composure and clearheadedness when Asher and Calhoun arrived to take her back.

She had decided to die.

275

Chapter Twenty-three

GRACE Marschak regarded Elizabeth dolefully. Since their earliest days as school girls in the Bronx, Elizabeth had been a maze of contradictions: sharply intelligent, yet naive; astute, but too trusting; independent, but so vulnerable; outgoing, but reclusive; perceptive, but, as now, totally unaware of what was happening in her own body. Grace wanted to shake her friend, but Grace Marschak detested displays of emotion; as the youngest of the ten children of a fervidly religious father, she remembered too well the killing effects of deeply felt passions. On rare occasions when she unwittingly thought of the past she could still hear the roaring, authoritarian voice of her father, and the quick anger of her mother.

No one who had known *Gittel* Marschak as a plump, dowdy teenager with wild, wiry black hair would have recognized the slim, modishly dressed sophisticate who sat behind the highly polished blonde wood desk arching in a graceful semicircle between the two women. Nor would they have recognized her carefully modulated and cultured voice. On the desk were neatly arranged stacks of file folders and medical journals. Beside the brown onyx desk set with its wood pens banded in gold was a silver bud vase containing a single white hyacinth, its fragrance scenting the office, which looked out onto the walled garden of the handsome Georgian townhouse on East 75th Street between Fifth and Madison. Grace Marschak had bought the building five years ago, and her offices and elegantly furnished apartment occupied all four floors.

She leaned now towards Elizabeth, her meticulously manicured hands calmly folded on the unblemished desk pad. Her high forehead was unruffled, rising into a fluff of frosted hair cut in the latest style. On the beige linen walls behind her, hanging in narrow gilt frames, were her diplomas: a bachelor's degree in science from Hunter College; a medical degree from New York University; a residency in obstetrics and gynecology from Mt. Sinai Hospital; her board certification plus other honors.

"Why did you wait so long?" Grace asked quietly.

Elizabeth flushed at her own stupidity.

"I had no idea, Grace. I often skip a month or two. I forget—and these past few years I had no reason to keep track. And I thought—at this age . . ."

"You're only forty-five!" Grace interjected. "My mother was forty-eight when I was born, and in 1956 a woman in California gave birth when she was past *fifty-seven years old!*" She settled back into the beige leather chair, and said more gently, "No, dear Elizabeth, you are not at all unique. Women are very vulnerable to unwanted pregnancies at your age, and if you do not want this child, you've waited longer than I like to see a woman wait. Certainly abortions can be performed in the fourth month and sometimes, if an amniocentesis test confirms a severe abnormality, even in the fifth month, but it is always a risk—especially if the mother is mature. I strongly advise against an abortion in your case."

Elizabeth looked at her sharply; she knew how sensitive Grace was to unwanted pregnancies, how, when Mrs.

277

Marschak died, Grace had come running to Elizabeth's house, screaming that her father had killed her mother with overwork and too many children. The two thirteen-year-old girls had clung to each other, sobbing. They had become closer than ever, and later when Elizabeth's parents died, again their closeness had been a source of comfort. Grace had always remained a good friend, and Elizabeth knew how strongly her friend felt about women birthing only those children they wanted. She knew also that before abortions were legalized, Grace had guided women to a clinic safely hidden and protected in a Mafia-controlled town in New Jersey. Although she would not perform the procedure herself, Grace once had accompanied a frightened fourteen-year-old, and had held her hand throughout the curettage. Elizabeth surmised Grace had become a gynecologist because of her mother. And so Grace's advice to her now came as a surprise.

Elizabeth leaned across the desk to her friend.

"Grace, I just can't have this baby."

"Neither can you risk endangering yourself at this time. You must think of Bonnie—she's suffered a terrible blow. What if something happened to you now, when she needs you so much?"

Elizabeth's mouth twisted at Grace's words. *I am thinking of Bonnie,* she cried inwardly, averting her eyes from the keen gaze of the woman across the desk.

Grace's voice softened even more. "I know this is a difficult decision, but you are a strong, healthy woman, Elizabeth, with the means and the energy to raise another child—it could be worse."

Elizabeth rose and shook her head.

"No, Grace, it couldn't—it's an impossible situation."

Light spring rain misted Elizabeth's face as she walked, hatless, the few short blocks to Asher's apartment; the cool drizzle washing the tender green of the trees across the street in Central Park did nothing to cool or cleanse the anger she directed at herself.

How could you be so stupid! she ranted silently. *Not to know you're pregnant at seventeen is understandable—but* now? Elizabeth could not forgive herself; that her periods

278

had always been erratic gave her no solace. For the past five years she had given her menses no thought at all, accepting the flow when it appeared, and grateful when it did not. She had her yearly checkups and then forgot about that part of her body. *But didn't you feel your clothes getting tighter?* Her mind was relentless. *Yes!* she cried to herself, *but I* always eat *when I'm upset, and since Bonnie's accident . . . and then I got so busy with the apartment, with teaching, I didn't care* what *I ate, or* when! *I never* dreamed . . .

So, idiot, *what will you do now?* her mind sneered.

"I don't know!" Elizabeth cried aloud. The sound of her agitated voice startled her, and embarrassed, she quickly looked around, but the few people hurrying by in the rain paid no attention; it was the least of what could be expected in New York.

"Good afternoon, Miss Banks," the doorman said as she came to Asher's building. She looked at the man blankly, and then she nodded wordlessly as he opened the heavy door for her.

Later, she sat on the cerulean velvet sofa and looked about the beautiful drawing room. She sighed deeply. At least the apartment was finished. On Friday, Asher and Tom would fly to Utah to bring Bonnie home. She was glad now she had agreed when Tom had, oh so carefully, suggested she wait in New York.

"Oh dear God," she whispered aloud. "What do I do now? How can I face Bonnie? How could she possibly understand?" Her mind gave her no rest, and she could not sit still. Nervously she got up and strode through the apartment, checking details she had just finished checking. She barely saw the remarkable transformation that she had wrought; for weeks she had worked feverishly, thinking of nothing else during the days she spent in New York, living in a haze, caught up in a secret joy. The apartment became an expression of love, and every room held its radiance—there was a warmth, a *luminosity* you *felt* as well as saw. What had been an odd assortment of furnishings was now a beautifully balanced, harmonious entity. The colors, textures, shapes pleased not only the eye, but

279

caught the senses, and you felt such serenity, you wanted to be nowhere else but *here*. It was a Walden of the heart as well as the mind, as if Elizabeth had finally written such a book and had spent hours reflecting, searching for what Maugham once remarked was the obligation of a writer: not merely to find the "right" word, but the "inevitable" word. The home that was to be her daughter's read like literature.

And Elizabeth had done her research. Working with an architect and a skilled contractor, she had made modifications in the living space to accommodate Bronwyn's needs. All the sliding glass doors opening onto the terrace were fitted with electric eyes so that Bronwyn could go in and out easily; the library had been moved upstairs and its space converted into Bronwyn's sitting room and bedroom —it opened onto the east terrace, from which she could enjoy the morning sun. All rugs were removed and the oak floors polished. Doorways were widened—there must be no obstacles for the wheelchair. Later, when Bronwyn was fully recovered, the exquisite Orientals could be taken out of storage. Elizabeth would not believe anything other than that *someday*, Bronwyn would walk again.

Asher had moved to a suite at the Warwick during the renovations, and Elizabeth stayed in Bronwyn's Village apartment when she was in the city. She had seen Asher just once since the day she agreed to redo the duplex, and that was at an initial conference with the architect and contractor. Since then, whenever she wanted Asher's approval, she phoned his office to arrange for samples of color and fabrics to be sent via messenger. Each sensed the uneasiness in the other and limited their communications to the telephone.

But this evening they had planned to meet at the apartment. Asher had not yet seen it completed, and it was an event to which he looked forward. Elizabeth turned on the lights as she went from room to room, dimming them to create special effects; she had had Ribbonlite installed in the overdoor arches, in the bookcases, in the ceiling coves, and in niches which held Asher's collection of antique Oriental sculptures. Now as she pressed the switches, an uninterrupted line of light illuminated the architectural beauty of the rooms and their contents, creating such a soft glow it completely dispelled the greyness of the rainy late afternoon. And it broke through her own gloom, awakening her to the beauty she had created.

She mounted the graceful sweep of stairs which curved from the white marble-floored entry to the upper floor and went down the wide, art-filled hallway to where the master bedroom looked west across the park. Going to the windows, she looked down on the terrace, now fully planted. It had looked beautiful from the drawing room, but she wanted to see it as Asher would see it from his room.

Wirtz Associates had created a remarkable garden, she thought. They had transformed the bare concrete terrace with its four-foot-high walls into a glen, as lush and green as any to be found in the English countryside. Everywhere spring was about to burst into bloom: terra cotta pots held tulips and hyacinths, still tightly wound, but daffodils, jonquils, and crocuses bloomed bravely, flaunting color in the still chilly air. In a corner, their newborn leaves shining in the April mist, dogwood trees sprouted tiny buds, ready to unfurl delicate blossoms as soon as warm May sun bathed the terrace. Wirtz had even managed a small pond, a rock garden, and a waterfall, and at night, concealed lighting subtly illuminated the garden so that when you strolled its paths, it was as though you wandered in moonlight.

From her vantage point, Elizabeth critically appraised the width of the paths, the ease with which Bronwyn could maneuver her wheelchair—all was as it should be. She turned to go, her eyes quickly sweeping Asher's room. A sense of pride rose in her—she liked this room more than any other. It was a handsome, urbane room—strong, like the man who would occupy it—done in warm earth tones and accented with blue, a blue as clear and calm as a cloudless sky. It was a masculine room, but a room in which a woman would feel welcome, a room in which to love and be loved.

To love and be loved! Her eyes went to the king-size bed. A slow, painful flush spread through her. *She could not show Asher his room,* or any room! She could not walk with him through this home she had created.

Hurrying into the library, she went to the Regency desk, grabbed some paper, and quickly wrote him a note, explaining she had to return home unexpectedly. She ran down the stairs and placed the note against a Chinese carving on the table in the entrance hall. He could not help but see it when he came in. She grabbed her raincoat and went out, closing the doors behind her. She paused momentarily as she heard the click of the heavy locks in the double doors. A firm resolve locked in her own mind. She would not come here again.

282

Chapter Twenty-four

BRONWYN wanted to be dressed and sitting in her wheelchair when Elizabeth arrived. She had only a vague recollection of seeing her mother in the hospital in Utah; this would be their first real meeting since the accident, and she did not want her mother to find her in bed. Being bedridden, like being short, put you at a disadvantage, and Bronwyn wanted to feel in control. Her purpose must not be weakened.

Morning sun streamed into the spacious corner room on the seventeenth floor of New York Hospital. It was more a suite than a hospital room, containing a sitting area with a sofa, easy chairs, and a small refrigerator for snacks and drinks. Since her arrival in New York a few days before, Bronwyn had given no thought to work, nor had she watched television or the tapes Asher supplied. She had

283

no interest in anything and whiled away those hours when Asher was not with her, staring out the tall windows which overlooked the East River, watching the boats, the traffic tie-ups and the red cable cars traversing the swift-flowing river, carrying passengers from 59th Street to Roosevelt Island.

"Helen, please hurry," she urged the woman washing her.

At first Bronwyn missed Maude, but she soon came to enjoy the amply proportioned Helen, who was as lenient as Maude was strict and as funny as Maude was dour. Bronwyn appreciated that she no longer had to guard her language or her temper.

Carefully the nurse pulled Bronwyn's hair up so that she could cleanse her back and neck. "If you'd let me cut that hair, honey, it would be so much easier."

"My husband better not hear that. It's what he likes most about me."

The woman chortled. "Don't wanna get that man mad at me! You shoulda heard him and Doc Calhoun! Whooo-eee! They was like two bull moose goin' head to head."

"What about?"

"You *know,* honey. Your man wants you home and Doc Calhoun won't release you until they clear up that urinary infection you got. No *way* does your husband want you here."

"I'd rather stay. I don't want to be released."

The woman dried Bronwyn's back and then began massaging, rubbing in a fragrant lotion with sure, strong strokes. "That halo must be pinchin' your brain. Why would you wanna stay here when you got such a beautiful hunk o' man dyin' for you to come home!"

"A lot of good my going home will do him or me," Bronwyn said bitterly.

The hands slowed their massage. Putting a sheet over Bronwyn's back, the nurse came around to where she could face her charge. "Honey, I may just be a practical nurse, and not as fancy as all those doctors who traipse in an' out o' here, but I think you 'n me's gonna have a talk about the birds 'n the bees. You know, that sounds like a pretty song." She laughed, but her eyes were serious.

284

"Forget it, Helen! I don't want to talk about it!"

"Listen, you better talk about it before you really begin to believe it! You're all wrong, Miss Know-it-all! You're not my first cervical, you know, and let me tell you, there's ways and *ways* to make you and your man happy!"

"Christ!" Bronwyn exploded. "My mother'll be here at eleven. What should I tell her? I look like a mess because my nurse was giving me a lecture on how to screw while stiff?"

Helen guffawed, her round breasts heaving in the white uniform.

"You sure got one weird sense of humor, Miz Jacobs." Helen turned Bronwyn as if she were a baby. "Okay. How much do you wanna bet on how fast I get you dressed?" The two women had found common ground when they discovered their mutual love for gambling.

Bronwyn gave her a sly look. "How much can you afford to lose today?"

"I'm winnin' today. I work too hard to lose. I'm bettin' a dollar to your two, I get you in that chair by ten forty-five."

Bronwyn lost—she almost always did. Sitting in the wheelchair, she looked in the mirror over the dresser. Helen had brushed her patient's hair until it shone and she had applied a soft, rosy makeup to Bronwyn's cheeks and lips. Bronwyn was pleased at her appearance, and she was also grateful for Helen's wisdom—the nurse had taken an early lunch so that Bronwyn could be alone with her mother. Bronwyn heard her mother's heels clicking down the hallway. There was no mistaking that rapid-fire walk. Putting a smile on her face, Bronwyn concentrated on her shoulder muscles; and the wheelchair moved into position, facing the door.

Elizabeth stopped in the doorway. In her hands was a small bouquet of flowers. As she looked at her daughter sitting in the wheelchair, her eyes filled with tears.

"Hello, Mother." Bronwyn smiled and then, totally against her will, her own eyes grew moist. She laughed lightly, trying to cover her emotion.

"I asked the nurse to put out a fresh box of tissues. I knew you'd need them—I'm afraid I need them too."

Elizabeth laughed self-consciously as she dried her eyes and bent to dry Bronwyn's. "I guess they should harness me to irrigate the Sahara." She gave her daughter a long, lingering kiss on the cheek.

Looking at the bouquet in Elizabeth's hands, Bronwyn smiled. "Crocuses?"

Elizabeth nodded. "I picked them this morning. They were peeking through the last traces of snow on the bank." She pressed the velvety purple and yellow buds to her daughter's cheek.

As she watched Bronwyn close her eyes to feel their touch and inhale the subtle scent of wild flowers, freshly picked, Elizabeth's throat constricted. Tears clouded her eyes again, and behind them she saw a young Bonnie, all arms and legs, running into the house calling, "Mommy, mommy, the crocuses are out all over the bank!"

Opening her eyes, Bronwyn looked at Elizabeth. "You need another tissue, Mom," she teased.

With an embarrassed laugh, Elizabeth turned away and searched for an empty vase in the flower-filled room. Finding none, she filled a glass with water and put the crocuses on the end table next to the sofa.

"Tom must have pulled rank to get this room. It's pleasant for a hospital." She pulled a chair close to her daughter and sat down. "Despite everything, Bonnie, you look beautiful. I'm so happy to see you at last."

Bronwyn's eyes swept her mother. She'd gained weight, but she looked healthy and tanned, and her new, shorter hairdo was becoming. A pride she had always felt whenever she looked at her mother rose in her, and Bronwyn was pleased. She was pleased also to realize the resentment she had felt about her mother and Asher was gone. It all seemed so petty now, and when she spoke, Bronwyn's voice held a sincere welcome.

"And you look terrific, Mom, even though you've been hitting the Häagen-Dazs, but I know it's because you've been worried about me. You always have such a vital look when you've been skiing a lot. The teaching does wonders for you."

Bronwyn's eyes held a warmth Elizabeth had not seen in

286

them since Asher came into their lives. Her heart quickened in response, and she leaned over and kissed her daughter full on the lips.

"That's from Blaze." They both laughed.

"How is he?"

"Loving and protective as always. I'll be bringing him in to visit you, once you're out of the hospital. I have a surprise I think you'll like."

"Don't tell me he's knocked up some beautiful bitch and you're getting a puppy!"

"No—" Elizabeth laughed, "but something almost as nice. It concerns something I've been wanting to do for a long time, and I'll tell you about it, but first I want to know about *you*. How are you, *really?* I don't mean physically, I can see that, and Tom's told me a lot. What I mean is, how do you feel *inside*—about yourself, about Asher—" she hesitated, "about me."

Bronwyn looked long and levelly at her mother. Unknowingly, her mother had asked the very question that opened a door Bronwyn had been seeking for days. *I've never lied to her*, she thought. *Even if I committed the most heinous crime, I could tell her, and she'd stand by me.* Love for her mother welled in her; it was as if nothing had happened between them, and they were as they had been—a mother and daughter bound not merely by blood, but by respect and affection. The feeling was so overwhelming that tears rose in Bronwyn's eyes. And she had so wanted to be cerebral!

Elizabeth leaned over and dabbed the tears away. "Now who needs the tissues?" she said softly.

Bronwyn gave a short, nervous laugh. "Oh, Mom, I'm so *glad* to see you, and I'm so sorry to have made you wait so long, but you know what a terrible patient I am, how I hate hospital visits. No one talks about anything that really matters, or tells the truth—it's such a charade."

Tells the truth! The words coiled in Elizabeth like snakes. There *had* been truth between them, but not now. *Never* could she tell Bonnie the truth about why she was going away. Unable to meet her daughter's eyes, Elizabeth looked away.

Bronwyn, caught up in her own feelings, did not notice.

"Mother." The word sounded so formal that Elizabeth looked at her daughter. Bronwyn continued.

"Mother, there have been no lies between us, and I won't lie to you now. I feel *rotten* inside. As for you and Asher, I came to terms with that in Utah. I was wrong, and I'm sorry. Whatever there was between you two before me is none of my business. What *is* my business, and what makes me feel so rotten, is what happened to me in the accident, and what's not happening to me now. Because you and Asher love me, and I *feel* your love so strongly, it makes everything worse, because I don't want to hurt you or hurt him."

A frightening intuition touched cold fingers to the back of Elizabeth's neck, and Bronwyn's next words made them tighten around her heart.

"Mother, do you remember what we talked about two years ago—when you found that lump in your breast?"

Elizabeth got up abruptly and went to the window. She looked out over the city, but saw nothing. Bronwyn's voice pursued her.

"You were lucky, Mother. What if it hadn't been benign? Would you have done as Fay did?"

Elizabeth shook her head from side to side. "I don't know, Bonnie. I really don't know."

"I know."

Elizabeth turned and looked at her daughter. "How can you know?"

Bronwyn's voice softened. "Because I know you, and I feel as you do. You can't stand the thought of mutilation; you would never have consented to a mastectomy. You would have tried all else, as Fay tried, even if it meant dying as she died."

"Bonnie, please. I don't want to talk about it. It's over."

Bronwyn persisted. She could not turn back now. "Do you remember what you made me promise when we saw her in the hospital?"

Elizabeth stared at her daughter, fear clutching at her. Bonnie couldn't mean what she was leading up to!

"You made me feel so close to you," Bronwyn said

desperately. "You entrusted your *life* to me, knowing I would never let you suffer as Fay was suffering."

"Oh, Bonnie!" Elizabeth sobbed, the tears rolling down her cheeks. "Please don't!"

"I have to. You're my *mother,* you're the only one I can turn to, you're the only one who would understand!" Bronwyn cried, feeling tears tighten her throat. "You *must* help me, as I would have helped you! How can you let me suffer? Do you have any idea what it means to want to scratch your nose and find you can't lift a finger?" Her voice cracked. "To have a foul stench wake you because you've shit yourself without *knowing?* And because they don't want you to mess again, they stick suppositories in you so that you'll shit on schedule? Do you know what it feels like to be spoonfed? Is *this* what you want for me? Is this how you want me to live for the rest of my life? This isn't life—it's *death!*"

Elizabeth buried her face in her hands, unable to stem her tears.

Bronwyn wept brokenly, pleading through quick, short gasps.

"You gave me life—a life so beautiful, I always blessed you for the happiness I knew. Maybe because I had so much, I can't accept living this way. Please, Mother—I'm begging you—*help me die!*"

Help me die. The words were like far-off thunder, barely breaking through Elizabeth's grief, but as they gathered in the layered, tension-charged space between mother and daughter, they crashed resoundingly. *Help me die!* A tongue of lightning licked through Elizabeth's tears, consuming them. She took her face from her hands and looked at her daughter unbelievingly. *Help me die!!* Thunder and lightning collided, shocking Elizabeth into reality. A reality so blazing it lit up her brain.

"Stop it, Bonnie!" Anger scorched her words. "Stop it this instant, or so help me, I'll shake that damn halo loose!"

Startled, Bronwyn stopped sobbing.

Cold rationality swept Elizabeth. She went to her daughter and dried Bronwyn's tears. Elizabeth forced herself to remain calm. Bronwyn was no hysteric. If she said she wanted to die—she meant it.

"Does Asher know how you feel?" she asked quietly.

"No, he'd never understand."

"And you expect me to?"

Bronwyn gave her a sardonic look.

"Be honest, Mom. If it was you in this chair, you'd ask for a hot fudge sundae laced with cyanide."

"No, I don't think so." Elizabeth's brow creased as she considered her words. "No, Bonnie, you're wrong. I don't think so."

"But you had to think about it, didn't you?"

"Of course! You wanted an honest answer, and I had to be sure."

"And are you sure?"

"Yes."

"How can you say that, in view of what you once made me promise?"

Elizabeth sighed. "That was totally different. If death is inevitable, I don't want to be kept alive on support systems. I was thinking as much of your suffering as mine. I don't fear dying, you know that, but I never want to hurt you."

"And letting me live this way is not hurting me?"

"No, it's something you were meant to deal with in this lifetime."

"Please! Spare me a reincarnation lecture," Bronwyn said shortly. Her eyes examined Elizabeth calculatingly. "If your belief in reincarnation is so strong," she said slowly, "can't you see all I'm asking is for you to help me have a chance at *life* once again? Or is it that now you can see what a crock all that reincarnation nonsense is! What's *real*, Mother, is that I can't lift my hands or move my feet, and *I don't want to live this way!* Can't you understand? I can't face being a burden . . . I can't bear being waited on . . . I'm no longer free!"

"Oh, Bonnie, darling!" Elizabeth leaned close and took her daughter's hands. "None of us is *free*. All of us know pain. I can't feel what you feel, but I know you're suffering. But I can't condone your wanting to die, not only because you're my daughter and I can't stand losing you, but because to me reincarnation is as true as sunrise, and I *won't* help you bring unfinished karma into your next life—you'll only have to face it again. Maybe this accident is because of something unfinished in a previous lifetime . . . you must work this out *now*, or it will follow you until you do. No, don't interrupt me, I'm not finished.

"As for your being a burden to Asher—or to me—that's *our* karma, something *we* must deal with. You're not a burden to me, and I'm sure not to Asher. You can't be a burden to those who love you."

Bronwyn's look repudiated all Elizabeth had said.

"I don't believe that any more than I believe in reincarnation," Bronwyn said derisively. "A burden is a burden. It kills love as surely as death ends life."

Elizabeth reached out and brushed back the hair which had fallen across her daughter's face. Her voice was composed as she spoke.

"Don't shut your mind and heart, Bonnie, to the infinite dimensions of life and the depth of human emotion. Just because you can't see, touch, or prove doesn't mean that certain realities do not exist. The more hidden, mysterious, and complex an idea is, the *less* it can be proved. Sometimes an idea is so profound it can barely be articulated, much less *seen*. It's like quarks—sound waves—electromagnetic energy. How can we, whose brain stems still contain physical evidence of our reptillian heritage, hope to know all there is to know? All we can do is fumble along and try to learn—and give of our love. I love you, Bonnie . . . I can't let you go!"

Elizabeth held Bronwyn's eyes so intensely, Bronwyn felt almost hypnotized. From her earliest childhood she had been a sounding board for her mother's ideas. Many times Bronwyn had felt it was *she* who anchored her mother to reality, but she had seen the duality Elizabeth felt permeated all life:

She was the yin to Elizabeth's yang, the negative to Elizabeth's positive. Were all mothers and daughters so opposite, she had wondered, or was it that daughters instinctively chose to be opposite? Was that choice not a

291

natural, protective instinct so that a child could find its *own* personality and learn by its *own* experience? Was not life a mirror in which one had to decipher one's own reflections?

Bronwyn's head ached with the thoughts streaming through it. She wanted only to get away—away from all pain—away from all thinking. Pressing her shoulders hard, she drove her wheelchair away from Elizabeth, to the farthest corner of the room. If Elizabeth could teach her to levitate away from all this, *then* she'd believe in the astral world.

Helen swept into the room, her arms filled with a large Styrofoam box from which came a delicious aroma. Chuckling, she went to the coffee table and began to undo the package.

"That man o' yours is *somethin'*, Miz Jacobs!" He's had '*Mr. Babbington*' cater a lunch for you and your mother!" She turned to Elizabeth with a broad smile. "You must be Miz Banks. How do you do? I'm Helen." She stuck out a huge, friendly hand, and Elizabeth shook it warmly.

"I'm pleased to meet you, Helen, and thank you for taking such good care of my daughter."

"She's a pistol, that one." Helen rolled her eyes towards where Bronwyn sat with her back to them. Going purposefully to her patient, she stood, arms akimbo. "Okay, Missy. Whenever you turn your wheelchair to the window like that, you're in a snit. So whatever it is, *forget it!* Your husband sent somethin' real good for you and your mom to enjoy, an' he tol' me to tell you he'd be by tonight, an' for me not to give you any supper—he's bringin' one. That man's got class." Deftly she spun the chair, propelling it to the sofa. "He's even sent along a portion for me, an' even though I ate, I'm sure gonna make room for '*Mr. Babbington*'!"

Elizabeth removed the magazines and books from the coffee table and, placing the crocuses as a centerpiece, she set out the silverware, the crystal, and the damask napkins the caterer supplied. Helen unwrapped the elegantly arranged dishes. Bronwyn watched silently, unable to control the response of her senses and her stomach to the

292

attractive array of food. There were delicious hot appetizers: quiche, bacon-wrapped water chestnuts, and spiced shrimp. The main course, served in green and yellow artichoke plates, was cold artichoke filled with an exquisitely curried crabmeat salad. For dessert there were small coupes of a darkly rich chocolate mousse, and in a silver pot, espresso.

Elizabeth smiled at Bronwyn. "And I was planning to grab a sandwich in the coffee shop."

Bronwyn looked briefly at her mother. Elizabeth had not seen her fed before. Well, maybe now she'd understand. Helen placed a napkin across Bronwyn's chest, and unobtrusively testing the warmth of the quiche, she held a piece to Bronwyn's mouth.

Elizabeth dropped her eyes, embarrassed for what she knew Bronwyn must be feeling. Suddenly she had no desire for food, but so that her daughter would not know, she put a selection of appetizers on her plate and nibbled at one. Then she said brightly, "Since Asher surprised us with this lovely lunch, I think now is the proper moment to tell you my own surprise." She took a long breath. She hated lying to her daughter, but she had no choice. She circumvented the truth with words that came too rapidly.

Bronwyn, listening, was reminded of a sparrow she had once watched as a child. It had been a bright spring day as now, and she and Prince lay on the bank upstream, lulled by the sound of the water, sated after eating the lunch Elizabeth had packed. Suddenly the anxious beeps of a bird overhead pierced the air, and looking up into the young green leaves, she had seen a sparrow flitting nervously. It was protecting its nest. She and Prince had moved upstream, and the bird quieted.

Watching her mother now, Bronwyn had the same feeling—why was Elizabeth so nervous?

"Bonnie, I'm planning to go away for a while. It's something I've been wanting to do for a long time—I hope you won't think I'm deserting you when you've been hurt—it's just that I feel strongly if I don't do it now, I never will."

Bronwyn knew immediately Elizabeth was hiding some-

293

thing. Her mother leave *now?* Her overprotective mother? It was out of character.

Elizabeth saw the skeptical look in Bronwyn's eyes, and she bent over her lunch. Bronwyn ate as Helen fed her, watching her mother silently. When they finished the mousse, Bronwyn let out a long sigh of pleasure.

"I feel human again," she said. She looked up at Helen.

"Would you mind leaving my mother and me alone? I think she'd like to tell me something personal."

Helen moved quickly and lightly despite her size.

"First I must take you to the bathroom, darlin'."

"I was hoping you'd forget that," Bronwyn moaned. "Excuse me, Mother. I can't upset their timetable."

While Helen took care of Bronwyn, Elizabeth cleared the dishes and glassware, repacking them into the caterer's box. Wrapping the leftovers, she put them into the small refrigerator. By the time she was finished, Helen had wheeled Bronwyn back to the sofa.

Picking up the caterer's box, Helen said, "I'll leave this at the nurses' station and then I'll visit Mrs. Greenstein next door. Call me if you need me."

Bronwyn watched Helen leave and then said, "Would you light a cigarette for me, Mom?"

"Are you allowed to smoke?"

Bronwyn laughed scornfully. "What difference would it make? They're in a drawer near my bed."

Elizabeth went to the bed, and Bronwyn observed her figure again. Elizabeth wore a light grey wool suit with a grey silk overblouse; her boxy, hip-length jacket hung on the back of her chair. Returning, she placed the cigarette in Bronwyn's mouth and lit it.

Dragging deeply, Bronwyn took a few puffs. "That's all, thank you."

Elizabeth took the cigarette and extinguished it.

"Are you going to a spa?" Bronwyn asked. "I know you get antsy whenever you gain weight."

"Perhaps . . . but that's only part of it."

"Why are you *really* going away?"

Elizabeth searched her daughter's face. "Do you mind? Do you think I'm being selfish to leave you?"

294

A thin smile edged Bronwyn's lips. "No, I have too many people taking care of me now. It's just that you've been a mother hen for so long, this turnaround seems strange. I'm glad, though, that you're thinking of yourself —it's about time. I'm just curious as to why."

Elizabeth shrugged and sat down, crossing her legs. She smiled. "I feel freer now that you're married. We've had an unusual relationship. Maybe it's because you never lived with your father or he with us. If he had, we might have been rivals and not grown as close as we have."

Again she smiled, only now it was shy, uncertain.

"You'll hate hearing this, but since you married Asher, I feel secure about you. I know it's silly to think marriage means security—or happiness—but it is warm and comforting for a mother when her daughter marries a fine man, a man of position and intelligence."

"And Jewish," Bronwyn said, laughing.

"Yes." Elizabeth smiled self-consciously. She leaned closer to her daughter.

"Bonnie, I know you were secure and successful before you married Asher, but I never felt I could *let go* before. Now, despite your accident, I feel *free*. I know that if I don't see you for a year, or longer, you'll be all right. What's more . . . I'll be all right."

Yes . . . she will, Bronwyn thought.

"Where are you going? What do you plan to do?"

If I could only *tell* her! Elizabeth thought. Instead she said, "I'm burned out writing romances. I need a change of pace, a change of scene. Maybe I'll try writing something more challenging. Maybe I'll just travel . . . or go to school. Bea has been after me to visit her. I love Paris, and I've never really spent enough time there. I plan to leave next week, after your birthday."

Bronwyn laughed out loud. "Bea? You want to visit Bea and try writing something more challenging than romance?"

Elizabeth realized how incongruous it was, and her lips twitched with amusement.

"Mother, you're the most marvelously paradoxical person I've ever known!" Bronwyn exclaimed. "You're fed up writing romance and so you choose to visit a woman who's been married three times, has had countless lovers, and lives off the fortunes they gave her!"

Bronwyn's laughter echoed out into the hall, and Elizabeth's mood lightened. It had been so long since she had heard her daughter laugh so freely.

"Would you mind taking care of Blaze?" Elizabeth asked. "I think Asher would agree—he'd really be no trouble. I don't want to take him abroad because he'd have to spend weeks in quarantine, and I don't like leaving him with Jesse for so long a time. The cats are no problem; they go in and out of the shed on their own, and they catch a lot of wild game. Jesse will supplement that with dry food—he'll come by three times a week."

Instinctively, the thought of having Blaze made Bronwyn smile, but then she suddenly realized what Elizabeth and the seductive lunch had made her *forget*—that she was *crippled* and bound to this chair! Her smile faded. How could she have been such a fool to be so easily diverted! Little more than an hour ago, she had been begging Elizabeth to help her die! She couldn't take Blaze if . . .

Angry guilt rose in her, and her face darkened with annoyance.

"That's impossible, Mother, and you know it," she snapped. "How could you even think of confining a dog who's always lived in the country to a city apartment? It would be cruel! No! I won't do it! Give Blaze to Jesse. At least Blaze likes the idiot, and I'm sure Mrs. Crouch would be kind to him."

Elizabeth was stunned. Bonnie hated Jesse! And she had always hated his taking care of the dog when they had gone away. Why would she want Jesse to have Blaze *now*? A terrible premonition skidded through her. Oh my God!

"Bonnie! Get those thoughts out of your mind! If you don't care about *yourself,* you *must* care about Asher and me! We couldn't take it, if anything happened to you. But we *can* live with *whatever* you have to live with . . ."

"But *I* can't!" Bronwyn shrilled. "And you've no *right* to lay that guilt on me! My life is *mine!* Not yours, not his, *mine!* What I do is my decision—*mine!* Please! I'm very tired. Oh Christ—I'd just like to sleep forever!"

296

Elizabeth stood fused to the cold, hard floor. And then she felt a touch on her arm. Turning, she looked into Helen's dark, brooding eyes.

"Go now, Miz Banks," the woman said gently. "Don't worry, she'll feel better after a long nap. I'm going to give her these pills."

But when Bronwyn awoke she did not feel any better. The more she thought about it, the more she realized it was foolish to have asked Elizabeth to help her. And it was better Elizabeth was leaving.

If I believed in God, Bronwyn thought wryly, *finding out how easily I can die without endangering anyone would be a sign that it's right. I can't ask Calhoun to shut off life supports, because I'm not on them. I don't need dialysis or a respirator, and there's little chance I'll get pneumonia in this damned hothouse! So, I've got to get someone to help me!*

Late in the day Calhoun surprised her by dropping in; he usually made his daily visit early in the morning.

"Hi," she said. "Can you stay awhile and talk to me?"

"That's why I'm here."

She glanced at him sharply. So, Elizabeth had spoken to him.

With a nod to Helen, he pulled a chair close to the bed. Bronwyn understood his signal and, as she expected, Helen left the room.

Mentally, Bronwyn prepared herself for a test of wills. Tom was not easy to deal with when he disagreed with you, and his demeanor suggested deep disagreement. He was too straightforward to conceal his feelings behind a bed-side manner.

She met his eyes challengingly. "When are you going to release me?"

"As soon as your urinary infection has cleared for seventy-two hours—I imagine sometime next week. We have to be careful with the antibiotics. We don't want you building up a resistance to them."

"And what about the halo and the leg casts? How much longer?"

"Another month, more or less, but Helen is going to be

297

taking care of you at home, and Asher has hired a physical therapist and an additional nurse, so there shouldn't be any problem."

"No problem?" Bronwyn said bitterly. "When the hell am I going to move my hands and legs?"

He looked at her squarely. "I don't know, Bonnie. You should have more movement by now. I've been considering a laminectomy, and I want to discuss it with Asher."

"*Asher?* It's not *his* body—it's *mine!* Why the hell don't you discuss it with *me?*"

"Listen to yourself! That's why. Bonnie, I've known you since you were a baby, and even in your crib you were impatient." His face softened, and he reached out to smooth the creases from her brow. "Under that shell you've built around yourself, my girl, beats a very tender and emotional heart, but you're your own worst enemy."

"This laminectomy—will it help?"

"It might—and it might also kill you. That's why we're so conservative with cervical surgery."

"I'll take my chances."

"But *I* won't! Until I'm *sure,* I won't operate. There's still a good chance you'll regain muscle movement without surgery. Your sensory reactions are positive and you're getting more and more movement in your hands and feet. Our biggest problem is your expectations and impatience."

The eyes which held his so stubbornly suddenly went liquid, and the fiery copper depths held such despair, he felt as though she had reached out and gripped his heart.

"No, Tom," she said quietly. "I'm not being impatient. I'm just being realistic, and I have *no* expectations. I know that the longer I have no movement, the less likely it is that I will ever regain full movement. It's something one of our coaches, Jonesy, talked about years ago when a racer we knew crashed. I don't want to go into it, or even have you explain it to me—I know I'll never be like I *was.* And you know something? I just don't want to live that way. I really would much rather die." She gave him an oblique look. "Why don't you *really* help me? It'd be so easy for you."

298

She said it so softly and surely, it shocked Calhoun more than if she had ranted. He looked at her bleakly and thought: *If she were some beautiful mare, injured the way she is, I wouldn't think twice. How often Pop watched them shoot T-61 into crippled thoroughbreds. We never let animals suffer—why humans?*

He took her hands and gently caressed her fingers.

"Bonnie, darling, listen to me. Your being hurt the way you are is terrible, and I'm not going to give you a lot of malarky about how great life is and why you should be glad to be alive—or even that you're lucky to be married to a rich man who can make life easy for you. The facts you've got to face are: if I help you die, my work is finished, and to me my work is my life. I won't sacrifice that for you or for anyone else. And if your plan is to commit suicide, then you leave a lot of suffering behind you, and that isn't fair; as a matter of fact it's downright *rotten*, because the people who love you will always feel guilty that they couldn't stop you, and your death will haunt them the rest of their lives. So while you may have a right to kill yourself, you *don't* have a right to inflict suffering on others, especially not on people you love and who love you. If you had no one, absolutely *no one*, I'd say, 'Do what you want.'" His eyebrows came together and his face took on a satanic expression. "But since there is someone—your mother and Asher—if you try to kill yourself, I will flay you with all the wrath only someone born of generations of Calhouns can foment! I will not permit you to destroy a healthy, intelligent mind! I don't hold with keeping bodies alive artificially when brains are dead, but I *won't allow* death when someone has a mind like yours!"

"Oh, Tom," she wailed. "It's because I *can* think that I can't live this way! If I were a vegetable, I wouldn't *know* what I was doing to my mother and to Asher! I hate myself for crippling them too. Don't you know they'll share this prison with me for the rest of their lives?"

It had been a long, demanding day, and Calhoun had little patience left. He got up heavily and stood looking down at Bronwyn. Sighing deeply, he said, "Yes, Bonnie,

299

I know. But we all live in prisons, and except for the poor souls born into poverty, ignorance, and bigotry, they're all of our own choosing.''

Bronwyn never planned to ask Asher. It just happened. When he arrived later that evening, he was dressed in jeans and carrying a large wicker basket covered with a red and white checked cloth. Slung over one shoulder was a bottle of champagne in a canvas cooler; over his other shoulder he carried a bulging tote. His face beamed with his surprises, and his hair fell over his forehead. He had let it grow longer, and Bronwyn liked the more youthful look.

Her senses stirred at his beauty and she felt a strong sexual urge rise in her. He put down his packages, and coming to her wheelchair, he kissed her warmly. She opened her lips, and her response thrilled him—she had not kissed him with such ardor since that last morning on the beach outside Darien.

When he finally took his lips from her she asked him what he had in the packages.

Teasing her, Asher slowly and deliberately undid the bulging tote. She goaded him until he withdrew a rust-colored suede vest lined with mink. Her eyes flew to him. What a beautiful present! She asked him to hold the vest to her face; he watched her close her eyes to the softness against her cheek. Then he put the vest on her, telling her it was a beautifully warm night for early April, and they were going on a picnic.

She laughed with excitement. Where? How?

Wrapping a blanket around her feet, he placed the basket on her lap and slung the tote with the champagne on his shoulder. He pushed her wheelchair towards the door, telling her she would soon find out.

At the end of the long corridor a set of doors opened onto a terrace overlooking the East River. She had sat in the sun on this terrace but she had never been permitted out at night. And it was at night that it was most beautiful. Tonight the sky was dusky; a full moon diffused the glistening web of stars and splayed the terrace with silver. A jeweled halo, prisms of ice crystals born of high, thin clouds, ringed the moon. Stroked with the moon's brightness, the city glimmered, the skyline a silvered shadow.

Asher unpacked the basket, setting out china, wine glasses, and silver. He covered the metal table with the checked cloth, unrolled red napkins, and took out two hurricane lamps. He lit the wicks on the fat white candles and Bronwyn watched him fold the napkins, candlelight playing on his strong-looking fingers.

She closed her eyes and felt those fingers enflaming her in the candlelight of the cottage in Connecticut. Her memory followed his hands stroking and fondling the insides of her thighs.

Asher spoke softly as he laid out the dinner, telling her Ruth had made the chicken, the broccoli soufflé, the Mexican corn bread. Bronwyn heard nothing of what he said. What she heard were his lips kissing her body as they lay before the fire—she felt his tongue weave in and out of her. At the sound of the champagne cork popping, her eyes flew open.

"It's not the right choice for a picnic, darling," Asher smiled, "but since I have a very special surprise, champagne is appropriate."

Memory flooded her—the night they had married, the night Asher had poured a magnum of champagne on their bodies and they'd licked each other clean. Her eyes devoured him. He gave her *so much!* What could she ever give him? Miserably she looked at the beautifully arranged table and the delicious array of food.

No! In the sterility of her room his feeding her was bad enough! Out here, where all was so lovely, she could not face that humiliation! Her agony spilled in a long, plaintive cry that arched over the parapet and fell into the void of night.

Astounded, Asher came to her, the opened bottle of champagne in his hand.

"My God, Bronwyn! What is it?"

Sobbing, she poured out her heart, crying out her anger, her hopelessness, begging him to help her die.

Chapter Twenty-five

WILLEM Van Zuye stood on the spiral stairs overlooking the studio, barking orders to the workmen crating the sculpture Tyler Oil had commissioned. His assistants scurried about making sure the moving men did not mar the massive marble work; they checked each wood brace, each wood panel of the crate. Van Zuye watched, a deep frown creasing his face. When he was certain the sculpture, shielded with foam on all sides, was secure, he waved his hand, and the workmen closed the crate, fastening it with long brass screws.

Van Zuye turned and began the climb to the aerie, where Asher waited to have lunch with him. Since Bronwyn's accident Asher had been a frequent visitor, seeking the solace a trusted friend brought. They had known each other more than thirty years; Van Zuye's sculptures graced the fountain and courtyards of the ICC buildings. The

302

frown on the sculptor's face deepened as he neared the aerie. When Asher had phoned the night before, Van Zuye had sensed a despair in him he had not heard since that terrible day the Cassidys died.

He found Asher on the roof garden, seemingly engrossed in the green shoots thrusting through the black soil of the vegetable patches laid out like a Mondrian painting. Asher looked up when he heard Van Zuye, and his face was dark, brooding.

"Would you rather talk first?" Van Zuye asked.

Asher put his arm on the small man's shoulders.

"You've been working hard all morning. Let's eat."

They ate at a small table in the sunny south end of the room where Van Zuye always had lunch. For him it was his main meal of the day, and he ate with concentration, chewing his food slowly. The elegant table setting was a sharp contrast to the simplicity of the food: on a gold-banded platter were raw sliced vegetables and mounds of alfalfa sprouts, in an antique tureen was steaming brown rice, and on abalone shells, broiled fish. A silver teapot contained a brew of comfrey, rose hips, and mint tea, and a blue porcelain bowl held fresh fruit. Van Zuye attributed his remarkable good health to his lifestyle and he had little patience with sick people and doctors. On the rare occasion when he felt ill, he took to his bed and fasted. Now he finished eating and said to Asher, "I know you are troubled. Tell me about it."

Asher fixed his eyes on the artist and said quietly, "Bronwyn wants to die. She's begged me to help her."

"And will you?"

Surprise crossed Asher's face. "How can you ask me that? Of course not! It would be murder!"

"Would it?"

"Stop being an inquisitor, Willem! I came here for some solid feedback!"

Van Zuye's words were clipped. "How would you feel in her place?"

Asher's expression was bitter. "But I'm not in her place! I love her—I want her just the way she is!"

The old man leaned across the table to him. "You'll never make her believe that."

303

Asher slumped in his chair.

"I know. I've tried, and all she says is that if I really loved her, I'd help her die."

"Even if it put you in jeopardy?"

Asher looked at him, and Van Zuye saw a grudging admiration in the green eyes.

"She's thought of that, it was her major worry, but she's come up with a diabolically clever idea. I'd be in no danger."

Van Zuye snorted. "All plans are clever until they go wrong."

"This one would work."

"How?"

Asher shook his head. "I don't want to talk about it. All I want is to get through to her that we can have a life together, that she is no burden to me, that her need only makes me love her more." His face took on a hopeful look. "Dr. Calhoun tells me we could even have a child! My God, Willem, do you know what that would mean to me? And what joy it might bring to her?" His eyes speared Van Zuye's. "I need your help, Willem! I know you hate hospitals, but if you visited Bronwyn, she'd be surprised and delighted. If you explained how I felt, she'd believe you. Her work has always been the most important part of her life—she no longer wants even that—and you could encourage her, give her good reasons for living!"

Van Zuye sat back and slowly began to revolve his head, relaxing the tension he felt building in him. He looked long and hard at Asher before he asked, "Did you mention having a child to her?"

"No. I was going to, and I also wanted to give her a ring I'd bought, but I never had the chance. For no reason she suddenly exploded and begged me to help her die."

"For no reason?" Sarcasm scored Van Zuye's words. He entwined his wiry, stained fingers and stretched his bony arms out on the table. "How can you be so *unaware?*" he said angrily. "And to even consider having a child! It's ludicrous! You can't know how the trauma might affect her kidneys, her liver, her entire system! Tell me, Asher, why are so many defective children born today? Do you think it's the will of God?" His eyes shone eerily. "God gave

304

man all he needed to reproduce healthfully, but man has polluted his environment and himself! God does not will sickness! It is man who pollutes his genes and pollutes his children! And you want to make a child with a mother who is so severely hurt? Don't you think she's had enough pain? Wake up, Asher! See life as Bronwyn sees it—as it really *is!*"

Asher opened his mouth, but Van Zuye held up his hand authoritatively.

"Let me finish! I can't help you. You see, I agree with Bronwyn, and were I so immured, I would make sure I died. There's no way she can concentrate on her work when she has no joy in life! And don't throw up examples of other people who cope so well with paralysis—each person is different. Bronwyn's a sentient, sensual woman, and she's more aware now of her body than she's ever been. The thought of you making love to her is probably excruciating, because she loves beauty and hates what she's become. I agree that if you loved her, you would help her, but you see, it's not just Bronwyn you want to keep alive—it's *Marguerite.*"

Van Zuye saw he hit a nerve, but he pressed on, his voice unforgiving.

"I never really noticed Bronwyn's resemblance to Marguerite until I saw the two of you together and saw the way you looked at her. And when you married so quickly, I knew *why.* You are *obsessed,* Asher. And now tragedy repeats itself, and you can't face losing Marguerite again. But you see, my dear and trusted friend, it may be your destiny *never* to have Marguerite. And what about *Bronwyn?* Do you have the right to make her live the life you wanted with Marguerite?"

Van Zuye's face sagged with enervation; his habits were disciplined and seldom disrupted, and usually he meditated and napped after lunch. He did not like this upset. Wearily, he said, "I'll visit Bronwyn, but not to plead for you. I want her to know how much I admire her courage, and that I understand."

He got up and went downstairs to his bedroom.

Asher sat lost in thought.

* * *

305

Bronwyn found Elizabeth waiting when she returned from therapy. As Helen wheeled her charge into the room, Elizabeth looked up from the book she was reading, a thoughtful expression on her face.

"I didn't expect you," Bronwyn said, surprised.

"I had lunch with Tom. He told me you could go home next week."

"Oh joy."

Elizabeth ignored her sarcasm and going to Helen, she handed her two books. "I hope you like them," she smiled.

The nurse beamed.

"Thank you, Miz Banks. Are they as sexy as that other one you gave me? You sure can write love scenes—and do they turn my husband on! I read them to him, and he's electrified!" She laughed heartily.

"I'm glad you enjoy them, Helen. Would you mind—I'd like to be alone with Bonnie. I'll let you know when I leave."

Bronwyn glanced up sharply at her mother.

Helen hesitated. After that first visit, Elizabeth had asked Helen never to leave them alone. Searching Elizabeth's eyes, she saw the dismissal in them, and with a shrug she went to the door.

"Call me if you need anything. I'll be in the lounge reading."

Frowning, Elizabeth looked at Bronwyn and then she went to the window and stared out at the city. The streets were wet and the spindly city trees bent in the wind. *Bent in the wind*. Was she, too, bending to an inevitable wind? Was there nothing she could hold on to for support? And none of her reading had helped. After that first visit with Bronwyn she had gone home and spent hours skimming Buber, Emerson, Adler, Tillich, Murchie, Kant, the Rig Veda, the Bible—looking for answers—but all she found were questions, and the more she sought solace, the less peaceful she became.

Bronwyn watched her mother, hope beginning to stir in her.

"Asher told me about the apartment, Mother. Thank

you. It was wonderful of you to take all that time. I'm sure it's even lovelier than he says."

Elizabeth turned, her eyes caressing the lines of her daughter's face. She never ceased to marvel that so beautiful a person came from her—and her daughter's beauty was so much more than her physical self. She came and sat down in a chair next to Bronwyn, and leaning close, she asked, "Do you still feel the same?"

Mother and daughter looked at each other steadily.

"You're thinking of helping me, aren't you?"

Elizabeth clasped her hands together and cried, "It's against *everything* I believe in, but I can't get it out of my mind! I can't sleep and when I do, I have terrible dreams. I hear you calling me, and then I run to you, but no matter how fast I run—I never reach you! I scream, *'Wait! Wait!'* and then I wake up screaming." Tears welled in her eyes. "My God, Bonnie! How can I help kill what I love most?"

"You can't, Mother." Bronwyn smiled gently. "And I was stupid to ask you. Forgive me. But it should be some measure of my love that I confided in you. Let's just forget about it."

"But *you* haven't forgotten, Bonnie!" Elizabeth despairingly shook her head from side to side. "I *know* it's in your mind. It's what you want, and you'll do something about it—and I won't be here . . ."

Bronwyn took a deep breath, trying to still the quivering in her stomach. She *knew* her mother. Despite everything, when it came right down to it, Elizabeth was the one person she could always count on.

Very softly, and trying to steady her voice, Bronwyn said, "I know how much you love me and what this is doing to you. I want you to know that. I also want you to know that I love you so much, I'm putting my life entirely into your hands. But first, thank you for not questioning my sanity. Not once did you say I was mad, or denigrate me, and I bless you for that."

"Oh, Bonnie," Elizabeth whispered, "I don't want to lose you."

"Mother, darling, what if I were terminally ill? You'd have to accept losing me then. And if you really believe in reincarnation, you'll *never* lose me—we'll meet again. Can't you accept that I'm ready for another life? If I'm willing to try and believe in that, because *you* tell me, and because *you* believe it—why can't you try and see that what I want is best for *me?* And even if you do nothing to help me *now,* I *can* help myself. When Asher told me about the terraces and the electric eyes which make it so easy for me to go in and out by myself, I realized I could sit out there some stormy day while Asher was at work and get so chilled I'd be sure to get pneumonia—that's the one thing they seem to be so afraid of in this hospital, that I'll get pneumonia. But then my death would be unnecessarily long and painful—for *everyone.* This way it's so quick and easy—why prolong the misery? Why make it so much worse for Asher—for me—for you? I know how you feel about him, and he doesn't even know how much he cares about you, but I see it in his eyes whenever he talks about you. When he told me about what you did to the apartment, his eyes *shone!* If I hadn't come along, you two would undoubtedly have gotten together. I'm just so tired of surviving. This isn't the life I want—it isn't life at all. I have a lot of pain and they give me this damn drug and it makes me groggy. I can't work . . . I can't even light my own cigarette. I can't do anything I want, when *I* want to. I just want to pack it in."

Elizabeth reached out and took Bronwyn's hands in hers. She held on to them tightly, her head bent, her tears falling on her daughter's fingers.

Bronwyn looked down at her hands; by concentrating hard and patiently she pressed her mother's hands. It was a small, puny movement, but Elizabeth was so grateful, she picked up Bronwyn's hands and kissed each finger.

"Oh, Bonnie, I love you so."

"And I love you," Bronwyn said. "And just in case you change your mind, I want you to know how easy it is to help me. Even if you don't, I bless you for considering it."

She lowered her voice.

308

Chapter Twenty-six

BRONWYN never expected Van Zuye to visit her; she knew his feelings about hospitals and sick people. He came without his usual entourage, striding into the sunlit room as if his very presence could make her whole again. He wore a turtleneck sweater as blue as a glacial lake, tight-fitting black pants, and a black beret. Louis had driven his employer uptown and he came in briefly to greet Bronwyn; then he left, saying he would wait for Van Zuye in the lounge.

The sculptor looked imperiously at Helen and said, "Please leave us alone."

The woman gave him such a withering glance, Bronwyn laughed.

"It's all right, Helen; this is Willem Van Zuye, the sculptor, and I'm very glad to see him. I'll call you if I need you."

Van Zuye pulled up a chair and sat down close to Bronwyn.

"I'm pleased to see you." Bronwyn smiled.

He fastened his beady eyes on hers.

"I'm not happy to see you here, and like this. I've come because you need a good friend."

They talked all afternoon, and Bronwyn could not believe this was the man she had known. This Van Zuye was open, charming, and made her laugh. He spoke of his boyhood in Holland, revealing stories she wished she had known when they worked together on his book. But the book had not been a biography, and Van Zuye had sheathed his privacy as though it were granite he refused to carve.

He began to speak of Asher as a young man, and Bronwyn was surprised to learn how long they had known each other. He told her of the Cassidys and of Asher's love affair with Marguerite and of her death, with Michael, in the plane crash. Then he told her of Asher's marriage to Eleanore and how Eleanore died. She grew quiet as he spoke, and a thoughtful sadness deepened the frown between her eyes. Van Zuye related how he had first met the Cassidys in Amsterdam in the thirties, when he had been an unknown artist, working part-time as a carpenter to pay his studio rent. Michael had bought two of his early carvings and later some of his paintings. When he gratefully told Michael he would like to paint a portrait of mother and daughter, Michael was delighted and invited him to Gstaad. After the war, Michael had arranged for his entry into the United States and loaned him the money to rent and equip his first New York studio.

Van Zuye's voice softened. "You cannot imagine what a golden child Eleanore was—I had never seen such a beautiful creature. There was a translucence about her, a light so pastel, I couldn't capture it. It was something you *felt*, rather than *saw*. I've never forgotten it, nor her."

His eyes held such melancholy, Bronwyn wanted to reach out and touch him. "You loved Eleanore, didn't you? Did you ever tell her?"

"No," he said more candidly than she expected. "To her I was a doting family friend, more than thirty years older, bald and short. But even had I been Adonis, the only man she loved, besides her father, was Asher."

"What happened to the painting?" Bronwyn was curious as to why she had not come across it in her research for the book. As an early work it preceded his abstract period, and she would like to see if indeed she looked like Marguerite Cassidy.

"I have it," Van Zuye said quietly. "If you wish I'll show it to you."

"Thank you." Bronwyn looked deeply into his ripe olive eyes, fascinated. "Tell me more," she urged.

"When the Germans invaded Holland I joined the resistance." He smiled with grim satisfaction. "My size proved very valuable—I could get into places grown men could not, and very often I disguised myself as a child." His face hardened. "But I could not save my parents. I was on a mission when the Gestapo came to my home. They'd found out my mother was Jewish, and when my father protested, they shot him. My mother screamed for them to shoot her too, and they did. They left their bodies right there on the stoop my mother used to wash every day."

His mouth was a slash and the words coming from it were knifelike.

"Others may have forgotten and forgiven the Germans, but not *I*. I remember how much the Germans loved Hitler—how they screamed in adulation, and how eagerly they followed orders. They were inhuman beasts, and I shall never *forget* or *forgive!* That is why I did not permit distribution of the book in Germany, and *none* of my work can ever be shown there!"

He shook his head as if to shake the anger from him. "But that's enough of me. I came to talk of you—and of Asher."

"Do I really look so much like Marguerite Cassidy?"

Van Zuye cocked his head and squinted.

"Yes, but not so much as Asher thinks. He sees you through the eyes of memory; I see you as you *are* because I *know* you—Asher does not. He's not had time, and memory deceives him. He sees only your coloring, your hair, your height, but you are not at all like Marguerite. You are a bold, independent thinker. You do not defer to a man, or to power, and you're not enslaved by religion." He ran his fingers along the lines of her cheek.

"Actually you're far more like Eleanore." He sat back in his chair and wove his fingers together.

"What was remarkable about Asher and Eleanore was that they never grew to hate each other—it could have happened so easily. Eleanore hated her mother for having Asher, and she knew Asher would never have married her, had Marguerite lived. And Asher could have resented Eleanore because she tried so hard to give him what he had wanted from Marguerite. As I watched Asher and Eleanore through the years, I was intrigued by how kind they were to each other, and I came to believe they were a *true* brother and sister—souls who had been siblings in another life, brought together again to comfort each other."

Bronwyn's mouth dropped open. *Van Zuye?* Cold, calculating Van Zuye? This was like talking to her mother.

The sculptor continued, his tone brooking no argument.

"Asher doesn't love *you,* Bronwyn. At least, not yet. To truly love takes time—it's like polishing marble. Asher was a boy who fell in love with an older woman. All young men do, and that's as it should be, for older women ripen young men, making them confident, strong, mature. But as men age they yearn for young women to refresh them with the audacity, the vitality, the splendor of youth. It is an ongoing, nourishing, natural phenomenon which nature abets and condones, for why else would she bless mature men with such attractiveness and punish mature women with the hateful strokes of *age?"*

He sighed and stretched his hands above his head, spreading his fingers, letting the tension flow from him. Again he fastened his black eyes on Bronwyn.

"But Asher's older woman died young, and he never came to terms with her death. Now he's met you, and he has the woman he lost, and a chance at his youth again. But—you want to die."

Her eyes flew to him. "How do you know that!"

"He told me."

"Everything?"

"Except how. Bronwyn, don't you see? If you die,

312

Asher will never rid himself of Marguerite. You will perpetuate a myth, and he will never know happiness."

Empathy filled his face and he leaned forward, taking her hands in his. He pressed her fingers tightly.

"Do you feel that, Bronwyn?"

She closed her eyes and nodded, trying to more firmly grasp the strong fingers which brought such life to stone, to steel. Could he bring life back into her hands?

He gripped her hands, his eyes slitted, seeing the depth of her concentration in the tightness of her brow. Finally she opened her eyes and he eased the pressure of his fingers.

Misery deepened the lines around her mouth. "How can I make him happy when I'm so desolate? Oh, Willem! I wish I could change my nature, but I'm self-involved. I love seclusion and being alone; living too close to someone irritates me, and I don't know *why* I allowed myself to marry Asher. I'm a difficult person, and you of all people should understand. I have no patience—now it's even worse. I dread waking up. I must wait for someone to empty my urine bottle, to wash me, dress me, feed me! I hate myself more each day, and Asher will grow to hate me, and feel even guiltier. He leads such a vital life. Every time he stays home because I can't accompany him will fill me with guilt. And his lavishness makes it worse. If I had only *myself* to think of, if I thought I was hurting *no one,* if I was dependent only on *me,* it would be easier, and it would be a challenge for me to take care of *myself.* But to enwrap others in my bondage is cruel, and what you've told me makes it even more imperative Asher have a chance for happiness. I must do this *now.* To prolong my life only means misery for everyone."

Van Zuye sat silent, his eyes sketching her face. He stood up and bent closely over her, running his fingers along the planes of her forehead, her cheeks, her jaw, around her eyes and over her eyelids. Closing his eyes, he traced his fingers, over and over, memorizing the contours. She felt a chill at the back of her neck.

"Why did you do that?" she asked.

"I want to do a sculpture of you."

"You don't do busts—iconographies—anymore."

313

"I do what I like." He pulled his chair close and sat down again. "Tell me what Asher wouldn't tell me. How do you plan to die?"

Her eyes measured him. "Why do you want to know that?"

"I might be the only friend you have."

Utter astonishment crossed her face. "But you disagree! Besides—I can't involve you, Willem!"

"Why not? You told Asher there's no danger to anyone."

An ironic smile curved her lips. "Even if there were, I can just see them incarcerating you!"

His laugh was short, grating.

Puzzlement etched lines in her wide forehead. "Why would you do this for me? You as much as said that if I died, I'd be hurting Asher more than if I lived, and since you seem to believe in reincarnation, wouldn't helping me hurt your karma and help me screw up mine?"

His thin lips stretched into a smile.

"Yes, my dear little skeptic, but you see, the *ultimate* decision is *yours,* and without a chance to make that decision, you will feel thwarted and bitterness will fester in you, making you incapable of being kind to yourself or to anyone else. I'm hoping that given the opportunity you will change your mind. I see it not as helping you die, but helping you *live.* If you opt for life, you will live with a more positive attitude."

"But what if I *don't* change my mind?"

He shrugged. "We all choose our own hell. I admire you, Bronwyn, but to me life is no more than a quark in time. I remember so clearly being young—all I did was turn around and I'm an old man. But I shall live again, and again, on into eternity, making my mistakes and learning with each lifetime. Death is no more than transport into another life, and if some choose to board earlier than necessary, it is a choice for this lifetime to be finished in another."

Her eyebrows arched.

"You sound like my mother."

"Really? But then, throughout the world, more people believe in reincarnation than do not."

"Well, I'm not a believer," Bronwyn said firmly. "And after what's happened, I'm not anxious to give it another try. You amaze me, Willem. I can't comprehend someone as pragmatic as you believing in the occult."

"I came to it late." He leaned back in the chair. "You're too young, Bronwyn, to remember the passion of the peace movement. I wondered why, after so many generations of war, an entire *generation* suddenly rose up and screamed *no*. Why did these young people let themselves be beaten and jailed? All they wanted was *peace!*" Sadness soured his voice.

"It hit me very hard, especially after what I had seen in the war. Nowhere in history could I find a parallel—thousands of children turning against their parents, against their government, against all tradition; dressing to torment the establishment—so keenly illustrating how shallow were our concerns. We cared more about how people *looked* and *dressed* than if they had bread, or a life worth living. Where did all this awareness come from? Why had it never happened before? And then I *knew!* It was a revelation so clear, it changed my life forever!

"These were the *souls* of the innocents murdered in a thousand places during the war: Auschwitz, Dachau, all the camps. These were the souls of the *children* who died in London, Leningrad, Warsaw, Dresden, Hiroshima, Nagasaki! Never in any war had so many innocent children been brutalized, and these children of the sixties, protesting in the streets and being beaten by police, were *souls* driven back to life to scream out against the senselessness of war and the heartlessness of poverty."

"If they were," Bronwyn said dryly, "their purpose was short-lived. They've succumbed to microwave ovens and video games like everyone else."

Van Zuye leaned over and kissed her forehead. "What did you tell Asher?"

"You really want to help me?" She held his eyes.

His face was grave. "What do you think?"

The birthday party Willem Van Zuye gave for Bronwyn the night before she was to be released from New York Hospital was one the staff of the seventeenth floor, used to

315

opulence, had never seen. Shortly before four, decorators arrived, and while Helen washed Bronwyn's hair and dressed her in another room down the hall, her bed was wheeled out and the suite transformed into a festive salon fragrant with fresh flowers and aglow with tiny lights and shimmering streamers. At five-thirty the caterers came with a sumptuous array of food and bottles of champagne in silver coolers. Van Zuye strode in soon after to supervise the final touches. He placed wild spring flowers around the towering, chocolate-covered birthday cake and critically smoothed the pink damask cloths on the buffet tables.

When Helen finally wheeled Bronwyn into the room, the nurse's eyes widened with delight and surprise. She gave Van Zuye a long and appraising look.

"I don't know how you got permission, Mr. Van Zuye, but I've gotta hand it to you—you're a classy man! And the staff wants me to thank you for the food you left at the nurses' station—there's enough there for all the shifts, and I can tell you, when those hungry interns hear about it, they'll be coming from all over the hospital. Too bad the champagne's off-limits to us—we can't drink on duty."

"That's all right, Mrs. Warder, please take home a bottle when you leave, and help yourself to dinner now. You won't have time once guests arrive. Perhaps you, too, Bronwyn, would like to eat with Mrs. Warder."

"Thank you, Willem," Bronwyn said gratefully. She knew he wanted to save her the embarrassment of being fed in public.

"Come," he said. "Jacques has prepared plates for you both. Please, eat by the window, so that I can sketch."

As Helen fed Bronwyn, Van Zuye sat on a stool catching their movements, and then he drew many versions of Bronwyn's face, her expressions, the slender arc of her neck, the tilt of her chin, and the way her hair, freshly washed, shone and fell around her shoulders. The two women, engrossed in the splendid variety and taste of the food, paid little attention to him. Bronwyn knew he did not like interruptions to mar his concentration.

Van Zuye paused to enjoy Bronwyn's beauty, and as his

316

eyes roamed her body seated in the wheelchair, a small nagging began inside him. It ate at him until he could not deny it. *She was dressed to die!* His adrenaline rushed, and he felt a momentary numbness in his toes. But he could not back out now—she had to have her chance! It had to be her decision! His hand trembled as he sketched the fine steel halo around her head—it made her look almost ethereal, as if she ruled some cosmic kingdom. Frowning, he carefully drew in the dress she wore, thinking she must have once found it in some antique shop. It was a fragile Victorian dress in ecru lace with a high collar and long, tight sleeves; its full-length tiered skirt hid the casts on her legs and she looked light, *spectral.* His pencil stopped in midair, and as he looked up he saw Asher staring at her from the doorway, his face so somber it seemed set in stone. But so quickly did it change into a smile, Van Zuye was sure he had been mistaken.

Going to Bronwyn, Asher touched her hair, running his fingers through its silky length. Bending, he kissed her, his lips moving tenderly on her mouth.

"Ummmm, you taste good," he said with a laugh, and then seriously, "I've never seen you look so lovely. You're like an exquisite daguerreotype. Wherever did you find that dress?"

She laughed happily. "In a thrift shop when I was still in school. I had Mother bring it in for me. I'm glad you like it; it's my favorite." And then, with feverish excitement, she said, "Can you believe this *room?* Isn't Van Zuye *incredible?* Oh, Willem, I can't thank you enough, for the party, for *everything.*"

They heard the click of heels and the chatter of people coming down the corridor. Van Zuye put away his sketch pad, and Helen cleared away their plates. Asher moved Bronwyn's wheelchair so that she faced the door, and soon she was greeting friends and colleagues, chatting animatedly, her cheeks flushed with excitement. Asher never left her side; he stood by her chair, his hand lightly on her shoulder, smiling at her gaiety. But deep behind his eyes was a cold emptiness.

When Elizabeth came in with Calhoun the suite was so

thick with people, she could not see Bronwyn. Calhoun preceded her, edging his way through the throng. Bronwyn saw her mother and called out to her.

Elizabeth turned quickly, and she stopped, struck by how beautiful her daughter looked.

"I'll get some champagne while you say hello to Bronwyn," Calhoun said, making his way to the buffet.

"Bonnie, darling!" Elizabeth said, carefully putting her arms around Bronwyn and hugging her tightly. "You look stunning!"

"Thank you, Mother." She looked up at Asher, an eager light in her eyes. "Don't you think my mother looks lovely in red?"

Elizabeth flushed at Asher's look, and she turned gratefully as Calhoun came to them carrying two glasses of champagne. He handed one to Elizabeth, and then, bending, Calhoun held the other glass to Bronwyn's lips.

"It's against regulations, but this is doctor's orders. You've earned a good time, Bonnie. Enjoy yourself."

"I hope my bottle's big enough," she said drolly.

He laughed, holding the glass until she finished its contents.

"Aren't you having any?" she asked.

"No, darlin'." A mischievous brogue tinged his speech. "Ya never know when I might be needed."

"Where's Mr. Van Zuye?" Elizabeth asked, looking around. "I'd like to meet him and thank him for this lovely party."

"You won't miss him," Bronwyn said. "Just find a circle and he'll be inside. He wants to meet you too. I told him how many strange interests you shared."

"Have you two eaten?" Calhoun asked.

"I have," Bronwyn said, smiling, "but Asher's been too busy standing guard."

"I'm not hungry," Asher said. "I'll have something later."

"Well, I am. I always am." Calhoun took Elizabeth's hand. "And that food looks fantastic. Besides, it saves me taking Elizabeth out to dinner. See you later."

Bronwyn watched Calhoun lead her mother to the

buffet tables, and out of the corner of her eye she saw that Asher watched them too. Drew Mednam and others from her office descended on Bronwyn, and she and Asher were caught up in their chit-chat.

Elizabeth was not hungry and she left Calhoun at the table, where he ate appreciatively and conversed enthusiastically with the caterer. She spied a small man standing alone, looking out the window, and with a faint smile on her face, she went to him.

"Bronwyn thought you'd be surrounded by people," she said. "I'm Elizabeth."

He turned and looked up at her.

"So—you're her mother." His eyes swept her boldly. "You're beautiful for a middle-aged woman."

She laughed. "And you look very fit and vital for an old man."

He chuckled. "You certainly are her mother."

"Thank you." She felt an immediate rapport with him. "Bonnie's told me about your parties, and I can see why—this is lovely. It's very kind of you to do this for her."

"She's my friend."

"I'm glad. She needs good friends."

Their eyes locked, and Elizabeth tried to see beyond his infinitely black pupils, but it was like looking into endless mirrors.

"I'm sorry we haven't met sooner," Van Zuye said. "I think we could have had many stimulating discussions."

Calhoun came to them, hand outstretched and with a broad smile on his face.

"You're Willem Van Zuye. I've admired your work for years, and I'm honored to meet you. I'm Tom Calhoun."

Van Zuye shook the large hand, his own disappearing in its mass.

"I know of you, Dr. Thomas Calhoun," he said formally, "and it is *I* who am honored to meet you. I say that of few medical men." He turned Calhoun's hand over and looked closely at it.

"You give life with this hand, Doctor. It makes my own feel very puny. Odd, is it not? Your hand looks more the sculptor's and mine the surgeon's."

319

"I have hands like my father's. He was a blacksmith, but he wanted me to be a doctor."

Van Zuye smiled, still holding Calhoun's hand in his.

"And I have the hands of my mother. My father was a carpenter, but my mother wanted me to be an artist."

The three of them fell into relaxed conversation, and Elizabeth wondered how and why Van Zuye had earned his forbidding reputation—he seemed so accessible. The evening wore on, and occasionally Elizabeth glanced back to Bronwyn and Asher, but they were always surrounded by people.

A bell began to signal the end of visiting hours, and Van Zuye excused himself. "I promised the floor supervisor we would leave on time, and I must keep my word." Again he shook hands with Calhoun.

"I would be very pleased, Doctor, to have you visit me at my studio. There is much I wish to talk to you about, and I would like to see you model something for me in clay. I want to see your fingers at work."

Calhoun grinned. "Do you have anything that looks like a brain?"

"We shall manage." The sculptor turned to Elizabeth and, taking her hand, he raised it to his lips, kissing it lightly.

"We have mutual interests, madame. Please call me when you plan to be in the city."

"Thank you, but I'm going away for a while."

"Then call me when you return."

"I shall."

"He's not at all as threatening as I'd heard," Calhoun said as Van Zuye gave instructions to the caterers and to his staff, who would dismantle the decorations.

Bronwyn still held court, but her smile looked weak. Asher bent close and kissed her cheek.

"You look tired, darling. Excuse me while I help Van Zuye."

Asher moved through the crowd, dispersing them, and soon the room emptied, leaving only Calhoun, Asher, Elizabeth, and Van Zuye. Helen had gone off duty.

"That's enough excitement for one night," Calhoun said. "I want you in bed as soon as possible."

She nodded. "I will. I promise."

He bent and kissed her on the mouth. Bronwyn looked up, surprised, and a capricious smile lit her face. He had never kissed her that way before.

"Why, Tom," she teased, "I didn't know you cared."

He looked at her solemnly. "You're a terrific woman, Bonnie. I just wanted you to know that, and to be happy. Sleep well." To Elizabeth he said, "I'll be at the nurses' station. There are a few things I must check on before we leave, and I want to sign Bronwyn's release papers tonight, just in case I get hung up in the morning."

He shook hands with Asher and Van Zuye.

"Make it quick. I'm going to send a nurse in shortly to put her to bed."

Van Zuye went to Bronwyn. He ran his fingers along her hair and then along her face.

"Are you my true and trusted friend?" he asked, his eyes riveted on hers.

She looked back at him steadily.

"Thank you for such a wonderful birthday."

He leaned to her and then he kissed her fully on her lips. When he raised his head, their eyes clung.

"Thank you, dear, dearest friend," she said, her eyes welling with tears.

He held her chin and kissed her forehead. "Goodnight, dear child."

With a nod to Elizabeth and Asher, he left.

Elizabeth went to her daughter and, folding her arms around her, she kissed her cheeks, her mouth. Bronwyn looked into her mother's eyes, her own shadowy.

"Hold me tight, Mama. Kiss me again."

Elizabeth's chin quivered. Bronwyn hadn't called her "Mama" in years. She hugged her daughter close. "Oh, Bonnie, how I love you," she whispered.

"And I love you." Tears glistened in Bronwyn's eyes. "When do you plan on leaving for Paris?"

"In a few days."

"Give my love to Bea, and take good care of yourself."

"I will."

Asher watched the two of them, a terrible coldness numbing him.

321

Elizabeth rose. "Goodnight," she said in a choked voice, and she left, tears blinding her.

Asher stood for a long while, staring down at his wife. He pulled up a chair and sank into it, lifted Bronwyn's hand to his lips, and kissed her fingers. He reached into his pocket and took out the velvet box he had carried for so long. He slipped the emerald ring onto Bronwyn's finger, just above her gold wedding band.

Her breath caught. "How beautiful, Asher. Thank you."

He took her in his arms and buried his face in her hair; his throat closed and tears stung his eyes. He kissed the fragrant softness of her hair, and all along the fine line where her hair met her face; his lips caressed her forehead, softly touching her eyelids, stroking down her cheek. He found her mouth and she parted her lips to meet his. A low moan came from her, and her eyes opened in surprise.

Asher raised his head, his eyes shining with tears.

Bronwyn smiled tenderly, her eyes holding a warmth he had never seen in them.

"Please don't cry, Asher. It's been such a beautiful evening, and I'm very happy."

He could barely speak, and his words came tightly. "You look so tired, I'm going to lift you into your bed."

"No!" she cried. "It's too ugly. Please, just wheel me to the window. I want to see the night on the river. I'll call the nurse later."

He got up and pushed her wheelchair to the windows. Bending again, he brushed his lips through her hair.

"Sleep well, my love."

She smiled up at him. "Take care."

Asher could not remember how he had gotten out onto the hospital terrace. A voice broke through the pounding in his head. He had not seen the woman standing in the shadows.

"Asher?"

Turning, he squinted into the darkness. "Elizabeth?"

"I'm still waiting for Tom. He had to look in on someone he operated on this morning."

She came and stood beside him, leaning her elbows on the parapet, looking out over the city.

He was silent for a long while and then he asked quietly, "Why are you going away?"

She didn't answer immediately. Finally she said, "I should have gone long ago. Now that I've made my decision, I'm anxious to leave."

"Does Bronwyn know where to reach you?"

"Yes. My friend's address and phone number are in her book."

"We'll miss you, Elizabeth."

She looked up at him, but his face was turned into the night.

"Thank you for all you're doing for Bonnie. You're very good to her. It's only because of you that I'm free to go away."

In the light reflecting from inside, Elizabeth saw Asher's jaw harden and a pulse begin to throb in his temples. His voice came hoarsely. "I want her to be happy. I want only what she wants."

"She was happy tonight—happier than I thought possible."

"Yes," he whispered, as if to himself.

Elizabeth felt suddenly bereft. How long would it be before she saw Bonnie again . . . and Asher? A chill April breeze spun off the river and across the terrace. She shivered. Drawing her light coat more closely around her, she was about to say goodbye to Asher when Calhoun's voice interrupted.

"So there you are, Elizabeth." Seeing Asher, he said, "I'm glad you haven't left. It's much too early for you to go home alone. I know a bar on Second Avenue with a terrific jazz pianist—let's unwind."

"No, thank you, Tom," Asher said, his face tired. "You and Elizabeth go ahead. I need a long walk."

"What you need, old man," Calhoun said, putting his arms around both their shoulders, "is warm company and hot music. Those are doctor's orders. Come on."

When the floor nurses came to put her to bed, Bronwyn refused, insisting she wanted to sit by the windows.

323

"I'm too excited to go to sleep. It's been such a beautiful night, and I've had such a good time. I can't face getting into that bed. Please—I'll buzz when I'm ready."

The women looked at each other, and then they shrugged. She was going home tomorrow—what difference did it make? They acquiesced.

"Please shut off the lights as you go out," Bronwyn said. "I want to look out at the city. It's so lovely tonight." They did as she asked and left, shutting the door partway so that the bright lights in the hallway did not reflect in the windows.

Sitting in the darkness, Bronwyn's fine oval face creased with the emotions careening in her. Puzzlement knit her brows, and questions clouded her coppery eyes. Why should she be so surprised? Hadn't she *begged* him to help her? But she'd pleaded with him in the throes of emotion —never had she expected he *would!*

Why did he do it?

Her frown deepened with her confusion. She had been so *sure*. It was what she wanted—it was *right!* Then—why did she hesitate now?

She curled her tongue, rolling two capsules from under its thickness. She maneuvered the two tiny cylinders until they settled against the inside of her cheek. There was no need to hurry. She had all the time she wanted—the later the better. That way no one could point a finger. The enteric coating would not dissolve until it hit her stomach. Even then it would take time, and then when the contents were released there would be pain, but not for long— nothing she couldn't handle. And then would come peace —sweet, lasting peace. Would she see a bright, beckoning light at the end of a tunnel, as some people had described after being revived from death? Well—she'd soon find out. Maybe she'd even find out if Elizabeth was right. A tiny smile touched her lips. If there was an afterlife, she wanted to spend it skiing. Yes, that would be fine—to ski all those beautiful clouds.

Why did he do it?

She had hoped, maybe, just *one* of them might help her. When she had told them how simple it was to fill enteric-coated capsules with cyanide and pass them to her with a kiss, she had hoped—maybe—just *one* would. And she had asked it be done *before* she left the hospital; with so many people around, no one could tell who had helped her. But never—*never* had she expected *two* of them would actually pass her the capsules!

Why did he do it?

She shuddered as she remembered his eyes when he placed the ring on her finger. It was as if every pain, every loss, every black day he had ever known shadowed those green depths—as if, with the ring, he pledged himself to her into eternity. She looked at the emerald ring; its facets caught a stray reflection in the room, and the jewel shone in the darkness. She shivered. The enormity of what she had asked of him and what he had *done* for her made her skin prickle. How could *anyone* be so selfless? Her lips curled bitterly. *She* certainly wasn't. Neither was MacCormack. Wait a minute, where did *he* come from? Why was she thinking of *him?* Beads of sweat broke out on her brow. *The hell with MacCormack!* And if there was a hell, she'd meet him there!

Like a bird confused by reflective glass, her eyes flew around the room, trying to see everywhere but inside herself, and when there was nowhere else for her to settle, she had to look into the blackness of her mind. What if *MacCormack* were in this wheelchair? Could *I* have done what Asher did? Could *I* have been so unselfish?

And from the blackness came a pinpoint of insight, lasering towards her, illuminating a truth so undeniable that shame coursed through her like scalding blood. *No,* I could *never* have done it! I'd want him *alive*—no matter what! I could never help him *die—I love him!*

She gasped aloud. Her face hardened into marble.

Love MacCormack? Now? After what Asher had done for her?

Angry, burning self-loathing seared her spine, her very being, tensing her body, flexing her strong shoulder muscles—her wheelchair began to move around the room. Her beautiful features twisted into an ugly mask.

"Damn you!" she cursed at herself. *"Damn you!"*

Think! Her mind reeled. *Think of what you've done to Asher!* He has to live with what he did for you! He'll never

325

be free of you! And he'll go on loving a dream, never knowing how false it was! He'll *never* know! No matter how close he is with Van Zuye, they'll never speak of it—he'll always believe *he* helped you die. You fool—you stupid, selfish fool! You and MacCormack deserve each other!

Her eyes tightened with self-hatred, deep, deep lines etching the once smooth skin. Her chair spun with the sharp, tense anger of her muscles. It picked up momentum —she became dizzy and disoriented. The chair hit the edge of the bed, jarring her—the capsules slid wildly in her mouth. The chair hit the bed again and her mouth fell open, the capsules ramming into the back of her throat.

No! No! Not now! It was a silent scream torn from a throat closed with horror. *Not now! I mustn't swallow them! I can't do this to Asher!* Her eyes rolled wildly and like a madwoman she tried to pull her fingers to her face—to her throat—to plunge them deep into her gorge and rip out the poison. But her hands lay still. She cursed her helplessness, her head splitting with screams she dared not scream.

Spit them out! Spit them out! her mind clamored. Her face grew crazed with her effort, her eyes bulged beyond their sockets. But her terror, her tenseness held her throat fast, squeezing the capsules. The chair spun; sweat poured from her. Panic-stricken, she tried not to swallow . . . she held her breath. She was so dizzy . . . so dizzy. Where were the nurses—couldn't they hear the chair? Couldn't *anyone* help her? Her heart hammered in her ears.

Desperately she tried to shake her head, to shake loose the capsules stuck like dry death in her throat, but the halo held her relentlessly. Tensing every fiber in her, concentrating on every muscle she could remember, she squeezed her eyes shut and forced herself to cough. She coughed— and coughed again. *Hard!* The capsules shot forward and she spat them into her open palm, closing her fingers to hide them.

A relief so sweet she could taste it cooled the sweat on her face. Slowly she relaxed. Her shoulders eased, and the chair stopped moving. Her face evened out, the carved lines of anguish receding. She took long, deep breaths, her mouth softening. She sat quietly looking down at her hands, staring at them. And then a faint, far-off, elusive memory flickered in her.

Where were the capsules? *Where were the capsules?* Little prickly pinpoints rose on her arms. She had to find them—no one else could! She had spit them out . . . into . . . her hand. *Her hand!* Every inch of skin rose on her body.

Her hand was closed! She had closed it!

She began to shiver. And shiver. And shiver. All of her vibrated like an overtuned harp. She held her breath, trying to stop the quaking which iced every goosebump on her flesh. Her eyes narrowed as she focused on her hands, afraid to breathe, afraid the image was false hope. Slowly, her eyes mere slits, she willed one finger to move, and when it *unwound* to the signal unwinding from her brain, she whimpered—frightened little cries of disbelief escaping from the ice of her insides. Gulping for air, she unwound first one finger and then another until her hand lay flat.

She saw the capsules in her palm.

Closing her eyes tightly, afraid that what she had seen was false, she concentrated on closing her other hand. When she felt it move she peeked from behind half-closed lids. She watched the fingers wind inward until her nails bit into her palm. She tightened her fist, unmindful of the bite of her nails, reveling in the sensation. Her eyes widening with realization, she slowly unwound each finger outward. Her breath came in quick, short gasps.

Like a baby discovering its limbs, she moved her hands . . . and then her arms . . . and then her toes. Not far . . . not high . . . awkwardly . . . but *moving!* She began to laugh with each small response, little, tentative laughs to match the little, tentative movements. Tears welled in her eyes.

"I can move," she whispered.

"I can *move!*" she cried exultantly.

"I can move!" she screamed.

"I CAN MOVE!" Her laughter clarioned down the corridor.

Chapter Twenty-seven

"CHECKMATE!" Calhoun said with satisfaction, an a-mused gleam in his eyes. He leaned back in the comfort-able leather chair, his elbows on the wide armrests, his chin resting on the pyramid of his fingers. "That's the fifth game I've won in two weeks. Do you concede?"

"Never!" Bronwyn exclaimed, her eyes scanning the marble chessboard with its carved marble chessmen. Where had she made her fatal move?

Calhoun watched her as she studied the chessboard. If you didn't look at her legs, he thought, you would never know she had been injured. She sat in her wheelchair, but she was dressed as though she were going to dinner at the Café Carlyle. She wore a jade-green silk dress with a high mandarin collar; intricate Chinese embroidery, hand-stitched in gold thread, outlined the deeply plunging narrow neckline. To complete the Oriental look, her hair

328

was coiffed into an elegant chignon and studded with black lacquered Japanese-style hairpicks. Calhoun was glad now he had dressed for dinner. He wondered if Asher would get back in time. The weather had turned mean, and Asher was flying in from the Coast.

Looking up from the chessboard, Bronwyn shook her head and gave him a hopeless smile.

"I don't know how you do it, Tom. I spend hours playing with that computer chess game, and still I can't beat you."

As if to commiserate with her, Blaze, who lay on the floor at her feet, lifted his cold wet nose and nuzzled her hand. She patted him affectionately.

"You will," Calhoun said complacently. "Look how you've beaten my predictions on getting well."

She glanced sideways at the crutches in a corner and then lifted her skirt slightly, revealing the steel braces on her legs.

"You call *this* beating you?"

"You're damn right I do! Not only have you beaten me out of a fat laminectomy fee, in less than a year you're pushing that chair on your own, and you can take a few steps on sticks. That's a lot better than I expected."

Her eyes clouded. "Can I expect more?"

Leaning across the table, he took her hands. "I hope so. God, I hope so. I know you're getting itchy because winter is coming and you dream of skiing. Maybe someday you will. The future holds great promise. We're experimenting now with lasers that act almost like soldering irons. Someday we may weld severed nerves far more precisely than the microscopic surgery we do now. We've known about lasers since the sixties, and we would be far more advanced with this research if the government had not been so much more interested in the laser as a possible 'death-ray' weapon."

He squeezed her hands. "Anything is possible. Haven't you learned that yet?"

Her eyes searched his. "Maybe . . . but if I ever get to *really* believing, it's because you're so Machiavellian, you can make me believe almost anything."

He got up and kissed her nose lightly. "What about a drink?"

"You bet." She lit a cigarette.

Calhoun went to the small bar near the library windows and looked outside. Sleet spat against the windowpanes like silver pellets.

"Asher will probably be delayed in this weather," he said.

"He'll call if he is."

"From the plane?"

She nodded. "Isn't it incredible? Probably because of your lasers. Asher says that with these new satellites, people will soon make phone calls on commercial flights."

"God, I'm impatient to make that kind of technological progress with brain and spinal cord injuries." He came back and handed her the drink.

"You will." Bronwyn smiled up at him. "Haven't *you* learned yet that anything is possible?"

He clinked his glass to her. *"Deo volente."*

"You really do believe in God, don't you, Tom?"

"I haven't found anything better."

"Not even computers?"

He gave her an arch look. "Computers have their limits."

"Not from what I've been reading."

"Remember, Bon, computers are only what man puts into them." He inclined his head and grinned. "And women. Computers can't think for themselves—they're dependent on human, God-given abilities. Computers without programmers and operators are useless." He smiled as if some inner, secret information gave him joy. "But God—God needs nothing more than his will, and his love."

"And what about his wrath?" Bronwyn asked softly.

An elfin gleam lit Calhoun's eyes. "No one's perfect."

Bronwyn giggled. "I'll never understand how a man of your intelligence can delude yourself with deities."

Calhoun settled back into the easy chair. "Ah, Bonnie. Remember 'A mind all logic is like a knife all blade—it cuts the hand of him who uses it.' "

330

"Where did you get that?"

"Tagore. Read him sometime."

"I have."

"Then read him again."

Their differences were what Bronwyn liked most about these hours with Calhoun. It was a welcome relief from the accord she knew with Asher. Asher always seemed to agree with her, to give in to whatever she wanted, and she never knew if it was because he did in fact agree, or that he did not wish to upset her. She was pleased he had not cut back on his work or his business travel because of her—she needed time alone and made good use of the days he was gone, reading, working, exercising. After she had left the hospital Calhoun had taken to visiting two, three times a week, insisting the reason he came was because of Ruth's cooking, but Bronwyn knew it was because he and Asher had developed a genuine friendship, and it had less to do with the new rehabilitation clinic Asher was subsidizing than that the two men held each other in high regard. And Bronwyn found that she, too, looked forward to Calhoun's company.

"What do you hear from Elizabeth?" he asked.

"You probably know more than I do. I think she writes to you more than to me."

"I haven't heard from her in over a month—but in her last letter she sounded busy and happy."

"I wonder if she'll come back for Christmas," Bronwyn mused.

"I don't think so. She seems to be caught up in a new life and new friends, and I expect . . ." He stopped, not wanting to tell Bronwyn he thought her mother would probably spend Christmas skiing.

But Bronwyn read his thoughts.

"Tom, don't be afraid of saying what comes naturally to mind because you think you're going to hurt me. You and I both know Christmas and snow are synonymous with my mother. If she doesn't come home, it's because she's skiing somewhere in the Alps. I'm happy for her—it's what I want for her." She smiled impishly. "Why don't you fly over and surprise her? Why don't you take her skiing?"

He chuckled. "Because, my dear little matchmaker, I'm too busy. Besides, I think your mother has found friends more interesting than me."

"Oh? What makes you think that? I read nothing like that in her letters."

Calhoun shrugged. "Male instinct. How can anyone as lively as Elizabeth live on the Left Bank, go to classes at the Sorbonne, and not meet hungry young Frenchmen? I'm sure she has the best-stocked refrigerator in the Quarter and poor artists and writers coming in for dinner every night."

Bronwyn laughed. "And breakfast, you think?"

"I hope so. I sure as hell hope so."

"Do you really?"

"Yes, Bonnie, I do. Your mother and I are close, but not that close."

"Why not?"

"That's an impertinent question."

"It's an honest question. Why can't you give me an honest answer?"

He looked at her speculatively. Lifting his glass, he squinted into the amber of the whiskey. Slowly he drank the contents, enjoying the pungent taste on his tongue and the heat of the liquor sliding down his throat. Generations of genes welcomed the warmth of the brew. And then he said, "She's afraid going to bed with me would destroy our friendship. Perhaps on her part she's right. Elizabeth is a woman who can't separate sex from love, and she doesn't love me, not that way."

"And what about you? Do you love her?"

He smiled, bemused. "The same way she loves me. But I could make love to her and have a damn good time, and still be her friend."

Bronwyn laughed. "We're very much alike, Tom."

He grinned back. "If you want to continue this wanton relationship, just don't beat me at chess." Getting up, he took her empty glass and his. "Would you like another?"

"Please."

Coming back with the drinks he said: "I'm looking forward to Van Zuye's Christmas party. I've heard it's quite an event."

332

"It is," she said offhandedly. "You'll have a great time." Something in her voice made him look at her probingly.

"Aren't you and Asher going?"

"Asher perhaps, but not me."

"That's a crock, Bonnie! Asher wouldn't go without you."

"He can. I like being alone," she said matter-of-factly.

Calhoun grimaced, his eyebrows knitting.

"That's an even bigger crock! You've had *too much* time alone. What you need are parties and people!" His eyes were pitiless and she looked away, unable to meet their challenge.

"Give me time, Tom. Seeing all those lithe young bodies hurts too much."

The heavy brows relaxed, and the strong, square face softened. "You can't avoid being hurt, Bonnie."

She lifted her shoulders, hunching them slightly. Her face was like a cameo with its finely etched features and peach-toned skin, and Calhoun's heart went out to her as she said, "I know that, Tom. I just don't want to go looking for it. I'm still trying to accept being crippled, and I think I've come a long way. At least I no longer want to die."

The sleet spat against the windows and December dusk turned instantly into night. The library was cozy with the fire lighting the room; the soft glow of lamps reflected on the cordovan leather furniture. Calhoun lounged on the sofa, his legs stretched before him.

His words were thoughtful and careful.

"I've often wondered what changed your mind about dying. Can we talk about it?"

She shook her head, but she met his eyes unflinchingly. "No. I will never speak of it. But I will tell you this: I was stupid and selfish, and you were right in everything you said."

Quickly, she changed the subject.

"You and Van Zuye have become quite the 'odd couple.' I can't believe he's doing a sculpture for your new clinic. He's very antagonistic to the medical profession."

Calhoun flexed his fingers. It was as if the very thought of Van Zuye made him more aware of his hands.

"I know." He smiled. "A lot of what he feels is valid. Doctors can be damn arrogant, and many are slow to accept alternatives to traditional medicine, and like every other profession, medicine has its share of charlatans. But I'm hoping when Van Zuye balances the good of what we do, he will soften his attitude. As for the sculpture—actually, I'm doing it. Van Zuye insisted I should create the piece and execute it, and he's encouraged me with his teaching and the time he's given me."

Surprise swept Bronwyn's face. "And you've said nothing in all this time!"

Calhoun suddenly felt shy; it was difficult for him to speak of the world Van Zuye had opened for him. The artist had made him believe he could mold inanimate mineral into something beautiful, something almost *human,* and he had made him feel that when he operated on organic, living matter, he was sculpting in yet another form. He had never consciously thought of his hands—the skill with which he used them was as involuntary as breathing—but in the weeks he had been working with Van Zuye, he had become aware of the broad palms with their freckled, red-haired backs, the strong, flat-tipped fingers, and of what they could do with clay and wax, and maybe, someday, even stone.

Sitting opposite, Bronwyn looked at his hands and she felt the sudden surge of a powerful attraction. She remembered how surely those hands had examined her legs after the casts were removed. It was as if they shaped the very bones under her skin. She felt again the fingers gently turn her neck when the halo traction was disassembled—she could still hear the bolts coming out of her skull. And then the fingers had traced each vertebra in the back of her neck, infusing such tactile strength, she felt sure they transferred life along with their warmth.

Asher had stood beside her bed, holding her hand as the casts and halo were removed. When it was over she turned her head for the first time in months. A smile curved her lips at the strange sensation, and she laughed nervously. Asher returned her smile, and she looked deep into the green depths of his eyes. In them she saw a welcome that made her heart tighten. He bent to kiss her, and as she

334

returned his kiss, she made a silent vow: she would do all she could to make him happy. And in his kiss she felt his promise, that never would he speak of what might have happened to change her mind.

Nor did Van Zuye. It was he she had first phoned in those early hours after flushing the pills down the toilet—even before she tried phoning Asher and later, when Asher could not be reached, asking a nurse to find Calhoun.

Van Zuye had listened so silently she could not even hear his breathing. Then he had said quietly, "Thank you. You've made me very happy." And her heart had swelled with affection for the truculent old man.

Now, months later, looking at Calhoun sitting across from her, she realized how different he was from the hard-driving professional who had raced back with Elizabeth and Asher from the jazz bar on Second Avenue, answering the nurse's summons. He was so much more *inward*, peaceful. Evidently, sculpting under Van Zuye's tutelage was an ideal outlet for a man with such awesome mental and physical energies.

"This is exciting news," Bronwyn said. "Are you working in stone—steel—what?"

"Clay. Its consistency is like the brain, and similar to sinew. After I finish the maquette, I'll translate it to plaster." He chuckled again. "Now *there's* a material I understand, and when that's finished, it will be bronzed."

Bronwyn's brow knitted with the ideas rising in her. Her eyes livened and she said eagerly, "Tom! Would you mind if I had a photographer shoot you at work in Van Zuye's studio? I can assure you, Tiu will not get in your way, and Van Zuye knows him. He's the man who did the photographs for Van Zuye's book and he works on cat's feet—he won't disturb you or Van Zuye. I'll bet there are all kinds of professional people who are unknown artists! All I have to do is some research and I bet I could come up with a book!"

Calhoun smiled at her enthusiasm. "It's fine with me, Bonnie, as long as Willem agrees. Actually, I know a pediatrician who does excellent sketches of children—I'll introduce you to him—and then there's a psychiatrist I've

335

heard of who's doing some beautiful bronze miniatures. I'm happy you've gone back to work. I think that's why you've made such excellent progress. The mind's power to heal the body has hardly been tapped . . ."

He stopped speaking as they heard voices in the down-stairs entry. Calhoun looked at Bronwyn expectantly. "That sounds like Asher. Good—Ruth'll serve dinner now. I'm starving!"

"There's someone with him," Bronwyn said, listening to the voices on the stairway. "He didn't say anything when he called about bringing someone home." She frowned. She was still uncomfortable with company, and now that she'd thought of the book, she had looked forward to retiring to her downstairs office after dinner and outlining her ideas. Asher and Calhoun had much to discuss. Calhoun had brought along architect's drawings for the new clinic building; they lay in thick rolls on the desk across the room.

Asher smiled broadly as he entered, and Bronwyn marveled that he looked so fresh despite his long day. His dark pinstripe suit was wrinkle free and even the collar of his white shirt was unwilted. The knot of his red print silk tie was perfect. As he came towards Bronwyn, he stopped to greet Calhoun, grasping the doctor's hand warmly.

"Glad you could make it tonight, Tom. I've a lot to tell you. I met a doctor in California who's doing incredible things with computers—he's actually programmed one to help a paraplegic walk! We'll talk about it."

The man behind Asher stood quietly in the background. His dark blue eyes briefly scanned the room and settled on Bronwyn. A light smile played on his lips. Bronwyn did not immediately see him because Asher blocked her view. Coming close, Asher bent to kiss her upturned face.

"I was hoping we'd make it in time for dinner—we hit rotten weather when we crossed the Mississippi. But I had good company . . . darling, may I present Douglas MacCormack."

Bronwyn had reached out for Asher when he kissed her, closing her fingers over his in welcome. He felt her hands tense and her grip tighten.

In pained surprise, Bronwyn looked from Asher to

MacCormack. She felt suddenly cold, and a nagging pain began in her neck—it always hurt when she became tense. Her eyes held MacCormack's defiantly. There were no lies between Asher and herself, and there would be none now. Controlling the annoyance in her voice, she said, "I know Douglas, Asher. We met years back."

She could not keep her eyes from sweeping the trim, compact body dressed in a dark grey business suit. Why was MacCormack dressed so formally? Had he been at Asher's meeting? What had brought the two of them together? Questions pounded in her head as she managed to say calmly, "You're looking well, Douglas."

Intrigued that by using his first name, she had indicated to Asher they were friends, MacCormack stepped forward.

"Hello, Bronwyn," he said easily, taking in how she moved her head, her hands, seeing the outline of her leg braces under the clinging silk. "It's been a long time."

Not long enough, Bronwyn thought, aware of how she was responding to his presence.

Asher saw how she had paled and the defiance with which her eyes had met MacCormack's. He thought of the day they had driven to Elizabeth's and how skillfully she had handled the Porsche. "I had a good teacher," she had said, and Asher knew now who that had been. Looking at the two of them, he also knew they had been lovers. MacCormack was not a man with whom a woman was merely friendly. Asher squeezed Bronwyn's hand reassuringly, pleased she had not pretended MacCormack and she were strangers. "Let's go down to dinner, darling. Charles tells me the poached salmon can't wait much longer."

Alone with Bronwyn in the small private elevator, Asher touched the crown of her head. "If I've upset you by bringing Mr. MacCormack home, forgive me."

Bronwyn pressed his hand to her cheek. "You never upset me, Asher. It's only I who upset myself."

Asher kept the talk at dinner as light as the fine Chablis Charles poured to accompany the salmon. Sensing Bronwyn's unease, Asher subtly steered the conversation so

337

that it floated in the high-ceilinged room. The three men ate heartily and conversed easily, but Bronwyn sat silent, barely touching her food. She burned to know just how MacCormack had managed to meet Asher, to be invited to her home. Careful of just how she phrased it, she said, "Asher, is ICC planning to cover Grand Prix racing? I thought ABC had that all tied up."

"We outbid them," Asher said with a smile. "ICC is expanding its sports coverage, and when Mr. MacCormack phoned me some weeks back to say he was planning to retire and would be interested in covering racing, I asked him to meet with our people. We signed the contracts in L.A. today, and beginning next season, Douglas MacCormack will be the ICC auto racing anchor. But since he's still competing he has to fly to Germany tomorrow to meet with the Porsche people, and I gave him a lift East."

Bronwyn's face froze with her amazement. "It's hard to believe. Douglas MacCormack retire from racing? Why?" Her tone clearly challenged him.

He shrugged carelessly. "It's time."

"Just like that?" She tried to keep her voice level, tried to subdue the anger rising in her. Damn him! She had never even dared to hope he might give up racing.

"Just like that," he said, spooning his soup.

What he could not tell her was that when he had seen her in the hospital, he had seen himself, and for the first time, had known fear. At his first race after that visit, the fear stirred his hands on the wheel and he had known . . . it was time to quit.

He smiled across the table at Bronwyn.

Caught in his steady gaze, she flushed.

From the corner of his eye, MacCormack saw how Asher watched his wife and he said casually, between spoonfuls of soup, "How's Elizabeth, Bronwyn?"

"Fine," Bronwyn answered, as cool as her untouched soup.

"There's an idea," Asher said to MacCormack. "When you're in Paris, why don't you look her up? She's living there now, and you can tell her you've seen Bronwyn, and how well she's doing. Letters and phone calls are fine, but there's nothing like an eyewitness account to satisfy the soul. I'm sure Elizabeth would be very happy to learn of Bronwyn's progress from one who's seen her."

MacCormack could barely contain a self-satisfied smile. "I'd be delighted," he said. He had always liked Elizabeth. Now, she might even turn out to be a valuable ally. "I plan to be in Paris for the holidays—I'd enjoy surprising her. Where is she staying?"

Bronwyn had seen the glimmer of satisfaction lift the corners of his sensual mouth, and her eyes lit with amusement. MacCormack had no idea how much Elizabeth disliked him. It would serve him right.

"She's staying with a friend," Bronwyn said smoothly, "Bea LeVine . . . I'll give you the phone number before you leave."

Later . . . late into the night, lying awake with Asher sleeping peacefully beside her, Bronwyn thought of the feelings MacCormack still aroused in her. *Why did I ever think it would be easy?* her mind rambled. She wished she slept alone, that Asher was in his room upstairs. Then she could get up and wheel herself outside to the terrace. Maybe the snap of chill winter air would still her thoughts so that she could sleep.

Closing her eyes, longing for oblivion, she tried to conjure the deep, delicious sleep she had known on winter weekends in the snow cave she had dug in the woods behind the house. After a week in the city, five days of smelling only the stale air of an office closed to the crispness of winter, she had looked forward to going home and sleeping outdoors in the purity of a winter's night, burrowed deep into the softness of a down sleeping bag with Blaze nestled warmly against her side, the white crystals of fresh snow inches above her head, the sound of the stream in her ears, and the clean scent of pine in her nostrils. The elusiveness of sleep now made her ache for the joy of the warm, wondrous sleep she had once known. If only she could get up and drag a sleeping bag outside. But that was no longer possible. And if she moved, Asher would waken instantly.

She could not sleep comfortably beside him—she worried about waking him with her restlessness. And knowing this, most often he slept alone, upstairs. But since she had made her decision to make up to him for all he had lost, and for the anguish she had brought him, she had not once rejected him when he wanted her. And he had wanted her tonight. She wondered if it was because of MacCormack. Asher was too astute not to have recognized her unease. Or was Asher trying to reassure himself? Lately their lovemaking had been less than satisfying. But what did it matter? She no longer really enjoyed sex. She hated her body—especially her legs, withered, their strength gone, two sticks that barely responded to her will. But heat had risen in her tonight, and she had cried out, as she had not in a long time. Asher had held her and loved her. Afterwards he had fallen asleep. And she lay awake—knowing that she had cried out for MacCormack, had fantasized it was he making love to her.

That was why she could not sleep—even if she had slept in a snow cave.

Chapter Twenty-eight

ELIZABETH hurried through wet streets just darkening with dusk, her lips curving with an inward smile of anticipation. Her blue knit coat flew open as she ran across Boulevard St.-Michel, snaking through homeward-bound students, edging between bumpers of closely crammed cars, their motors panting, their drivers' fingers drumming on gear shifts as they waited impatiently for the light to flash green. And when it did, if some poor pedestrian was not quick enough, *trop mal*.

Elizabeth gathered her coat around her, securing it by pressing the books in her arms close to her body, trying to seal out the damp wind blowing across the vast green swath of the Jardin du Luxembourg. But she raised her face to the freshness of the chill air—it was a welcome relief after the closeness of the classroom and the pollution on Boul' Mich', so thick she could taste it.

Crossing onto Rue de Médicis, she skirted the beautiful park surrounding the Luxembourg Palace. Her pace slowed as it did every time she walked this way. Even in December the lawns were lush and green, and fragrance filled the air. Even in December, even at dusk, Paris held a light found nowhere else. Why had she waited so long to come? She stopped and looked back towards the gentle rise of land swelling upwards from the Seine—Montagne Ste.-Geneviève. Through the mist she could make out the domineering cupola, the carved statues, and the baroque facade of the Church of the Sorbonne looming amidst the cluster of stone buildings she had just left. The Sorbonne! Buildings which had stood for 700 years. She could still not believe that she attended the University of Paris, walked its ancient corridors, sat in its gaunt classrooms and vaulted lecture halls. She shivered with pleasure. But enough of this! She was late!

She had not meant to get into a discussion after class, but the subject fascinated her: were the artisans who carved or cast for the sculptor less the artist than those who created the original concept? The differences of opinion had been high-pitched and emotional, and she had stayed until the dampness in her shirt alerted her to how late it was. *Joshua!* Joshua waited hungrily. His tiny fist would be crammed into his mouth, his forehead creased with irritation—waiting for her nipple—waiting to drain the milk which filled her breasts.

With a quick wave she had left her friends to hurry home, and now as she walked up narrow streets to Rue Racine, warmth lit her eyes as she thought of her baby. How considerate he had been to arrive before classes began. That he had arrived at all was a miracle! And she had not wanted this marvelous child? At first she had hoped the amniocentesis test would reveal an abnormality and she could prevail on Grace for an abortion. But when the test showed she carried a normal child, her natural instincts took hold and she began to cherish her pregnancy. Grace had warned her she might not carry full term, and indeed Joshua was born prematurely—at the end of her seventh month—but he had been a strong preemie, weighing five and a half pounds, and she was permitted to nurse him immediately. He was beautiful—as beautiful as all of Paris!

Elizabeth stopped at a stolid, Renaissance-style, four-story stone building with deeply recessed windows and formal, carved cornices. She took a key from her pocket and turned a heavy lock in one of two huge, paneled oak doors. She pushed hard and the door squeaked open, revealing an inner cobbled courtyard, in the center of which was a carved stone fountain surrounded by stone urns which in summer contained a profusion of red geraniums and white petunias. Elizabeth ran up the curving outside stairway to the second floor.

How lucky she had been to find such a charming and spacious apartment so close to the park and the university. Actually Bea had found it. The building belonged to Lillianne Gerard, a good friend of Bea, and when the apartment's occupant for many years, Professor Vachon, followed his wife in death by just a few weeks, Lillianne was distraught. The couple's married children wanted no part of their parents' fifty-year accumulation of possessions—Madame Gerard could keep it all! But Lillianne was leaving to spend the summer at her vineyard in Ribeauvillé, in the Alsace, and she had no time for such things! She could not take time to clean out the *appartement!* Fuming, Lillianne phoned Bea, and Bea told her of the friend visiting from the United States who needed an apartment.

C'est vrai? Was it possible this friend wanted a furnished flat?

Oui! That's exactly what she wants—and she wants it right now—*le plus tôt sera le mieux.*

Mais non! C'est impossible! Lillianne was astounded—no one spends the summer in Paris!

D'accord, agreed Bea, *mais Madame Banks est enceinte.* She refuses to come with me to Cap-Ferrat! *Bêtise!* Foolish!

Enceinte? All the more reason not to suffer the heat of summer!

Despite Bea's objections, Elizabeth spent the summer in Paris. She moved into the apartment in late May, just weeks after her arrival in France. Apartments in Paris,

343

especially on the Left Bank, were as scarce as twenty-inch waistlines after forty-five, and Elizabeth was grateful to find living space. She liked the scholarly, lived-in look of the six-room flat. It comforted her as though old friends wrapped warm arms around her. And Professor Vachon's books, scattered on shelves, on tables, and on the floor welcomed her.

"You must do it over!" Bea said. "You simply cannot entertain the way it is! *Cela ne se fait pas!*"

Elizabeth laughed. "Some people spend fortunes to achieve this antiquated ambience. I'll clean it up, but I'm changing very little."

Bea left for Cap-Ferrat and Elizabeth spent long, leisurely days strolling throughout the city. At night she studied French and read Professor Vachon's books until her eyes closed and she could fall asleep without thinking of the past . . . or the future. The apartment and the professor's books planted in her mind the first seeds of attending the Sorbonne. Her early weeks in Paris had been a social whirl. When Bea learned Elizabeth had not merely gained weight, but that the boxy suits and dresses concealed a pregnancy, her chagrin and surprise ·almost peeled the flocked paper off the walls of her ten-room *"pied-à-terre"* facing Place Victor Hugo. Elizabeth firmly refused to discuss the matter, and Bea stopped questioning her friend. Elizabeth's stoicism told her how unexpected this pregnancy was. To Bea all pregnancies were an inconvenience she had made sure she would not suffer. *Quelle gaffe!*

Bea was determined Elizabeth would have little time for reflection, and soon Elizabeth felt like a character in a Noel Coward farce: telephones rang, people came and went, and servants scurried about with canapes and cocktails. Elizabeth would not have been surprised to awaken some morning and find a tousle-haired young man in tennis whites, a silk *foulard* around his throat, saying, "Tennis anyone?"

Bea LeVine lived high and well. She was a woman who from her earliest days had attracted men. She was not beautiful, but she had an exotic, sensual quality that

344

promised endless pleasure. Her dark brown eyes were almond-shaped and smouldered with sexuality. Her nose was long and sharp, but her mouth was as generous as her soul, and when she smiled, her eyes shone with warmth and her olive skin drew back tightly over high cheekbones, giving her a sculptured, Egyptian look.

Everything about Bea LeVine seemed to have been designed for the enticement of men. Her walk, even now at fifty, made many a *boulevardier* turn and smile. So rhythmically did she glide by on spike-heeled, size 4B Ferragamos, her rounded, feminine calves flowing into slender ankles, her full hips swaying, that one felt almost inclined to raise a baton. And cinching her small waist was always a belt—*"ma ceinture d'amour"* she'd laugh. From her low-cut necklines swelled full breasts kept firm with cold baths and daily pectoral lifts with ten-pound weights. Even Bea's low, gravelly voice was an instrument of seduction. And seduce men she did, for in Bea LeVine swam the active genes of Eve, Bathsheba, Delilah, and Cleopatra. She made men feel as if nothing else existed but them. And for Bea, nothing else did. Her life revolved around men—she was seldom without husband or lover, and often she possessed both. From the first day she had walked into Emil Holzer's office at eighteen to take dictation, men had taken care of Bea. Emil, a sixty-year-old widower, proposed two months later, and when he died of a coronary at sixty-two, the former Beatrice Tannenbaum from Brooklyn inherited his real estate millions. Her last marriage had been to Étienne LeVine, who brought her to Paris. Étienne had also left her millions. And there had been two face-lifts and a tummy tuck, and although the once black hair was now dyed and the glow of eighteen had become the pampered gleam of fifty, men still adored Bea LeVine.

Elizabeth had met Bea in Chamonix when Bea was between marriages and Elizabeth between books. They sat drinking wine on the terrace of the Savoy after sharing a guide for skiing the glistening sixteen-mile glacier run, down the Valle Blanche from the 12,600-foot Aiguille du Midi. Bea twirled her wine glass, the late afternoon sun catching its ruby contents. Her eyes roamed the taut young men sitting nearby, and she had said drolly, "Darling, don't tell me you've come just to ski!"

Despite their different outlooks, the two women enjoyed each other's company, and two days later, when Elizabeth was late coming in from the mountain, Bea, waiting in the lounge, gently bumped her chair into the gentleman drinking alone at the next table—it was Étienne LeVine.

Bea nourished the seeds of the Sorbonne in Elizabeth's mind.

"Why not? Don't ever deny what you'd like to do, especially when you have the means to do it! You've got the time, the money, and now, an apartment within walking distance! And think of the *men* you'll meet! Young—vital—interesting men! To a Frenchman, Elizabeth, a woman is like wine, and the best wine is from fully ripened grapes."

"And so is vinegar," Elizabeth had said.

With a Gallic shrug that belied her Brooklyn background, Bea retorted impatiently, "You're at your sexual peak, Elizabeth, and even if you choose to ignore it, the European man *knows* it the moment he sees you. What you need is a good nurse—one who will take superb care of the baby while you're in class and who won't stick her nose into your bedroom—so don't hire a Frenchwoman! What you want is an English *nanny*—they're extraordinary with babies and absolutely discreet."

Joshua's early arrival made it all possible.

Bea flew up from Cap-Ferrat and took charge. By the time Elizabeth left the hospital, Isabel Jameson, a grey-haired Englishwoman with impeccable references, arrived from London. Bea flew back to her villa and Elizabeth enrolled in the Sorbonne.

A baby's impatient cries sounded through the apartment as Elizabeth opened the door. Tossing her books on a carved ebony table in the entrance, she removed her coat, and unbuttoning her shirt, she hurried down the hallway, where a room overlooking the rear garden had been turned into a nursery. Sitting in Professor Vachon's mahogany rocker was a portly woman holding an infant to her shoulder—she patted the child's back and crooned softly. Seeing Elizabeth, the woman stood up and with a scolding look handed the baby to its mother.

"Really, Mrs. Banks," she said stiffly, "if you insist on nursing, you *must* be home on time!"

"I'm sorry, Isabel; it won't happen again."

The baby felt his mother's presence and stopped wailing. He tossed his head around, seeking her nipple, his tiny lips sucking at the air. Undoing the damp panel of her nursing brassiere, Elizabeth settled into the rocking chair and put the child to her breast. He sucked feverishly, kneading tiny fingers into the fullness of her flesh. The nurse went out of the room, turning off the lights, leaving only one dim lamp which softly illuminated mother and child.

Elizabeth smoothed back the damp, dark curls on her son's forehead, and smiled tenderly down at him. He fed so eagerly, droplets of creamy milk spilled from the corners of his mouth, and he grunted hungrily. She felt the strength in his lips and the solid weight of his body. He was thriving. At first she worried that at her age her milk might not be nourishing or plentiful—evidently it was, for Joshua was healthy. She wanted to nurse as long as possible. With Bonnie she had lost her milk too early, but then there had been so many problems—trouble with Danny, money worries, and finally she had had to get a job. Working was one thing—*having* to work was totally different. She was a lucky woman, so many mothers *did* have to work. Thank God, she was no longer young and poor, or even worse, poor at this age and with a baby!

Elizabeth put her head back against the wine velvet upholstery of the rocker and let the thoughts spin out in her head. How ungrateful to regret what might have been, or to worry about the future. *The future is* today; *I can handle that. And wouldn't today fade into yesterday—and aren't all yesterdays filled with regret anyway? So . . . I will think only of* now *. . . of how beautiful this moment is.* She closed her eyes and gave herself up to the joy of her son's lips at her breast.

347

When she felt Joshua's mouth go slack Elizabeth knew he had fallen asleep. Reaching out, she took a small towel from the nearby table and put it on her shoulder. Lifting the child, she gently patted his back until he awakened and burped. Then she put him to her other breast, where again his lips closed busily. After a while his breathing deepened and once more he drifted off to sleep. She ran her fingers around and around the softness of his cheek.

"Wake up, darling, don't be lazy. You're not finished yet."

She stroked the small ears lying flatly against his finely shaped head. His mouth closed again on the nipple. When he had drained her breast Elizabeth put him to her shoulder and burped him again. His head nestled into the warmth of her neck and she felt the softness of his hair under her chin. She kissed the top of his head—how sweet he smelled. She had missed his bath tonight but tomorrow was Saturday and she had all weekend to be with him. Next week there were examinations, and she would be busy. But after that came Christmas vacation! Christmas! So soon? She hadn't even thought about it!

But Bea had.

Bea planned her days with the smooth precision of a Patek-Phillippe. Whenever days slowed down she wound them up again, for to her, each party, each social encounter had to be a jewel in the timepiece of her life.

This Christmas Bea decided to stay in Paris. She was bored with St. Moritz, and snow conditions were bad. And she had not given a Christmas party since poor Étienne had collapsed into the Lobster E'Toufée, Christmas Eve four years ago.

"Well, cher Étienne," she sang out, "c'est soirée est pour tu!"

But only she would know that—never would she bore her friends with sad thoughts. The biggest bores in the world were those who, when you asked how they felt, told you, n'est-ce pas?

On Christmas Eve, when Elizabeth walked into Bea's salon with its frescoed ceilings and mirrored walls, Bea greeted her happily, her smile as bright as the silvered

348

Christmas tree standing before the French windows. Elizabeth wore a red and purple silk dress with matching, silk-strapped, high-heeled sandals. The sleek, uncluttered gown clung to her now slim figure, flaring at the hemline into a slitted skirt which ended in asymmetrical triangles at her ankles; the long slits revealed flashes of her shapely thighs.

Her hair was swept back and brushed into a crescent which curved behind her ears and back towards her face, the ends turned under into a sleek and shining pageboy cut. In her ears were gold hoop earrings and around her smooth forehead was a twisted coil of the same silk as her dress, wound with a slender gold chain.

"Marveilleuse—très chic!" Bea exclaimed, her dark doe eyes snapping with approval.

The two women kissed each other on the cheek.

It was a stunning party, and Bea reigned supreme. Her silver turban emphasized the Nefertiti look of her face, and her close-fitting silver gown with its long sleeves and low-cut neckline undulated like a second skin as she glided through the crowd, introducing Elizabeth. Around her throat Bea wore the magnificent emerald necklace Étienne had given her when they married. She looked barely forty and from across the room, no more than thirty. And from that far side of the room, a man with dark blue eyes stood in a corner and watched the two women. When Bea saw him she smiled and put her arm through Elizabeth's.

"Come, I have a surprise for you. There's a marvelous looking young man who phoned to say he was flying in from Stuttgart especially to see you . . . naturally, I invited him to the party. How romantic! And you never said a word! But I can't blame you. If I had someone like that, I'd keep him on a very short and tender tether."

Elizabeth halted. "I don't know what you mean, Bea . . . I'm not expecting anyone, and I know no one from Stuttgart."

"I know; he said it was a surprise. And, darling, he's not from Stuttgart, he's an *American* . . . and he certainly knows *you*. Ah, here he comes."

Douglas MacCormack made his way to them.

Elizabeth's eyes filled with surprise—and disappoint-

349

ment. Of course, she'd known it could not be Asher . . . but . . .

"Hello, Elizabeth," MacCormack said with a warm, engaging smile.

He took Bea's hand and kissed it. "Thank you again for inviting me . . . it's a wonderful party."

"*Pas de quoi* . . . have fun," Bea lilted, turning away and greeting new arrivals.

"May I get you a drink?" MacCormack asked.

Elizabeth stared at him, puzzled. Why would Douglas MacCormack make a special trip from Stuttgart to see her?

He laughed at the expression on her face. "Don't be so serious, Elizabeth. I've come to bring you special greetings from Bronwyn, and this was a wonderful excuse for me to get out of having to spend Christmas and New Year's in Germany. I leap at any opportunity to be in Paris."

"When and why did you see Bonnie?" It was an accusation more than a question, but MacCormack was unruffled.

"I'll tell you all about it over a drink." He cupped her elbow and led her to a mirrored table where a young man tended bar. "What would you like?"

"Perrier and lime, please."

"Rye and soda, and Perrier with lime," MacCormack said to the bartender. "On the rocks, please."

Handing Elizabeth her drink, MacCormack smiled with admiration.

"You've never looked better—you look incredibly young—but Paris does that for everyone. Bronwyn and I had our best times here."

"Thank you," Elizabeth said, sipping her drink. "Now tell me about Bonnie."

He stirred the ice in his glass with the tip of his finger.

"Like you, she's never looked better. If she weren't in a wheelchair with braces on her legs, you'd never think anything had happened. I couldn't believe the incredible progress she's made since I saw her in the hospital in Utah."

Elizabeth's head came up sharply. "You saw her in Utah?"

350

"She didn't tell you?"

Her eyes raked him. "No. She must have hated your seeing her that way. She wouldn't allow any of us to visit. It was the most difficult thing I ever had to do, to stay away like that. But you . . . you of all people . . . should have known better."

"I couldn't help it, Elizabeth. I had to see her."

She turned on him angrily. "Why? You must have known she was married! And you certainly knew how she would feel about being so severely hurt!"

His eyes shifted, unable to meet hers.

"And why are you seeing her now?" she persisted. "Can't you let well enough alone? She's married to a man who adores her, and if she's doing as well as you say, it's because of all he provides for her. What did you ever give her but grief?"

He hadn't expected her tirade. This was not the Elizabeth he knew and hoped to influence. She made him feel like a heel, and he felt compelled to redeem himself in her eyes. Slowly, seeking his words, as if by talking aloud he could explain to himself what he feared to admit, he said, "Elizabeth, seeing Bronwyn so hurt scared the *hell* out of me. Christ! I saw my father maimed after a race . . . two of my best buddies killed outright, and it was as if it was inevitable . . . something I *expected*. But seeing *Bronwyn* like that was something I could never imagine!" He shuddered. "She's always been such a strong, willful woman—she makes you feel she can do *anything*, and what's more important, that *you* can do anything! She's one of the rare women you believe in—she doesn't castrate you with her strength, she makes you feel invincible!" His voice broke. "When I saw her so helpless, not able even to lift her hands, it tore the heart out of me! And I knew what I'd lost and what an ass I'd been. For the first time, I looked into *myself*, and it wasn't a pretty picture. I can't even hack it behind the wheel anymore. I'm quitting at the end of this season, and I called ICC and told them I was available. Asher's offered me a golden rice bowl—I'll be the racing anchor for ICC. That's how I saw Bronwyn in New York. I'd flown back from L.A. with Asher the day we signed the contracts and I was at their house for dinner.

351

I never expected to see her so vital—so beautiful—" His voice trailed, and his eyes rested on Elizabeth's. He bent his head and kissed her lightly on the lips.

She drew back. "Why did you do that?"

"You make me think of her."

"We're not at all alike!"

"Yes, you are, in many ways."

"No! We're not!"

He laughed. "Hold on, Elizabeth. I'm not trying to come on to you—not that it wouldn't be a pleasure. Maybe I kissed you because I wanted to *feel* Bronwyn. I want her. She shouldn't have married Asher. That was all wrong—she doesn't love him!"

The color drained from Elizabeth's face. "How can you know that?" she asked, an unexpected anger rising in her.

He went on, unperturbed. "A man *knows*, Elizabeth, just as a woman *knows*. I saw Bronwyn's eyes when she looked at me across the table. Maybe she married Asher to get back at me, maybe she married him because she *wanted* to love him. But she *doesn't*. But neither will she hurt him, because he's so obsessed with her."

"Obsessed?"

"Yes. He walks on eggs with her. It's not natural. He does all the giving and she's uncomfortable with the taking. Bronwyn needs the dissension, the disagreement, the truth of a real relationship. She'll never know a fight with Asher, or have the stimulation she needs—that's why *we* were so good together. We belong together."

A frown knifed Elizabeth's brow.

"You want Bronwyn now? You couldn't commit to her when she was whole!"

"We couldn't commit to *each other,* Elizabeth. Neither of us felt we needed *anyone*. But seeing her crippled made me realize how much we need each other, and I love her more than I thought possible. When I first walked into that hospital room and saw her, before she even knew I was there, I thought she'd be better off dead. I wouldn't want to live, hurt the way she was. But then, despite that, I was *glad* she was alive. And I wanted her!"

Elizabeth's throat tightened and her head began to throb. His words brought back a terrible memory.

352

She had been sitting in the jazz bar with Tom and Asher when the call came summoning Calhoun back to the hospital, and she had hoped—just for a split second—that Bonnie had died. *Oh God forgive her! Just for an instant she had wished her daughter dead!* But—wasn't that what Bonnie had begged for? And she had not helped her! She had done nothing to relieve her suffering. She had sat in the cab speeding back to the hospital, huddled between two silent, grim-faced men, sweat pouring from her, and when the cab drew into the hospital's circular drive she could not move. Tom had leapt out first and reached an insistent hand for her. Asher, too, had sat unmoving, his face a stone. Tom spoke sharply and they had rushed inside and found Bonnie *alive, moving her hands, crying with joy!* Relief had swept her, so overwhelming she fought to keep from fainting. If she passed out, they might discover she was pregnant.

A week later, she had left for Paris.

And now sometimes, deep in the night—so deep, dawn lay sleeping just below the horizon—Elizabeth awakened and remembered what she had thought the moment Tom had been called to the phone.

MacCormack's voice came from far away.

"Elizabeth, I just wanted you to know how I feel—how it is—and to understand how I want Bronwyn."

She forced herself back. Her eyes came alive, anger filling them. She flung her words: *"How you feel? How it is?* Who the hell do you think you are? Priapus? How *dare* you think you can just step back into Bonnie's life! What *is* Douglas, is that Bonnie is *married*—you've no right to come between her and Asher! Understand? What I understand is that you've always been a self-centered bastard!"

Furiously she turned from him—furious not only with him, but furious with herself. She still wanted Asher.

353

Chapter Twenty-nine

Wᴵᵀᴴ a yawn Isabel Jameson put her book down. Taking off her reading glasses, she leaned her head back on the pillow and closed her eyes. Then she opened them wide—then shut them tightly, repeating the sequence a number of times. Isabel always exercised her eyes whenever she read for any length of time. She finished the ritual by rotating her pale grey eyes, circling first in one direction, then in another. Her round, fleshy face with its short, wide nose and thin lips remained passive. Her long grey hair, which daytimes she wore in a tight bun, flowed around her shoulders. It was her nicest feature, heavy, wavy hair framing her face with a well-defined hairline, culminating in a widow's peak above her squarish forehead.

Bored with the book, she put it on the night table. The French settings were interesting, especially now that she

354

was living in Paris, but weren't all romance novels alike? Yet, she liked the Barclay novels, and here she was working for the woman who *wrote* them! When the Gillian Agency had contacted her to inquire if she would consider a position in Paris, she had been surprised and pleased to discover her employer was actually *Ellen Barclay!* She had read almost all her books. They were a bit more real than the run-of-the-mill, but still, like the others, there was too much emphasis on sex—as if that was all there was to life!

Sex! Isabel sniffed in disdain. That was all anyone thought about today! Even Monsieur Serbie upstairs— even at his age! Her mouth narrowed, the lines around her lips deepening as she thought how brazen he had been! She didn't want *sex*—what she wanted was *romance!* There no longer was romance—only *sex!* Like those pill-popping punkers she had worked for last year. Imagine! Degenerates like that making *millions* and making babies—poor, poor babies, born addicted. Raised in an ear-splitting world of dope, drink—and *sex!* Isabel shuddered.

How had she stood it? Because she had loved the children, she supposed. But that last, wild party, when the punkers had broken almost every stick of beautiful antique furniture in the centuries-old mansion, had been too much. Of course, she regretted losing the money—never had she earned such a handsome stipend—but one had to live by principle!

And then came this offer to work for Mrs. Banks. What she would have preferred was a traditional English family, where the old values were respected, where a woman knew her place, where the man was *master*. That was the way life was meant to be. No wonder the world was in such a mess—no one lived by standards or morals anymore. No one even wore white gloves when they served! Nothing was like it had been! But the thought of caring for Ellen Barclay's baby had sent a little quiver of excitement through her—was the child the result of a *romantic* liaison? Did the author live the life of which she wrote? She must have loved the man to have had his child at her age.

And Isabel Jameson, born into a family of unbending

355

pride and unbending tradition stemming from having been "in service" for generations to the best families in Britain, accepted the offer to go to Paris to care for the baby of Elizabeth Banks—a.k.a. Ellen Barclay.

Getting up, Isabel drew her nightrobe around her and went into the adjoining room to check her charge. In the soft glow of the nightlamp on the dresser she saw all was well. The child slept on his back, his face rosy in peaceful repose. His small hands were curled, resting on top of the blue blanket. He breathed quietly and evenly. To be sure, he was a beautiful baby, Isabel thought fondly. Gently she adjusted the covers, being careful, as she bent over the crib, not to engage the mobile of colorful birds and flowers hanging from a support affixed to the rail. She felt the infant's hands, making sure he was warm enough. Mrs. Banks insisted on keeping the window in the room open slightly—even in winter! Isabel did not approve. But he was a healthy, contented child, not like the colicky, sickly babies of the punkers; but then Mrs. Banks was not a pill-popper or a drinker, and this baby was breast-fed. Isabel preferred to care for breast-fed babies; they were happier, more tranquil, and there was less work. And it was the *right* thing to do—what nature intended. If a woman was to have a child, the least she could do was nurse it. Yes, Elizabeth Banks had some good qualities, Isabel had to admit, even though she was not married and had been so foolish as to have a child at her age—and then attending the Sorbonne! Did she think she was a young girl? It was important in life to know your place and your limitations.

With the comfort that comes from knowing you're right about absolutely *everything*, Isabel went back to her own room. She took off her robe and folded it neatly across the foot of her bed—it would stay that way, for she did not permit her body to move freely while sleeping. She bent to place her orthopedic slippers in exactly the spot that would allow her to slide into them when she rose. The covers drawn back, she got into bed, reached out, and turned off the light.

* * *

From under the long velvet drapery in the parlor poked a pale, twitching nose and strung-wire whiskers. And then a pair of tiny, jet-black rat's eyes. They glittered malevolently in the reflection of the lamp left burning for Elizabeth. The rat scurried across the room, out the door, and down the hall, the dark grey body hugging the baseboard, long whip tail trailing. Passing the nursery, something bright and colorful flared in the hard, rifle-shot eyes. The rat spun sharply and stopped, ears alert, nostrils quivering, BB eyes transfixed on the sway, sway, sway of the mobile over the crib. The rodent rose on his hind legs, mesmerized. A puff of air snaked through the partially opened window and the plastic birds fluttered. The rat's eyes shone and darted. He dashed to the baby's bed, racing up the maple legs onto the narrow rail. The birds and flowers danced and the rat stopped, his eyes piercing, his ears peaked, his nose shivering. The whip tail flicked back and forth. Another bare breeze caught the mobile. The rat hunched tightly. *He leapt!* Into the shrouds—into the birds—into the flowers! His squat feet tangled in the lines—his strong, compact body floundered in the web of plastic shapes. The mobile bent with his weight. He struggled, squealed, and snapped the slender support. Enmeshed in the mobile, the rat fell into the crib, landing on the face of the sleeping child. Needle-sharp paws clawed wildly, savage teeth snapped. The baby awakened, screaming in terror.

The screeching cries slammed into Isabel's sleep. She leapt wildly from bed and ran to the room, switching on the lights. When she saw what was in the crib, she shrieked, her own cries of horror drowning out the child. Tearing the mobile from the baby's face, she grabbed him close, in her haste knocking over a lamp; it fell, its shade awry, into the soft cushion of an easy chair. The freed rat bounded from the crib and in its own terror raced across Isabel's bare feet. She screeched and turned to run, her feet catching in the long hem of her nightgown. She tripped, falling headlong, hitting the heavy chest near the door. Her head struck hard on the sharp corner of the bureau and she blacked out from the blow. Flailing his

357

arms and legs, the baby screamed and rolled from her grasp.

In the chair the exposed light bulb burned into the cotton cushion. The pillow began to smoulder, a charred ring spreading, blackened edges sparking. Soon tiny flames ate outward; wisps of smoke rose to the high ceiling, and the air in the room caught the fingers of light and heat, fanning them into hungry flames.

Bea LeVine's servants had been trained not to call their mistress to the telephone during a party. They were to take a message, and the call would be returned. Consequently, when Monsieur Serbie, who lived in the apartment above Elizabeth, phoned, he was told Madame LeVine would call back. But Mariel, who answered the phone on her way to the kitchen for a fresh tray of hors d'oeuvres (Claude, the butler, had gone to the wine closet for more champagne), forgot about the phone call by the time she returned to the salon.

Just before the midnight supper was to be served in the oval-shaped dining room the doorbell chimed and Claude opened it to a blue-clad gendarme.

"Madame Banks est ici?"

Claude's thin eyebrows arched slightly, but his voice betrayed no surprise. *"Un moment. Attendez ici, s'il vous plaît."*

His face impassive, Claude sought out his employer. Bea listened to his clipped words and without any semblance of hurry she followed the butler into the marble-floored entry.

Her face and manner were composed, her French as fluent as a native Parisienne's. "Yes—may I help you?"

"Madame Banks?" the officer asked, removing his hat.

"No—I am her friend. Is something wrong?" A small pulse began to tick in her throat.

"I must speak with Madame Banks."

Ice edged up Bea's back. She turned to Claude but he had already gone to find Elizabeth.

"Can't you tell me what it is?" Worry creased the makeup on Bea's face.

358

"It is best we wait for Madame Banks."

Bea clasped her hands together and found they trembled.

Elizabeth entered, and when she saw the gendarme she stopped abruptly. Claude had said only that someone was at the door asking for her. Her heart began to hammer, and she came running. Bea grabbed her hand, but Elizabeth shrugged loose.

"What is it?" she cried. "Is it my baby?"

Guests began to gather in the doorway behind them and MacCormack, seeing the uniformed gendarme, shouldered his way through and came quickly to Elizabeth's side, just as she said those words.

MacCormack looked at her sharply.

"Calm yourself, madame," the gendarme said officiously.

"*Nom de Dieu!*" exploded Bea. "Say what you have to say!"

"There's been a fire . . ."

"Oh my God!" Elizabeth's hands flew to her mouth, choking back the screams she felt tearing loose. "My baby . . . my baby!"

MacCormack stared at her. He took her hand and she clung to his.

The gendarme said more kindly, "Your baby and the nurse are in hospital. Please, if you will come with me, I have a car downstairs."

"Claude!" Bea said, but he already had her wrap and Elizabeth's.

"No, Madame LeVine," said MacCormack. "You can't leave your guests. I'll go with Elizabeth." He put the coat around Elizabeth's shoulders.

"But—I must go," Bea implored.

He squeezed her hand. "What you must do is see to your guests. Leave everything to me."

Shaken, Bea nodded. "Yes . . . you're right . . . thank you."

His arm around Elizabeth's shoulder, MacCormack led her out the door. They followed the gendarme to the elevator.

CHOICES

MacCormack's thoughts raced even more rapidly than the police car speeding through the Paris night, its blue lights spinning, its alarm sounding.

Baby? Elizabeth's baby? When? Who?

He looked at Elizabeth sitting next to him, hunched forward, as if by sitting so, she could make the car go even faster. He knew anything he might say to comfort her would be useless and he sat silent, listening to the questions in his mind.

They reached the hospital and Elizabeth ran ahead of the gendarme and MacCormack into the emergency room. A large, squarely built woman sitting at the desk told her to sit down and wait.

"Wait!" Elizabeth cried. "I want to see my baby *now!"*

MacCormack took her arm, but Elizabeth pulled loose.

"Now!" Tears streamed down her face.

"Calm yourself, madame," the woman said sternly. "The doctor is with the child, and you must wait for him. He will take you in to see your baby."

"Is he all right? Was he burned?"

"The doctor will tell you everything. Please—do not make a scene. Please, sit down."

But Elizabeth could not sit. She paced the waiting room, clasping and unclasping her hands. Suddenly she stopped, embarrassed. She had never even asked about Isabel! Hurrying back to the desk she said, "The nurse—Miss Jameson—how is she?"

"She, too, is being looked after. Please—it should not be much longer."

Elizabeth paced and MacCormack watched her in silence, aware of her anguish, wanting to help her, but not knowing what to say or do.

The gendarme joined them and, opening his notebook, said, "And now, madame, I will tell you what occurred:

"At twenty-four hundred hours an alarm was phoned in by a Monsieur Serbie, who lives on the third floor at number Three Rue Racine. Smoke was coming through the register of his bedroom and earlier he had heard screams. When the firemen arrived, they broke in the front door of the apartment below and found a woman and child

360

on the floor in a back bedroom. A chair in the room was ablaze—the woman and child were carried out, given oxygen, and taken by ambulance to hospital. Monsieur Serbie insisted on accompanying them, saying he was a friend of the woman's. Fire and smoke damage were confined mostly to the rear of Apartment two-B, which I understand is your apartment."

Elizabeth nodded and looked around. "Is Monsieur Serbie still here? I would like to thank him."

"I do not know, madame. Perhaps he went to get a coffee."

A small surge of hope coursed through Elizabeth. From what the gendarme said, Joshua and Isabel had to be all right—please, dear God, they had to be all right! A chair burning? How? Isabel did not smoke. She was just about to question the officer further when a man and a nurse holding a clipboard emerged from a room down the hall. She rushed to them.

"Are you the doctor? Is my baby all right? May I see him?"

The short, plump man smiled benignly. "Ah, you must be Madame Banks. How do you do? I am Doctor Georges Marius. Yes, your baby will be fine. Just some smoke inhalation and a few scratches on his face. Fortunately he was on the floor, where the smoke is not so thick. He is on oxygen and doing well."

"Thank God! And Miss Jameson?"

"She took a bad fall, and has a nasty bruise on her head, as well as smoke inhalation, but she will be fine. She told us the baby was born in this hospital, and I've already seen his records. This is fortunate—it helps when we know a child's history."

MacCormack had come to Elizabeth's side and the doctor nodded to him. "Ah, Monsieur Banks, I wish the child to stay in hospital until we know for sure there is no lung damage, and no infection from the scratches on his face. We have given him antibiotics."

Fear crossed Elizabeth's face. "But I thought you said he was doing well."

"Madame, he is an infant, just four months old, and his

361

respiratory system is still fragile. Also, he was premature. We must be certain there are no complications. He must be monitored until all danger is past."

Elizabeth could barely speak, but she managed to say, "I'm nursing him. May I continue?"

"By all means, it is important you continue. We wish to make no changes in his normal routine. You will pump your breasts and fill the bottles mamselle will give you. If you've not done this before, the nurse will instruct you. I will be in touch, and the desk will give you my phone number, and now, monsieur, madame—you may see your baby. But be quiet—he's sleeping now. Later he will be transferred to the pediatric section. If you will excuse me, I have other duties."

She did not even think of correcting the doctor's assumption that MacCormack was the father—she wanted only to see her child. MacCormack followed her into the room. He, too, wanted to see her child.

Elizabeth's heart turned over and tears stung her eyes at the sight of her son lying pale and still, plastic tubes taped to his tiny nose. The baby's dark hair was brushed back from his wide forehead, the curls falling in waves, his small, dark eyebrows arching slightly over the closed, translucent lids. Looking at the infant, MacCormack felt a strange sensation, as though he knew the child. There was something so familiar . . .

Elizabeth stood in silence, wanting to touch her baby, but not daring to waken him. The baby sensed her presence and stirred, beginning to whimper in his sleep. Elizabeth could not contain herself and she reached out, taking his hand, stroking the tiny fist. His fingers curled on hers and he stopped whimpering. He opened deep green eyes and looked sleepily at his mother. Slowly the eyes cleared and became alert, and then a smile—a beautiful smile—the special smile which bonds only mothers and babies, curved his mouth, and his cherubic face came alive, the green eyes shining happily.

"Oh, darling—darling," Elizabeth crooned softly. "You're going to be fine—just fine." She caressed his cheek, her tears falling lightly on the blanket as she bent to kiss him. "Mama loves you—Mama loves you."

MacCormack felt the hackles rise on the back of his neck.

The green eyes, such a rare green—the wide smile—and the expression! He looked so much—so much—like Asher? *Asher?* As soundless as a panther, MacCormack came closer. The child saw him, and another dimpled smile spread across the small face. MacCormack smiled back, his eyes crinkling. He touched the baby's hand, and the infant caught his finger, gripping it tightly. MacCormack stared at mother and child. Had Elizabeth known Asher? *She must have!* The baby had to be his! The resemblance was too striking. Was this why Elizabeth was in Paris?

He studied the infant's face and saw the man in the child.

Did Asher know?

Did Bronwyn?

A pulse began to throb in his head. Mixed feelings, as though he froze on a hot stove, seared him. He didn't like what he was thinking, or the hope rising in him—it was like being second in a race, just yards from the finish, when the lead car blows a tire.

Elizabeth raised her head and saw the look on his face, and she feared the time she had tried to buy had been cut short.

Chapter Thirty

WHEN she was young Bronwyn had always looked forward to Christmas and New Year's. She never knew how her mother managed it, but even before she became a successful novelist, Elizabeth took off from work for the holidays, and they would go somewhere wonderful to ski: in the early days, before there was much money, to nearby places like Hunter and Camelback, and then when Elizabeth hit it big, to St. Anton, Aspen, Sun Valley, Tahoe, Lake Louise, Vail. Bronwyn was keenly aware of the charmed childhood she had known, and she thought often of those happy days when she and Elizabeth had been more than just mother and daughter, they had been *comrades*. And this year as the holidays approached and Elizabeth did not call, Bronwyn felt a sense of loss.

Thoughts of Elizabeth came randomly, many times breaking into her concentration while she worked, other times as she sat reading before the fire after dinner. One night when she had put her book down to stare into the flames, Asher had said, "Anything wrong, darling?"

"No, I was just thinking."

"About what?"

"Nothing really."

She hadn't seen Elizabeth in more than eight months! Stop being a dunce! Bronwyn told herself. Your mother is doing what she's always dreamed of! You've been separated before. *But this is different,* her mind nagged. *This time* Elizabeth *has left* me! So? Must it always be you who goes away? How do you think she felt when you went off to school, when you went off to race, and when you moved to New York? *Well, at least she was* home. *If I wanted to talk to her, I just picked up the phone!* Really? How often did you call her? She always called *you*—and when she did, you were teed off! *But she called at the damnedest times. I was either getting up, getting out of the shower, going out, going to bed, making love, or maybe just sitting down with a drink after a rotten day, when I didn't want to talk to* anyone! But with *anyone,* you were *polite;* with your mother, you were *impatient!* How many times did you just say, "What's up?" So who are you to feel lousy because your mother doesn't call?

Bronwyn looked at the phone, wishing it would ring, wanting to hear Elizabeth's voice. Why hadn't Elizabeth given her an address and phone number other than Bea's? All she really knew was that Elizabeth had an apartment near the university. Why was Elizabeth being so secretive?

She had called Bea on Christmas Eve, sure that her mother would be there, even timing her call so that it would come shortly after midnight, Paris time. But Bea had sounded strange, and Elizabeth had not called back. It just wasn't like Elizabeth not to wish her a happy holiday. Still, Bronwyn said nothing to Asher, and she tried to seem cheerful and filled with Christmas spirit. They would spend a quiet Christmas at home, and Bronwyn was grateful they were alone.

At her suggestion Asher had given Charles and Ruth a holiday cruise as a gift. The couple was surprised and delighted but they worried whether Bronwyn could manage. She had reassured them and Asher it would work out. Helen had a cousin who could fill in, and between the three of them—Helen, the cousin, and herself—all would go well.

"Besides," Bronwyn had teased, "there's always the Stage Deli and 'Mr. Babbington' for takeouts."

Giving a man who had everything a Christmas gift presented a problem Bronwyn had never faced, and she racked her mind about what to give Asher. And finally it came to her—she contacted a rare book dealer and he came up with a signed, first-edition copy of Wallace Stevens' first published work, *Harmonium*.

They were in the library Christmas Eve, where Asher had just finished trimming the fat green spruce that stood before the window. Bronwyn had been helping, handing Asher lights and ornaments, exclaiming over the many fine antique pieces, some of them handmade.

"The Cassidys collected them for years," he said. "I never could give them away." He reached up to put the last few brightly colored, intricately decorated glass balls on the tree. "I never celebrated Christmas, of course, until I went to live with them, and it set a pattern for me—even though I feel strongly about my Jewish heritage and my own traditions."

Bronwyn smiled at him. "I know what you mean. My mother and I always had a tree. She's very Jewish about so many things, but she loves Christmas. I think she soothed her conscience by lighting the menorah and celebrating Chanukah. When the holidays coincided we had both a menorah and a tree in the window."

Asher laughed.

"That's it," he said, stepping back. He handed Bronwyn a clicker switch. "And now, madame, the lights, please."

She pressed the switch and the tree came alive in a rainbow of colors. "It's lovely, Asher—thank you!"

"Thank *you*, darling, and happy anniversary."

"It's not till next week."

"Tonight's our true anniversary. It's tonight that we met."

She looked at him, her eyes suddenly solemn.

366

Quickly he bent and kissed her. "Have I told you, Mrs. Jacobs, how absolutely beautiful you look tonight? You're even lovelier than the night I first saw you."

She touched the strong face and kissed him back. "And you, Mr. Jacobs, are absolutely stunning in that green velvet smoking jacket. I've always wanted to spend an evening with a man who wore a smoking jacket and see if what my mother writes about is true."

Bronwyn felt better than she had for days. She sat in her wheelchair wearing a white silk and wool sweater with a low-cut bodice of openwork lace that bared her shoulders and ended just above the bustline; her long wool skirt was a bright red, green, and navy plaid, and she had tied back her shining hair with a red velvet ribbon. Now she took a gold foil-wrapped package from behind her back and handed it to Asher.

"Happy Christmas."

He tore the wrappings off eagerly and when he saw the Stevens book, his eyes flew to hers in delighted surprise. He opened the book carefully, saw the Stevens signature, and drew in his breath. Lightly he traced the autograph with his fingers, handling the book with such reverence it could have been the Dead Sea Scrolls. He bent and kissed Bronwyn again, and handing the book to her, he said huskily, "I'll always cherish this. Thank you. Please—read it to me. I want to hear 'Sunday Morning' from your lips."

"Would you mind, Asher? I'd like to sit on the sofa, near the fire."

"Of course, darling." He lifted her from the wheelchair, placing her on the couch so that the firelight came over her shoulder and illuminated the book. Blaze, who had been lying near her chair, got up lazily and, with one lumbering move, settled on the couch next to her, shoving his head into her lap.

She began to giggle and looked at Asher, a mischievous gleam lighting her eyes. "I feel just like Elizabeth Barrett Browning, but Blaze is certainly no Flush." Opening the book, she began to read in a soft cadence, her hand trailing on Blaze's ears. Her voice rose and fell, mirroring the beautifully imagined words.

The glow from the fireplace cast an aura about her face and Asher, sitting in the leather chair opposite, watched the movement of her lips. His mind wandered . . .

He sat in the jazz bar, hearing nothing, not Tom or Elizabeth, not the music. And he saw nothing . . . *there was nothing* . . . even he no longer existed. Whatever human there had been of him, he had left behind in the hospital. *Why had he done it?* But even that memory no longer existed. And then someone came to the table to tell Tom there was an urgent telephone call for him from the hospital. Asher felt himself sinking into a black hole. He remembered no more—not even how he had gotten to the hospital. But there was Tom tugging at him—pulling him inside. And then there was Bronwyn—*alive!* Crying and smiling, holding out her hands—curling and uncurling her fingers, and he had wept, long, wracking sobs. He had held her close, their tears mingled, and once more came *feeling.*

Since then, he often wondered, but never asked—had she spit out the capsules *before* or *after* she knew she could move? And he had told himself it didn't matter. But—it did. And they had settled into a pattern of kindness and gratefulness, and as the days and weeks passed he found himself cheering her on as a proud father cheers on his child—as Michael had cheered Eleanore.

But months later, he awakened one dark morning with a strange feeling of unease. He lay listening to the November sleet drop like shot on the terrace. Why this oppressive weight? Why this sense of something wrong? And then he remembered! And an embarrassment even deeper than the night before made his face flame. He tried to think logically. It happened to all men—it had happened to him before—but never with someone he loved! And last night she had wanted *him*—she had come to *him!* He closed his eyes, shame running through him. Now! He would take her now and love her as she had wanted him to love her last night! But he lay flaccid. A terrible fear rose in him. What if last night had not been just a momentary aberration? He glanced at Bronwyn, her head resting on her curled arm. How peacefully she slept, like a child. Lightly he touched her cheek. *Like a child.* A sudden, abhorrent feeling rose in him. Abruptly he pulled his hand away and stealthily he got out of bed. He felt as if he slept with his daughter.

"You're not listening, Asher." Bronwyn's voice broke through the maze of his wanderings.

He sat up sharply. "I'm sorry. Please go on."

She put down the book and shook her head. "No, I've finished."

He got up and went to her, and kissed her head. The gesture startled him. Goddammit! He had to rid himself of this damn paternal feeling which had plagued him for weeks! She was his *wife*, not his *child!* And then he thought of the Christmas gift he was about to give her. It was the gift of a father to a child! Chagrin creased his face.

Bronwyn stared at him. "Is something wrong, Asher?"

With an effort he pulled himself together. "Forgive me, darling, I've been preoccupied all day, and your gift was such a wonderful surprise, I lost myself in it." He forced a smile. "Now it's time for your present."

"What is it?" she asked excitedly.

"Hang on to Blaze. I'll be right back."

He returned carrying a small wicker basket. The moment he walked into the room Blaze's head came erect, his ears standing. The dog's nostrils twitched and he would have bounded from the couch had not Bronwyn held his choke collar. Bronwyn, too, came alert, leaning forward, her eyes widening as she heard small, low sounds coming through the wicker.

"Is it what I think it is?" she exclaimed.

One day they had gone down to the Village to pick up some books from Bronwyn's apartment. Driving along Hudson Street, they passed a pet shop she had not noticed before. Ordinarily she disliked pet shops; she thought too many proprietors cared little for the animals they sold, and she hated to see animals in cages. As a child she had cried when Elizabeth had first taken her to the zoo—she never went again. But this shop looked clean and spacious. It sold only cats and kittens, and a new litter played in the window, scampering wildly, boxing at each other, cata-

369

pulting and attacking from behind and under scraps of torn newspapers.

"Asher—look!" she had cried. "Please—oh please, stop!"

Asher pulled over and double-parked. Nowhere along the street was there a parking space, and Bronwyn sat in the car laughing at the crazy antics of the kittens.

"They're Abyssinians," she said. "They're very doglike for cats. They have a low voice and they're affectionate like dogs. You can even train them. They're supposed to be very smart. I had a friend once—Jeff was his name—he was wild about them. He said they were the only cats in the world smart enough to run a computer. I could never tell if he was joking or serious. Aren't they *gorgeous?*"

"Would you like one, darling?" Asher asked.

"You wouldn't *mind?*"

He kissed her cheek. "Not at all. But what about Blaze?"

"He'd *love* them! He's used to cats. I'm sure he misses Archie and Orrin."

And Asher went inside to ask the owner if he might take the litter out to the car so that his wife could choose a kitten. The man laughed dryly.

"Those cats were sold before they were born. They're very rare and very expensive. I have a waiting list for Abyssinians, but I'm expecting two more litters to come in by December. They'll be ready for Christmas. Let me have your name and phone number, and if I have a cancellation, I'll give you a call."

Asher could not believe what he was hearing—he had no idea these cats were so popular. Disappointment on his face, he returned to the car and told Bronwyn the kittens were sold. He did not tell her more were expected by Christmas and that he was determined she would have one.

Asher placed the basket on her lap.

"Down, Blaze!" she said sharply, but the dog excitedly nosed the wicker, his tail wagging. He let out a small, plaintive yelp, and Bronwyn heard growls from within. Asher took hold of the dog's collar and pulled him away as Bronwyn opened the lid.

She looked up, astounded. "You got *two* of them!" Laughing with pleasure, she picked up two tiny kittens. "Oh—they're so *beautiful!*" But the kittens heard the dog and their heads twisted nervously, their tiny noses quivering, their bodies shaking. They clawed the air but Bronwyn knew how to avoid those sharp little needles, and she held them close, stroking their fluffy, coffee-colored bodies, crooning to them until they settled against her. They began to purr, and when they had quieted she held them out, kissing the dark brown tips of their ears, the dark brown of their eyes, and their little pink mouths. "Oh, I love you . . . I love you!" she whispered. She looked up at Asher with such happiness his throat constricted.

"Are they males or females?" she asked.

"One of each, and from two different litters. If you wish, you can mate them."

"How did you manage *that?* They seldom sell males and females from different litters. They're afraid you'll take their business away!"

Asher laughed with amusement. "I'm sure Mr. Medina knows I'm not going into the cat business."

Bronwyn giggled. "And I'm sure you must have paid Mr. Medina a small fortune. Oh, thank you, Asher. They're the loveliest present you could have given me."

And Asher felt a warm contentment now about his gift. "By the way," he said, "they're already litter trained."

Bronwyn nuzzled the kittens. "Of course. They're so smart, they're born trained."

"What are you going to call them?"

She thought for a moment and then she laughed. "Albert for Einstein—and Apple—for you know what." Tickling the female behind the ears she said, "Little Apple, I'm going to teach you to use my computer." She held up the male. "And as for you little Albert, you'd better come up with something other than E equals mc squared."

Cautiously, taking one kitten at a time, stroking it, soothing it, she held first Albert and then Apple out to Blaze. Paws flying, the little animals hissed and bared their teeth, but as Blaze nosed them gently, the kittens quieted.

"Soon they'll be jumping all over him and sleeping with

371

him, and he'll run off to a corner to try and escape them. Oh, what fun it's going to be watching them grow up!" Bronwyn patted and kissed the dog. "Good boy, Blaze, good boy. I love you, too." She pulled him close and he lumbered back onto the couch and settled again with his head in her lap. Eyeing him warily, the kittens bounded onto a pillow out of reach. When they were sure the dog would not bother them, they began to play, boxing and tumbling with each other. Bronwyn watched, laughing.

Relaxed now, Asher sat back in the leather chair, and opening the Stevens book Bronwyn had given him, he began to read.

Bronwyn sat near the sliding glass doors watching light snow dust the evergreens on the terrace. She had gotten up early. Normally she liked sleeping late on Sunday, but today she wanted to review the final draft of her outline for Calhoun's book before Asher, sleeping upstairs, awakened. They were going to Van Zuye's for lunch, and Calhoun would meet them there.

The snow began to fall heavily and the kittens playing at Bronwyn's feet scampered to the glass, leaping at the flakes, boxing the pane, trying in vain to catch the crystals. Laughing, Bronwyn slid the door open just enough for the curious kittens to test their paws in the snow—and then she opened it wider. They stood uncertainly on the jamb, their backs arching, their tiny heads bobbing up and down as they watched the snowflakes descend. Reaching out, then, they took small, tentative stabs at the strange white dusting, and with a quick leap they soared into the air to catch a snowflake—but they tumbled into the snow. It was cold, wet, and they darted back inside to the warmth of the pillow in their wicker bed. Busily they licked their paws and bodies clean.

Bronwyn smiled and reached out to grab a handful of snow—it melted on the warmth of her fingers. Her face grew solemn. She slid the door closed and stared outside.

The phone rang, but so deep was her reverie, for the moment she did not hear it. Finally its soft, insistent tone got through to her, and wheeling herself back to the desk, she picked up the receiver.

"Hello," she said.

The line crackled with interference, and then it cleared.

"Bonnie? It's me. What's up?"

The words slapped back at her, and Bronwyn was so startled she didn't answer.

"Bonnie? Are you all right? Hello? Hello?"

Bronwyn smiled ironically at her mother's greeting. "I'm here, Mother. You took me by surprise."

"I got your message. Sorry I couldn't get back to you sooner."

"Where have you been?"

"Busy—and then Bea gave this big party . . ."

"I know," Bronwyn interrupted, "but Bea said you'd left. She sounded unlike herself. Did you take off with one of her men?"

Elizabeth laughed lightly. "Happy New Year, darling, and to Asher. And also, happy anniversary."

"Happy New Year to you too, Mother. When are you planning to come back?"

"How's Blaze?"

Did they have a bad connection, Bronwyn wondered, or was Elizabeth avoiding the question?

"He's fine. He has two new playmates. Asher gave me two Abyssinian kittens for Christmas."

"How lovely! Blaze must be ecstatic."

"He is. If he were a female, he'd nurse them—he watches over them like a mother hen. But that's enough about animals. How are *you?*"

"Fine; just fine. And you . . . and Asher?"

"Okay. I'm working on a new book. Tom's doing a sculpture for the new clinic, Van Zuye is supervising, and I'm doing a book about it, plus bringing in other professionals like Tom who find an outlet in art."

"That sounds terrific! Well, darling, I have to go. Give my regards to everyone . . . and . . . be happy. I love you."

Why was Elizabeth cutting her short? She'd never, *ever* made a *three-minute call*—Elizabeth was the reason AT&T made *millions*.

"Mother?"

"Yes?"

". . . Nothing. Have fun."

"Thank you, darling. Goodbye."

"Goodbye."

Bronwyn heard the line go dead, and she held the phone in her lap until it began to buzz. She replaced it in the cradle, her brow creasing. She knew as much as she did before the call: *nothing*. Bronwyn didn't like it.

"I'm not sure I'll forgive you for not coming Christmas Eve," Van Zuye said, affecting a glacial demeanor. But then he kissed Bronwyn on the cheek.

"Oh yes, you have already." She smiled as Asher took her wrap and handed it to Louis. She sat in her wheelchair in Van Zuye's studio. Van Zuye still wore his workcoat, and she and Asher were dressed casually, as befitted a lazy Sunday after Christmas. They were waiting for Calhoun to arrive.

Two covered shapes sat on nearby stands. Bronwyn knew one of them was Calhoun's maquette—what was the other?

As if she transferred her thoughts to his, the artist went to one of the shapes, and turning to face both her and Asher, he said to Bronwyn with a hint of a smile, "Your Christmas present."

"Mine?"

With a swift movement of his agile hands, Van Zuye whisked the cover off, revealing a life-size bronze bust.

Bronwyn gasped. How strange it was to see yourself through someone else's eyes! So—he *had* made use of the sketches he'd drawn so quickly that night in the hospital. A chill of pleasure raised the flesh on her arms.

"Oh, Willem! Thank you! It's magnificent."

Asher went to the sculptor and, putting his hands on the small man's shoulders, he bent and kissed Willem's cheeks.

"Thank you, dear friend. But it is much too generous a gift. Please, permit me to do something in return."

"Nonsense," Van Zuye said shortly. "Do not deprive me of the pleasure of giving. But, if it makes you feel better, you can pay to have it moved to your apartment. Art movers charge a fortune."

374

Asher laughed—he knew how paradoxically frugal Van Zuye could be. "With pleasure."

"I know you are anxious to see Dr. Calhoun's maquette, but it is for him to unveil it. We will wait here until he arrives. He is a remarkable man, and it is a remarkable work for a nonprofessional."

Van Zuye took off his workcoat and hung it on a peg. Underneath he wore a bright green turtleneck and black corduroy trousers. Through the pant loops he had drawn a pink slash of silk, and on his feet were the black Chinese slippers he always wore.

"I like the book idea," he said to both of them. His eyes went to the briefcase in Bronwyn's lap. "You've brought the outline? Good. We'll have plenty of time to discuss it at lunch. Dr. Calhoun has no commitments today and neither do I. It will be a relaxing afternoon."

The buzzer sounded and Louis went to the elevator to open the downstairs door and admit Tom Calhoun.

"Has Calhoun told you, Asher, that he wishes his royalties on this book, if any, to go to the new clinic?"

"That's Bronwyn's department, Willem. It's her imprint."

"Yes," Bronwyn said to Van Zuye, "Tom and I have discussed this, and fifty percent of our profits, too, will go to the clinic. I plan for the book to make money. It's not just an artistic endeavor—we're going to promote it."

The elevator doors clanged open and Calhoun strode into the vast studio, his face ruddy, his down jacket damp with snow. He had walked from the subway station at Canal Street. There was nothing he liked more than walking the streets of New York in the snow. With one broad stroke, nature brushed the city clean, and Calhoun reveled in its freshness. Pulling the knitted wool hat off his head and shrugging himself out of his parka, he greeted them warmly.

"You missed quite a party."

"I know," Asher said, "but it was very pleasant at home."

"And just wait till you see what Asher gave me for Christmas," Bronwyn smiled.

"Oh?"

"I'm not telling. You'll have to see for yourself."

Calhoun ruffled Bronwyn's hair. She wore it loose today, and it fell like a shining cloud around her face. His eyes went to the uncovered bronze.

"Well, now you know what *Van Zuye's* given you for Christmas."

"Yes—isn't it marvelous? I still can't believe it!"

"I watched him work it, and nothing could be more intimidating. God! If I had that kind of talent!"

"Enough—enough," Van Zuye said with a wave of his hand. "You've more than enough talent for one man, Dr. Calhoun. And now, please unveil your maquette. That is the reason we are all here."

Calhoun seemed suddenly, uncharacteristically uncertain. He stood hesitantly, rubbing his hands together. "Look," he said, "I want you to be totally honest with me. If you think it's—uh—not the kind of thing that would be suitable—uh—please, say so. Or—uh—if you feel it needs some changes—that's okay too."

"It's not okay!" thundered Van Zuye. "An artist does not change his vision to suit anyone but himself! Your art, Dr. Calhoun, is the expression of your soul, visualized through your eyes, your fingers. All that is important is what you feel inside, and if *you* are pleased with what is under that cloth, so will we be! And if we or anyone else is not, it does not matter!"

Van Zuye held Calhoun's eyes fiercely, and a slow smile flickered on the big man's face. Taking a deep breath, Calhoun went to the large wood stand and withdrew the cover.

Asher's sharp intake of breath was the only sound in the studio.

Bronwyn stared transfixed, small shivers running up and down her arms and spine. She looked quickly from Asher to Van Zuye. There was a smug smile of satisfaction on the sculptor's face and a look of sheer astonishment on Asher's. And then she looked at Calhoun. How could it be that someone with absolutely no art training had created a grouping of figures that could—that could—*no!* But *yes*— not quite as sharply defined, more impressionistic, but

Calhoun's grouping of five figures—a child, a young woman, a young man, and an old couple—were reminiscent of *The Burghers of Calais!* She shivered again with inner excitement. Like the Burghers, Calhoun's people were dressed in the style of *their* day—*today*—and, as in Rodin's piece, they revealed an individuality, a strength that was awesome. But there was something more. She moved her wheelchair close, narrowing her eyes, trying to determine what else it was she saw in the greyness of the clay. What was it? Her eyes widened. Pathos. That was it. The figures, all of whom were handicapped, had a pathos that tore at your heart! But yet it was not sentimental, designed deliberately to evoke the emotions—it was a simple statement of how life *was,* and in the simplicity of that statement lay its strength and its nobility.

Bronwyn looked at Calhoun, seeing him as she had never seen him before, and her eyes filled with tears. She fought to keep her voice steady. "What's the scale, Tom?"

"One to four. I hope to do the plaster four times larger. I want it to be slightly bigger than life-size."

"It is now," Bronwyn breathed.

"My God, Tom!" Asher said. "I had no idea!" He turned to Van Zuye. "Did you?"

"When I saw him work with clay, I *knew*. What does it remind you of?"

Asher did not even hesitate. *"The Burghers of Calais."* Van Zuye nodded.

"You can't be serious," Calhoun said uneasily. "Rodin was a genius."

"And you, my dear friend, are a *savant*," said Van Zuye. "Well then, since we are all in agreement concerning Dr. Calhoun's sculpture, I see no reason why we can't go upstairs to lunch."

They ate on a low, square table Louis had set before the fireplace in the living room. The fire dried out the dampness of the day and they relaxed on colorful, plump cushions, enjoying fresh Dover sole served with black Chinese mushrooms and artichokes stuffed with creamed celery and spinach. Louis poured glass after glass of a Montrachet Marquis de la Guiche and the conversation flowed as freely as the wine. For dessert there was a delectable chocolate rum cake. Bronwyn felt herself sink into delightfully carefree comfort.

After coffee was served, Van Zuye said, "Well, Bronwyn—now tell us about the book."

Reluctantly Bronwyn pulled herself back to the business at hand. But it all went quickly. Van Zuye agreed to cooperate, and as she asked Calhoun to give her his schedule so that she might plan a timetable for the photographs, Asher said, "Try not to arrange anything between February fifteenth and twentieth."

His words encompassed them all.

"The F.C.C. is paving the way for the licensing of three to four thousand new television stations across the country. It will take place in the next three years, and there's also the ruling on satellite home transmissions coming up. It's a changing world for television, and there's to be a conference in Paris to plan worldwide for these changes."

He leaned over and took Bronwyn's hand.

"I want you to come to Paris with me. We'll be there for Valentine's Day, and while I'm busy at the conference, you can visit with Elizabeth." He smiled, his green eyes teasing. "You two should have a lot of fun at the new collections."

A thousand thoughts spun suddenly in Bronwyn's mind. "I can't, Asher."

"Why not? It's only for a week, and we'll use the ICC plane. You'll be as comfortable and as private as at home."

Bronwyn looked deep into the smiling eyes. *Why not!* She didn't care a whit about the collections but she did want to see Elizabeth and find out what was really going on!

She glanced at Van Zuye and Calhoun, and their faces encouraged her. She smiled at Asher.

"You're right. I'd love to go!"

378

Chapter Thirty-one

Iᴛ was not a subject Asher had considered discussing, but when Van Zuye said, as they sat at lunch a few days before Asher and Bronwyn were to leave for Paris, "I'm pleased all goes well. I was not happy with your quick marriage, but you've proven me wrong," Asher, frustrated by weeks of painful introspection and no solutions, found himself asking his close friend, "Are you still sexually potent, Willem?"

The sculptor's small eyes widened momentarily; he measured Asher intently. When he spoke he chose his words carefully.

"No man asks that question, unless it is *he* who has a problem. Do you want to talk about it?"

Dark color rose in Asher's face. "No."

Van Zuye stopped eating. He wiped his small mouth with the linen napkin and, putting it down, he said in a calm, unemotional voice, as though discussing the weather, "I know it is a private, sensitive subject, but evidently you are troubled." He leaned across the table. "All men know impotence at one time or another. As for me, on occasion sex is good, but I expect no more at my age. As you know, there are many ways to compensate."

"It's not the same!"

"Of course not! But all life is compromise."

"I'm still too *young* to compromise."

"Yes, you are. Therefore, whatever is wrong is something other than physical, and for that answer you have to be brutally honest with yourself. Have you the courage?"

Asher said nothing.

Van Zuye regarded him closely. Since Asher was reluctant to speak, so was he, but it had to be said.

"You realize what's happened, don't you?"

Asher could not meet Van Zuye's knowing eyes.

"You're treating her like a handicapped child, and it is very difficult for decent men to be sexually potent with their children."

Asher's face paled.

"But it is even more than that," Van Zuye continued, not wanting to reopen old wounds, but seeing no other way.

"Everyone repeats their mistakes, Asher. That is why history is so repetitious. We tend to live in patterns. Few have the insight, the intelligence to recognize destructive patterns, and even fewer have the *will* to break them. When you met Bronwyn, she fit perfectly into the pattern your mind had carved for Marguerite. When she was injured, the protectiveness you had for Eleanore surfaced. And now Bronwyn has slid, without your consciously knowing it, into Eleanore's slot."

Cold recognition edged, unwanted, into Asher's mind.

Van Zuye spoke even more quietly.

"You can fool yourself, Asher, but you can't fool your body. You do not love Bronwyn the way you think you do. Love has many faces, many feelings, and your feelings are all mixed up with compassion—duty—and guilt. This is why you're having trouble in bed."

* * *

"I think that does it!" Bronwyn ran a pencil through the last of her notes.

The dark-haired young woman sitting on the other side of the desk finished writing memos on a yellow legal pad. She looked up.

"Are you sure? Is there something else I can do while you're away?"

Bronwyn smiled. Mary was so eager—just the way she had been.

"You're bored, aren't you? You'd really like to do more."

The girl's young face colored. "I'm sorry. Is it so obvious?"

Bronwyn leaned across the desk to her. "I'm truly grateful you've stayed on this long—I knew you were ready to move on even before I got hurt. You've been tremendously helpful to me, but don't let me hold you back now. If something good turns up, take it."

Mary Turner's lips twisted.

"Things are lousy in publishing. Many houses are laying off editors, and you pay me more as your assistant than some editors are making."

"Well then—" Bronwyn smiled. "—when I get back from Paris, I'll just have to expand the job to fit the money—okay?"

"It's a deal!" And for the first time that day, Mary Turner smiled happily.

The intercom on Bronwyn's desk buzzed, and she flipped the switch.

Charles's voice came through crisply. "I'm sorry to disturb you, Mrs. Jacobs, but Mr. MacCormack is here and he would like to speak with you."

Bronwyn frowned. Asher had said nothing about expecting MacCormack. And *she* certainly did not want to see him. But out of the corner of her eye she saw the look of quickly masked surprise which crossed Mary's face. Bronwyn knew her romance with the highly visible MacCormack had been a source of gossip with the girls at Mednam, and she did not want Mary to think he had come back into her life, or that his visit was unexpected or unwelcome.

"Would you please ask him to wait, Charles? We're almost finished, and I want to gather the papers Mr. Jacobs left for him."

"Very well, madame," Charles said, and the line went silent.

"Well," she said, looking directly at her assistant. "Can you imagine? Douglas MacCormack is retiring from racing and joining ICC as a sportscaster." She began stacking some papers in a gesture of dismissal. "Anyway, Mary, thanks for doing such a good job. I know I won't have to worry about the office while I'm in Paris."

Mary put a sheaf of papers and the legal pad into her attaché case.

"Shall I stop by here tomorrow morning or go directly to the office?"

"The office," Bronwyn said. "I've a manuscript I want to finish editing and another one I'd like to read quickly. I'll call you if I need you. Have a nice evening."

"And you too," Mary said, going out the door.

Bronwyn lit a cigarette, collecting herself before she faced MacCormack. This was her favorite part of the day, and she resented his disturbing it. Helen and the day maid had gone home. Charles would soon leave to pick up Asher, and Ruth was busy in the kitchen preparing dinner.

It was a private time when Bronwyn enjoyed having a drink, playing with the kittens, and just letting herself relax. Well, Douglas could just sit and wait—she'd see him when she was ready. She whistled softly to catch the attention of the kittens. Blaze, sleeping in a corner, lifted his head, opened one eye, and went back to sleep. But the kittens scampered from their wicker bed and, leaping lightly onto a chair, onto the desk, they landed in Bronwyn's lap. She nuzzled them and they rubbed themselves against her.

"It's time to go out, you rascals." She raised her voice, addressing the dog. "And you too, Blaze. Come on—wake up! You need your exercise."

The dog lumbered heavily to his feet. Putting his front paws out, he took a long, long stretch, and then he yawned. She shook her head at him. "My, you're getting lazy. This city life is ruining you."

She wheeled herself to the glass doors, and as she went through the electric eye, the doors slid open. Immediately Blaze rushed past her and out onto the terrace, going to a special spot where Bronwyn had trained him to relieve himself. The kittens also had a litter box hidden under the trees. Bronwyn felt the animals were her responsibility, and she cleaned up after them. It was a chore she felt she had no right to impose on the servants.

The night was cold and windy, and she shivered in her sweater and wool slacks. Leaving the animals to romp, she turned her chair to go back inside and saw MacCormack standing in the open doorway.

"I thought you'd forgotten me," he said with a slow smile.

She wheeled past him without answering, and the door slid closed behind her. She spun her chair and faced him.

"What do you want, Douglas?"

He put his hands up in mock defense. "Is that any way to greet a friend?"

"I don't like surprises."

"You used to."

She sighed exasperatedly. "Look, Douglas, what's past is past. I'm interested only in *now,* and living *now* as best I can." She looked at him, and suddenly she remembered what she had read. Her face softened. "I'm sorry about Daytona."

He shrugged. "You can't win 'em all."

"Was it the car?"

He avoided her eyes and said slowly, "No, it was me. It's the reason I'm quitting. I just don't have it anymore."

Empathy checked her annoyance. She had never seen him so diffident.

"Would you like a drink?" she asked.

"Yes, a stiff one. But here, let me make it."

"No, sit down. I'll do it."

MacCormack sat in the large lounge chair near the window. "This is a terrific setup," he said, scanning the room. "Do you ever go downtown to your office?"

"Sometimes, but mostly I work here. I have everything I need—a copy machine, a computer terminal with a direct line to the office and to the printer—my mother did it all.

From what Asher tells me, this part of the apartment was originally the library and dining room, but since it opens directly onto the terrace, and Mother knows how I love to be outside, she turned it into a suite for me."

Bronwyn handed MacCormack his drink. He closed his fingers on hers, holding her hand along with the glass.

"Don't," she said, pulling her hand away. She wheeled the chair back to the bookcase, which held a small bar, and poured a double Bourbon into a heavy tumbler.

"Are you and Elizabeth still close?"

Bronwyn hesitated. "Yes . . . I think so." She looked out into the night. Outside the terrace was lit, and she could see the animals chasing each other, teasing, playing. She turned and wheeled her chair back to face MacCormack. And then she laughed, a small, nervous laugh.

"You know, it's almost as if she ran away from home! So many times when I was young, I had the feeling I was the mother and she the child, and now it's as if she's run off somewhere to assert her independence from *me.*"

"I saw her in Paris."

An amused, expectant look rose in Bronwyn's eyes. "I was hoping you would."

MacCormack gave her a quick, sharp glance. Something about the smile playing on her lips—had she set him up? Elizabeth's angry words still rang in his ears, but she had been kinder, though still distant, after they had left the hospital. Wanting to spare her the shock of seeing her apartment, he had prevailed on her not to go home. Instead he had taken her back to Bea LeVine's, where the party was still in progress, but after hugging Bea and assuring her the baby and the nurse would recover, Elizabeth had retired to a guest room, and he had left. He had called her a number of times before he had left Paris, but she had not returned his calls.

"How is she?" Bronwyn asked.

MacCormack tried to fathom what went on behind her eyes.

"Well, she looks fantastic—very young and very French. I've never seen her dress like that." Slowly and deliberately, not taking his eyes from Bronwyn's face, he said, "I saw Joshua too."

384

Bronwyn frowned. "Who's he?"

"You don't know?"

"Oh Christ, Douglas, I don't know *everyone* my mother knows. She's probably made many friends in Paris."

It was what MacCormack had thought. It was why he had come.

He sipped his drink and toyed with his glass, twirling the liquid. He had known what he would do the moment he saw her, and he had no qualms. Sooner or later she'd have to find out.

"Your mother knew Asher before you married him, didn't she?"

Resentment flared in her. How dare he! "Spit it out, Douglas. You've never been subtle."

"I don't want to upset you, Bronwyn—"

"That's a crock! You don't give a damn for anyone's feelings but your own!"

"That's not fair!"

"It's true!"

"I've never hurt you!"

"How can you *say* that?"

His voice quieted. "If I did, I didn't mean it."

"You didn't *know* it, you mean!" Her voice cracked slightly with the emotions she tried to control. "That's what's so hurtful. You're not even aware of how unfeeling you are."

"I don't buy that!" MacCormack shot back. "I feel things as much as you! Maybe I'm self-absorbed, but so are you. When you wanted to do something, go somewhere, you did it! You never asked *me!* Who you kidding, Bronwyn? We're *exactly* alike!"

Her eyes wavered, and he knew he had hit home.

"I asked you about your mother and Asher because it's important to me, to you, and to them."

"Whatever it is, it's none of your business!"

"It sure as hell is, because I *love* you, and dammit, you love me!"

She gave him a bitter, sardonic look, and when she spoke her voice had dropped two decibels. "No, Douglas, you're wrong. We're not alike, because if you really loved me, you wouldn't speak to me this way. I wouldn't do this

385

to you." Her lips curled with her anger. "I'm not interested in any further discussion. Please—leave. And if in the future you have to see Asher, see him at his office. I'm finished with you."

MacCormack slowly shook his head from side to side.

"It's not that simple, Bronwyn," he said quietly, his eyes darkening. "Despite what you think, I'm not an unfeeling bastard. It was when I saw you in the hospital that I realized I loved you, and what I told you then, I meant—I still do. I was angry because you'd married Asher without telling me, or giving me a chance, and I hated losing. I can't help that. I've worked too hard all my life to win—I'm not a good loser." He sighed deeply, bending his head back and looking at the ceiling. And then he continued.

"I can't explain what seeing you hurt did to me. Even when my father was hurt it didn't hit me so hard. Maybe it was because I was so much younger, and I felt so invincible. But when I saw *you*—I became afraid." He took a deep breath, avoiding her eyes, which did not leave his face. "I could never endure not being free to move. But it wasn't pity I felt for you. I just wanted to take *care* of you. I thought being with me would make you happy and make you work hard at getting better. And I needed you! I need someone to love, someone to be there for me. I planned to break up your marriage. Oh, the bid to ICC was sincere; I wanted that job, I need to be a part of racing. But I engineered Asher into bringing me home for dinner. I wanted to see the two of you together and what my chances were. And when you looked at me that night, I knew you loved me. And Asher knew it! I saw how he watched you at dinner." He rose impatiently and began to pace the room, stopping finally to face her.

"Dammit, Bronwyn! Do you think you can really make him happy? Or yourself? Maybe, if I hadn't learned what I did in Paris, I'd bow out. You have a comfortable life— Asher certainly does a lot for you—and I'd have no right to break that up, but what I know now changes everything."

She stared at him. A faint throbbing of apprehension ticked in her stomach.

386

MacCormack gulped the last of his Scotch, wanting the liquid to burn away what he was about to tell her. With a slow, measured step he went to the bar and put the glass down. Dammit! He was a *heel*, but it was better she heard it from him. With him, she would be free to vent her feelings. Returning, he stood close to her chair, looking down into her eyes.

"I went to Paris to see Elizabeth because I wanted to tell her how I felt about you, and because I wanted to win her over." He smiled crookedly. "I never realized how much she disliked me. But you knew, and if it gives you pleasure, she really laced into me—not that I didn't have it coming. I had no idea, however, it would be Elizabeth who would make it right for me to speak to you like this."

"What the hell are you talking about?" Bronwyn tried to keep her voice steady.

"Don't you have any idea who Joshua is?" MacCormack's voice was gentle. "Why do you suppose your mother went to Paris after you'd been so badly hurt? Why has she stayed away this long?"

It was a question she had asked herself many times, and now she feared the answer. Her eyes skidded nervously as she said, "I've never heard of Joshua. Who is he?"

"Elizabeth's baby. He's about six months old."

Bronwyn's mouth dropped open.

"And who the father is—is unmistakable."

Bronwyn's drink fell from her hand, the glass rolling unbroken on the soft carpet.

"You're *crazy*," she choked, her eyes twice their size.

"I wish I were."

"*You're crazy!*" she cried. "I don't *believe* it! It's not possible!"

Furiously, she spun her chair away from him. She would *not* believe what he was saying! He was *insane!* She had to get out—she couldn't breathe.

The doors to the terrace slid open as her chair passed through the electric eye, and before MacCormack could move, she was outside. The dog bounded eagerly to her, his movement so abrupt, so swift, he frightened the kittens. With a squeal they leapt into the dogwood tree, scampering to the topmost branches arching out over the parapet. The brisk wind swayed the slender, leafless bough, and the kittens froze with fear, meowing shrilly.

"Oh—no!" Bronwyn screamed. Pushing strongly on the arms of the wheelchair, she tried to stand up, but the braces, heavy on her legs, caused her to flounder and fall back.

"Help me! Help me!" she screeched.

MacCormack raced to her.

"The kittens! The kittens!" She sobbed, pointing frantically to the tree. The terrified animals clung precariously to the windswept branch.

Reaching the tree in swift strides, MacCormack climbed easily into its crook, stepping from branch to branch, thinking only of the tiny creatures at the end of the bough. He heard the crack of the limb he was on only as he reached far out over the brick wall.

Bronwyn's scream echoed into the night, and then she fainted.

Chapter Thirty-two

SHE did not want to wake up.

But Asher persisted.

"Wake up, darling, wake up. Everything's fine."

No—it wasn't! She had seen Douglas *fall!* No—she wanted only this sweet, sweet blackness. Tears stole from under her tightly closed lids.

She heard a soft, familiar chuckle, and familiar hands rubbed hers. "Wake up, Bronwyn, it's *me*—I'm all right, and so are the kittens." And then familiar lips kissed her tears, and her eyes struggled open.

She saw his dark head bent over hers. There was a blue welt on his forehead and scratches on his cheek. Her fingers went to his face, searching its planes, touching his lips.

"How?" she gasped. "You *fell*—I *saw* you! I thought—"

He laughed softly, his dark blue eyes very much alive. "I

know, and for a split second so did I. But you didn't see it *all*—I twisted and fell backwards."

Her eyes held his.

Asher watched the two of them. He had heard Bronwyn's screams as he'd gotten off the elevator, and he had rushed to her rooms, his heart pounding so heavily it thundered in his ears. The terrace doors were open, and the sharp wind scattered papers on her desk. Outside Blaze barked loudly. Bronwyn lay slumped in her chair and MacCormack lay in the shrubbery, a broken branch beneath him. He was bruised, scratched, and the sleeve of his tweed suit jacket was torn, and he was holding tightly to two writhing kittens.

"See to Bronwyn," he had said. "I'm okay."

Asher had carried her inside and laid her down on the sofa, then covered her with an afghan. Now, as she regained consciousness, MacCormack, kneeling by her side, helped her sit up. Asher stood nearby, a frown between his eyes.

"I think we could all use a drink," he said, going to the bar and pouring whiskey into three glasses. "What happened out there?" he asked.

MacCormack told him.

"You were damn lucky," Asher said grimly, "and lucky to be blessed with splendid reflexes. I can't thank you enough for saving the kittens." He handed them the drinks. "Tomorrow I'm calling the garden people. I'll have them prune every tree so that no branches extend beyond the wall."

"That's a good idea," MacCormack said.

"Are you sure you're not hurt?" Asher asked.

"My back aches, but I've known worse."

"You'll feel better after a hot shower and some dinner. I'll have Charles lay out some fresh clothes."

"No—thank you, I can't stay. I only stopped by to tell Bronwyn I'd seen her mother in Paris."

"Oh? How is Elizabeth?"

MacCormack glanced at Bronwyn.

The impact of what he had told her hit her now with full force. Blood rushed to her cheeks and her eyes sought his, imploring him to say nothing.

390

"She's fine, just fine. If you'll excuse me, I'll wash up and take off."

"Are you sure you won't stay?" Asher asked. "It's no trouble."

"Thank you, no. I have things I must do tonight."

"As soon as you're ready, Charles will drive you to your hotel."

"It's not necessary. I'll grab a cab. New York cabbies are used to seeing men in my condition." He laughed lightly. "Even this early in the evening." He went to Bronwyn and took her hand. "Are you okay?"

She met his eyes, and he saw withdrawal like a steel door shutting, closing off the warmth and concern they'd held a few moments ago.

"Yes. Thank you."

"Well then, goodnight."

She didn't answer, but her eyes followed him as he went out the door. Asher accompanied him, waiting in the entry while MacCormack washed his face and hands. When he returned, Asher helped him into his trench coat. As MacCormack shrugged into the sleeves and tied the belt in a loose knot, Asher said casually, "Were you and Bronwyn in love?"

The younger man paused, surprised. And then he replied.

"Yes."

"Do you love her now?" There was no resentment or accusation in Asher's voice.

MacCormack faced him squarely. He wasn't as tall as Asher but their eyes met. "Yes," he said firmly.

Asher's face was drawn as he searched MacCormack's eyes.

"You know she may never walk again."

MacCormack's sharp-peaked lips curled with irony. "When I realized I loved her, I didn't think she'd ever move her hands again." He grimaced and shook his head. "Crazy, isn't it? You can be with a woman for years, and you get so used to her. Then something like this happens, and you wake up to what you had, and what you lost." His gaze sharpened. "I was teed off when she married you, but what the hell—I deserved it."

"And now?" Asher asked.

MacCormack shrugged. "She's made her choice. I just came by to tell her about Elizabeth."

Asher nodded. His body seemed tired, as though only his dark business suit held him together. He moved towards the doorway.

"We'll see Elizabeth in a few days. Bronwyn and I leave for Paris on Saturday."

MacCormack had been following him, but now his step slowed and his head came up abruptly. Asher did not notice, though. His mind was elsewhere.

Reaching out his hand, Asher said, "Goodnight, Douglas, and thank you again for what you did."

MacCormack shook the hand, concentrating on what he saw in Asher's eyes, in Asher's face. He had not been mistaken about the baby. He had told Bronwyn the truth.

"Goodnight, Asher." What the hell could he say about Paris? Enjoy yourself? When the elevator came, he stepped into the car. As the door slid closed, he turned the back of his coat collar up. It was cold outside, and he wanted to walk.

His face lined with his thoughts, Asher returned to Bronwyn's study. He stood in the doorway looking at her. She held the kittens in her lap, stroking them gently. Her head was bent, and the lights in the room caught the titian of her hair. She sensed him watching her, and she raised her head.

"We have to talk, Asher."

He nodded. "I know."

Since he had left Van Zuye's earlier that day he had not been able to shake off the depression which had gripped him after their conversation. He had been short-tempered and impatient in the office. There were two meetings he could barely sit through, and there were details he had to finalize before he left for Paris. He gave up finally in frustration and took a cab home, not waiting for Charles.

Bronwyn sensed a difference in him; he was clearly troubled. He had never seemed so closed-in, so unapproachable. She observed him carefully, her mind clamoring to speak with him. She felt as though MacCormack had stripped bare the myelin sheath of her nerves and that they sparked and short-circuited. Questions and answers collided crazily in her mind, but as she measured Asher's mood, she realized this was not the time to discuss what MacCormack had told her. Even if it were true—and the more she thought about it, she knew it *had* to be true—Asher need not know, not yet.

He came and stood by her chair, looking down at her. His face and eyes were unfathomable.

"What's wrong?" she asked.

He gave her an oblique look. "I'm not sure."

He sank down on the sofa. "That's not true," he said. "I had lunch with Willem today, and he made me face what I've been trying to ignore."

Bronwyn said nothing.

Asher sighed. "He sure can put burrs under your seat." He raised his eyes, catching hers.

"Van Zuye thinks I treat you like a handicapped child."

She looked away, and he saw immediately that she was uncomfortable.

"Do I?"

"Yes—at times."

"Do you resent it?"

"I try to tell myself it's because you care for me, and—you've never had a child . . ." She stopped, annoyed at what she'd said.

"I'd like to."

Angry at the slip of her tongue, Bronwyn did not hear him.

Asher leaned towards her, his eyes taking on a hopeful expression. "Bronwyn, I'd very much like to have a child."

She stared at him.

A light, teasing smile formed on his strongly defined lips.

"Perhaps then I wouldn't be so overprotective of you. Maybe I'd treat you more like a wife." He chuckled, feeling better than he had all day. "We might even have a good fight or two."

But there was no humor in Bronwyn tonight, and it was not a subject she could laugh about, especially now.

393

"That would be all wrong, Asher."

"Why? Look what we can offer a child."

"A crippled mother?"

"A mother with a loving heart, and a fine mind."

"We can't!" she cried.

"We can! You can have a child—and a healthy one."

"I don't *want* a child! Not *ever!*"

"Darling," he soothed, "you're just overreacting, and that's understandable."

"*You* don't understand," she interrupted. "I've *never* wanted children. They're mewling, selfish animals—no, that's unfair. Animals are kinder—children eat you alive!"

Asher's face paled. "You can't be serious!"

"I'm damned serious! I had my tubes tied years ago!"

Her words scored him, and an unreasoning hostility surged through him. "That's a hell of an unfair thing to do!"

"Unfair to whom?"

"To the man you marry!"

Her eyes blazed.

"It's *my* body, Asher. Besides—you never asked!"

"It's not something you *ask* about—it's what you *expect!*"

"*What you expect?*" She boiled over. "*I* didn't *expect* to marry you, and who the hell are you to *expect* or even assume that *my body* is a receptacle for your seed? Is that the only reason for marriage? Is that what your grandmother told Jenny?"

He stood up abruptly, his face dark with anger. He couldn't believe the rage rising in him. He began to pace, clenching and unclenching his hands.

Bronwyn had never seen him like this, and a strange, thrilling sensation crept up her spine.

Their eyes met, the animosity between them so palpable, the room seemed charged with their energy. They glared at each other, and Asher felt a sexual hunger he had not known for weeks. Without a word he strode to her wheelchair and picked her up roughly. The kittens bounded from her lap, disappearing under the sofa.

She was so astonished she did not realize what was happening, and when she did, she pounded at him.

394

"No! No!" she raged, furious not with him, but that she *wanted* him!

He trudged purposefully to her room and almost threw her onto the bed. Her leg braces clanged as she hit the mattress.

"Don't you dare!" she cried, painfully aware of the tingling, the throbbing in her.

He thrust himself on her and she felt the heat of his surging power through the layers of their clothes. She pushed hard against his chest, turning her face aside, not daring to meet his demanding lips.

Desire flamed in her, and she sobbed angrily, trying to quench her own unexpected passion.

"No! . . . Don't! . . . We can't!"

He tore at her sweater.

And she knew what she must do.

"Asher . . . STOP! . . . Please! . . . You must! . . . Elizabeth has a *baby!* . . . It's *your* baby . . . *your baby!*"

It was as if her words were a shearing, jagged iceberg striking below the water line. He froze—and then he sank heavily on her.

She felt the strength leave him, and she pushed him off her.

He rolled aside, lying on his back, staring into the darkness, breathing raggedly. And then he began to laugh, short, sarcastic sounds that didn't seem like laughter at all.

"Oh, Willem," he said aloud, irony rusting his tongue. "Wait till you hear *this!*" He turned his head to Bronwyn. "Is this what MacCormack came to tell you?" he asked bitterly.

"Yes," she murmured, tears stealing from under her closed lids.

He got up and stood looking down at her. "We do have things to talk about," he said.

Chapter Thirty-three

PARIS shimmered. Days of rain had washed the streets clean as fresh canvas, and now the warm May sunshine brushed a full palette of color on the sparkling city. In St. Germain-des-Prés people strolled along the wide boulevard and filled the small tables of the sidewalk cafés. There was an almost pink-tinged clarity in the air; even the pollution which hugs the narrow streets of the Left Bank seemed to have been swept aside by the breeze wafting up from the Seine.

Everywhere one felt the vitality of spring! In the quick, Gallic walk of passersby; in the swift Gallic gestures of friends chatting and drinking in the cafés; in the bob of the pigeons competing for crumbs tossed by an old, bent man sitting in the sun.

In the plaza across from Les Deux Magots adjacent to the eleventh-century Romanesque Church of St. Germain-des-Prés, tourists encircled a group of jugglers and street performers. The sunshine danced in the sequins and spangles of the entertainers' garish homemade costumes, reflecting flashing prisms of blues, reds, greens, and yellows onto the faces of the applauding crowd who laughed and tossed coins into the black top hats and bowlers on the sidewalk.

Elizabeth sat at a small table against the grey wall of Deux Magots, sipping a glass of Macon Blanc. She preferred the ambience at Café Flore but Bea had insisted they meet here.

"I'll be exhausted—I have three fittings," Bea had said. "Magots is livelier. It will resuscitate me."

Bea was late but Elizabeth did not mind waiting. The afternoon was hers. Earlier that morning she had gone to the Sorbonne to receive her final grades. She had done well, and she felt proud of the folded card in her handbag. Nor did she have to be home on time to nurse: Joshua was nine months old, and she had weaned him just before examinations. Isabel had urged her to enjoy the day.

"I plan to spend a very peaceful afternoon with Joshua, sunning right here in the patio. Take all the time you want."

Were it not for the letter in her purse, all would be nearly perfect.

She tried not to think of the letter, focusing instead on the animated scene in the café and in the streets. Two men at a nearby table gazed at her with frank admiration; she glanced away, uninterested, but pleased. She liked the way she looked today, and an admiring glance was pleasant confirmation. The dusty pink silk knit dress she wore was her favorite—what she liked even more was that she could now wear the wide wrap belt. When she had tied the soft leather twice around her waist this morning, it made up for the days and weeks of dieting.

Elizabeth's thoughts veered back to the letter. A letter she had read four, five times and still did not fully comprehend. She had not been so foolish as to expect to keep Joshua a secret for long, but she had hoped to postpone the confrontations by living in Paris. The night of the fire, when MacCormack learned of Joshua, her first instinct had been to ask him to say nothing, but as they walked out of the hospital and waited for a cab, she had decided seeking his silence would make it worse. Then he would know without doubt that she had something to hide. All he actually knew was that she had a child. So what? It could be anyone's. In this day and age, having a child out of wedlock was commonplace. As for Joshua's resemblance to Asher, which she saw all too clearly—well—MacCormack could *prove* nothing. And if he found out she had not told Bonnie about the baby—well, she would just brush it off as not wanting to disturb her daughter when Bonnie had to concentrate on getting well.

After MacCormack left for the United States, Elizabeth told Bea the truth. Though they had known each other for years, theirs had been an on-the-surface relationship. Now it became a true friendship in which each felt secure enough to say exactly what she thought. Elizabeth found Bea's frank "live and let live" attitude very comforting.

"Ah, cherie, this is not an easy situation," Bea had said. "But admit *nothing*. The closer you keep truth to your heart, the less hurtful it is. But who am I to tell you or anyone what to do? We do what the heart directs. Yet, permit me one tiny suggestion: Life is like being in a witness box. If you say only 'Yes' or 'No,' what can they do? *Don't ever explain!* Let them wonder. To *wonder* is one thing—to *know* is another. And even better than 'Yes' or 'No' is a half-smile—a Mona Lisa smile. It drives people wild!"

When Bronwyn phoned early in January, Elizabeth, the baby, and Isabel were still living at Bea's, waiting for the repairs to the apartment to be completed. Elizabeth had answered the phone.

"Well!" Bronwyn teased. "Imagine finding you *in!*" She sounded happy, and Elizabeth felt relief flood her. Evidently MacCormack had said nothing.

"It's good to hear from you," Elizabeth answered, smiling into the phone.

"Guess what!" Bronwyn laughed. "Asher and I are coming to Paris!"

Elizabeth gripped the receiver, her knuckles whitening.

"When?" she managed to say.

"Valentine's Day! There's a conference Asher wants to attend, and while he's busy, I'll visit with you."

Elizabeth could not speak.

"Mother? Is something wrong?"

"No . . . it's just that I'm very busy at school . . ."

"Don't worry about that," Bronwyn ran on. "While you're in class I'll be at the Louvre. I never had time before to spend hours there, and now I won't even have to walk those hard floors—I can ride around in comfort. See you in February, and say hello to Bea."

And they had hung up.

Elizabeth yearned for the days when her phone conversations with her daughter ran on and on and on—when she spoke openly of what was in her heart and on her mind. She had never withheld anything from her child; even when Bronwyn had been a youngster they had confided in each other. Many times she had been surprised by what Bronwyn admitted—other times chagrined. But they had always been honest. And she had told Bronwyn what she could never tell another. Elizabeth hated her dissimulation now. How she wanted to tell Bonnie the truth. She needed her understanding ear, and her loving heart.

She had cried to Bea, "What am I going to do? We'll be back in the apartment by then. I can't invite her there! And if I meet her here, or at her hotel, or at a restaurant, she'll want to *know* why I don't show her my home. And if I do, even if I tried to hide Joshua, what if he cried? Do I just shrug and say . . . 'Oh, that's only your baby brother!' And when she sees Asher's imprint on that little face, I can say . . . 'By the way, he's also your stepson!' My God, Bea! What do I do? I thought I'd be able to face her and tell her . . . but I can't . . . I just can't!"

"First, you stop pacing—before you wear a hole in the carpet," Bea said firmly. "And then you *think!* You must tell her eventually, and the sooner the better. It will be more difficult later."

Elizabeth sank onto a chair and shook her head, her shoulders sagging. "It's too soon. She needs more time. I need more time."

"It will always be too soon." Bea's voice was quiet and kind.

"I know that, but I'm not ready—I'm just not ready, nor is she."

Bea sighed with resignation. "Then take a trip. Say you must do some research for class, for a new book—whatever." Her dark eyes lit up with a sudden thought. "Better yet—say *nothing*, until the very last minute. Call Bronwyn the morning they leave and tell her you've met a *fantastic* man who insists on taking you to Ibizia for Valentine's Day, but that you'll try and get back to see her before she leaves. Then you take Isabel and the baby and go *somewhere*—and the day they are to fly back home, you show up at the hotel, breathless. You've flown back just in time to say hello and goodbye!"

Slowly the worried frown on Elizabeth's face eased, and a faint smile touched the corners of her lips.

"You're incredible, Bea. Do you think it would really work?"

"Why not? The unexpected always does!"

Elizabeth decided to go to the Auvergne. She had always wanted to see the Romanesque churches of St. Nectaire, Le Chaise Dieu and Orcival. She hoped, if the weather permitted, she might also explore the ruined castles of Murol, Tournoël, and Cordés.

"In February?" Bea exclaimed. "You're mad! You'll freeze! Go to Nice or Cannes!"

"That's just where *they* might go after Paris! Besides, it's a good time for the Auvergne. There won't be any tourists."

In the intervening weeks Elizabeth acted decisively. She moved back into the refurbished apartment and made arrangements for the trip. She even managed to obtain leave from her classes, explaining it was a family emergency. But none of this was necessary.

Two days before she was to leave, Bea called and said Bronwyn had phoned and left an urgent message for Elizabeth to return the call immediately. Elizabeth's hands trembled as she dialed, and when she reached Bronwyn, her daughter's voice was so distant and cold, Elizabeth's throat constricted.

"What's wrong, Bonnie?"

"We're not coming to Paris. Something's come up, and Asher has decided someone else could cover the conference for him."

Elizabeth's heart soared with relief, and she ignored Bronwyn's tone.

"It's just as well, darling. The weather is cold and nasty, and my classes are getting difficult. It will be so much more enjoyable later on . . . perhaps in summer . . ."

"Perhaps." And then there was silence.

"Bonnie?"

"I'm here, Mother."

"I thought you'd hung up."

"No—I'm here."

Elizabeth heard her heavy breathing.

"Bonnie, are you sure you're all right? Is there something you want to tell me?"

A short, dry laugh crackled in her ear.

"I'm okay. But isn't there something you'd like to tell *me?*"

Elizabeth was so relieved that Bronwyn was not coming to Paris, she barely heard her daughter's question.

"Take care of yourself, darling. Maybe we'll get together this summer."

Elizabeth could not see Bronwyn biting her lip, nor the emotions contorting her face. All she heard was a subdued, "And you take care." And then a click as Bronwyn hung up.

Quickly Elizabeth dialed Bea. She never even thought about MacCormack.

But Elizabeth's heart darkened with the lightening days. As February trudged into March, March into April, April into May, and Bronwyn did not call, Elizabeth thought often of that last phone conversation, and she felt certain MacCormack had told her about Joshua. She could not bring herself to call her daughter. She feared that if Bronwyn did indeed know about the baby, she would get her to admit it; it was so easy to fall into a verbal trap. Yet, Elizabeth could not close off all contact. Instead she wrote to Bronwyn frequently, brief, breezy letters which Bron-

401

wyn had not answered until today. Even that was unexpected.

Sitting in the café now, Elizabeth opened her purse and fingered the letter inside. Bronwyn's letters were as rare as snow in the Mediterranean, and for years Elizabeth had fought her resentment at this quirk in her daughter's nature. Despite her language skills Bronwyn seldom wrote personal letters. Elizabeth's mind wandered. Danny had been like that—even though Bonnie had never known him, it was as if she had grown up at his side. Researchers should ask *mothers*, Elizabeth thought, about whether it's nature or nurture that molds a child. Elizabeth grimaced with her thoughts. She *knew* Bonnie's nature—it was unfair of her to expect more.

When Bea had given her the letter, Elizabeth had opened it with trepidation, wondering what had impelled Bronwyn to write. Its contents were as terse as Bronwyn's phone calls and utterly surprising. Elizabeth had read and reread the single page, astonished, trying to understand.

She withdrew the buff-colored business envelope from her purse. Bronwyn did not even have personal stationery, and she had used her office letterhead to type the letter, even typing the "Bon" which closed it instead of a signature.

Elizabeth began to read:

Hi—I have a favor to ask. I want to move home—office and all. Blaze is getting fat in the city, and I'm getting bitchy. And the kittens are almost cats and too rambunctious to leave out on the terrace anymore. We all need fresh air! . . . and space! Would prefer to go West, but work demands I be close to New York. I can hire a secretary from town, and with my computer terminals and phone modules be in touch with the office and even with the printer. And you've got a dandy word processor gathering dust, which the secretary could use. And since Purolator calls at the ski area they can service me too. I'd have a ramp built from the parking circle, across the bridge, up the hill and onto the deck, and my electric wheelchair could handle that easily. AND BEST OF

402

ALL! Helen and her husband want to live in the country! They would live-in—Helen to care for me, cook, etc., John to be handyman, caretaker, chauffeur. And I'll keep the apartment in the Village for a pied-à-terre. Tom thinks it's a great idea . . . he'd be up every weekend (so he says). We have an ongoing chess game. (I'VE BEATEN HIM TWICE!) What about it? I'd be where I love to be, and you can stay in Paris as you've always wanted. Let me know quick . . . I want to see the trees budding!

Take care—Love—Bon

Elizabeth frowned, fine lines cutting across her forehead.

Why not *one word* about Asher?

And, "Tom thinks it's a great idea?"

What does Asher think?

A shadow fell across the typed page.

A voice said, "May I sit down?"

Engrossed in the letter, Elizabeth shook her head.

"I'm sorry, I'm saving that seat for a friend."

"I know. She asked me to come instead."

This time Elizabeth recognized the voice. The letter in her hand shook. Slowly she raised her eyes.

Asher smiled down at her.

"May I sit down?"

Color flooded her face. She nodded, unable to speak.

He pulled back the slatted chair opposite her, easing into the seat. Glancing at the letter still in her hand, he smiled again.

"I was certain I'd be here before that arrived."

He knows what's in this letter, her mind clamored, but all she could do was stare at him.

"It's good to see you, Elizabeth," he said. "You look lovely. Healthy and happy." He signaled to the waiter.

"Would you like some more wine?" he asked.

She heard herself say: "Yes, please . . . Macon Blanc."

He smiled. "Ah, a good wine, but may I recommend one of my favorite Alsatians?"

I don't care about wine, her thoughts cried, *I want to know why you're here!* But her lips said, "By all means."

403

"Cuvée Fredrick Emiles, s'il vous plaît," Asher told the waiter.

A small smile of approval touched the man's face and he made a note on his pad.

Asher leaned back in the chair and crossed his legs. He steadied the questions churning in him. Looking out over the crowd, he said with a casualness he did not feel, "It's an incredibly beautiful day. I've been walking since morning."

He couldn't be here on business, Elizabeth thought. Not dressed like that. He wore a blue open-necked sports shirt under a grey cashmere sweater and grey flannel trousers. His hair was slightly windblown.

She was just about to ask him about Bronwyn when he turned and said, "Are you busy this evening?"

Why don't you say something about Bonnie? her mind insisted.

Her eyes met his and she replied wryly, "Bea asked me to dinner, but it must have been a ploy since she seems to have arranged all this."

Amusement curved his lips. "You're a perceptive woman," he said.

"I'm not." Mind and voice answered simultaneously. "Seeing you is very surprising."

Why are you here? Why this letter from Bonnie? The questions showed clearly in her eyes, but she found no answers in Asher's.

The waiter returned with the wine, placing the cooler between them. He set two glasses on the table and poured a small amount of the pale liquid into Asher's glass. When Asher tasted it and nodded his approval, the waiter smiled and poured wine into Elizabeth's glass, then into Asher's.

Elizabeth felt as if she watched the ritual from afar.

Asher twirled the glass but waited until she tasted the wine before he sipped it. His eyebrows arched as he awaited her reaction.

She was glad the wine gave her something to do. She turned the stem, releasing the bouquet, and took a sip. Looking at Asher, she said, "It's lovely—so much drier than most Rieslings."

"Maybe Izzy carries it," he said with a straight face.

For the first time since he had surprised her, she smiled, and then she laughed, her face softening, her eyes lighting with warmth. Asher bent his head slightly so that he could see her face better under the ivory-toned fedora hat she wore tilted over one eye.

"You have an incredible memory!"

"For trivia," he said dryly, raising his glass to his lips.

Elizabeth wondered what lay behind his cool green eyes. She wanted to know so *much,* but she fought the questions arcing from her brain to her lips. She wanted it to come from *him.*

He looked at her, his mind scudding. *Why—why didn't you tell me I had a son? Why didn't you let me help? I should have been there when he was born!* He wouldn't push her—it would have to come from *her.*

He put down his wine glass and said lightly, "I have tickets for *Amadeus* tonight at the Marigny. Would it be convenient for you to accompany me? I'm curious to see Polanski play Mozart. It seems so out of character for him."

But what you're doing is so out of character! her mind flared. *Why are you talking of such trivialities?*

She answered coolly. "It is different. I went with Bea on opening night, and Polanski is remarkable. He makes Mozart pathetic, rather than ridiculous, which is what the British production did. You'll like this French version."

"Ah, then if you've seen it . . ." Disappointment tinged his voice.

When are you going to tell me? her insides cried, but her eyes under the hat revealed little.

"I'd like to see it again," she said. "My French is far from fluent, and I enjoy hearing the language spoken so beautifully."

Elizabeth—Elizabeth, he thought. *Tell me about my son.* He smiled at her. "Good! After the performance we'll go to a favorite haunt . . . it's a jazz club on St. Benoit. I never miss it when I come to Paris."

"You don't mean Le Bilboquet?" Elizabeth asked.

He was pleased. "Then you've heard Militia Battlefield?"

"Yes, she's wonderful. Isn't her name incredible?"

405

He nodded, smiling. "She insists it's real."

Guilt rose in Elizabeth. She should not be feeling this good—she had no right to the warm, wonderful feeling suffusing her. She could hold back no longer.

"Why isn't Bonnie with you? What's happened, Asher?"

It was as if he had been waiting for her questions. The eyes lost their cool casualness. He put down his wine glass and, leaning towards her, he took her hands in his.

"Bronwyn and I are divorced. We received the final papers just a few days ago."

Everything in Elizabeth went limp. "What?" she stammered. "Why? When?" She pulled her hands away.

Asher's voice was quiet and unemotional.

"I'm sorry to shock you, but it's best I told you straight out." His eyes gripped hers. "Bronwyn and I discovered that our feelings, affectionate and caring though they are, could only hurt us in the long run. What I had wanted no longer existed. It stemmed from a neurosis I should have admitted long ago, a neurosis I projected unfairly onto Bronwyn. What she felt for me was a result of my own problems, along with her sense of obligation—guilt—oh, so many emotions, Elizabeth, that can be mistaken for love. She is a wonderful woman, but I was not being fair to her—or she, to me. And the fault is entirely mine. It was I who impelled her to marry me, and our decision to divorce was the first really mutual decision we made since we met. She is much more content now that she is free, and I, too, feel peaceful and optimistic. We each look forward to the future. She is very enthusiastic about moving back to the country, and she hopes you will agree."

Elizabeth could not believe what she was hearing. Her head throbbed, and she knew it was not the wine.

Divorced? Now she understood the letter! It still lay in her lap. She looked down at it, and folding it carefully, replaced the sheet in the envelope. Slowly, she opened her purse and tucked the envelope inside. She found it very difficult to speak, but she said, haltingly, "If that's what Bonnie wants . . . of course . . . it's as much her home as mine . . . she was always so happy there . . ."

Tears sprang to her eyes, and lowering her head so that

406

he could not see beneath the brim of her hat, she brushed them away. Striving to think clearly, she took a deep breath and said, "It had to be more than just a sudden discovery that you were not right for each other. What *really* happened, Asher?"

Her heart told her he knew about Joshua.

His gaze wandered out to the crowd thronging the plaza in front of the church. He could not meet her probing eyes. *She would have to tell him about Joshua.* His eyes misted at the thought, and he said, looking into his wine glass, "Every action has a catalyst, Elizabeth, and for Bronwyn and me the catalyst was merely coincidental." He took a deep breath. "But it was powerful enough to break through the prison we were building around ourselves and make us see how wrong we were for each other. I'm very glad it happened, Elizabeth . . . and so is Bronwyn."

And Elizabeth was sure he knew.

Now it was she who avoided his eyes.

He saw her discomfort and, putting a sheaf of folded francs on the table, he pushed his chair back. Getting up, he said, "It's such a beautiful afternoon—let's walk."

Elizabeth did not have the strength to rise.

Asher came around to her chair, took her arm and helped her up, then led her through the closely set tables, out to the street. His hand under her elbow, he kept up a steady stream of conversation as they crossed Boulevard St. Germain and walked up Rue de Rennes.

"Van Zuye asked me to give you his very special regards. He hopes when you return to New York that you will come and see him . . . Tom is working with Van Zuye and doing some truly amazing sculptures . . . he's talking about giving up his practice someday to concentrate on art. Meantime he's very busy with the new clinic . . . it opens officially in September and his sculpture will be in the atrium . . . He and Bronwyn have become very good friends . . . they have a great deal in common . . . they're always laughing and arguing when they're together . . ."

Elizabeth stopped in her tracks.

"Tom . . . and Bonnie? What about Douglas MacCormack?" she asked.

Asher smiled down into her eyes.

"There's love, Elizabeth—intense, passionate feelings —and then there's a genuine love relationship. Perhaps what Bronwyn feels for Douglas and what he feels for her is too demanding to weather well. Who knows? Maybe what she has with Tom will grow into a comfort and a need that neither will want to give up. All three are remarkable people and free, independent spirits."

"I know," Elizabeth said. "It's difficult for free, independent spirits to meld and give to each other."

He looked at her steadily, and placing his forefinger under her chin, he lifted her face so that she met his eyes. A smile played on his lips.

"How free and independent a spirit are you, Elizabeth?"

She was warmed by a feeling as if all of springtime had somehow miraculously seeped into every cell of her being. A happy smile touched the corners of her mouth and illuminated the green flecks in her hazel eyes. Moments passed before she spoke, and when she did, her words were strong and sure.

"Free enough to give love, and independent enough to need love."

His smile was dazzling.

"Come," she said, laughing, entwining her fingers in his and turning towards Rue Racine. "There's someone I want you to meet."